PRAISE FOR SUSAN ISAACS AND
AFTER ALL THESE YEARS

"A sure candidate for the bestseller lists. . . . Isaacs shows herself in top form. Once again Isaacs proves a dab hand at rattling skeletons in the closets of Suburbia—here murder and adultery are skewered with this author's typically savvy wit. . . . A heroine who gives new meaning to the word 'feisty.'"
—*Publishers Weekly*

"Isaacs is at the top of her form. . . . Bursts with energy, razor-sharp dialogue and memorable characters."
—*Detroit News*

"This is a mean, funny book. . . . Susan Isaacs, author of *Compromising Positions* and *Magic Hour*, is building a reputation for writing savvy, intelligent and wry entertainments. . . . What makes Isaacs both interesting and fun is her addition of sardonic humor and dead-on social commentary. . . . The book takes gleeful aim at excess wherever it finds it."
—*Houston Chronicle*

"Who couldn't love a heroine who lives in a mansion yet still teaches high school and wisecracks like your best girlfriend?"
—*Glamour*

Also by Susan Isaacs

NOVELS
*Magic Hour
Shining Through
Almost Paradise
*Close Relations
Compromising Positions

SCREENPLAYS
Hello Again
Compromising Positions

*Published by HarperPaperbacks

Susan Isaacs

AFTER ALL THESE ❤ YEARS

HarperPaperbacks

A Division of HarperCollinsPublishers

This is a work of fiction. The characters, incidents, and dialogues are products of the author's imagination and are not to be construed as real. Any resemblance to actual events or persons, living or dead, is entirely coincidental.

HarperPaperbacks   *A Division of* HarperCollins*Publishers*
10 East 53rd Street, New York, N.Y. 10022

A hardcover edition of this book was published in 1993 by HarperCollins*Publishers*.

Cover illustration by Neal McPheeters

First HarperPaperbacks printing: May 1994

Printed in the United States of America

HarperPaperbacks and colophon are trademarks of HarperCollins*Publishers*

❖ 10 9 8 7 6 5 4 3 2 1

To my aunt and uncle,
Sara and George Asher,
who saw to it that I was not an only child

ACKNOWLEDGMENTS

I needed facts, assistance, wisdom, and technical expertise, and I found precisely that from the people listed below. I want to thank them—and apologize if I twisted their truth to fit my fiction.

Arnold Abramowitz, Janice Asher, Mary Elizabeth Bliss, Barbara Butler, Edmond Coller, Jonathan Dolger, Mary FitzPatrick, Nancy Frankel, Lawrence S. Goldman, Leonard Klein, Edward Lane, John McElhone, Gail Mallen, Mathias Mone, James Nininger, Bill Scaglione, Cynthia Scott, Chris Speziali, Connie Vaughn, Susan Zises, and (of course) Justin Zises, Lara Zises, Samantha Zises, and Jay Zises.

Thanks also to Susan Lawton for the antiques and interior design and to Anthony Lepsis and Brian Whitney for the landscaping.

I am grateful to all the people who helped me at the Port Washington (N.Y.) Public Library and at the Audubon Society of Huntington (N.Y.), the New York Public Library, and the Billy Rose Theater Collection of the New York Public Library for the Performing Arts (Theater Research Division).

Here's to my friends the English teachers, who inspire their students—and me: Barbara Kaplan-Halper, Edith Tolins, and the wonderful, awesome Teacher of the Year, Mary Rooney.

Speaking of friends, the real Jane Berger is a delightful human being.

I want to thank my children, Andrew and Betsy Abramowitz, for their love, companionship, and editorial advice. And a special thank you to their high school and college friends for being such good company.

My assistant, AnneMarie Palmer, has saved my sanity too many times to enumerate. As always, I am grateful for her good humor and hard work.

My agent, Owen Laster, is not only a wise and honorable gentleman but a doll.

Larry Ashmead, my editor, has seen me through five novels now. I don't think there is any finer person in all publishing.

And after all these years, my husband, Elkan Abramowitz, is still the best person in the world.

One

After nearly a quarter of a century of marriage, Richie Meyers, my husband, told me to call him Rick. Then he started slicking back his hair with thirty-five-dollar-a-jar English pomade.

Okay, I admit I was annoyed. But in all fairness, wasn't Richie entitled to a life crisis? He was just two years from fifty. His jaw wasn't so much chiseled from granite anymore as sculpted from mashed potatoes. His hairline and his gums were receding at about the same rate. And when his shirt was off, he'd eye his chest hair in disbelief, as if some practical joker had plunked a gray toupee between his pectorals.

Well, I could empathize. At eleven months younger than Richie, I didn't exactly qualify as a spring chicken. Still, unless a man's taste ran to pre-pubescent milkmaids with braids, I would probably be considered somewhere between attractive and downright pretty. Shiny dark hair. Clear skin. Even features. Hazel eyes with green specks that I liked to think of as glints of emerald. Plus one hell of a set of eyelashes. And not a bad body either, although in the fight between gravity and me, gravity was winning; no matter how many abdominal crunches I did, I would never again be tempted to include getting my panties ripped off in broad daylight as a detail of a sexual fantasy.

Like Richie, I wasn't so crazy about growing old, especially since I had at last come to appreciate the unlikelihood of immortality. A person who can laugh in the face of eternal nothingness is a schmuck. So my heart went out to him. And I made a sincere effort to call him Rick. But after all those years of "Richie," I'd slip up every so often—like in bed. I cried out, "Oh, God! Don't stop, Rich . . . Rick." But by then he was shriveling, and seconds later, it looked as if he'd Scotch-taped a shrimp to his pubic area.

The signs were there, all right. I just didn't read them. That's how come I was surprised when, on the bright blue June morning after our silver anniversary party, which we'd celebrated on what our real estate broker had called the Great Lawn behind our house, in a white tent festooned with creamy roses and thousands of twinkly white lights, Richie told me he was leaving me for his senior vice-president, for—his voice softened, then melted—Jessica.

Jessica Stevenson had been one of the two hundred guests the night before. In fact, Richie had foxtrotted with her to a Cole Porter medley that had included "You'd Be So Nice to Come Home To." Yes, Jessica was a younger woman. But not obnoxiously so. Richie wasn't one of those fiftyish guys who run off with twenty-two-year-old Lufthansa stewardesses. At thirty-eight, Jessica was a mere nine years younger than I. Unfortunately, she had luminous aquamarine eyes and was learning Japanese for the fun of it.

At what turned out to be the final party of my marriage, I kept waiting for Richie to say: "Look at you, Rosie! As beautiful as the day we were married!" He didn't. In the humid night air, the pleated, Grecian-style white silk gown that had caressed my curves in the fitting room at Bergdorf Goodman clung to my bosom and legs with crazed malice.

Jessica, naturally, did not look as if she'd wrapped herself in a wet sheet. No. She glowed in a gold lamé off-the-shoulder bodysuit tucked into a transparent cream chiffon skirt that hung, petal-like, in soft panels; her top was divided from her bottom by a four-inch-wide gold leather belt. It goes without saying she had a slender waist—although to be perfectly candid, her bosom was nothing Richie would normally have written home about; she was fairly flat, except for those overenthusiastic nipples men go crazy for, the kind that look like the erasers on number two pencils.

I had actually blown her a kiss as I raced by, searching for the caterer to tell him that a guest, Richie's banker's girlfriend, had converted to vegan vegetarianism the previous weekend. Jessica, in awesomely high-heeled gold sandals, was standing with a couple of the other Data Associates executives, laughing, squeezing a wedge of lime into her drink. She waved back with her usual energy: Rosie! Hello! With her gold bodysuit and the bronze highlights in her dark-gold hair, she looked shimmery, magical, almost like a mermaid.

But that Richie would actually leave me for her? Please! He and I had a history. We'd met in the late sixties, for God's sake, when we were both teaching at Forest Hills High School in Queens. We had made a life together. A rich life—long before all the money. We had children. So yes, I *was* surprised. Okay, stunned.

Across our bedroom, Richie's black-olive eyes were overflowing. He gulped noisy mouthfuls of air and was so choked up I could barely hear him. "I can't believe I'm saying this, Rosie." As he wiped his tears away with the heel of his hand, he turned crying into a manly act. "What gets me"—his chest heaved—"is that"—he sobbed, unable to hold anything back—"it sounds so damn trite."

"Please, Richie, tell me."

"For the first time in years, I feel truly alive."

The late-morning air was hot, sugary with honeysuckle, a reminder that lovely, sweaty summer sex was just weeks away. But, as the song goes, not for me. In spite of the season, I shivered and pulled the blanket tight around my shoulders. Sure, I was cold, but I suppose I also had the subconscious hope that all bundled up, lower lip quivering, I'd be an irresistible package.

I wasn't.

Richie was. With his combed-back steel-gray hair, his rich-man's tan, his hand-tailored white slacks and crisp white shirt and white lizard loafers, he looked like an ex-husband who had outgrown his wife. But his face was wet. His tears were real. "Rosie, I'm so sorry."

I couldn't think of a comeback. I just cried. He shifted his weight from one loafer to the other, and then back again. The confrontation was either horribly distressing or it was running longer than he'd expected and he had a lunch date. "Richie," I sobbed, "you'll get over her!" As fast as I could, I changed it to "Rick, please! I love you so much!" but by then it was much too late.

That summer, I went through all the scorned-first-wife stages. Hysteria. Paralysis. Denial: Of course Richie will give up a worldly, successful, fertile, size-six financial whiz-bang for a suburban high school English teacher. Despair: spending my nights zonked on the Xanax I'd conned my gynecologist into prescribing, regretting it was not general anesthesia.

I was utterly alone. Husband gone. Kids grown and off on their own. And our beagle, Irving, died the first week in August. I wandered through the house, weeping, remembering Richie's body heat, the children's warmth, Irving's cold and loving nose.

At least wandering was exercise. When Richie hit it big, he did not believe that less was more. More was more. One day we were in our Cape Cod, with its original, early sixties all-avocado kitchen, its off-the-track storm windows, its cockeyed basketball hoop over its one-car garage. The next, we were two and a half miles north, right on Long Island Sound in Great Gatsby country, in a Georgian-style house so stately it actually had a name. Gulls' Haven.

Admittedly, a nocturnal wanderer in a New York Shakespeare Festival T-shirt, pointlessly sexy black panties, and Pan Am socks left over from our last first-class flight to London (before Richie got even richer and we started taking the Concorde) given to rambles through a deserted house clutching a wad of damp Kleenex wasn't the picture "Gulls' Haven" ought to have evoked. But it was the truth. That's how it was on that fateful night.

Fateful? To tell you the truth, that night didn't seem any more or less ominous than any other. When we'd moved, Richie had ditched the digital radio-alarm on his night table for a brass carriage clock, so I'll never know the precise time I woke up or, more important, what wakened me. But it was around three-thirty. I realized I wouldn't get any more sleep because I was scared to take any more Xanax. My luck, the next pill could be the one to put me in what the doctors would diagnose as a persistent vegetative state. Richie, driven by guilt, would pay for the best custodial care, so I'd spend the last three decades of my life cosmically desolate and unable to read, a prisoner in the solitary confinement of my own body.

I wandered some more. When Richie had taken the hike that last week in June, he'd made the twenty-six-mile trip west into Manhattan with just an overnight bag. How could a guy want to leave nearly his whole life behind? But I was past sniffling in front of the closets full of his custom-tailored suits, touching the toes of his handmade shoes. I was able to get past them, and past his bathroom too, all rich green marble and chunky gold fixtures; we'd made love in his stall shower the first night we'd moved in.

At that point, my stomach rumbled. I thought: A container of nonfat yogurt couldn't hurt. Deep down I knew, as I descended the curving flight of stairs, that I'd go to the freezer and—Oh! Would you look at this!—find one of the sausage-and-meatball pizzas I'd bought to have in the house for when the boys came home. Or maybe I'd microwave a hot dog, which would turn out to be three hot dogs. Since Richie left, I'd developed a tummy. Well, tummy is too diminutive a word. Another few weeks of compulsive snacking, and I'd look as if I was at the end of the first trimester of pregnancy, not a great look for the menopausal.

I walked into the dark, basketball-court-sized kitchen wondering whether I had any hot dog rolls or if I'd have to beat the hot dogs into submission so they'd curl into hamburger rolls and also, as a matter of intellectual curiosity, if a person could whip up a really thick malted in a Cuisinart. And I tripped.

Tripped? God almighty! Tumbled over some huge—what the hell was it?—*thing*. My close-to-insane cry of terror frightened me even more. I scrambled backward until I crashed into the warming oven of the big iron stove. Whatever it was didn't move. I heard my own whimper, a pathetic, bleating sound. Frantic, I looked over at the readout panel for the security system near the back door. Green light, which meant someone had turned the alarm system off. I was positive I'd turned it on. Another whimper. Dear God, no. But then it hit me . . .

Alexander! Of course! He had run out of money, so he'd come back home and, as usual, dropped his backpack on the floor, no doubt cradling his guitar and tenderly conveying it up to his room. I said "Shit!" over his carelessness. But I was so full of joy that one of my kids was home. I reached out and switched on the light.

It was not Alex's backpack on the floor.

It was Richie. He was lying on his back. His lips were a narrow line of displeasure.

No wonder. He had a knife right through the center of his body.

Oh, how I screamed! "Oh, God! Oh, God!" And I ran all about for a minute, flapping my arms, witless. I banged into the maple Welsh dresser so hard that a platter painted with blue and white Dutch girls and a soup tureen shaped like a turkey crashed to the floor. Then I screamed some more. Maybe I'd seen too many movies. When a woman encounters a corpse, what does she do? She emits a shriek so bloodcurdling it could almost persuade God to change his mind.

I bent down, touched Richie's cheek. Cold. But listen, he was lying on a tile floor. "Richie?" I whispered. Then I screamed: "Richie!" No response. No sign of life. I put my finger near his nose to see if there was breath. No. There had to be a chance; he *could* be alive. "Richie, please!" Driven by hysteria— no, by hope—I grasped the knife handle, trying to pull it out. It made a squishy, rocking motion, but it wouldn't move. Neither would Richie. I knew then that he was, truly, dead.

What did I really feel? My heart turned to cold stone. I felt dead. No, that's not completely true. Richie was definitely the dead one. Looking down at him, though, it wasn't his absolute stillness that made me keep screaming his name over and over, but how alive he looked. Any minute he would gaze down, scowl at such domestic theatrics, and wrest the knife out of himself. Except he didn't.

The blood on his torso formed a three-petaled red flower, with the black knife handle as a giant stamen. Horrible. I felt so dizzy; I cupped my hands over my mouth and nose so I could take in a couple of lungfuls of carbon dioxide. It was only then that it hit me. What I was staring at was not exactly a self-inflicted wound. If the world's most sensitive microphone had been clipped onto the neck of my T-shirt, it would have picked up my whisper: "Murder!"

Richie was dead because someone had killed him.

I forced myself to look at him. His body lay across the planks of the dark wood floor. His fists were loosely clenched. His right hand was bent at the wrist and his fingers curled into a thumbs-up sign that, considering the circumstances, seemed in terrible taste. My own fingers flexed, wanting to fix it.

But I'd already touched the knife. I knew the police wouldn't be thrilled about that. See, I wasn't what you'd call an innocent when it came to homicide. I read too many crime novels for my own good. Dick Lit, my best friend, Cass, the English Department chair, called the genre. Derisively. But I'd read all those whodunits and watched so many detective movies in my life that even in that terrible moment, I should have known not to taint the crime scene. What if I'd smudged the killer's fingerprints? Or knocked off a crucial skin cell the cops could send for DNA analysis?

I inched back very carefully and made myself look—an objective look. All right, not so objective, since the first thing I noticed was that Jessica had been picking out his clothes: magazine clothes. I'd never seen a real man dressed so fashionably. High-top sneakers, not the dingy, gray-black frayed kind he would have worn for basketball in junior high, but jet black, sleek, modern. They probably cost more than the monthly rent on our first apartment. Deliberately baggy dark-gray cotton pants drawn tight at the cuffs. A form-hugging pullover.

I glanced around him: dirt on the floor—dark, loamy bits of soil in an erratic path that began at the kitchen door. My stomach flip-flopped. I couldn't take it anymore. A howl of horror caught in my throat, choking me. But I had to look. The dirt could be a clue. I took a long, quavering breath and walked around Richie in a wide arc. Sure enough, the dirt was stuck in the grooves of the soles of his sneakers, particularly the left one. Obviously, he'd tracked it in.

That was it. No more evidence that I could see. But Homicide would find something. I turned my back on Richie and waited in the silence for the cops to come bursting in. It was going to be so awful having to admit that I'd touched the knife handle. Where were they?

Finally I realized why I was waiting. It was only Richie and me—and he definitely hadn't dialed 911. So I did. A woman with a Hispanic accent answered

"Police. Emergency." I said: "I want to report a murder." Then I began to babble: There's no street number, but if you drive to the bottom of Hill Road and go along Anchorage Lane and then up the gravel road on the right—the one with a Private sign—you'll come to Gulls' Haven. Then I added: "Oh, the victim. . ." She waited. I couldn't say anything. I was hypnotized by a copper skillet hanging from the pot rack. It reflected a tiny, distant image of Richie's dead body. "The victim?" she insisted. So I told her: "My husband."

I always preferred art to life, because art seemed more sensibly constructed. Also, it was usually less boring. In English-country-house murder mysteries, for instance, someone finds the body and says, "Egad, the vicar!" No slogging through sixty more pages while you wait for the police to show up. No tedious wait: the chapter ends, and the next one begins right away; in the first sentence, someone is pouring tea for the constable. Film noir doesn't diddle around either. The camera cuts from a mouth contorted by a scream directly to the cigarette between the lips of a cynical private eye.

It would have been so natural to hear, instantly, the *whaa-whaa-whaa* of a siren and the reassuring crunch of gravel as police cars sped up to the house. But after I hung up the phone, I was alone. The silence was spooky. In a grim, cobwebby corner of my mind, I envisioned a translucent Richie arising from the mortal coil of his body, drifting over the center cooking island, curling around the brass chandelier over the table until—with a hellish *whoosh*—the spirit was drawn into the grillwork of the air register near the baseboard. I heard myself say: "Oh, boy, I don't like this."

But then I got really scared. Because how did I know how long he had been dead before I tripped over him? Five hours? Ten minutes? Just in case, I called out: "The police are coming!" My voice lacked conviction, though. It was all trembly, Marilyn Monroe-ish.

Nerves, I told myself. Relax. But just as I closed my eyes to draw a deep Lamaze cleansing breath, my lids fluttered. Something was wrong. What? I scanned the kitchen: On top of the white-tiled center island, between the extra stovetop we used for big parties and the small fruit and vegetable sink, there it was. Another clue: the oak knife block. It had one empty slot, the one for the big carving knife—which was in my husband.

Oh, God, was I getting dizzy!

Stop with the vapors, I ordered myself. And don't start with the ghost business again. Think! Was it a burglar who grabbed a convenient weapon when Richie surprised him? Could it have been someone who came in with Richie? Wait a second! What had brought Richie back to the house? My lawyer, Honi Goldfeder—a woman who appeared to use throw pillows for shoulder pads—had insisted I change the alarm code so he couldn't get in: "Babes, change the code and let him know you changed it. And don't tell me he has no interest in getting into the house, because *you never know,* and if he *does* sneak in, it won't be to tickle your fancy, *if you get my drift.*" I'd refused: "Men sometimes change their minds. I wouldn't want Richie to think I've locked him out." She'd pointed an inch-long coral finger-nail at me: "You cannot afford to be a cream puff!" Naturally, I was.

But what *had* brought Richie back?

The chime at the front door pealed out its Protestant, grace-before-meals four-note chime. I ran toward the front door. The chill from the marble floor of the center hall rose through my Pan Am socks. My thighs broke out in goose bumps. I sprinted over to the guest closet and grabbed a trench coat, one of the three expensive Burberrys Richie bought in his first paroxysm of Anglophilia, after his ship came in.

I flipped on the outside lights. Six uniformed police stood beneath the three arches that consti-tuted Gulls' Haven's front portico. As I opened the door, one of them, slightly older and more thickly mustachioed than the others, stepped forward and inquired: "Mrs. Meyers?" I let them in and turned on the hall lights. Slowly, appraisingly, they examined the sconces, the dentil moldings, the green-and-white checkerboard marble, as if they had dropped by for a late-night Decorators Showcase.

"Mrs. Meyers?" The cop was much taller than I. He stood so close that when I looked up I could see he combed his nose hair over his mustache. "Mrs. Meyers. We got a call about your husband. Ma'am, could you show us where he is?"

I pictured the blood on Richie's shirt turning brown, forming a cracked crust around the blade.

"Mrs. Meyers, we're here to help you."

Some lines from *Othello* popped into my mind. I'd recited them to Richie once, after a whole night of making love. We were both so amazed and resentful to see daylight. "Perdition catch my soul / But I do love thee! And when I love thee not, / Chaos is come again."

"Mrs. Meyers!" The cop's voice was much too loud. That's probably when I fainted.

TWO

Sergeant Carl Gevinski of Nassau County Homicide would have been good-looking if it weren't for his face. He had nice floppy, graying blond hair that he had to keep brushing off his forehead, crinkly Walter Cronkite eyes, and a friendly big belly. But his face was a circle, with a bulbous clown's nose, the kind you're tempted to squeeze so you'll hear a loud honk, although some accident or fight had squashed it so it hardly rose above his cheeks. In fact, when you looked straight at him, he appeared flat, existing in only two dimensions, like the face of the moon.

"Y'okay?" he asked.

"I'm fine. I blacked out for a second."

Somehow, the cops had hauled or guided me into the library. More police cars had pulled up. About twenty minutes later, Gevinski and his technicians from Homicide had arrived.

I wanted to get out of Richie's trench coat, but as I tried to think of a way to excuse myself to change clothes without appearing frivolous, my legs started to tremble violently, as if I were deliberately banging my knees together in some desperate Jane Fonda exercise. I grabbed the nearest chair at the reading table and lowered myself onto it. The table and chairs were one of Richie's first English antiques. The drawers of the table were inlaid in brass with letters of the alphabet. For a while he took to telling company: "Amusing, isn't it? We bought it at auction in London." But then his cousin Sylvia, who was in the acrylic nail business, laughed in his face, so he'd changed "amusing" to "interesting." Of course, Cousin Sylvia was off the guest list forever.

Gevinski sat opposite me. "I don't like to intrude on you like this, but time is a factor," he said.

"I know. I ought to tell you, before we talk, that I did something wrong."

He bobbed his head in encouragement. "Tell me about it," he urged, tolerant and forgiving, a worldly priest ready to hear the most gruesome confession.

"Don't get the wrong idea," I reassured him. "What I meant was, I may have interfered with your crime scene."

"What did you do?"

"I thought for a second that Richie might be alive, so I . . ."

"So you what?"

"I tried to pull the knife out of his chest." He didn't yell or even snarl at me. He didn't say anything at all. "I knew I shouldn't have, but I was irrational. I thought: He's so still, but maybe he's still alive. If I can just pull out the knife, he'll give this big sigh of relief. I'm sorry, Sergeant Gevinski. I'm really sorry."

"What made you finally decide he was really dead?"

"I don't know. I think I must have known it right away, but for that one irrational second I hoped . . ."

"I understand. Can you face a few more questions now?"

"Sure." My mind was clear. I was neither hysterical nor overcome with grief. My hands were steady. Except, when I tried to cross my legs, I didn't have the strength.

Gevinski peered at his watch. Its face was one of those yellow smiley things, with two eyes and an upturned semicircle for a grin.

I read police procedurals: Time was a factor. I knew the Seventy-two Hour Rule: If the police don't find the perpetrator of a homicide within three days of the murder, the odds against their ever doing so increase astronomically.

"Could you give me the full name?" Gevinski spoke so suddenly I flinched.

"Rose—" Dear God, how could I break this to Ben? And to Alex? He and Richie had been so angry at each other. How in the world could I explain it to my mother?

"The deceased's name, please."

"Richard Elliot Meyers."

He didn't look like a lead detective, a cop full of unrelieved sadness at the human condition, the kind always played by depressed actors like Dana Andrews or Tom Berenger. No, Gevinski was another stock character—the pudgy, asexual, dough-nut-eating partner.

"Occupation?"

"He was president of a company called Data Associates."

Gevinski's eyes swept the library. It was an immense, wood-paneled room, with three couches and God knows how many chairs, ottomans, and side tables. A palm tree that my next-door neighbor had grown in her greenhouse. Two chandeliers. Books, naturally. When Richie decided to bid on Gulls' Haven, I challenged him: This place isn't for us, and you know it, Richie. His expression had turned only slightly surly; he'd been expecting something like that from me. I went on: It could take us an entire generation just to find our way back from the wine cellar. And what the hell are we going to put in that library? Your *Introduction to Differential Calculus?* My *Complete One-Volume Shakespeare?* My paperback mysteries? This is a strictly hardcover room—although maybe your mother would consider donating her Reader's Digest Condensed Books. He countered with: At least *my* mother reads.

But the owner of Gulls' Haven, the executive pro-ducer of a canceled soap opera (who had bought the property from the estate of a robber baron's compulsive-gambler great-grandson), was thrilled to sell Richie the contents of his library; he had bought them from a company called Books by the Yard. Which of course led to a fight. I might have started it by calling Richie a parvenu. It ended with him turning purple and yelling that I had no right to make him feel pretentious just because he happened to appreciate nice things.

So he bought the manor to which he wasn't born. And I got a collection of leather-bound volumes on aeronautics, Catholic saints, the history of Spain (in Spanish), and numismatics. Only the most shallow breather could ignore the occasional whiff of mildew wafting up from the bindings, but as long as you weren't dying for something to read, the library was pretty grand.

"Did the money come from business or family?" Gevinski asked.

"He and a partner started the company. My one hope was that it would do well enough so we could send the boys to good colleges and maybe redo the kitchen. Who could have imagined all this?"

"What does the company do?"

"Research. They'll find out whatever you want to know on any subject. Their motto is 'Knowledge Is Power.' It's on all their stationery. With quotation marks, but without citing the source." Gevinski kept silent, so I guessed the lack of attribution didn't trouble him. I added: "Francis Bacon. *Meditationes Sacrae*."

"They do hush-hush work?"

"No. Just in-depth research. They started out as a computer search company, but they expanded. Now they have four hundred full-time researchers working in regular libraries all over the world, plus another hundred who tap into data bases."

"They make this kind of money from research?"

"Their clients are Fortune 500 companies, law firms, political candidates. Educated people, although none of them seem able to use a card catalogue." Suddenly my elbow slid off the arm of the chair, and I was tilted sideways. When I straightened up, I realized my arms and shoulders were shaking. My legs started banging again too. "I'd like to get something," I told him. Gevinski's face was blank. "I want a tranquilizer."

"Just one more question, Ms. Meyers. Were you awake the whole night?"

"No. I just got up and went downstairs. I was hungry."

"What time did you go to sleep?"

"Early. I was tired. I guess about nine-thirty or ten."

"And got up?"

"Around three-thirty."

"You hear anything?" I shook my head. "Could you have maybe heard something that woke you up?"

"I don't think so, but I can't be a hundred percent sure."

"Maybe you heard a fight. Some dishes got broken."

"No, that was my fault too. I'm sorry—I forgot to tell you about it. When I first saw him, I suppose I went a little crazy, running around, not knowing what to do. I banged into the hutch. A platter and a tureen came crashing down."

"Was anyone in the house with you?"

"No. Our kids are grown. We used to have a couple who lived in, but now they're working for my husband in the city." He nodded. "I have someone coming in twice a week." I waited for him to offer a cop quip, like: Bet it takes more than two days just to vacuum this joint; but he didn't. "We have a fairly sophisticated alarm system," I went on. Gevinski sat there and listened, occasionally stroking his tie, its dark gray broken up by small yellow maple leaves. "The alarm was on when I went to bed," I said. "I'm positive of that. But Richie knew the code."

"Why wouldn't he?"

"He doesn't live here anymore."

He stopped playing with his tie. "Where does he live?"

"In the city."

"You divorced?"

"Separated. Almost divorced. The lawyers have just about finished fighting over the separation agreement. But he moved out the end of June."

Gevinski's fingers counted off the months: one, two, three, four. October! "Did you throw him out?" He sounded so sympathetic that if I'd said "Yes," he'd have said: "You did the right thing!"

"No. He left me. Another woman."

He reached into his inside jacket pocket and pulled out a spiral-bound notepad. "I guess that's an old story," he said kindly.

"I guess so."

"You know her name?" I gave him Jessica's name, the address of her duplex, and her phone number; I knew it because that's where Richie had been living while they looked for what he called "a place where we can spread out." In the interest of full disclosure,

I also told him that Richie planned to marry her as soon as our divorce was final. Since I wasn't asked—and I knew it was routine police procedure—I gave him my name, my age, and my occupation. He thanked me and jotted them down. "Can you wait here for just a minute?" Gevinski asked. I told him I could. "I really appreciate your cooperation." He walked out.

I drummed my fingers, but the old polished wood muffled the sound. I paced the room. The Persian rugs muted my tread. Every room in Gulls' Haven was designed to refine whatever was in it. But that had been Richie's point. I remember how he had brightened when the decorator told him, in her nasal, upper-crust voice, that one of the upholstery fabrics—bolts and bolts of cabbage-rose chintz—might take "a tad longer than usual"; it was being custom-dyed in vats of tea so it would look yellowed, slightly shabby. The old-money look.

But by the time the material arrived, Richie loathed it. He despised the decorator, too, and told me that her attempt to make new money look like old money was strictly to appeal to nouveau riche types. He said she was a condescending bitch and said: "Fire her." I would have loved to, but she had dilated, disapproving Faye Dunaway nostrils and she scared me, so I told him he'd have to do it. "My pleasure," Richie said. But he never got around to it, so we spent another small fortune in damask curtains and Adam mantels before she finally disappeared.

To hell with this, I thought. I've got to get dressed and tranquilized. I strode over to the door, but as I walked out, a uniformed cop put up his hand in a broad Stop! School Crossing! gesture.

"I have to change," I explained. He shook his head. "Why not?" He shrugged. His face was absolutely empty. "Please. I'm just going upstairs."

"I have to ask Sergeant Gevinski if it's okay." But he stayed right where he was.

I stomped back into the library, trying to keep my mind off Richie. Impossible. Someone had *murdered* him. In the moment of his last breath, his final heartbeat, had he locked eyes with his killer—or was he still hoping he could find a way out? Had it hurt, the knife point piercing the skin, slicing through muscle, puncturing bone, or had it happened too fast? Was there time for Richie to comprehend he was dying? A pulse like a frantic heart raced in my throat.

Why was this cop being so boorish? And Sergeant Gevinski: He'd taken the news that I'd grabbed hold of the knife with such equanimity. Could he really be that understanding? Did he view what I'd done as a common housewifely reflex, like pulling out the meat thermometer when the roast is finished?

I couldn't stand being in a dead man's trench coat another minute. I strode back to the subanthropoid at the door. "Did you ask Sergeant Gevinski if I can go upstairs?" I asked.

"Not yet. He said he'd be back soon, so you might as well relax and wait for him."

I backed down, too rattled to assert myself. Well, why shouldn't I be rattled? My man was dead with a carving knife from Williams-Sonoma in his chest. My knife, or almost. According to the separation agreement the lawyers had promised would be ready for us to sign by the weekend, Richie and I would divide the money from the sale of Gulls' Haven. I was to get the contents of the house, which happened to include a great set of knives. Plus. His lawyer offered what my lawyer called an insult—two million dollars. But instead of acting insulted, Honi informed me she simply laughed in the other lawyer's face—and said eight million or no deal. She explained that meant they would split it down the middle by Friday.

My last words with Richie had taken place two nights earlier. He had screamed over the phone: "Jessica did not want to believe what your lawyer is asking! Do you want to know what she said?" I said I didn't, but of course he told me anyway: "She said the one thing she admired about you was that you seemed content with what you were!"

"Calm down, Richie."

"Who the hell are you to tell me what to do?" His yelling was approaching the falsetto range. His last words to me were: "What did you ever do that was worth millions of dollars?" Now he lay on our kitchen floor with a bunch of Nassau County civil servants tape-measuring him and photographing him and probing under his fingernails with tweezers.

What exactly was going on here? What kind of cops were these? Gevinski had seen I had the shakes; his heart should be going out to me. He should have been hollering: Hey, somebody get her doctor on the phone, fast. Poor dame, she oughta be sedated. Instead, he was indifferently polite.

Gevinski returned, treading noiselessly in black orthopedic shoes. They were the molded kind, where each individual toe is given special treatment. "Sorry. Had to talk to the assistant D.A. on the case."

"Any news?"

"What news could there be?" He glanced at his watch. "Did Mr. Meyers have any enemies?" He didn't seem to expect any revelations; his notepad was back in his pocket.

"No."

"Did you hear him recently expressing anger or upsetness at someone?"

"We didn't talk much anymore. As far as I know, the only person he was angry with was me."

Gevinski's eyebrows began as two minuscule tufts of hair on either side of the bridge of his nose and ended as long lines that shot upward; they looked like blond check marks. He lifted them a fraction of an inch. "How angry was he?"

Gevinski, I decided, was not fascinated by the subtleties of human relations. With Richie lying *en brochette* just across the hall, and with my having touched the knife, I realized I ought to amend my answer. "He was angry, but it was normal pre-divorce hostility. Our lawyers were still discussing the final details of the monetary settlement, so naturally it wasn't all sweetness and light." I offered a wan, widowy smile. "As far as him being angry at anyone else, I don't know. He'd stopped confiding in me."

It wasn't that Gevinski didn't smile back. He did. But it worried me that beyond his reflexive smile, he clearly did not find me the least . . . I tried to come up with the precise word. Sympathetic? Appealing? Right: He found me neither sympathetic nor appealing. But there was more. He accepted whatever I said—Uh-huh. Right. I hear you—but he didn't seem to believe it.

Extreme stress, like that brought on by being doubted by an officer of the homicide squad, serves as a cue to every symptom of menopause: You're on! Suddenly light-headed, desperate for sleep, I clamped my jaws shut to suppress a yawn. Simultaneously, I had a hot flash. An instant later, as I grabbed onto the back of a chair for support, I was as wet as a marathon runner. I wiped my forehead on the back of my sleeve but then realized it wasn't my sleeve; it was Richie's Burberry's sleeve, and it was water repellent. Gevinski watched closely.

"Let me think. Did Richie have any enemies . . . " I began again, trying to come up with something to offer him. It wasn't that Richie hadn't been likable. Great guy, people always said. *Charm*ing. No enemies.

But no friends either. Even in our first years in Shorehaven, in the Cape Cod, where the nearby houses were so close you could look into your neighbors' kitchen window and see what brand of frozen waffles they were serving for breakfast, where familiarity bred a gung-ho, all-American, we-have-no-secrets friendliness, where neighbors routinely dropped in to borrow tarragon mustard or a snow blower, Richie wasn't one of the guys.

Not that he was an outcast. He was the man you'd go to if you needed someone to calculate how many square feet of Mexican tile you needed to redo the downstairs bathroom, definitely the fellow to talk sports with, because who else could quote the most arcane fielding stats on the 1947 Brooklyn Dodgers and be interesting? Everyone said: No wonder he's such a good teacher. He's not just good at math; he's *terrific* with people. And he was. Great company at a clambake, a smart fan at a Super Bowl party. But in all the years we were together, I don't think any man ever asked him to take a ride over to the lumberyard or confided in him about a nagging wife, an unstable child.

In those days, before big shots like Carter Tillotson would even give him a nod at the drill bits display in the hardware store, much less want to play tennis with him, Richie didn't even have a regular partner among the regular guys; he filled in for the sick and the lame at the public courts in Shorehaven Park. Sometimes I'd watch him washing the car or mowing the lawn and worry why he wasn't liked more. Popularity was something the kids I taught were obsessed with, and I was ashamed of myself for wishing that Richie were more like the men on our block who, without self-consciousness, could wear a barbecue apron appliquéd with a moronic message.

Once, I asked him who his best friend was. He tossed it off: You are. So I said: Come on, Richie. What if you had a serious problem with me? Whom would you talk to? He smiled. That tantalizing, lopsided smile. I'd still talk to you. Now lay off, Rosie. You know men don't have friendships the way women do—and don't give me that fear-of-intimacy stuff. He drew me toward him and placed my hand on his intimacy. Richie had never been a man's man.

"I don't know if you'd call him an enemy, but Richie's former partner was very angry at him. His name is Mitchell Gruen."

"Go on," Gevinski said, more resentful than curious, because now he'd have to type up another page for his report.

"We were all teaching in a high school in Queens in the late sixties. Richie became a teacher to get out of Vietnam. He was certified in math and social studies. Mitch taught math. And he was crazy about computers." Gevinski crossed his arms over his belly and glanced again at his smile watch. I talked faster. "Anyway, after our first child, money was tight. I was taking a year of maternity leave, and Richie had to get a second job. Mitch already had one: going to people's houses and demonstrating home computers. If a client bought one, a teacher would visit once a week until he learned to use it."

"So?" Gevinski said.

"So Mitch was a terrible salesman. He loved computers, but he wasn't so crazy about people. The company said if he didn't start making some sales, they'd have to let him go. He was desperate for money to pay for his computer habit, so he begged Richie to go on calls with him, to be his partner."

"I hate to pressure you, Ms. Meyers, but time's a factor."

Gevinski wasn't being curt exactly, but he seemed genuinely indifferent to what I was saying. I told myself it was silly to feel nervous. Still, a spouse, especially a jilted spouse, is usually the prime suspect in American detective fiction. More so when the murder takes place at home, with a piece of the family cutlery as the weapon. And when the spouse's prints might be on the weapon? Forget it!

It wasn't that I believed Gevinski would actually

consider me a suspect without knowing more about Richie's life, but I did wish he would be more conspicuously curious as to who done it.

"Richie went in with Mitch," I pressed on. "They worked until ten or eleven, four nights a week. After about six months, they were a big success. The company expanded their territory. But after another year, Richie realized the money wasn't in computer hardware, or even in the rent-a-teacher concept."

"Where was it?"

"Information. One of their clients was a man in the garment industry. He asked Richie and Mitch if they could do some research for him; there was a California textile design company he wanted to buy. To make a long story short, Mitch checked the data bases. I did the library work. I wrote the report too. Richie could express himself, but he hated to write, and Mitch never caught on to the concept of complete sentences."

"What did Mr. Meyers do?"

"He was the people person. He was great. Absolute strangers . . . He'd call people in California whose names came up in the computer check, and they would wind up telling Richie their life stories. And he was terrific with the client too, dropping tidbits of information Mitch and I dug up, in a way that got the client terribly excited, wanting more. See, Richie was a born seducer; he knew exactly what to put in the report to get the client excited. Short, punchy sentences. No big, intimidating words. Computer jargon to make it sound scientific. And every now and then, he wouldn't let me footnote a reference; he made me write: 'Our sources inform us . . .' And it worked! Instead of giving them the five-hundred-dollar fee he promised, the client wrote out a check for a thousand. He hired Richie and Mitch to research some new process for matching plaids, *and* he recommended them to someone in his country club—who recommended them to somebody else. The clients always came back for more. By 1977, they were making an extra twenty thousand a year apiece. By 1979, Richie finally convinced Mitch to quit teaching. They opened up Data Associates."

"With this Mitchell Gruen the inside man and Mr. Meyers working the clients?"

"Yes. After a few years, the firm was grossing around ten million dollars a year. Twenty million by the mid-eighties. Meanwhile, all Mitch was doing was the same basic research he'd always done—and getting half the profits. I suppose that wasn't fair to Richie. The company had hired about a hundred teachers by that time, and they all were doing the exact same work as Mitch."

"So your husband squeezed him out?"

"Yes. I think it was the following year. He hired an investment banker who did an analysis of the company. A brilliant job. Richie took the analysis, went to Mitch, and said: 'I'm ready either to buy the company from you—or to sell it to you. Either way, the price is seven million dollars. But we can't go on being partners.' Well, Data Associates had become Mitch's whole life. He had complete access to all the equipment he could ever dream of, *and* he was rich. He even took to riding around in a limo. Poor Mitch, he was having such a good time.

"Anyway, after Richie bought him out, Mitch set

up his own company. It failed. Then he made some bad investments. Big investments. He was a born patsy, with no business judgment. He ran through the entire seven million dollars and probably went a little crazy. He blamed all his problems on Richie. Then, about three years ago, he tapped into the computer and got the new master password for Data Associates' whole system. He wiped out their entire program library. It probably was just a nasty little trick to Mitch, but it took six months and about two million dollars to fix things."

"Did Mr. Meyers call the police?"

"Yes."

"This Mitch go to jail?"

"No, but he was fined a hundred thousand dollars—which he didn't have. After he lost his appeal, he called Richie and said: 'I gave you your life. You took mine away.' He had to sell off most of his computer equipment to pay the first installment of the fine."

At last, Gevinski took out his pad: "Spell this guy's name." I did. "Where is he now?"

"I'm not sure. He lives in the city. Oh, I know who might be helpful: Data Associates' public relations person. Jane Berger. She knows Mitch better than anybody. It's interesting: she's the busiest woman in New York, but for some reason she still has time to keep in touch with him—by modem. I never could figure out that friendship. She's totally sane; Mitch is light-years beyond eccentric. Anyway, she told Richie that Mitch has become a recluse. He keeps the blinds drawn and doesn't leave his apartment for months at a time. He even orders his meals by fax so he doesn't have to talk on the phone."

"Did he ever make threatening remarks to your husband or gestures?" I rarely failed anyone in English, but I would have loved to be able to flunk Gevinski for that sentence.

"Not that I know of."

All of a sudden, without a word, Gevinski stood and strode toward the door. Give the guy the benefit of the doubt, I told myself, watching him leave. Maybe he's going to put out an all points bulletin on Mitch.

I called out: "I think he's probably listed in the Manhattan phone book." The corners of Gevinski's mouth turned up into his automatic smile. "I forgot to mention something," I added, much louder. He nodded to go ahead, but stayed where he was. "The investment banker: the one who did the analysis of Data Associates. It was Jessica Stevenson. The woman he left me for. Richie was so impressed with the way she solved the Mitch problem that he spent a year wooing her to leave her firm and join Data Associates."

"Be patient," he called back to me.

So I was patient—for about two minutes. I examined a few shelves of books. Then I examined the telephone. I knew I had to face calling the boys. Boys? Well, on matters close to the heart, I suppose I still thought of my sons the way I thought of my students: large, interesting, sexually active children. So how the hell do you tell a child his father has been murdered?

Ben was a fourth-year student at the University of Pennsylvania's medical school. I dialed his apartment, knowing he might be at the hospital at five-thirty in the morning, but I soothed myself by imagining his resonant, reassuring Hello. When I heard his lady friend, whom Alex had nicknamed Suspicious Foods, I almost hung up. But I said: "This is Rose Meyers. I'd like to speak with Ben."

Usually I was able to manage a relatively cordial "How are you?" to Suspicious. Occasionally, I'd inquire how hay fever season was going. It wasn't scintillating repartee, but what other conversation could I make with a thirty-five-year-old extremely boring allergist who was living with and wanted to marry my twenty-four-year-old son?

"Mom?" Ben got on almost immediately.

"Ben . . ."

He knew it was something bad. "What is it?"

"Daddy," I said, and only realized then that I should have said: Your father.

"Is he hurt?" He didn't wait for me to answer. He whispered: "Dead?" I nodded. "Mom?"

"I'm so sorry, Benjy."

"What was it?" He sounded crisp, clinical, as if waiting for a report on a patient who had not lived through the night.

"He was killed, sweetheart."

He couldn't say anything at first. By the time he could, his voice squeaked. "An accident?"

I told him, briefly, what had happened. He asked about the knife. Where and how deeply had it gone in? Did I know at what angle? I understood Ben. His wasn't a doctor's infatuation with blood and guts; it was a need to reassure himself that his father could not have been helped. "It sounds as if it sliced into the aorta," Ben said. "He wouldn't have had a chance." Then he added: "Mom, are you okay?"

"I don't know. I keep thinking I might go off the deep end with the horror of it. But then I feel so detached, almost as if I were reading one of those drecky true-crime articles in *New York* magazine where they toss around words like 'hubris'!"

"Easy, Mom."

"I am easy, for God's sake! But I went down for a yogurt and wound up tripping over—Oh. I'm so sorry."

"It's okay. Did you call Alex?"

"Not yet." If any words of mine could alleviate Ben's pain, those would.

"Do they have any idea who could have done it?"

"I doubt it. It's too soon. Oh, Ben, he's still in there! In the kitchen."

Neither of us could speak for a minute. Finally Ben found the strength to break the silence. "Listen, Mom. I'm getting dressed and getting right into the car. I'll be there before you know it. Okay? You won't have to be alone. We'll all be together."

Which sounded comforting, except I had a feeling Ben was conjuring up not Mom and Her Boys Consoling Each Other but, rather, a threesome of him, me, and . . . I could never remember her name. Melissa? Marissa? Miranda? She'd once had a heart-to-heart with Alex, after he sneezed three times, and she said: "Something you're eating. No excuse: I want you to make a list of suspicious foods." So Alex called her Suspicious Foods behind her back and went on sneezing. I had sneezed too, but she never told me to make up a list.

She could kill all conversation at a family gathering simply by announcing: "You'd be amazed how many

corn products I can find in the average person's diet."
Ben said he loved her.

I called Alex, but naturally he wasn't home. At
twenty-one, on a leave of absence from the
University of Massachusetts, he was earning his living as guitarist and lead singer in Cold Water Wash,
a group he assured me was starting to make its name
in New England alternative-music circles. The message on his answering machine was a cool "You
were sayin' . . . ?"

What could I be sayin'? "Just called to let you
know you won't have to buy a Father's Day gift next
June"? As it was, I was so unnerved by his machine's
honking electronic you-can-talk-now tone that all I
could do was mutter something like Call home, it's
urgent. It did not surprise me that the one time I
wanted Alex at five-thirty in the morning he was not
to be found.

Maybe something terrible had happened to him
too.

At five forty-five, Gevinski returned to the library,
loudly sipping what smelled like overboiled conve-
nience-store coffee from a cardboard cup. I smiled,
graciously and, I hoped, cooperatively. "I'd have
been glad to put up a pot of coffee or make some
tea."

"You think it would be a good idea if I let you
have the run of the crime scene again?" he joked.
"The kitchen *is* a crime scene, you know."

"I said I was sorry."

"Sure. No problem." Only Gevinski's words were
laid-back. He pulled out his pad and whipped
through it with such urgency he ripped one of the
pages. "Your husband left you for Jessica Stevenson?"

"Yes," I said. "Have you spoken to her yet?"

"Let's just finish up here, if you don't mind."

"Sure."

"Thanks. You said Mr. Meyers moved out in late June?"

"That's right."

"What have you been doing since that time?"

"I went back to teaching right after Labor Day, when school opened."

"What did you do all summer?"

"Well, Richie and I had planned a cruise around the Greek islands in July, and I was going to spend August rereading some nonfiction. *The Silent Spring, The Fate of the Earth, Mornings on Horseback.*" I must have been hoping that Gevinski would jot down the titles, because I was disappointed that he didn't. "I wanted to work at least one of them into the curriculum."

"So what did you wind up doing?"

"I sat on the stairs that go down to the beach and stared at the water for two months. I was a wreck."

"Your husband moved out totally?"

"His clothes and just about everything else he owned are still here, but he was out."

"But was it *totally?* He didn't come back once he moved out—you one night, Jessica the next night?"

"No."

"Did you see him since he moved out?"

"Once, at my lawyer's. He was with his lawyer."

"And other than that?"

"No. He said it would be less painful for both of us if we discussed whatever business we had together on the phone."

"There's one thing I don't quite get, Ms. Meyers."

"What is that?"

"Help me figure it out. If Mr. Meyers moved out so totally, how come he dropped by last night, uninvited—and just in time to get himself killed?"

Three

A little after six-thirty, one of Gevinski's men, who was wearing something I'd never seen before, a maroon suit, returned to the library. He said if I wanted to go upstairs for a few minutes, I could. It was only when I was listening to the water beating on my shower cap that it dawned on me that the police probably wanted a few minutes to poke around in the library. But what was there to poke through? Six leather-bound, gold-tooled volumes on the life of Saint Bruno of Querfurt? Family photos of happier times, the four of us grinning and googly-eyed in snorkel masks? The restaurant matchbooks in the bottom desk drawer that Richie collected until he realized collecting matchbooks was gauche? I'd always been a little nervous that they would spontaneously combust, and Gulls' Haven would wind up like Thornfield.

I put on school clothes—plaid slacks, a yellow silk blouse, and a sweater—took a Xanax, and stowed another in my pocket. I hated being such an upper-middle-class namby-pamby, gulping tranquilizers instead of tossing back a shot of whiskey, but I was no longer tough enough for a snootful of booze.

When the American Dream came true for Richie and me, we stopped being stand-tall Americans and became human lapdogs. First, other people cleaned our house. Then they cooked our meals, arranged our flowers, fertilized our tomatoes. More people came along; they balanced our household accounts, vacuumed our pool, paid our taxes, invested our money. We had a French tutor for Ben, a psychiatrist for Alex, a personal trainer for Richie, a visiting manicurist for me, and a family therapist for us all. I had insomnia on Egyptian cotton sheets and pillowcases ironed by a laundress.

I never realized how money complicates life. Forget tax returns as thick as a Trollope novel. I'm talking about how we slowly lost touch with the world as it was and wound up living in the scented-candle universe of other rich people.

This is how it happened: When our old friends saw a chauffeur driving the family Mercedes, or the cook preparing a Pritikin tuna fish salad, they laughed and said: "Give me a break!" This angered Richie and embarrassed me, so we began to spend more time with other people with chauffeurs and cooks, people who also lived in twenty-room houses or thirty-room co-ops. Slowly, we ditched the old friends. It was surprisingly easy to do. We told each other it was hard to be with them because they envied our success, or because they would not see that despite all the money, we were still the same old Richie and Rosie.

Instead of spending Saturday night barbecuing chicken for a couple of neighbors, we went to a charity benefit in a tent in East Hampton. Someone we met there, a man from Athens, Georgia, who'd made it big in shopping malls, invited us on his yacht for a Mediterranean cruise. So we gave up going to the cabin in the Adirondacks where we'd gone fishing for the last fifteen summers. Dazed from too much sun and Dramamine, we hung out on a big ship with a dozen strangers in white linen slacks. I never got to read *The Wings of the Dove*. I didn't have time; I had to finish an exposé of the machinations of an odious arbitrageur that everyone else was reading so I could be part of the dinner conversation over a too-small portion of bass baked in parchment.

Gulls' Haven, our dream house, stood on a ridge that jutted ever so slightly over Long Island Sound. If you woke in the master bedroom in time for sunrise— and with the gulls screeching as they made their first sweep of the day to defecate on our roof, only the soundest sleeper made it through dawn undisturbed—you could gaze out the rear windows, over the lawn, westward across the blue-gray water, and see Manhattan in the distance, a golden city shining in the early sunlight. If you wakened in Ben's or Alex's room, in the east wing, you could take in the green velvet grounds of the waterfront estates of Westchester County.

If you never left the back half of Gulls' Haven, you would spend your entire life believing America was always beautiful.

But it wasn't so pretty up front now. I pressed my nose against the glass of the tall windows near the head of the staircase. Straight down, I could see police cars, a crime-scene van, an ambulance, and, barreling up the drive, a WCBS-TV mobile unit with a dirt-smeared eye on its side. Two uniformed cops trotted over to greet it with shaking heads and you're-out-of-here thumbs; after completing a reluctant U-turn by backing over a thicket of azalea bushes, it disappeared down the drive, toward the road.

I stomped back into the library, ready to confront Gevinski: Who called the press? What's going on here? He wasn't there.

Thank God, my friend Cass was. "How did you hear about it?" I asked her.

"Rosie," she began, "this is dreadful." Cass was a very grande dame. Definitely not in height, although with her steel-rod spine, she did seem taller than the broad-beamed five foot three she was. But her ebony features were so finely chiseled that people rarely noticed that her exquisitely molded Yoruba carving of a head was attached to a Buddha's body.

And when she spoke: definitely grand. "We came to get you for the walk at six forty-five. When you didn't appear, we decided to trot up here and hurl rocks at your window." Cassandra Higbee talked in that leisurely, good-liberal-arts-college way that assumed the world would wait until she phrased her thoughts just so, which, in fact, the world seemed willing to do.

Cass may not have been an actual aristocrat, but she'd been born a class act. Yes, the morning's three-mile walk had just been canceled because of the murder of one of the participants' husbands. Yes, at that precise moment, two beefy men wearing blue "Medical Examiner" jackets clomped past the open library door, wheeling a gurney. Cass, unperturbed, gripped my shoulders, spun me around, and shepherded me toward the couch. In doing so, she almost succeeded in cutting off my view of the third man, who was carrying a black plastic sack.

"A body bag," I said.

"Hush, Rosie."

"Well, it *is* a body bag."

"If you spent more time reading Edith Wharton instead of those dreadful novels where the alcoholic detective kisses his old flame goodbye on her decomposing lips, you would not possess such hurtful knowledge."

"Edith Wharton was an anti-Semitic bitch."

"So you have said," she soothed me. "Now, I am here to help you. What can I get you? An early-morning cognac?"

"I had an early-morning Xanax."

"Sit, then. We can talk if you like, or I will just keep you company."

The other two women who walked with us, Stephanie and Madeline, could never have been so in command. Stephanie Tillotson, although the perfect woman, would only have kept her composure long enough to make two or three pâtés and bake a half-dozen baguettes, for those pre-autopsy guests who unexpectedly pop in and want a nibble. Madeline Berkowitz, on the other hand, would probably lock herself up for three weeks and emerge with yet another work of alleged art—something like "Himicide: Ode on the Execution of an Errant Husband."

But Cass stayed cool, although the body bag did, for a moment, bring out a grayness in her skin—the way a black person gets pale. But with effortless grace, she placed one Niked foot behind the other and lowered herself onto a couch. Despite navy sweats and red turtleneck, she was, as always, self-possessed and so proper that it seemed liveried servants might materialize to wheel out a formal tea for her to pour. She breathed: "Imagine. When we arrived at the top of the drive, we were stopped by a yellow plastic streamer emblazoned 'Crime Scene.' "

I could hear Gevinski and his men in the kitchen. They were having some sort of conference, although the rumble of male voices was so low I couldn't make out the gist of what they were saying. "The cops didn't try to stop you from coming in?" I asked.

Cass flicked away an imaginary mosquito, thus illustrating the difficulty she'd had with the Nassau County Police Department. Then she patted the cushion beside her; I sat. She took my hand in hers. "I am sorry, Rosie."

"I thought his leaving me was the worst thing that

could ever happen." Cass reached under the cuff of her shirt and withdrew a hankie; she didn't believe in tissues. I pressed it hard against my eyes. I wanted to cry, but I couldn't.

"This is devastating," she said. "But you will get through it, you know. And when you think you will not, I will be here to help."

I'd only cried once in front of Cass, the Sunday Richie walked out, but that had been a good test; she was the best person in the world to fall apart in front of. She didn't sniffle in sympathy, babble heartening bromides, shift in chagrin at my ethnic loss of control, or clasp me to her bosom to make me an honorary soul sister. Instead, she just sat by me.

She took back her hankie, limp from my sweaty hands. "No," she said, before I could say a word. "I do not want you to have it laundered, thank you." She slipped it back inside her sleeve. "Oh, I forgot to mention that Madeline and Stephanie send their sympathy."

"Are they here?" I asked, my voice probably full of foreboding.

"Of course not. Madeline said she had to get home. I am sure she will want to get in touch with her inner child-woman so she can create Literature. Is there no one who can stop her?" Cass's chilly Eastern Establishment preparatory school enunciation was warmed by a touch of Bedford-Stuyvesant drawl; she'd spent her first fourteen years there. "And Stephanie." She exhaled an exhausted sigh at the mere thought of Stephanie's vigor. "As we speak, she is probably reading a tome on Jewish mourning practices."

"While simultaneously pickling lox. Can you picture

the platter she'll bring over?" Stephanie had given up a career in litigation to become the paradigm of suburban womanhood.

Cass said: "Rosie, tell me what I should do for you. I would hope it would not involve lox, which may be beyond my competence."

"Can you fix things at school for the next . . . " The enormity of what had happened in my kitchen was dawning on me.

"You will need at least two or three weeks," Cass decreed. "Perhaps until the end of the semester. Or it might conceivably take the entire school year." When your dearest friend is also your department chairman, it can be touchy. In the ten years we'd been teaching together, though, I had never asked Cass for any favors. "Take all the time you need. If any rules get in the way, I shall bend them or break them."

Cass's hand was large and warm and comforting. All of a sudden I realized I was still squeezing it. I let it go. "Cass?"

"Yes?"

"I may be in trouble."

She displayed her gift of being able to raise one eyebrow. "With whom?"

"With the police sergeant in charge of the case. I don't think he believes me."

Cass stretched out her neck and lifted her double chin as if listening for vital data being transmitted on a frequency inaudible to the ordinary human ear. When she'd heard enough, she looked straight at me. "Rosie, a gentle reminder. This is life, not Dick Lit."

"I know, but I can feel that things aren't going well."

"Why do you think you are in trouble with him?"

"He thinks it's significant that Richie came over here just in time to get killed."

"Not an altogether ridiculous observation."

"Could you manage less ironic detachment? Maybe whip up a little more sympathy?"

"The substance of what he is saying is not without merit. It does not mean he is about to take you to a small room and beat you with a rubber hose. Why *was* Richie here?"

"How should I know?"

"You didn't invite him? Not even a coy 'Drop by whenever you are in the neighborhood'?"

"No. He knew he didn't need an invitation. But how come he showed up in the middle of the night?"

Cass gnawed on the inside of one of her cheeks. She was born to chew. Her mind worked better when her jaw was moving. Gum was on her list of unspeakable vices, but she rarely left home without a Charleston Chew in her handbag.

"Do you want a pretzel or something?" I asked.

"My cheek will do for now, thank you. Tell me, why would Richie want to skulk about your house?"

"Maybe he wanted to see me."

"In the middle of the night?"

Words tumbled out. "Listen, if Richie for some reason decided to come back to me, I wouldn't put it past him to sneak upstairs and slide right into bed. He was ... dramatic, exciting. I mean, look around Shorehaven. You know how different he was from the rest of the guys his age. Ninety percent of them: eunuchs with deep voices. Sexless. Gray."

"Theodore is beige, actually." Cass's husband was

the publisher of a conservative magazine, *Standards*. "And he is not sexless, although unfortunately he does disprove the myth of black male sexual superiority."

"But Richie was different. He was—"

Cass spoke kindly. "Last week, when we had dinner at that new Japanese place, you said you finally understood that he no longer loved you, that he loved Jessica and was going to marry her."

"So maybe I was wrong last week. He could have been getting tired of her."

"Why?"

"Well, don't laugh."

"I will restrain myself."

"She's really not a warm person."

"Did his lawyer telephone yours and suggest that Richie wished to reconcile because he missed your warmth?" The fact was, Cass knew damn well that my lawyer had called me the day before, cackling that Richie was so desperate to marry Jessica that he was caving in to nearly all of our demands. "Is it likely that he came to ravish you and thereby declare his love?"

"I guess not."

"Then where do we go from here?" Cass inquired. I managed a listless shrug. "Rosie, you cannot afford to be passive at a time like this. Think! Look to your dicks! What would . . . who is that tedious character in that Dorothy Sayers novel you forced me to read?"

"Lord Peter, and he's not tedious."

"These books have turned your mind to mush. In any case, what would Lord Peter do?"

"He would try to find out why Richie was here. Probably he'd be curious to know if Richie came with anyone. . . . Oh! Cass! Maybe he came with Jessica!"

"Why would he do that?"

"How should I know?"

"To have an aberrant sexual encounter with her on your kitchen table? To mock your taste in place mats?"

"I have nice taste in place mats."

"The ones embroidered with fruit designs? Please! However, to the matter at hand: Richie would not have brought Jessica here. You know that, I know that, and no doubt the police do as well."

I put my face in my hands, massaged my forehead, and mumbled: "Maybe he didn't bring her. Maybe she *followed* him." I glanced between my fingers. Cass did not seem any more electrified by this hypothesis than by my others. "Just listen to this scenario. Richie told Jessica he'd made a mistake. He was still in love with me. Or maybe he just couldn't stand the thought of losing a big hunk of his fortune. In any case, he's coming back to me. So she follows him here and kills him!"

"Why?"

"*Why?*"

"The woman is quintessentially cool. She is making an annual salary of . . . "

"A half-million bucks."

"Thank you. She could easily make the same elsewhere, if not more. Correct? Why would a woman of her ilk murder a man simply because he wanted to return to his wife?"

"Maybe she was crazy—" I started to say crazy with jealousy, but I knew it couldn't be. Jessica might be enamored of Richie's wealth, pleased by his vitality,

delighted by his talent in bed. But if he did leave her
... I truly believed Jessica would not fall to pieces.
She'd probably be upset. Not eat for a couple of
days. Lose five pounds. "Okay, maybe she wouldn't
go crazy. But she'd be supremely pissed off."

"Pissed-off people do not stab, my dear. Pissed-off
people have their attorneys negotiate a severance
with highly favorable terms."

After Cass left to get dressed for school, I waited for
Gevinski to come back. He didn't, but since no uniformed hulks tried to keep me in the library this
time, I went upstairs, to my office. It was a room
that, for Gulls' Haven, was pretty cozy, although by
any objective standard it contained enough square
footage for a full production of *Aïda*. In the house's
Edwardian heyday it had been the mistress's dressing
room. Now all it had was an old desk and chair and
a crimson couch that was more suitable for a weary
hooker than a proper lady. I stretched out. Less than
twelve hours earlier, I'd been sitting at the desk sipping Lemon Zinger tea, marking the last of "The
Gamut of Love in *Pride and Prejudice*" papers.

From the window opposite, on the side of the
house, I could see the low stone wall that separated
Gulls' Haven from the higher ground of the
Tillotsons' Emerald Point, the thick woodland that
lay between the two estates, and, following a dirt
path up the promontory, the stately linden trees that
shielded the Tillotsons' court from whatever tennis
courts have to be shielded from. Their house was so
far away from the court that all I could spot was a
thin slice of blue-gray slate roof.

It was a comforting, familiar view. But something was moving beneath all those autumn-colored trees. I was off the couch in a flash. On the edge of the wood, in the no-man's-land between the two properties, right next to the road, a couple of men in orange-and-blue windbreakers were on their knees. A giant blue spruce rose beside them. I couldn't make out what they were doing, so I ran across the house to Ben's room, found his bar mitzvah binoculars, and raced back to my office.

The blue-and-orange jacket turned out to be a piece of particularly hideous official Nassau County haberdashery. I adjusted the focus. A black guy was spreading white glop over what was probably tread marks from automobile tires; the other guy's job seemed to consist of talking to the glop-spreader. I eased open the window as quietly as I could; I couldn't hear a thing.

I couldn't really see anything either, at least not anything significant. The glop guy was probably wasting his time. The wooded area wouldn't have any clues, since nearly everybody who played tennis with Stephanie Tillotson or her husband, Carter, parked on just that spot—because it was closer to the tennis court than the house was. According to Stephanie, who, by birthright, knew everything about Old Money, the builders of the North Shore estates had been passionate in their conviction that if you could hear the *thwomp* of the ball as it hit the racket, the court was too damn close to the house.

But then I readjusted the focus. What I had first thought must be one of those big black boxes for cable TV connections right next to the road, half hidden by the branches of the spruce, was actually the side fender of a car. A sports car. I ran into the next room, my bathroom, to get a better view. There it was: so low and aerodynamically correct it wasn't much more than a black scalene triangle. True, I didn't know shit from Shinola about sports cars. Nevertheless, I knew it had to be a Lamborghini Diablo. Richie had once confided that the Diablo was his dream car, but it was so expensive it went beyond mere self-indulgence: It would have been morally wrong to buy one, he explained. A $239,000 outrage. Maybe he'd gotten a good buy.

I was thinking some more about what money had done to me and Richie, so it wasn't until I started down the big, curving stone staircase that I heard the shuffling below. I leaned over the railing just in time to see the attendants from the medical examiner's office wheeling out what had once been my husband, wrapped up to go in a body bag. A uniformed cop sprang forward to open the door.

In movies, body bags always have nice tailoring and a thick zipper that makes a cruel rasping noise on the sound track. But that's Hollywood. This was Long Island. From where I stood, I didn't see any zippers; it looked as if the Nassau County P.D. was using Hefty bags. Richie would have been indignant, being carted out like that. Such a squalid exit for such a stylish man! The uniformed cop kept watch as the medical examiner's crew rolled the gurney up to the ambulance. I craned my neck. The rear doors of the vehicle were open, ready to receive the body.

I squinted. Something familiar . . . right behind the yellow crime-scene tape but way off to the side. Wraparound sunglasses with mirror lenses. Black spandex legs. Black Gore-Tex windbreaker and a black motorcycle cap. Madeline Berkowitz. Her angry-poet look was undermined somewhat by pink angora earmuffs. She had told Cass she was going home, but there she was, taking in every second of Richie Meyers' final moment at Gulls' Haven. She winced as the ambulance doors slammed shut, then about-faced and ran down the drive, kicking up gravel as she went, faster and faster.

The phone rang and a voice said: "Hey."

Alex, of course, would never say anything simple or direct, like "Hello" or "The message you left said urgent and I'm terribly worried, so please tell me what's happening."

"Alex?" I asked, even though there was no mistaking the voice, a full baritone with the slightest hint of hoarseness. A great rock-and-roll voice. If he ever became a famous rock-and-roller, fans would turn on the radio, hear just one note, and say: "Alex Meyers!"

"What's goin' on?"

"Where the hell were you? It's eight o'clock." Silence. "Alex, listen to me. Something terrible has happened."

"Who to?"

"To whom. Your father."

"Like what?" Studied indifference. A customer waiting to hear the choices of entrées in a lackluster restaurant: heart attack, car accident, street crime. Relations between Alex and Richie had been bitter since high school, when the police brought Alex home at three in the morning stinking drunk. Richie grounded him. Alex responded by stuffing his bed with pillows and sweatshirts, taking the Sav-Ur-Life fire escape ladder from under his bed, and continuing his after-hours social life with his bass-playing, dope-dealing friend, Danny Reese, and the other guys in his band. We learned about his excursions one morning after a night of heavy rain, when the housekeeper pointed out a muddy footprint on his windowsill. So Richie installed sensors on Alex's windows; opening them would set off harrowing alarms. Alex retaliated by concocting a device with magnets to circumvent the sensors.

Miraculously, Alex had not only graduated high school but got accepted to the University of Massachusetts—where he'd been put on academic probation three times. He claimed the third suspension was grossly unfair. To get even with U Mass, he left Amherst and moved to a slum near Cambridge and sent the dean of students a notice that he was taking a leave of absence. He called Richie to tell him he was going to be a full-time musician. Richie expressed his opinion of this decision by canceling Alex's American Express card. Alex expressed his by stealing—he called it "borrowing"—Richie's platinum card and charging a new amplifier, as well as a dinner at a Boston restaurant that included a two-hundred-fifty-dollar bottle of Château Margaux: this from a kid whose true taste ran to wine coolers with names like Strawberry Spittle. Richie then mailed Alex a certified letter saying that if Alex did not shape up, he would be cut off without a cent.

I told Alex what had happened to his father. No "Oh my God!" Not even a quick gasp.

"I want you to come home," I told him. Silence. "Alex, I want you home today." Nothing. "Do you understand?"

"Yeah."

"Do you need me to wire you money to get home?"

"No."

"Do you have enough to pay for a shuttle ticket?"

"Yeah. But I'll have to get back to Boston first."

"Where are you now?"

"Where? New Hampshire."

"You had a gig there?" No answer. "Get home as soon—" I never finished the sentence. Alex banged down the phone.

Whom could I turn to? All summer long, I'd devoured how-to-survive-divorce guides with the intensity I'd once devoted to *The Tempest*. They all offered the same wisdom: You're on your own, toots. But ever since I'd been twenty-two years old, I hadn't been. Richie had always taken care of me: my social life, family life, and sex life, my financial well-being. He was the one I'd call once a year to announce, Hey, my mammogram's okay.

I knew the how-to books were right, that I was my own person; I had no choice, since I was no longer anybody else's. But even after Richie left, if the worst had happened with the stock market—or with the mammogram—he would have been the one I'd call once the meanness of the divorce blew over. Sure, I knew that high over Gracie Square he'd probably roll his eyes and mouth a weary "Rosie" to Jessica (who would sit on his lap and give him supportive kisses as he spoke to me), but in the end he would help. So okay, he wouldn't help personally anymore. He'd assign a thirty-two-year-old Wharton M.B.A. to my case. But within hours, teams of accountants would be summoned or entire staffs of hospitals would be called upon. This woman needs help! Do something!

Who could help me now? I had one kid with a ponytail and a guitar who thought it was witty to rhyme "scum" and "come." I had another kid who gazed, lovestruck, at a woman with false eyelashes, ten years older than he, while she spent half an hour at a family dinner recounting a fifteen-minute consultation with a patient whose neck was covered with pustules.

My father couldn't help. He'd been dead for fifteen years. My mother was alive, but her mind was dying fast. She did not have the dreaded Alzheimer's, merely senile dementia. On those infrequent occasions when she was able to remember my husband-less state, she became furious at me, convinced I'd thrown Richie over—so I could continue a flaming affair with a man she called Lover Boy. She shouted in the intimate apparel department of Lord & Taylor, where I'd taken her to buy her a new bathrobe: "What does Lover Boy have that your husband doesn't have?"

Richie's sister, Carol, had been a friend as well as my sister-in-law. We'd bought layettes for our first babies together. A week after Richie left, she took me to lunch in the city, where, over angel hair with baby asparagus and pygmy eggplants, she told me to let go gracefully. For my own peace of mind. This was no infatuation. Rick was in love with Jessica. Madly in love. Hopelessly in love. Completely in—I simply got up and walked out. I never heard from her again.

Could I turn to Richie's business associates? After all those dinner parties, hundreds of nights of rubber *coq au vin* we foisted on each other, not a single person at Data Associates—and not a single spouse—had called since the day Richie left. To tell you the truth, it wasn't such a big surprise, or such a big loss.

The closest Richie came to having a real friend was his pal of the last seven or eight years, Joan, the wife of his biggest client, Tom Driscoll. I'd been the one who actually made the introduction: Years earlier, back in Brooklyn, before Tom became an Ivy League snob and then the coldest fish in Manhattan, he had been one of the world's best kids. We'd been great pals in elementary school, and although we grew apart, we came back together—briefly—to be boyfriend and girlfriend in our senior year of high school.

Joan Driscoll was thin, shrewd, and cruel, the prerequisites for social success in New York. During her first visit to Gulls' Haven, she called Richie "Squire Meyers." Instead of tossing her out on her bony backside, Richie laughed. He thought Joan was the epitome of sophistication. Maybe she was. After he left me, I called her, imploring her to please put in a good word for marriage. She and Tom had been together for ages; maybe she could persuade Richie that he and I should at least try—maybe go for counseling. She said: "At the risk of sounding harsh, lovey, the *last* thing Rick wants is counseling. The man is as happy as a clam."

My old friends? My closest friend from Brooklyn College was now an exercise machine wholesaler in San Diego. My second closest had been tied up for the past two years with a torrid love affair, a divorce, a remarriage, and a change-of-life baby, and was currently recuperating from a nervous breakdown in an ashram in the Berkshires that had no phone.

I had Cass, but how much could I ask of a woman who had a full-time job, a husband, and three kids who, while ostensibly away at private schools, seemed a near-perpetual presence in the house, with their mid-semester breaks, pre-finals breaks, Christmas breaks, winter breaks, and spring breaks?

I had my fellow teachers, but unlike Cass and me, they had no household employees to cook, clean, iron, take care of their children, and go to the super-market for them. Their lives had been my life not so long ago; I knew they had, tops, a half hour of free time every day.

There were my other two walking friends. Stephanie had given up writing legal briefs for needlepoint. Her current project was a rug with a border of plant symbols, from Easter lilies to Valentine's Day sweetheart roses, which represented A Year in the Life of the Tillotsons. Stephanie and I baked together every Friday afternoon, we shopped together—although the closest we'd ever come to exchanging confidences was when she confided that her mother had refused her request to borrow her golden sable, but that was no surprise, because her mother had always been unnurturing, superselfish, and superficial.

Or should I turn to Madeline the Poet, who, two days after Richie left, asked me: "'Alone / In the king-sized cosmos of / The Posturepedic / Why?'"

Actually, the only person around at the moment was Sergeant Gevinski. He must have been eating something. He'd tucked his tie into his shirt, so only the knot showed. A roll or bagel, I decided as he approached; there was a sprinkling of poppy seeds on his chin. Could I turn to Sergeant Gevinski?

"Ms. Meyers."

"Yes?"

"I'd appreciate it if you could stay close to home the next few days. Not that you'd probably want to go anywhere, but things come up. You know how it is. We may have some more questions."

"I'll be here," I told him.

"Good," he said. "Wouldn't want you to run out on us." He winked: a joke. Neither of us laughed.

Four

I should have been pledging allegiance with my homeroom class. Instead, I was getting Sergeant Gevinski's permission to visit my next-door neighbor. Two seconds later, as the kids say, I was off like a prom dress.

As the crow flies, Emerald Point, although on a higher bluff than Gulls' Haven, was not far at all. But even if you weren't tripped up by clinging vines and centuries of dead, fallen trees, the woods that separated us were so choked with nettles and poison ivy that a single step could result in a rash, so there was no real shortcut. The easiest route was down the flight of wooden stairs at the end of our back lawn, onto the beach, across the sand, and then up the Tillotsons' stone staircase to the back of their house—a schlepp when one of us ran out of ketchup. Stephanie and I usually drove. But this time I took the long route, down our nearly quarter-mile-long drive to Anchorage Lane and then up Hill Road toward Emerald Point. I had to get out for a while. I was not sure if I was looking for distraction or for clues.

Nothing fascinating in front of my house, just knots of uniformed police and strolling plainclothesmen. Their almost unrelieved whiteness seemed to indicate that while the Nassau County Police Department was adept at recruiting adorable blue-eyed men, it was a long shot to win any prizes on Martin Luther King Day.

The crime-scene van, which had looked full of promise from the house, kept its secrets behind dark-tinted windows; the maroon-suited cop I'd spotted earlier slid open the van's door just wide enough to slip in; then he yanked it shut.

The glop-spreader on Hill Road was not so secretive. By the time I got all the way over there, he was troweling on the last of the white stuff. Then the man who had just been keeping him company leapt to work. He turned out to be a photographer. He seemed to find his subject enthralling; he crouched, he stretched, but instead of shooting the deep reds, golden yellows, and rich oranges of the woods, he shot angle after angle of the wide white strips and the area around them. I squinted: sure enough, tire tread marks. I was a little nervous about hanging around and arousing any more suspicions than I had aroused already, but the two appeared used to an audience; Shorehaven Estates, with a population density of one tasteful person per tasteful acre, was probably pretty dull for them. They nodded—gracious hosts. I nodded back—refined guest—and checked out their work. Besides Richie's tire prints, there were others. To me, one set seemed as prominent as Richie's, the tire impressions around the same depth in the dirt, and about as wide, not eroded by wind or autumn rains.

"How do you know which marks to put the glop on?" I asked.

"We do 'em all," said the photographer.

"Yeah," said the other guy, "all." They both chuckled at what must have been vintage forensics humor. "But these are numero uno," he added, pointing at the marks that led directly to the tires of the Lamborghini.

It seemed pretty clear that Richie simply drove in off the street and parked behind the line of trees closest to the road. Not a brilliant hiding place, but effective enough. Having played tennis with Carter hundreds of times, Richie would have known that spot, right next to the road, so you wouldn't have to ramble through poison ivy to reach the packed-dirt path that led up to the court—but where your car would not be seen. Not that any of the Tillotsons' tennis friends had anything to hide. They just didn't want to tempt a cruising car thief with their new flamingo-red Jaguar, or have the local cops ticket them for street parking, which was considered lower-middle-class and therefore illegal in the Estates.

The tire men packed up their glop and cameras and moved on. So did I. Onward and upward— except the road to Emerald Point had never been that steep before. Even though I walked a brisk three miles every day, my calves burned with every step, my chest squeaked with each breath. The road that led up to the house seemed infinite, a *Twilight Zone* walk out of time and space that continued without meaning or end.

Panting and a little frightened, I finally spotted the house. When I made it up the high stone steps, I leaned against the huge mahogany front door. The Tillotson house itself, a Tudor, was so damned solid; the deep *bong* of the door chime resonated inside. It always amazed me how that bong provoked the semieducated to show off: "'Do not ask for whom the bell tolls . . . ,'" they'd intone, while waiting for the latest in the long line of Tillotson servants to open the door.

I couldn't catch my breath, and it didn't help when I felt a stab of chest pain. Desperate, I was trying to recall what I'd read in the Living section of the *New York Times* about how to tell if you're dying, when the male half of the Tillotsons' most recent couple opened the door. According to Stephanie, he wasn't exactly a butler. He was more what is described in glitzy novels as a Japanese houseman, except he was a Norwegian: Gunnar, a stringy man in a white jacket. He apparently came from that one square hectare of Scandinavia where people did not speak English as a second language.

"Ja?"

"Stephanie?" I inquired, to keep things simple. But just then Stephanie herself came rushing from the back of the house. She'd changed from her usual walking outfit—spandex pants and University of Michigan Law School T-shirt and a windbreaker—to a rose-colored turtleneck and denim gardening overalls with lots of pockets in front. She'd obviously been cross-pollinating again; the tip of her nose was a powdery yellow. She could spend hours in her greenhouse with a magnifying glass and a cotton swab, performing what I guess was the botanical equivalent of artificial insemination—while a servant kept little Astor amused building mansions with Creative Playthings blocks.

Clippers, Q-Tips, a miniature spade, peeked out of Stephanie's pockets; a clawed implement shaped as if it were giving you the finger hung out, marsupial-style. "Rosie!" She threw her arms around me. I just had time to swivel to avoid being punctured by the finger thing. Stephanie was young, only thirty-two. She was also beautiful to the point of being flawless, a five-foot-ten-inch wonder of a woman. A wellborn wonder, a Long Island blueblood. Her father, John Foster Dulles's first cousin once removed, was Mr. Securities Law on Wall Street. Her mother, a descendant of a lesser Astor and a middling Whitney, had been Deb of the Year in 1957 as well as a ranked tennis player. Being so gorgeous and privileged, Stephanie was not expected to be capable of normal human emotion. But she was. I was comforted by a surprisingly hearty embrace, although she was such a strong athlete that her hug was a little too crushing.

"Thank you, Gunnar," she said, as she let me loose. The houseman evaporated. "A nightmare," she murmured. This time, she appeared to mean the murder, not her servant problem. "Come into the music room. I have brioches in the oven. I made them just for you. A total nightmare! I'll have Inger bring them in. With cappuccino? Coffee? Tea?"

The music room had been designed in the days when music meant having fifty guests in to hear Schubert's *Trout* Quintet. The Tillotsons' latest purchase, an extremely grand grand piano, could have been built for a doll's house, for all the room it took up. Unlike Richie, who had become profoundly rich, Dr. Carter Tillotson, thirty-three years old and already the third-most-sought-after plastic surgeon in Manhattan, was merely stunningly well-to-do. He'd been born to a family that had settled on Long Island in 1697. Unfortunately, the Tillotsons, who became one of the first families in Shorehaven, lost their feed stores in the crash of 1893—and the rest of their small fortune thirty-six years later in the Great Depression. Carter had been born so poor, Stephanie once confided, that his parents couldn't afford to send him away to boarding school. Luckily, he was not socially doomed. Stephanie was enough of a rebel to marry a man who had needed financial aid to go to medical school. To Stephanie's family's chagrin and the Tillotsons' delight, both the marriage and Carter himself seemed a huge success— although he was still struggling to pull together his fourth million.

To camouflage their temporary deficiencies in the furniture department, Stephanie had filled the music room—and the rest of the house—with potted trees.

She knew this was not the way to furnish what her mother called a proper home, but she was counting on Carter, after another couple of hundred more liposuctions, to permit her to go off on another six-figure shopping spree for cabinets and couches, chandeliers, and chairs. But those, too, would be sucked up and lost in the gaping hugeness of Emerald Point.

However, considering that it was a mansion, Stephanie's house felt reasonably homey. We sat on matching raw-silk club chairs surrounded by a rain forest of Chinese fan palms, parlor palms, and sago palms. The pale moss-green carpet beneath our feet was so thick and reassuring it could almost have grown up from the floor itself.

"Do you want to talk about it?" Stephanie asked. By high school standards, Stephanie would be a very close friend: not only did we bake together; we antiqued, visited flea markets, and drove into Manhattan to meet our husbands. But I didn't want to talk about Richie with her, mainly because she never had anything particularly insightful to say. I did want to be with her, though. More than anything, I needed a dose of her shoulders-back, head-up, girl-jock, nothing-can-touch-us WASP confidence.

"Is it true you found him, Rosie?" I nodded. I really couldn't talk; my throat had closed down. And Stephanie wasn't in such great shape either. For once, she couldn't come up with any rah-rah, stiff-upper-lip support. "I'm so . . . so *upset*," she said. As if to prove it, she began to cry. Tears spilled over her prominent cheekbones and meandered down her face. "I'm sorry to be carrying on like this," she apologized. "You're the one who should be crying."

"It's okay, Stephanie."

"I know what Richie turned into," she acknowledged. "But for the longest time . . . he really was super."

"He was," I managed to say.

Stephanie groped in her five zillion pockets and finally came up with a rag she'd probably used to clean off clay pots. She was about to wipe her eyes with it, but I grabbed it away.

"It's filthy. You'll get that oozy-red-eye thing."

She glanced at the cloth for the first time and shoved it back in her pocket. Then she brushed the last of the tears away with the back of her hand. Still sniffling, she reached over and pinched off a brown-edged leaf from one of her pots-de-fleur, a ceramic bowl filled with foliage plants and a small florist's tube that held a single flower to glow against the dark greenery. "Sorry I started bawling, Rosie."

"I wish I could cry. I guess I'm in shock."

"You must be. Do you have any idea how it happened?"

"I always thought Richie would drop dead of a heart attack," I mused, avoiding her question. I didn't tell her how fervently I'd wished it on him. During sex with Jessica. "Oooh!" he'd shout, and she'd say something youthful, like "Go for it, Rick"—except he wouldn't. Or he'd clutch his chest as he was jogging along the East River promenade, or while playing tennis in the Hamptons. Or, skiing in the Rockies, he'd start making fish-mouths, vainly trying to extract more oxygen from the thin air.

"Of course you're in shock," Stephanie said. "Who wouldn't be? But you'll be fine. Trust me." That helped a little, but I hadn't hiked up to Emerald Point only for a quick fix of Wasp aplomb, although God knew I needed all the aplomb I could get. I wanted advice.

Before she'd taken to spending her life hiring and firing The Help, driving two-year-old Astor to play dates, growing palms, bromeliads, and lemon trees in her greenhouse, needlepointing, embroidering, flavoring her own olive oils, and working for battered women and groundwater, Stephanie had been a litigation associate at one of those gigantic New York law firms that, with great pride and fervor, defend petrochemical conglomerates in lawsuits brought by cancer-riddled former employees.

"I think I may need legal advice," I said. So I brought her up-to-date on Sergeant Gevinski.

She said "Yikes!" a couple of times and "This is incredible!" once. When I finished, she said: "I'd watch out for him."

I was so relieved; I wasn't paranoid. I was right. "You really think so?"

She rubbed her perfect although slightly-too-full-to-be-fashionable upper lip with her index finger. A stranger might think Carter had gotten in a couple of collagen injections just to give her face interest, but the stranger would be wrong. All over the house there were hundreds of framed photographs of Carter and Stephanie at every stage of their lives except *in utero*. Carter was good-looking in the bland, blond, short-haired style of models in Cadillac advertisements.

But Stephanie was different. From her class picture at the Greenvale School to her Miss Porter's field hockey team photo to a snapshot taken of her in a toga at some college party to her engagement portrait, she was genuinely beautiful. Beautiful, Richie had concurred, but not at all sexy. I hadn't disagreed. Men gaped at Stephanie from a distance, but they rarely got close, the way they did with less stunning, more accessible women.

Stephanie did nothing to play up her beauty. She was too athletic to waste time on elaborate hairstyles. She walked with us in the morning, played tennis or rode at a nearby horse farm every afternoon, worked out on the StairMaster at dusk, and, for a while, until even she admitted it was excessive, put on a reflective vest and ran at night with a lawyer friend, a woman named Mandy, who worked in the city. Stephanie's clothes were always simple: even socializing with the jet-setters who were Carter's patients, she never got dressier than basic black and her grandmother's pearls, or a pair of simple but very large diamond earrings. She never, ever, wore makeup, and that made her beauty all the more intimidating. Feature by amazing feature, Stephanie was perfect. Cass and I wondered if Carter had married her so he could stare across the breakfast table every morning, memorizing each part, saying to himself: *This* is what a chin should be. Or had he married her to entice prospective patients: Gosh, they would think, can he make me look like that?

But besides being beautiful, Stephanie was smart.

"Yes," she said. "I think the man from Homicide is crazy to suspect you of *anything*. But *I* know you."

"Should I get a lawyer?"

"I don't know what to tell you, Rosie. I was a civil litigator. We *never* did criminal stuff."

"Stephanie, I need help."

She started the lip massage again, more intense this time. "Well, it might make this Gevinski think you have something you want to hide.... Calm down. Let me finish. But you're a woman of means, of standing in the community. You're not accustomed to being pushed around by the police. Since he's acting really icky, as if he has major doubts about you, you might as well have someone to protect your rights, someone to stand up to him—you know, to demand to speak with the lieutenant or captain or whoever is really in charge." Nervously, she rubbed her hands up and down the legs of her overalls. "Your trying to pull out the knife might be a problem."

"Maybe I should find a detective."

"What for?"

"To find out who done it."

"Rosie, in real life, do you know what detectives do? They take pictures of adulterers *in flagrante,* or they look for runaway husbands." She must have sensed how disheartened I was, because she added: "Maybe I'm wrong. I'll put out feelers. Maybe there is a Sherlock Holmes for you."

"Should I be worried, Stephanie?"

"I wish I could give you a flat-out no. But I can't imagine what's on this policeman's mind. Is there any evidence that connects you to Richie?"

"Of course not." Then I thought. "Except for the knife."

Her entire body shuddered. "I won't ask you anything more about what you saw. It must have been supertraumatic, and the last thing you'd want to do is relive it." Stephanie didn't push, but then, she never had to. Who wouldn't try to please her? Her face was a classic oval. Her eyes were a luminous blue-gray, large, with a perpetual sheen, so she always looked as if she'd just finished laughing or crying. Her glossy dark-brown hair (in the same to-the-shoulders blunt cut as in her toddler pictures) framed her marvelous face. Although much too well-bred to be a busybody, Stephanie attracted confidences because people yearned for her approval. Fortunately, she was always generous with it. I couldn't imagine anyone in the world *not* wanting to bend over backward for her. Except Carter. He was polite to her. He bought her beautiful jewelry, although, as Stephanie once disclosed while we shelled black walnuts, not *important* jewelry.

But Cass and I both agreed that Carter didn't seem smitten. Maybe, Cass conceded, he was simply not demonstrative. But after Richie left, the thought did cross my mind that Carter was working suspiciously long hours too. Still, who knew? Being a big-city Somebody was no nine-to-five job; in Manhattan, maybe all plastic surgeons routinely saw their very important patients at ten at night.

Stephanie never complained. In fact, she spent hours preparing exquisite little suppers for Carter, three or four small courses to tempt him when he walked through the door at eleven-fifteen. "Richie was stabbed below his chest," I told her. I touched the midpoint of my torso. "Ben thinks the knife must have hit the aorta and he bled to death."

"What was he doing at your house?"

I was tired of people asking me that, so I answered a little too forcefully. "How should I know?"

"Of course. Sorry I asked." She paused and then shifted into her gung-ho mode. "I know how stressed out you must be, Rosie. Beyond stressed out. Why don't I bake a few things for when you get home from the cemetery? Jewish pastry is fun. Babka. Rugelach—" Before I could get the rest of the menu, the other half of the Norwegian couple, Inger, brought in a tray with brioches, jam, and coffee. "Thank you, Inger," Stephanie said. Inger, a tiny, silver-haired woman who resembled a sardine, gave a nod so curt it bordered on rude; then she disappeared. Stephanie's exquisite nostrils flared a thirty-second of an inch. I couldn't tell if she was reacting to the housekeeper's snippiness or if Inger had committed some upper-class atrocity, like folding the napkins for morning coffee into rectangles instead of putting them in rings. "I'll call the senior litigating partner at the law firm, have him recommend a criminal lawyer in Nassau County. Someone local would probably be best. Someone who has a relationship with the D.A."

I guess I gasped.

"I'm sorry," Stephanie said. "That was thoughtless. What I meant was, you need someone who can pick up the phone and make the right call. Stop this Sergeant Gevinski from going after you. Get him on target."

"But who's the target?"

Stephanie lifted a silver pincer and put a brioche on a plate. I broke off a piece. It was hot, fragrant, fresh from the oven. "The target is anyone but you, Rosie."

I needed solace—a lot of it—and was hoping Ben would be there when I got home. But I could not find a single comforting face. In fact, the first thing I noticed as I walked into the house was the number of cop faces that suddenly turned right, left, up, down: any old way to avoid making eye contact with me. I felt that butterfly flutter in the stomach that precedes overt panic. I tried to wish it away: No wonder they averted their faces. They knew by now that Richie had walked out on me. What message of sympathy could they offer? Better he's dead, lady: Can you imagine your having to deal with whether to buy a baby gift for little Stevenson Meyers a year from now?

Except, even before Sergeant Gevinski crooked his finger and motioned me into the dining room, I comprehended the real reason the cops weren't looking at me. To them, Richie's murder was no longer a who done it. It was a she done it.

I walked in, remembering, for once, not to trip over the fringe of the red-and-blue Sarouk rug that had finally arrived the day before our silver anniversary party. Before Gevinski got a chance to offer me a seat and display his authority, I grabbed the Papa Bear chair at the head of the table.

"Just a couple of things I'd like to get clear, Ms. Meyers. You went to sleep at nine-thirty or ten?"

"About then."

"And woke up at three-thirty?" If I'd been having a

dinner party, he'd be four guests away from me. Not far enough.

"Yes."

"You're not sleeping so well since the divorce?"

I'd read enough mysteries in which perfectly innocent people got into deep trouble by talking too much to an unimaginative cop. They were always absolved by the last chapter, but, I reminded myself, this was real life. Watch out!

Still, no matter what conclusions Gevinski drew, in a couple of hours I'd have the name of some lawyer who could make Gevinski's superiors tell him to get down to his real business—finding a killer. I assured myself it was okay to feel reasonably confident. There was no case against me, for the simple reason I hadn't done anything.

But meanwhile, I had to deal with a dry mouth, a punching bag of a heart—and Gevinski. "I asked if you were having trouble sleeping," he said.

"I assume I was asleep by ten. I don't know why I woke up."

"I see. You didn't hear anything when you were awake. What I'm having trouble with is how come you go to sleep and, like magic, your ex—okay, your almost-ex—drops in." I thought of a few responses: smart, smart-ass, downright nasty. But I kept quiet. "You're sure the alarm was on?"

"Yes. Almost positive."

"How do you account for the fact that it didn't blast you out of bed?"

"Richie knew the code."

"You never changed it after he left?"

"No."

He looked up at the ceiling, then down at his

reflection in the table. "Oh, by the way," he said offhandedly. "The guys at the lab had a quick look, and they say it seems to be your fingerprints on the knife." He watched me try not to tense up.

"I explained about that last night."

"Right. You know, anybody would be tempted to pull a knife out of a body—the body of someone they had feelings for. But the word is 'tempted.' You actually did it. It's a problem, Ms. Meyers. And then there's another problem."

"What?"

"Your separation agreement."

"What about it?"

"According to Ms. Jessica Stevenson, you and Mr. Meyers were going to sign the agreement this weekend. Right? She swears—and we can check further if we have to—you and your almost-ex had a verbal agreement that Mr. Meyers wouldn't change his will until you signed the agreement. Am I on target here? You'd had words because he'd wanted to treat your sons different in the will because one of them"—he pulled out his pad and leafed through his notes— "Alexander was a problem kid. You wanted Mr. Meyers to treat Alexander and Benjamin the same. So a big part of the negotiation between your lawyer and his lawyer was getting Mr. Meyers to agree to treat both kids equal. Like to come into trust fund money at the same ages, to get equal percentages of his estate. Then you'd agree to sign off on his estate, even before the divorce became final. Right?"

"Yes. Richie and Alex weren't getting along, but I knew it would blow over. But if anything happened to Richie in the meantime, it would hurt Alex beyond belief and hurt the boys' relationship with each other."

Like a nursery school kid at naptime, Gevinski put his forearms on the table and rested his head on them. I wouldn't have minded punching him in his squishy nose. "I'm more interested in you, okay? Once you'd signed the agreement, you'd be totally out of the picture."

"Out with about five million dollars." So much money. It had made me a little sick. If it hadn't been me, I would have said precisely what some of our old neighbors, some of the teachers at school, would say: Poor Rosie. She'll cry all the way to the bank. Or: At least Rosie can afford to take a nice vacation to forget her troubles. Ha-ha, *thousands* of nice vacations.

"Well, Ms. Meyers?"

"Well, what?"

He sat up straight. "Instead of getting a *part* of Richard Meyers' money after this coming weekend, now you'll be getting it all. And 'all' is major, major money. I'm sure you can understand that might raise a few eyebrows." I thought: Give him nothing. Like the couple of stinkers I'd run into in the classroom, Gevinski was gifted at getting me so upset that I felt on the verge of doing precisely what he wanted me to do: lose control. "Is there anything you can tell me to lower those eyebrows, Ms. Meyers?" I didn't respond. He pointed to his smiley-face watch. "Mr. Meyers is being autopsied now. They're taking out your kitchen knife with your fingerprints on it. Very, very carefully."

"What do you want from me?"

"A better explanation of what happened than

the one you gave me. Not for me. I'm on your side. Really I am. For my superiors in the department— and the D.A. They're not buying your story. So talk to me, Ms. Meyers. Be open. Let me help you."

Five

I'd had natural childbirth, and I was wide awake when they placed a baby boy with pale fuzz and a button nose in my arms. So even though he looked like a Southern Baptist, I knew Benjamin was mine. He had been adorable from birth. Women were forever wanting to pinch his cheek, except his cheek was hard to reach. He was the size of a small Alp. Six feet six. Two hundred and twenty pounds. From Richie all he'd inherited was soulful black eyes, but at least they established his paternity. "Mom." His voice was deep and gentle. "Try to calm down."

"Sure. It's always better to face life in a maximum-security prison when one is calm."

I'd spent a good part of the morning going through closets and drawers, peeking under seat cushions, probing every pocket in all the clothes in Richie's closets, to try and find what he'd been looking for. Other than his entire wardrobe, all he'd left behind was a 1969 World Series yearbook and a snapshot of the two of us he'd kept in his wallet years earlier. Our arms were around each other, our fishing gear lay at our feet. It had been taken one summer in the Finger Lakes, sometime in the seventies. Richie had a walrus mustache, and I wore bell-bottom jeans and a blouse with giant daisies; we both looked hideous and very happy.

It was sometime around noon. A halfhearted sun cast dusty white light through the library windows. Suspicious Foods returned from the kitchen empty-handed, having failed to seduce Gevinski into allowing us to take three diet Cokes from the refrigerator. "He said it's all evidence from a crime scene," she apologized.

"Right," I said. "There might be fingerprints on the broccoli."

Ben flashed Suspicious a smile that meant: Be tolerant. Whenever he smiled, his eyes crinkled up and became little smiles themselves. I tried to figure out what she had that made him smile so. She seemed absolutely ordinary, with thin brown hair, unexceptional eyes, an average figure, and a flat, middle-America accent. Her only bow to liveliness was her makeup, which was far too flamboyant, as if she'd lost her mind at the Estée Lauder counter: blackberry eyelids, raspberry cheeks, strawberry lips, all on a vanilla face. At last, Ben stopped smiling and gazing lovingly and remembered lunch. He'd stopped at the fancy takeout store in town, a place that had somehow survived the decline of yuppie civilization. He untied a red ribbon from a brown bag that had "Recycled!" stamped all over it, and pulled out environmentally correct containers of couscous, wheatberry salad, and something that looked like celery strings in a mysterious maroon-flecked tan sauce. As he unwrapped the sandwiches, he read the labels: "Chicken and grilled vegetables. Let's see . . . Thai tuna salad. And mozzarella, tomato, and basil. What do you want, Mom?"

My stomach felt as though I'd swallowed a dirty sponge. Also, I was not unaware that Suspicious had her eye on the chicken sandwich. I decided it was all right to be selfish. "I'm not going to be a gracious hostess. Gevinski may be off my back in a couple of hours, but in the meantime, I'm being threatened with a lifetime in the company of women who do not care about Jane Austen. I want the chicken sandwich."

"It's great that you can keep your sense of humor under these circumstances," Suspicious declared. She held the salads, one by one, up to the light—part of her unending search for lurking allergens.

"Mom," Ben said patiently. "Everything's going to be fine. I'm sure this is standard operating procedure to rattle people so if they are hiding anything it'll come out."

"No. Normal police procedure is *not* to polarize a

suspect; it puts people in a defensive stance. He should be treating me as the grieving widow."

"But he isn't. That's good."

"No, that's bad. It means he doesn't have doubts."

"Honey," Suspicious said to Ben, "if you let me have the car keys, I'll drive into town and pick up some bottled water." ·

"That's okay, honey," he said.

"It's no bother at all."

"Good idea!" I cut in, and gave her a beverage list that included Snapple French Cherry, Diet Mandarin Orange Slice, and Schweppes Bitter Lemon. "Thanks so much." With any luck, I could get an hour alone with my son.

"You're probably concerned about the age differ- ence," Ben said the second she left. "And maybe the religious difference."

"Not now, Ben."

"If you'd just give her a chance."

"I'm sure she has wonderful qualities, but I don't give a damn about them now. Get your priorities straight."

"Like what do you mean?"

"Like your father's been murdered and the cops are blaming your mother."

"Mom, don't you think you're being a little melo- dramatic?"

"No, I don't. But even if I am, indulge me."

"Fine."

"I want you to tell me the truth."

"I always do." Almost always. Ben was as close to being essentially truthful as a person can get. Also, he was so fair-skinned that on the rare occasion when he did try to lie, his cheeks turned bright red.

"When was the last time you talked to your father?"

"Last Sunday."

"Who called whom?"

"He calls me every Sunday." He stood and bounced on the balls of his feet a few times. He had the edgy look of an athlete expecting a surprise play.

"Did he mention anything at all connected with the house?"

"Nope."

"I'm not going to ask you what he said about me . . . unless you feel it's germane." Ben didn't sit back beside me on the couch. He moved into the protective embrace of a big yellow wing chair. "It's important we share information. We have to figure out what was going on in Daddy's life. We want to help the police find whoever did it. And we want to save my ass. Right?"

"Right. Dad told me you were at each other's throats over money but that he understood it was your way of trying to hold on to him."

"That's absolute horseshit!"

"I knew you'd say that."

"Benjy, I was entitled to a healthy settlement. I helped him start Data Associates. I wrote all their reports the first three years, and after that I edited all the important ones. I wrote the brochures they sent to clients, wrote the 'This Is Data Associates' handbook they give to all the new employees. I got him his first important client."

"Right." He'd only heard the story five hundred times. "Tom Driscoll."

I'd known Tom Driscoll all my life. We grew up in the same apartment building in Brooklyn; he lived directly upstairs from me. We'd been best friends as little kids. Once we hooked up a telephone made of frozen orange juice cans and string and called each other at night. We were so thrilled by our technical wizardry that we were oblivious to the fact that our phone didn't work at all and that we could hear each other only because we were shouting into the cans next to an open window.

But Tom and I drifted apart by the time we went off to different high schools. Well, not completely apart. We became close again senior year. But we lost touch completely after Tom went off to Dartmouth on a track scholarship and I went to Brooklyn College. Over the years, though, my mother kept passing along updates with calculated casualness, pretending to doubt that I'd be interested: Tom married, Tom the vice-president of a very posh, very private bank. Tom the president. Tom out on his own, the venture capitalist. So I knew he'd made it. Big.

I don't know where I found the courage, but after Richie and Mitch began Data Associates as a full-time operation, I decided to call Tom; all it took me was half a year to get up the nerve to ask if I could take him to lunch. I used a personal day and spent twelve dollars to have my hair blown out. And I sold him on Data Associates. "You know," I told Ben, "Tom offered an annual retainer right there in the restaurant when we had lunch. And you know what I said?"

"You said absolutely not, to try Dad's company first."

"I told you that too?"

"Yes."

"Your father would have had a fit, but I knew Tom would go for that; it meant I wasn't asking him for a handout, that I believed in what Dad and Mitch were doing. And he did try us. He became Data's biggest client, and his name attracted other big firms. So I did make a major contribution to the company. Nowhere near what your father did, but he wouldn't have made it—or made it so big—without me."

"Easy, Mom." I realized I was in one of those fight-or-flight positions: shoulders hunched, jaw clamped, head jutting forward. I closed my eyes and took five slow, deep relaxation breaths.

"Sorry for waxing wroth, kiddo," I added, dizzy from too much oxygen. "I'm in a wroth mood. And sorry for not being more—you know—maternal. My God, you've lost your father. I'm so sorry. But I'm not myself. I'm not sure who I am at this point."

"S'okay," Ben responded.

"Tell me what else you and Daddy talked about."

"He went on about you having to accept reality and that he hoped you could make a life for yourself. Then—let's see—about how he wouldn't try to force me to have a relationship with Jessica but that he was sure I'd come to care for her. And we talked about the Giants-Eagles game. You want to know about that?"

"Of course not."

"Then that's it." He draped his endless legs over the arm of the wing chair and tapped his size-fourteen sneakers together to signal the discussion was over. But it wasn't.

"Did he say anything about Data? New clients, old clients?"

"No."

"New tensions, old tensions?"

"Not that he talked about. He didn't talk about business at all."

"Anything about Mitch Gruen?"

"No. He hasn't mentioned him in ages."

"Was he angry or upset about anything?"

"Only about you," Ben answered softly. "Sorry, Mom."

About five minutes later, as if to absolve me of the melodrama charge, Gevinski invited me down to police headquarters. "Invited" is overstatement. What he said was: "I'd like you to come with me over to headquarters." I told him I had to wait and speak to a lawyer and asked didn't he have to read me my rights under the Miranda decision. He asked: "How come you know all about Miranda?" He didn't seem to listen as I explained that I was a great mystery buff, so naturally I'd know about the Miranda rule. He informed me that Miranda did not apply at this point and I was to go with him to headquarters. *Now.* And no, my son Ben could not come along.

The interrogation room at headquarters did not have a dangling bulb to glare in my eyes, but its two-tone green walls, gray metal table, gray metal chairs with leatherette seats, and large, dirty black wastebasket were forbidding enough.

"Make it easy on yourself," Gevinski said.

"I might say the same thing to you," I answered. "This is obviously a high-profile case. If you arrested the wrong person, a lot of careers would be ruined."

"I know that, Ms. Meyers. Don't you think we've

thought about this?" His tie was still tucked inside his shirt. I kept hoping a homicide lieutenant who resembled Harrison Ford would materialize and say: I'll take over from here, Sergeant. But the door remained shut.

"I realize you're having trouble with the coincidence," I said. "Richie coming to the house and getting killed."

"Right."

"But life is full of coincidence."

"I'm sorry. This seems a little too full."

I should have been angry, but I was too scared. I tried to swallow so I could start talking again, but my throat was tight. When I finally managed, I made a loud sound that in comic strips is represented as "Gulp!" "Did you ever think my husband might have been tailed?" I asked.

"We thought about it and rejected it. There's no evidence to that effect."

"Please, just think about it again. Maybe someone was out to get him—"

"And followed him to Long Island to kill him in your kitchen?"

"What if the person knew he was coming to my house? What an opportunity! Kill Richie there. I get blamed and they go free."

He sat back, laced his fingers together, and rested his hands on his belly. "Take it easy, Ms. Meyers. I'm not a bad guy. All I know is, you have a problem. Maybe there's an explanation. Maybe he socked you. Threatened you. Was it some kind of self-defense thing?"

I knew I should be quiet. I'd told Ben to get Stephanie moving on finding the lawyer's name. Any minute, someone with an attaché case could be walking through the door, saying: From now on you talk to *me*, Sergeant. Except this would be my last chance to convince Gevinski. Or at least plant a seed of doubt in his mind.

"There was more than one set of tires."

"What?"

"I saw your people spreading white paste over tread marks from my husband's tires. But his weren't the only tire marks there."

"People park there all the time to play tennis at your next-door neighbors'."

"But there was one set that looked as new as Richie's did. I mean, I passed the spot and wondered why your men weren't making as big a deal over those tread marks. They were probably making molds of them because that's what the rulebook says to do."

His chest rose with his slow, I-am-being-patient breath. "Those marks could easily have been made earlier, a couple of days ago." He was so uninterested. "And even if somebody did pull in there last night—so what? Your husband's car was on an angle that any car going uphill could have seen the reflector light on his rear side bumper through the trees. If I was in a patrol car myself and saw that, I'd check it out. But all I'd see was that it was an expensive car, locked, with nobody in it. I'd figure one of the neighbors had car trouble and left it overnight. When I called the license plate in, I'd know the name Meyers, so I'd think, No big deal, and drive away. And that's what those other tread marks are: No big deal."

After your scalp tingles and your heart misses a

beat and your hands start to shake, you rise to a new level of panic where you feel nothing at all.

"Someone *had* to have planned this whole thing out," I told him.

"You're going to tell me it was his girlfriend, right? She knew he was coming to you. Maybe she encouraged him to come. Then she followed him there, grabbed your carving knife, and killed him, then she threw a few dishes around to make it look good."

"I told you. I broke the dishes."

"That's right. I forgot. Anyways, she killed him."

"I'm not saying it was she."

"Well, I have to go along with you on that. I don't think it's her either. Look, you're no dummy. You're well-informed. And you like mystery books. So you know all about motive. What in God's name would be her motive? She loses a megabucks boyfriend who's crazy in love with her. And *you* wind up with the megabucks." He combed back his hair with his fingers. "Now, from our point of view, what could have been *your* motive? He ditched you for a younger woman. He was going to make a generous settlement, but hey, maybe you felt you deserved it all."

"You're not thinking! I *am* a smart woman. If I wanted to kill him, why would I do it in my house?"

"Because what you did had nothing to do with smarts, Ms. Meyers. I don't think you spent months planning the perfect crime. You found him in your house, you lost control, and you killed him." He offered an expression of regret for what I was going through, a sad sigh. "Believe me, I know life isn't black and white. It's grays. You could have a perfectly reasonable explanation. So I'm asking you: tell me now and maybe I can do something for you. Tell me later, no deal."

"There is nothing to tell."

He stood and waited for me to get up. "They'll release the body this afternoon. So I guess the next time we see each other will be at the funeral." He shuffled to the door and held it open. "Too bad we couldn't work something out, Ms. Meyers."

Six

"They had cops tailing me on the way home!" I didn't even try to get the screech out of my voice. Ben squeezed my shoulder reassuringly, but his lips were white, the way they used to get when he was in nursery school and had a stomach virus and was about to throw up. "Two guys in a gray car!" Poor kid: Mothers were supposed to be bland, the warm milk of humanity, but there I was, squawking and trembling.

Suspicious seemed on the verge of contributing something but then reconsidered; probably what she had in mind wasn't boring enough. Just then, Alex strolled in.

Forget the shoulder-length hair, the three-day growth of dark beard, the torn, bleached jeans, the dirty, cracked leather boots. With his black, hooded eyes and the deep lines that ran from his cheeks down to the edges of his jaw, Alex was so much like Richie I had to turn away for a second. When I looked again, I saw my kid, his wild, rock-star hair hiding his stick-out ears. Gently, he laid down his guitar on the library table, then he dropped his backpack and leather jacket on the floor. I threw my arms around him.

"This is a nightmare, Alex."

"I know, Ma."

I think he wanted to hug me tight, but his older brother was in the room, so he just kept patting my back, the way you burp a baby.

Alex and Ben then engaged in mutual manly arm-punching, followed by a fast kiss.

"Hey, Alex."

"Big Ben."

"Can you believe this?"

"No," Alex replied. "No, I can't."

"The last time I spoke to him," Ben said, "the very last talk we ever had, I asked for money. For one of those TV-VCR combos, with stereo speakers. I didn't even need it. Who the hell has time to watch TV?"

The right side of Alex's mouth edged up into a half-grin, a ringer for Richie's. "The last time I spoke to him, I told him to drop dead." His smile turned into a nervous twitch.

Ben put his arms around Alex, enveloping him. I couldn't believe how different my sons were. Big, small. Light, dark. Muscular, wiry. Open, closed. They could have belonged to different species.

For the moment that Alex relaxed in his big brother's embrace, I gave Suspicious Foods a look that said: This is a private family moment. She fluttered her furry false eyelashes. So I said: "If you don't mind, I'd like to be alone with my sons." She seemed to understand. She muttered something about having to call a man with a rash under his arms and left.

I took the boys' hands. Ben's hand was huge, strong, his skin chapped from all the washing up he did at the hospital. Alex's hand was smaller, more finely sculpted. His fingertips had rock-hard calluses from playing the guitar. I gave him the once-over. He was wearing a dingy undershirt; curly chest hair peeked out from two rips. "Alex," I said.

"Yeah?"

"No matter what happens, I'd like you to put on a tie and jacket for the funeral."

"'No matter what happens'? What more can happen?"

"Mom has a little problem," Ben began.

"Mom has a big problem," I cut in. I brought them both up-to-date on what had occurred in Gevinski's office. Alex lowered his head and studied his boots. Ben sat on a couch and put his face in his hands. When his shoulders started to shake, I realized he was crying. I sat beside him, hugged him and smoothed his soft hair. "Easy, Benjy."

"Oh, Mom. What are you going to do?" he asked.

I glanced up at Alex. He came over and sat on the

other side of me. "I don't know what to do." We were quiet for a few minutes. "I can't believe this is happening," I told them. "I've got to speak to the lawyer. I wish Stephanie would get moving."

"How can they arrest you?" Alex demanded. "That's the stupidest goddamn thing I ever heard!" He kept blinking his eyes. Maybe he was fighting back tears. Maybe he was stoned on something. It was hard to read Alex.

There was more than just the physical resemblance to Richie; Alex was so much like his father. As with Richie, you could sense Alex was feeling something intensely, but since he wouldn't consider confiding in anyone, you had no clue as to what it was. The only person who really understood him had been Richie—who'd always said Alex was a sneaky little bastard. Like father, like son: born game players, seducers, charmers, men seemingly not burdened by too rigorous a conscience. What Richie never understood, however, was how much Alex loved him. And that, I assured myself, was where the resemblance stopped. Richie's loftiest emotion was passion. Alex had a loving heart.

Naturally, Ben loved his father too. Still, while his athletic and academic achievements had gratified Richie, he was much too nice a person to be of serious interest to his father.

"Alex, about that last conversation you had with Daddy . . . " I said. "When was it?"

"When he reamed my ass about using his American Express card, a couple of months ago."

"No letters from him?"

"Just the one I had to sign for, that said if I didn't cut the shit—"

"Do you have to talk like that?"

"Ma, you know the word."

"Of course I know the word. But you shouldn't be using it in front of me."

"All right, Mother. The letter said if I didn't shape up, he would not only stop supporting me, he'd disinherit me." As an afterthought, he inquired: "Did he?"

"No. Now listen, both of you. I don't want to upset you more than you already are, but you have to know everything." The boys nodded. "I hope it goes without saying that I didn't kill your father."

"Don't be ridiculous," Ben said.

Alex twirled a lock of his long hair around his finger. "You're not getting it, Ma."

"What aren't I getting?"

"As long as this Gevinski thinks you're the murderer, he isn't going to look for whoever did it."

"Believe me, I get it."

"Jesus Christ," Ben said, "then the case will be closed forever!"

I sent the boys upstairs to call Richie's sister, Carol the Cashmere Queen, and make funeral plans. I sat so still I could feel all the pulses in my body throbbing. I listened to the grandfather clock chime quarter hours.

A little before seven, Cass, Stephanie, and Madeline brought dinner over. Stephanie, naturally, had done all the cooking, but Cass helped her carry in the platters. Madeline folded and refolded napkins. She rolled one into a cylinder and held it so it drooped. "The male organ!"

"How clever," Cass muttered. She had served on a library committee with Madeline years earlier.

She hadn't known her well but knew she was an avid reader. So when Madeline asked her if she could join the three of us on the walk, we'd all agreed: A good mind would be good company. And Madeline was thoughtful, clipping book reviews for us or calling when a favorite author was being interviewed on an obscure cable channel. On the other hand, just when we were huffing along at a good pace, she'd stop short, possessed by Art. We'd jog in place as she'd recite: "'There is no frigate like a book . . .'" However, since her divorce two years earlier, she had become a feminist *artiste* herself, and now she quoted her own poetry.

"'My Marriage,'" she suddenly announced.

"Is this one of your poems?" I inquired, trying hard to keep fear and loathing out of my voice.

"Yes. But it's not just about *my* marriage."

"It has a certain universality," Cass said wearily.

"Yes!" Madeline glanced at me and bit her lip. "I'm sorry. Maybe this isn't the right time for it."

"No," I said. "Go ahead." She was such a sad sack in her black pants and sweater and Hell's Angels leather vest. None of us ever had the heart to tell her to stuff it.

Madeline cleared her throat. "'I dared not breathe / For fear my soul / Would explode / From all the emptiness it contained.'"

I waited until I realized that was the entire poem. "Very good," I said.

"Then how come *The New Yorker* rejected it?"

"They're very mainstream," I replied.

Madeline had never been a fun person, or even a vaguely amusing one, but she had been sweet. Then her husband left, not for another woman but for other women, lots of them. She soured. I don't know if that abandonment was more or less hurtful than what Richie did. In any case, Myron Michael Berkowitz, D.D.S., moved into a singles condo that boasted an indoor pool with a waterfall. Madeline's work, creating crossword puzzles, had never been a full-time job, but instead of making up more puzzles to compensate for her sudden drop in income, she stopped working entirely to become a full-time alimony poet.

I glanced from Madeline, blotchy and bitter, to Stephanie, with her peaches-and-cream face. She had set all the food out on the dining room table and was pulling a mesh vegetable bag from her canvas tote. Extracting a wad of watercress, she made a leafy circle around the grilled marinated vegetables. She scattered random sprigs of dill on top of the poached salmon and, after a moment's thought, stood a fir tree of rosemary in the middle of the red potato salad. "Thank you," I breathed, while she arranged in a wicker basket *ficelles* of sourdough bread and seven-grain rolls she'd baked.

"Don't thank me. I have all the menus planned, so you won't have to cook while you're doing your week of mourning. It's really such a sensible custom." She handed me a slip of paper, which turned out to be the name of a lawyer in Manhattan. She said no one she knew could give her the name of a good criminal lawyer on Long Island, and she thought I needed representation right away. "He's senior litigating partner at my old firm," she confided. "I never worked with him, but he has a super reputation."

I couldn't help wondering if Stephanie ever regretted giving up her legal career for puff pastry. Not for the first time, I felt sorry for her, for her unappreciated beauty and her uninterested husband. But sympathy can go just so far. After her remark about the mourning period, I knew that in a matter of seconds she'd launch into one of her pro-Semitic discourses on Superior Jews I Have Known, None of Whom Are Pushy. I wondered if I could manage to take a little poached salmon on a plate up to my room.

Fortunately, just then, Alex and Ben—and Suspicious—came in. Amazingly, Alex not only had shaved but had slicked back his hair with about a quart of gel, which made his resemblance to Richie even more startling. Even Cass, who knew him best, did a double take. Madeline smacked her forehead with the back of her hand, amazed. "You are a carbon copy of your father!" Stephanie's jaw actually went slack; she looked as if a hundred points had been knocked off her IQ. "Oh my God!" she gasped.

"How're ya doin', ladies?" Alex asked them all. He had picked up a generic rock-and-roll accent somewhere and sounded as if he'd been raised in a New Orleans whorehouse.

"Fine, Alexander," Stephanie said, unable to stop gaping at him.

Meanwhile, Madeline was on a roll. "I hope you aren't like him in your dealings with women," she said to Alex.

"Madeline," Cass interjected, "might I suggest a muzzle?"

She sniffed at Cass and turned to me. "Remember

'Hu*man* Being'? I wrote it last year: 'You left / Not in silence / But in loud malignity. / You did not return. / So you could not observe / The hole that opened in my heart.' "

"I remember," I said. "Very moving."

Cass gave a weary sigh and went over to kiss the boys. Ben seemed genuinely heartened to see her. She had met Suspicious once before, and she shook her hand, a little too enthusiastically. Alex wasn't exactly thrilled to see Cass. Four years earlier, she'd had the courage his other high school teachers lacked; she tossed him out of her Advanced Placement English class, telling him that her colleagues were in error, that he was not an underachiever. He was an ass.

The seven of us sat down to dinner. For a few unendurable seconds, we were able to hear the tinkle of chandelier crystals stirring from our breathing and our shifting uncomfortably in our chairs. No one had anything to say. At last, Cass asked Ben about his internship plans and Alex about what sort of audiences Cold Water Wash attracted. The tinkle was lost in conversation. It almost began to feel like a normal dinner.

Of course, with Madeline inadvertently spilling Stephanie's yogurt-dill sauce onto Cass's lap, followed by her demand, a few minutes later, for "Quiet! Please, I need quiet"—presumably to listen to her muse—it couldn't be called completely normal. But at least, with her mouth full, she could not recite.

Cass claimed that behind her artsy facade, Madeline was seething because she could no longer blame her husband, Myron, for mocking her artistic ambitions, thereby causing her to have a thirty-year-long writer's block. Now, divorced, she had to put up or shut up, and her work was so dreadful that not even the ever-tolerant *Shorehaven Sentinel* would publish it.

My theory was that she had spent so many years being Mrs. Berkowitz that she had trouble remembering her own name. After Myron and his dazzling bonded teeth left, she was desperate to find an identity. What was so terrible if she thought of herself as a poet? But two years after her big rejection by M.M.B., D.D.S., all she had was a pile of pink slips.

I pushed a slice of eggplant around my plate. It had dark grill marks. Like iron bars, I thought. Or prison stripes. I couldn't eat. I couldn't believe what was happening to me.

"I used minimal oil," Stephanie said encouragingly. "Extra-virgin olive."

"Maybe you're being just a little egocentric," Madeline suggested to Stephanie. "I guess that's inevitable for somebody like you. But it's not your food; Rosie is incapable of eating. Did any of you ever read Angela Davis's *Women, Race and Class?*" She waited for us to admit we hadn't.

"I have," Cass replied. "What could it possibly have to do with Rosie not eating Stephanie's vegetables?"

"You of all people should understand," Madeline responded.

"As well I do," Cass snapped.

"I am beside myself," I said quietly, cutting them off.

"Oh, Rosie!" Cass said. "Forgive us for being frivolous."

Stephanie looked as if she longed to be in her greenhouse, shoveling compost.

Madeline shook her head in grief at the human condition. "Would it ease your pain if I reminded you what he was?" she asked me.

"He was the father to my sons, Madeline, who happen to be here right now."

"They're not children!" she responded. Ben stared down at his plate. Alex hefted the bowl of potato salad in his palm, weighing whether or not to slam-dunk it on Madeline's head. She saw him and added quickly: "I hope no one thought I meant he deserved to be killed for what he was."

"Anything new with the police?" Stephanie was much too chirpy, but in all fairness, she may have been trying to discourage Madeline from a potential haiku.

I shook my head: nothing new. I couldn't tell them about Gevinski. I didn't think I had the stamina to endure their compassion.

"Who do they think did it?" Madeline asked. "That woman of his?" I shook my head. "Who?"

"They have a suspect," I said softly.

"They're really serious about this, Rosie?" Stephanie seemed shaken.

"Very serious."

"Alex," Suspicious said, "could you please pass the potato salad to your brother."

"Serious about *what?*" Madeline demanded.

"They think I did it," I managed to say.

"It's so crazy," Ben remarked, holding a piece of grilled red pepper aloft on his fork.

"No matter what you did, there isn't a woman alive who would convict you!" Madeline said. "Cheating on you. Remember the poem I wrote the day he left you—after that mockery of an anniversary party? 'A silver celebration / A night of love / Yes, love and golden laughter / Until leaden daylight / When the iron man / Without irony—' "

"Mrs. Berkowitz," Alex said in his glorious baritone.

She was angry at the interruption. "What?"

"Shut the fuck up!"

I froze. Madeline froze. We all froze. Then Madeline pushed herself up with such force her chair crashed to the floor. She waited, hands planted on her hips. One second, two, three. She glared at Alex. He glared back, so she averted her eyes and glared at me. I said nothing. Madeline stormed out.

Stephanie leapt up, put on her zestful let's-get-organized voice, and asked if the police had given permission to use the kitchen. When I said yes, she got busy clearing the table. Alex, I noticed, kept sneaking glances at her each time she came in for more dishes. It wasn't only Stephanie's beautiful face he found so compelling; he was intent on checking out what was going on beneath her loose-fitting blue sweater set and baggy tweed slacks. At one point, he actually offered to help her, but she said please, don't bother. He stared into her big, luminous eyes. For a fraction of a second, drawn in, Stephanie stared back. Then, flustered, flushing, she retreated to the safety of the kitchen to Saran-wrap the salmon. Ben, of course, didn't even notice her; he and Suspicious were holding hands beneath the table.

"I saw some men outside," Cass said to me quietly. "In a gray car at the foot of the drive. Two more in front of the house."

"What? Just now, when you came in?"

"Yes. Is it customary for them to camp out in this fashion?"

"No. This is twenty-four-hour surveillance."

"Fools!"

"Don't you have any doubts, Cass?"

"About what?"

"About whether I did it."

"Not a one, Rosie."

It rained that night, a cold autumn downpour that sounded like drumming fingers as it hit the dry leaves. My last thoughts, before I fell into what was more of a stupor than a sleep, were that the night air smelled good and that I should have put up a pot of coffee for the cops who were staking me out, standing in the rain.

Forrest Newel, Esq., of Johnston, Plumley and Whitbred, looked like a pompous establishment lawyer from a Ross MacDonald novel who knows disgusting secrets about all his clients. His old-fashioned wire-rimmed spectacles were perched precariously on his high-bridged nose. A gold watch chain dangled from the vest of his pin-striped suit. I was wearing a suit too, my only one: last year's trendy taupe thing. It itched.

Behind Forrest Newel, a window framed the towers and turrets of the Manhattan skyline as if it were a painting he owned. He listened to my story at four hundred dollars an hour, cleared something huge and moist from his throat, and announced: "It would seem you're in a bit of a pickle, Mrs. Meyers."

Usually, I'm not the rational, sequential kind of dame whose mind goes A, B, C and immediately recognizes the inevitability of D. Nor am I the kind who thinks in whole sentences. But an instant after Forrest Newel spoke, a rational thought that was also a complete sentence popped into my mind: If I go to jail, I will come out an old woman.

Calm down, I cautioned myself. This is not the time to get theatrical. "And they can just arrest me?"

"Probably not until after the funeral, and of course they would need a warrant for your arrest."

"Is that hard to get?"

"In your case, I regret to say, not terribly. It's that"—he caught himself before he could say "damn" in front of a lady—"that knife with your fingerprints that makes things sticky." I wished he would frown or wring his hands in anguish over my predicament, but he sat perfectly composed on his throne of brown leather, his hands loosely clasped in front of him. Forget anguish: Forrest Newel was so unruffled he didn't even move. When he spoke, his words slipped out between his barely parted lips. I could hardly hear him. "I wouldn't preclude my having a go-round with the district attorney, but arrest is, if not inevitable, at least likely."

"But the evidence is all circumstantial! He was stabbed in my house with my knife. That's all."

"That's all? Your fingerprints were on the murder weapon."

"I told you—"

"Mrs. Meyers, the problem is, there is no evidence of anyone else being in your house."

"But there *had* to have been someone, goddamn

it!" I roared. Forrest Newel's head jerked back. "The killer was *there!*"

"Mrs. Meyers, please. Get a grip." I had to lean forward to hear him. "If a killer was in your house, the police will learn of it soon enough. Don't forget, there are the results of the autopsy to come, to say nothing of the other forensic tests. Maybe one report will say: 'The knife was moved *post mortem.*' Wouldn't that be dandy?" Dandy? I thought. This is some fancy-pants *schmendrick* who's probably never tried a criminal case.

"Do you handle murder cases?" I asked.

"Not recently. But I had three years under my belt as an assistant D.A. under Frank Hogan here in Manhattan, back in the fifties." My complexion must have gone from sick white to sicker green, because he added: "Murder, insider trading, tax evasion . . . they are all the same to a litigator. Underlying principles of law and all that. Now let's keep our fingers crossed about those other tests—but let's not be cockeyed optimists either."

I tried to be an enthusiastic advocate for myself. "The tests will probably show that there was more than one set of tire marks near Richie's car." If Forrest Newel's eyes hadn't been open, I would have sworn he was sleeping. His vested chest rose and fell. He was absolutely relaxed. So I spoke with all the fervor I could muster. "*Please.* There was dirt on the kitchen floor. I've been thinking: Richie's car was right near the road. Why would he have so much dirt on his shoes? It hadn't been raining. Don't they do tests on that sort of thing?"

"As far as the tire marks go," Forrest Newel said, "you yourself told me that particular space is often used for parking by people playing tennis at your neighbors' court. As for the dirt you seem to believe is exculpatory evidence, the police will say your husband tracked it in."

"You think I killed my husband."

"I tell all my clients, it doesn't matter what I think. It's what the *government* thinks."

"I did not kill him!"

"Don't get yourself distressed, Mrs. Meyers. This isn't the end, you know. This is the beginning of a long process."

"Do you think I'll go to jail?"

"I would certainly hope not."

"Do you think it's likely?"

"If we can find some evidence to indicate you are not implicated in your husband's death, or if we can convince the police that another suspect is more deserving of their consideration, you would be, as it were, off the hook. If not, then I would have to advise you to plead guilty in return for reduced charges. In that case, I am sorry to report, you would have to spend a bit of time in jail."

When I was able to speak, I asked: "What's a bit?"

"In the worst of all possible worlds?" He smiled, but quickly recovered and switched to his bad-news face. "Not more than twelve to fifteen years." I got up. "But that's not likely. I'm certain it would be less."

We said our goodbyes. I was sick to my stomach. My breakfast bagel and fat-free cream cheese felt stuck in my trachea, which was probably the only thing preventing me from heaving the bitter dregs of my morning coffee all over the gleaming black floors of Johnston, Plumley and Whitbred's foyer. My

reflection—an ordinary woman in a too-stylish suit—
was trapped in the granite.

The final lurch of the elevator before the door
opened did me in. I stepped out onto Park Avenue.
It appeared to be peopled solely by women with
important careers. They were interchangeable, elegant, multibraceleted women with hawk-thin faces
and shining hair. No taupe suits for them. Not this
season. They knew to wear plaid suits with long
skirts that came down to the middle of their dark-
stockinged calves. I pushed through the crowd and,
believe me, those women knew to make way for
me: Look out! they telegraphed each other.
Hyperventilating suburbanite!

But I couldn't hang over the curb and heave, not
with those hotsy-totsy dames as witnesses. I held on
to a street light. Their outlined-in-lip-pencil lips com-
pressed in distaste when I let out a groan. I was so
sick. If I threw up, they'd pucker their faces, avert
their heads, and demand of each other: "Can you
believe how much she ate for breakfast?" I swallowed
the acid in my throat. I took a deep breath. Don't, I
willed my body. It will be like getting sick in front of
a hundred Jessicas.

Jessica: I rested my back against the street light.
Think. Had Jessica been at the house with Richie?
Did she know he was there? I started walking. My
legs knew where I was headed two blocks before I
did.

I sat in my itchy suit on the sticky seat of a taxi.
Around the time Richie started hating his life, probably
the same night Joan Driscoll mocked Gulls' Haven

and called him Squire Meyers, he started collecting snobbish facts about Manhattan. Like the good addresses on Beekman and Sutton Places are the odd numbers, because they have the river views. Like there are stylish little streets like Sniffen Court and Henderson Place and Gracie Square, and if you give one of them as your address to another chic person, they'll say "*Mar*velous."

He had moved to Gracie Square, to a building as tall and graceful as Jessica. She owned a small duplex there overlooking the East River. In the days when she was just another executive at Data Associates (to me at least), she'd throw what she called "little dinners" for thirty. I'd stand in her living room during cocktails and try to make conversation with one of her irreproachably suave friends, most of whom had been cued to demand of me: What is happening in the high schools of America? They'd also been cued to act enthralled no matter what I answered, since I was the president's wife. I tried to pretend I didn't know they found me tedious. I tried not to be seduced by the spectacular panorama of tugs and barges gliding up the East River outside her windows. Instead, I forced myself to make animated conversation. And I judged my social success by whether Richie slept with me when we got home. He never did.

I got out of the cab and walked up to the iron gate in front of the building. The doorman came over, weighing whether my suit was expensive enough. I said "Good morning" because I decided it sounded more urbane than "Hello." He was dressed in a navy-blue uniform with epaulets that resembled giant, upside-down gold toothbrushes.

"May I help you?" he inquired.

"Ms. Stevenson, please." His fluffy white eyebrows went up; obviously he'd heard about Richie. My heart started pounding. What if Gevinski was up there with Jessica right now? What if she called the police and ... "I'm Ms. Meyers." The doorman's lantern jaw dropped. "Mr. Meyers' *sister*," I confided. His color faded from crimson to a less life-threatening pink.

"Sorry for your troubles," he murmured. He hauled open the gate and ushered me into the building. I thanked him as he picked up the phone. "I have Mr. Meyers' sister, Miss Stevenson." He nodded deferentially as Jessica spoke.

Fortunately, the elevator man had already descended, so he didn't hear Jessica scream when she opened the door saying "Carol!" and spotted me. She emitted a woman-spots-mouse *Eeeek!* and was still at it as she tried to slam the door in my face. It could only have been desperation—and the sight of her in mourning attire, a white cashmere cat suit unzipped halfway down her rib cage—that made me throw myself with all my might against the door. The pain shot through my shoulder, up my neck, and down my arm, bringing tears to my eyes. But I was in.

"Get out!" She'd stopped eeeeking. Her tough tone was enough to make the average junior executive burst into tears. But all of a sudden I realized I was in charge. She was afraid of me!

"I can't believe you're afraid of me." Jessica did not reply. I noticed no redness or puffiness around her eyes. If she had fallen to pieces over Richie's death, she had managed to pull herself back together. "You can't honestly think *I* did it," I went on. But she was acting as if she did, eyes darting back and forth around the marble entrance gallery, looking for help from all sides. There was nothing except a very modern metal table, a painting of black scribbles, and an enormous sculpture that looked like a bronze scrotum.

"You think I did it," I said. "Do you know what's ironic? I think *you* did it."

That got her hot under the collar, causing the worst of her fear to evaporate. She put her hands on her hips. I noticed her waist was so small her fingers almost met in front. I also noted a knuckle-to-knuckle emerald-cut diamond on the ring finger of her left hand. "*I* did it?" she demanded. "Are you quite deranged?"

"Stop with the Briticisms. You're from Ohio." I wanted to add, "you whore," but figured it might antagonize her.

"Out!" Her eyes blazed. I hated to admit it, but even in a rage she was really great-looking. I bet Richie told her: It excites me when you're mad. I, on the other hand, would have told him the word was "angry," not "mad." That's what happens after twenty-five years of marriage and twenty-seven years of teaching English—which may, in part, explain his attraction to a beautiful, young, I-can-wear-a-cat-suit-with-no-underwear investment banker who didn't know beans about diction.

I'd held back on "you whore." But what about "murderer"? Yes, Jessica was scared of me. But did that mean she thought I was guilty? Could it instead mean that she thought I was an implacable Fury, unwilling to rest until I exacted vengeance for the crime of murder—or for her other crime, adultery.

"Tell me why he was at my house."

"I'm going to call the police." I think she took a step backward. It was hard to tell because she was dressed in white and the floor and walls were glossy white. It sounds overly stagy, but, unfortunately, the apartment was fairly subtle, to say nothing of stunning in the extreme. Fashionable but not at all ostentatious. Spare. Elegant. All those wonderful, classy attributes Richie hadn't been able to buy with all his Georgian silver and Chippendale chairs.

"Jessica, *please*. I'm about to be arrested for a crime I didn't commit. I need help."

"You certainly do."

"Why won't you tell me the reason he came to my house?" She pretended to be riveted by the alignment of the deep V of her décolletage. What was she hiding? "Is it because you didn't know that Richie was going? Because he didn't confide in you?" She shook her head as in: You're hopeless. But maybe she was just covering up that Richie hadn't played it straight with her either. "The last few years," I said gently, "he never let on to me what he was thinking. If he was holding back on you too—"

If she hadn't laughed with that dismissive honk, I wouldn't have hauled off and smacked her. But she did. *Whomp!* I slapped her across the face. Her head bobbled as if there were a spring in her neck. *Boing, boing, boing.* Then she screamed—and loud.

Suddenly, from inside the apartment, a man

appeared. Barefoot, still tying the bathrobe sash as he rushed in. "Jessica?" he called.

"Oh, God," she whimpered. He put his arm around her. She shrunk against him, pressing her hands against his chest, burrowing her head under his arm.

"What happened?" he demanded. He was much older than she, late fifties or early sixties, with pouchy bags under his eyes, little purses. His hair was so thick and white it was hard to believe he wasn't wearing a wig. "Jessica, who is this?" He was tall. The bathrobe didn't cover his knees.

"She hit me!"

Then it dawned on me. The reason his bathrobe was so short was because it was Richie's. "You don't waste any time, do you, Jessica?"

She withdrew from the man's embrace. I thought she was going to spit at me. The left side of her face was bright red. I was simultaneously relieved and disappointed that there was no handprint. "This is my *father*," she said. She took his hand and said to him: "This is Rick's former wife."

"Not former," I retorted.

"Why are you here?" the man snapped. Despite his pale, naked legs, he had an authoritative, Chairman of the Joint Chiefs of Staff voice.

"Please, I'm in terrible trouble." I waited for his better nature to react to my being a damsel in distress, but he just drew Jessica's hand tight against his chest.

"Look," Jessica said. She displayed her unfortunately-still-red cheek.

That did it for dear old Dad. And for me. He

dropped her hand and in a flash grabbed the collars of my jacket and blouse so tight I started to choke. Then he hauled me to the door and threw me out.

Seven

"I've gotten the ball rolling, Cassandra," her husband said. "I'm waiting for a call back."

Cass, the straightest of the straight arrows, gazed at him. "I hope you will be able to subvert the criminal justice process, Theodore. Rosie is in trouble."

Theodore Tuttle Higbee III glanced over at me. "Do you think they'll actually arrest you?"

"Not right after the funeral. Probably late today or tomorrow."

Still, I was managing. Right? In spite of being followed by two cops, this time in a white car, I'd gotten myself over to Cass's house early enough to borrow one of her church hats for the funeral, a small black saucer with a short veil. I was even able to sit in the glassed-in, skylit sun porch of the Higbees' sprawling ranch house, chatting and drinking coffee. But I had become a robot called Rosie Meyers, a machine without sensation.

"I hope you can strong-arm some of your crackpot political friends on her behalf," Cass said to Theodore.

"I'm trying, Cassandra."

"Try harder. Are you going to allow them to handcuff her and lead her away? To whom will I talk? Whom will I get to teach Honors Shakespeare in the middle of October?"

"The district attorney is a Democrat," he explained.

"I know that, Theodore. But I thought your influence extended beyond mere provincial boundaries."

"I've heard Forrest Newel is a good man," he said defensively. "I'm sure Rosie will be fine with him."

"He is a dolt. And you are a nincompoop, " Cass said.

But a well-connected one. Theodore III, while agreeable company at a dinner party, would never be called a profound thinker—or even a thinker. But if you needed to reach any reactionary anywhere in the world, he was your passport. "Newel was a major muckety-muck on Reagan's New York finance committee in '84," he mused. "I hear the fellow's as sound as they come." Translated from Right-speak, that meant that Forrest Newel, like Theodore, was against government spending on any program that might benefit the poor, the sick, the old, the young, the homeless, the helpless; he was for any policy that encouraged massive spending on megadeath weapon systems.

"Forrest's Harvard, you know." So was Theodore.

"Naturally," Cass remarked. "The most overrated institution in America." She crossed her arms over her substantial chest. "Is he at least a good criminal lawyer?"

"I would assume so." Theodore smoothed his mustache, which looked like a strand of licorice glued to his upper lip. "Why wouldn't he be?"

"I haven't the foggiest notion why I ask his opinion," Cass remarked to me as she refilled my coffee cup. "The man knows nothing."

Theodore smiled indulgently at his wife across the red-and-white gingham tablecloth. "Cassandra is so tart," he said, with evident pleasure. Each made it a practice to discuss their marriage as if the other had just stepped out of the room. "Tart and feisty."

Cass, who was on another of her diets that would last no longer than three days, sipped from her cup of hot water and lemon juice. "It is hard to believe," she said to me, "that in this last decade of the twentieth century, an Ivy League–educated African-American can be, concurrently, so obtuse and so smug, but Theodore manages it."

Theodore, a light-brown version of Fred Astaire, dapper, slender, and graceful, beamed at his wife. The heir to the magazine-publishing company his grandfather had founded, he had met Cass at a Christmas party the year she arrived at Goucher after three years on a get-them-out-of-the-ghetto full scholarship at Choate. Ignoring reality, disregarding their vast differences in class, style, intellect, and temperament, eschewing common sense, he cast her as his pudgy Ginger, pursued her, and married her the day after her graduation. "She's really crazy about me," he informed me.

"Do you see?" Cass exclaimed. "He does not converse. He banters. And I am *not* crazy about him. The truth is, he needed me to prove he was not ashamed of being black. Still does. And I was enamored of his money and social position when I was still a silly girl. That was when I agreed to his proposal."

"She keeps saying that, but then why has she stayed married to me?"

"Theodore," Cass said, ignoring his question, "I want you to find out what this Forrest Newel's reputation is. He sounds like a bubble-brain."

We had nothing more to say. The only sound in the sunroom was Theodore's knife scraping excess peach preserves off his English muffin. Then, from someplace deep inside the house, I heard a delicate pinging, like a triangle being struck repeatedly. Theodore bounded out of his chair and hurried inside. "His private line," Cass explained. "He had it installed so he could tell people to call him on his private line. This is the call he's been waiting for. If it is possible for strings to be pulled for you, he will pull them. The party of Lincoln owes him."

"For what?"

"For being its Negro all these years."

Outside the glass walls, a brisk wind slapped dead brown leaves against the thick trunk of an oak.

"You are wondering why I stay married to him."

"You're happier than you think you are."

"My dear," she said slowly, "the only people who are truly happy are the people we do not know very well." I stared down at the crumbs of cranberry bran muffin on the translucent white china plate before me. "Perhaps there are exceptions," she conceded.

"You're only saying that to give me hope."

"Yes."

"It doesn't."

Cass sighed, then reached over to Theodore's plate, took his English muffin, and, forgetting her diet, spooned a mound of preserves on it. She took a large, contemplative bite. "Maybe we can outfox the police."

"How?"

"I don't know." She took another bite. "How about arson? We could burn down your house! They might believe you perished in the flames."

"And then what do I do for the rest of my life?" She put the half-eaten muffin on her plate. I grabbed it and stuffed it in my mouth before she could get it back. "Sling hash at a truck stop in Sioux City?"

"Let me think. Ah! You could get a wig and blue contact lenses, and when they come for you . . ." Her voice faded. She had no more real hope than I had. "Between the two of us we ought to come up with some sort of nefarious scheme. We will talk after the funeral."

"I may be in jail."

She pulled off the checkered napkin that she'd been using as a bib to protect her funeral dress, a navy jersey with a white shawl collar. She looked very proper. "Do you have access to a great deal of money?" she asked.

"I'm not sure. The last I heard, the lawyers were duking it out over some assets Richie shifted around the month before he kissed me off. Anyway, why would I need a great deal of money? For a whole team of criminal lawyers?"

"No. For a bribe."

"Cass, you know from George Eliot. You don't know from graft."

"You do, though! You read those books."

"But I don't live in a George V. Higgins universe. Can you see me slipping Gevinski a wad of C-notes in a men's room?"

We heard Theodore's light footsteps on the flagstone floor of the hall outside the sun porch. Quickly, we agreed on how to contact each other, to use the old trick half the teachers at Shorehaven used when they wanted to receive personal calls during the school day and not, for example, have to discuss a yeast infection with their gynecologist on the English office telephone. If I could get to a phone, I'd leave a message for Cass that Dr. So-and-so's office was calling to confirm an appointment for, say, eleven o'clock. At eleven, she would be at one of the pay phones at school—we used the one outside the cafeteria—to receive the call.

"Rosie," Theodore said, before he sat down. He spoke my name so coolly that I knew there was no hope.

"What is it?" Cass asked him.

"My friend assured me the D.A.'s office and the police will not alert the media. No handcuffs either. They agreed that Forrest Newel can bring her in tomorrow evening, after dark, so if photographers are watching the house, he can sneak her out through the garage and drive her there in her own car. But that's all I could do."

"That is *all?*" Cass exclaimed. "With your connections, I assumed—"

Theodore looked only at his wife. Already, I was history. "The results of the forensic tests came in, Cassandra. There is not a shred of evidence there was anyone in the house the night before last— except Rosie and Richie."

The cops who'd followed me to Cass's kept close behind me as I left. They stopped, pulling over to the side of the road, only after I passed through the open iron gates at the entrance to Emerald Point. The gates were emblazoned with a heraldic device, a lion and a bunch of leaves. In profile, the lion had a delicate, upturned snout—a subliminal reminder to Carter Tillotson's wealthy, socially ambitious, assimilating neighbors that he was New York's nose-job king.

I sat in the car in front of Stephanie's grand Tudor. I had fallen off the edge of the earth and entered a new world in which a neighborly favor was no longer lending a Weedwacker but convincing an ultraconservative politician to put in a good word so I would not be photographed in handcuffs as I was arrested for murder.

I wondered which of my fellow teachers would be the stinker who went on Eyewitness News to tell them that beneath my cheerful facade there was seething rage. I thought about which of my students would be the most damaged by my arrest and disgrace. Joey, in my sophomore writing class, who was so fragile? I'd been working with him after school so he wouldn't fall behind—and, as the school psychologist had suggested, so he'd have an outlet for expressing himself, as well as a project that would keep him engaged and too busy to dwell on suicidal thoughts. I thought about which student would feel the most betrayed. Elena, from Guatemala, a senior in my honors class? Her Spanish accent was still so heavy I sometimes couldn't understand her, but her papers! The kid was born to be a Shakespeare scholar. Of course, I knew exactly which wise-ass would start the first "What did Mrs. Meyers say before she stabbed her husband?" riddle.

Someone in town was burning leaves. The air was pungent and cold, hard on the throat, but irresistible. I took a deeper breath. I remembered when I was eight or nine, walking home from P.S. 197 with a construction-paper pumpkin, stopping to pick up acorns from a pile of leaves so I could throw them at Tom Driscoll and the other Catholic boys on their way home from Saint Aloysius. I had once been a bright and lively girl who knew how to get a guy's attention.

I thought about whether the jury would look at me when they returned and what that terrible instant would be like, between the time the judge asked: "Ladies and gentlemen of the jury, have you reached a verdict?" and the response. And whether prisoners in a maximum security prison were allowed to meet visitors in a dayroom, or if there would be bars between me and my sons, me and my grandchildren.

I rang Stephanie's doorbell. I waited. I rang it again. Finally, breathless, cheeks flushed, she pulled it open. She wore a pale-yellow bathrobe with blue piping. Her wet hair was wrapped in a pale-yellow towel. "Sorry. I was all the way upstairs, getting ready." She shivered. The wind was getting stronger, one long, cold gust. I remembered our first morning at Gulls' Haven, when Richie stood out on the back terrace, the wind coming in off the Sound, whipping at his undershorts. He'd yelled up to me: Hey, Rosie! It's all mine!

"How come Hansel or Gretel didn't get the door?" I asked Stephanie. "Did you fire *them* too?"

"Gunnar and Inger. *They* quit. Found a job in Arizona paying twice what we're paying. Good riddance, but Carter is in a snit. Says no more couples. Just a maid, and a nanny for Astor." She stopped and looked at me. I must have looked like hell, because her jaunty manner suddenly fell flat. Her voice grew dull, thick, full of dread. "It's not going well, is it?"

"They'll be arresting me in the next couple of days."

"Oh, God. Oh, Rosie. Come in."

"I can't. I have to go home and get dressed for the funeral. Please, Stephanie, you have to help me."

She pulled the sash of her robe until it was so tight she had to release it to breathe. "Of course. I want to help you. Just tell me what it is you want me to do."

"Find me another lawyer. I'm stuck with Forrest Newel—"

"I know he's a little old-fashioned, but he's supposed to be the best."

"He thinks I'm guilty. He's not even trying to get them to find who did it. He just wants to get a good deal for me."

"Rosie, that's what lawyers *do*."

"Fine, and I'll be out of the jug in time for the Miss Osteoporosis Pageant in 2025. Please, Stephanie, you've got to get me someone else."

"I will. You have my word. Now take a deep breath. You have to get a grip on yourself."

The services for Richie were held about fifteen minutes from the house, at Eventide East in Manhasset, a funeral home whose exterior seemed to be modeled after Monticello—if Jefferson had had a cousin in the aluminum siding business. It was one of those dreadful nondenominational places with lots of little rooms paneled in blond wood with fake stained-glass windows in an innocuous floral pattern, so none of the bereaved would be made even more hysterical by an unseemly menorah or an inappropriate cross.

Naturally, it was a nightmare. I had a fight with Ben because I told him Suspicious could not be seated with the family for the simple reason that she was not part of the family. He, usually the most reasonable and polite of young men, called me a bitch. I suggested he take Suspicious and sit with Jessica; since the two were almost the same age, they might have a lot to chat about. He informed me that, in fact, he and Suspicious and Jessica and Dad had spent time together and that the two women had really enjoyed each other's company. In the end, he stood beside me in the reception room but would not acknowledge my presence. Alex, on the other hand, leaned on me. But that was because he was so high or low on some controlled substance that his legs could not quite support him. My mother—a short, bottom-heavy woman who resembled one of those inflated toys you punch down only to have it spring right back up—was displaying nearly all the symptoms of senile dementia, including incontinence on her own shoes. She insisted on knowing, in her not-so-sotto voce: "Who's dead?"

"Richie."

"Richie?"

She had once been zestful and good-humored, a born man-pleaser, with a button nose and happy hazel eyes. She was not an intellectual, nor even particularly intelligent, but she'd been sharp enough to be a great cardplayer; if there had been a canasta event in the Olympics, Pearl Bernstein would have brought home the gold. She'd been a fashion plate, too, and an ardent movie fan, who could describe every outfit worn by Bette Davis in *Now Voyager*. My father, a social studies teacher, remained smitten with her until the day he died. He'd buy her perfume or a half-pound box of Barton's chocolates for no reason at all. Although my mother hadn't been conceited about her prettiness, she had been pleased by it. She used to say: Rosie, you know what the word "a crime" means? To let yourself go. I put on my face every single day, including mascara, even if the only place I'm going is out to the incinerator.

"Richie was my husband, Mom."

"You think I don't know Richie?"

Richie's sister, Carol, dressed in what appeared to be black crepe swaddling, ostentatiously kissed the boys. Not only did she not kiss me; she did not look at me. "Looks like she's going to a funeral," my mother announced, in a voice that could probably be heard in Miami Beach. "Who's she?"

"Richie's sister," I whispered. "Carol. The one whose husband was Richie's accountant." I tried to peer over the heads of the crowd. I did not see Jessica. But I thought I glimpsed Tom Driscoll out of the corner of my eye. I controlled myself for five seconds, then glanced over to the spot where I'd seen him. He was no longer there.

A few friends and neighbors came over. They murmured: What can I say? I can't believe it. A horror. What does this say about our society? But they checked around first to be sure no one was watching, and they murmured fast. They didn't want to be seen talking to me. Or kissing me. They threw their arms around Ben, squeezed Alex's droopy hand. But few gave me more than a perfunctory peck. Except for Cass and Stephanie, hardly anyone looked me in the eye.

A black-suited, needle-nosed Eventide employee shepherded the visitors into the chapel. As they were filing out of the reception room, my mother blared: "So where's Richie?"

"He's inside, Mom. Come on. We'll go in."

"Why isn't he here with us? Is he playing tennis?"

Ben took her hand. "He's dead, Grandma."

"Who's dead?"

"My father. Richie."

"No!" She shook her head so hard her jowls flapped back and forth. "Oh, God in heaven!" she screamed. "Oh, God. Richie's dead!"

She was still inconsolable when, to a hideous chorus of whispers, we walked into the chapel, although by that time she was muttering, "Charlie,

Charlie," and seemed to think we were at my father's funeral.

I have no recollection of what the rabbi said. He was a kid not much older than Ben. He looked like a Beach Boy in a yarmulke. He made veiled references to "all those who loved Richard," thereby not only including Jessica by default but also deftly avoiding the Richie-Rick controversy.

I finally saw her. She was in a mist of melancholy gray silk, all the way in the back, by herself. A brilliant ploy, sitting isolated, lovely, lonely, young. The rabbi was so moved he immediately disengaged his Intermarriage Alert System and delivered his eulogy straight to Jessica. Heads kept turning, every eye was drawn to her—and to the tears that meandered down her face.

In the limousine on the way to the cemetery, Alex dry-swallowed another pill, an act at which he seemed particularly adept, then denied he had taken a pill. Ben mumbled that he was sorry, that I wasn't a bitch, that I had been a wonderful mother, loving, supportive, and fun. Hadn't we had wonderful times when I taught him to ride a bike, when we went to the city to see Shakespeare in the Park, when we went looking at colleges? His apology, although heartfelt, sounded too much like a rough draft of his first letter that I'd get at mail call in my cell block. I asked him what kind of pills Alex was on. He said probably some sixties- or seventies-style designer drug, similar to Quaaludes, and that I shouldn't worry; Alex didn't seem near overdosing. My mother wept most of the way, then roared at the punch line of a joke only she could hear. As the limo driver and I helped her out at the cemetery, she announced:

"Now that he's dead, don't let yourself go. You gotta get a new boyfriend."

"Stop it!" I glanced around. Thank God, no one seemed to have heard.

"You *always* had boyfriends." She cackled. "You think I didn't know? You think the whole world didn't know how you carried on?"

Ben looked ill. "She's senile," I told him. He nodded, mechanically. "Come on, Benjy. You know me. Do you think I ever cheated on your father?"

It got worse. Somehow, between the funeral home and the cemetery, the jury of my peers had gone out, deliberated, and found me guilty beyond a reasonable doubt. Alex, Ben, Suspicious, my mother, and I stood alone on the left side of the coffin, along with Cass and Theodore, my relatives, a few teachers, and two old friends from my college newspaper.

On the other side of the coffin, arrayed in a consoling semicircle around Jessica, staring at me across the freshly dug grave, were Richie's city slicker friends. There were so many of them. It hit me then that long before Richie moved out, he had left me; he had an entire life I knew nothing about. Mitchell Gruen, of course, was not there. Behind those two hundred gorgeously dressed people were all his business associates—and behind them, shuffling, sniffling, whispering, and checking out the Manhattan outfits, our neighbors and friends.

The rabbi lifted his head. His sun-bleached hair fell over one eye. He brushed it away and explained why the Mourner's Kaddish was really a prayer for the living, not for the dead—whom he called "those who have gone before us." I watched Jessica. She wasn't really beautiful, not in the pure, invulnerable way Stephanie Tillotson was. Her forehead was too high, her chin too small, her arms and legs too long. But with her lean body, streaky mane of hair, and startling aquamarine eyes, she was better than beautiful. She was fascinating; a man would resent anything that made him stop looking at her.

Out of respect to a quarter century of marriage, I should have prayed along with the rabbi. I closed my eyes, but I could not dismiss Jessica's image. I tried to come up with a reason Richie might leave her to come back to me; I couldn't find one. Nor could I find a reason why Jessica would follow Richie to my house, pull a carving knife out of the big oak block, and stab him to death.

Ben had his arm around Suspicious. Alex was concentrating on not swaying. I was left holding my mother's cold, dry hand. She lifted it and wiped her eyes and nose with it. "Sad!" she announced.

Ben brought his finger to his lips. "Shhh, Grandma."

"Shhh yourself, Big Mouth, Big Feet, whoever you are."

"I'm Benjamin."

She gave him one of her old, flirty smiles. "I'm Pearl."

"God of Abraham, Isaac, and Jacob," the rabbi was intoning. The coffin rested on a metal frame directly over the freshly dug grave. I tried to make myself look back, past the last few months, and remember that inside that pine box was the person who had been the center of my life for twenty-five years. But I couldn't concentrate; standing near the back of the semicircle, behind a tight pack of Data Associates secretaries, was Sergeant Gevinski, and with him was a young, burly detective with a see-the-pink-scalp crew cut. They were there to guard me. The young one's body was angled forward, one foot in front of the other, ready to sprint if I did what they obviously expected: made a break for it.

What the hell did they think I was going to do? Pull out a hand grenade, make my getaway, and then lie low in the Feinberg family mausoleum until the heat blew over?

Gevinski saw me looking at him. He gave me an acknowledging nod. My heart raced. I was so frightened. So angry at Richie. He had destroyed my life by being faithless, then by leaving me, and, if that weren't enough, by driving someone crazy enough to kill him.

"We have to say goodbye," the rabbi droned.

The killer had to have been someone with a purpose. I could not accept that it had been a burglar lurking behind a sycamore who thought "Goody!" when he saw Richie sneaking in. What kind of burglar doesn't burgle? Gevinski had left a receipt for Crime Victim's Valuables beside the toaster-oven in the kitchen. Richie had been wearing a Cartier watch. Besides his credit cards, a picture of him "with his arm around a woman," and his driver's license, it listed his wallet as containing three hundred and forty dollars in cash, all in twenties. There were also keys in his pockets, ninety-six cents in change, and Certs sugar-free breath mints.

"Rose!" my mother shouted, even though I was right beside her. "Who's that skinny marink over there, bawling her head off?"

"The wife of a client," I said in a hushed voice, but of course, by then everyone had followed my mother's eyes to Joan Driscoll, Richie's dear friend.

"Would you look at those knock-knees!"

"Mom, this is a funeral. You have to be quiet."

There was nothing that could be done to a human being that Joan Driscoll had not done to herself. Her straight hair had been permed only enough so that it curved under just before it grazed her shoulders. It was colored a blue-black that had never occurred naturally on any living person. She resembled Veronica, the rich girl in the Archie comic books, grown to bulimic middle age. Her nose had been refined, her chin redefined and clefted, her thighs suctioned, and most recently, from the looks of things around her always-plunging neckline, she had brand-new breasts. Two volleyball-sized objects swelled under the jacket of her stylish, short-skirted black faille suit.

Alex saw her too. His eyes widened. He tried to elbow his brother but missed. "Hey," he drawled to Ben, "get a look at Hojo's nouvelle tits." In his drugged serenity, Alex only intermittently seemed to comprehend that he was at his father's funeral. I turned to give him a warning look just in time to see him trying to catch Joan Driscoll's attention, running his tongue over his lips in mocking sensuality. "Hojo," Alex said, but his voice was soft, to say nothing of slurred.

Hojo was Alex's nickname for her. Jo for Joan. Ho for whore. He'd started calling her that after she came to dinner one night in a low-cut dress and said hello to him and Ben by lifting their chins with the side of her index finger and kissing them lightly on the lips. I'd wanted to deck her.

Richie had been amused. Tolerant. Joan's little games. Harmless teasing. The boys weren't children anymore. His dear friend Joan. He'd gotten the "dear friend" from her. So sophisticated. Everyone in New York was either a nonentity or a dear friend.

Joan was crying too hard to notice Alex. However, almost nothing escaped her husband, Tom. But nothing seemed to touch him either. Not a zonked-out rocker ridiculing his wife's sexuality. Not my presence. Not Richie's death. He saw it all: the rabbi, Jessica, the jurors who had come in with a guilty verdict, me, my mother. He saw his wife's new Grand Canyon of a cleavage. How could he miss it? How could he have married her? What had made the boy I knew choose the life the man was living? How could he stand it?

But Tom's arm was around her, jiggling slightly with each of her sobs. The rest of him was absolutely still. No emotion crossed his lean face. He had dead man's eyes.

The rabbi chanted a protracted Amen. The crowd shifted, waiting for him to dismiss them, which he did with a nod that caused his surfer hair to bounce again. That instant, as Hojo raised her head and Tom dropped his arm, my mother had one of her increasingly rare moments of lucidity. She looked from Hojo's white, ageless, lineless, lifted face to the man beside her. She squinted. She gawked. She grinned. "Tommy Driscoll!" she called across the grave. "He has his father's face," she announced.

"Don't, Mom."

"Same nose," she boomed. "A big schnozz for an Irisher. Everybody in the building always said they must have Italian blood." Then she called even louder. "Tommy!" The crowd froze in place.

"Mom, please be quiet."

"Shut up, girlie," she said, and jerked away. She made a megaphone with her hands and thundered across the grave: "Tommy!"

I caught up with her and took her arm. "Mom, you don't have to talk to him today. You talked to him at our silver anniversary party. In the big tent. Remember? That's how come you recognize him. I brought you over and introduced you. He said it was good to see you again, and you said you wouldn't forget him in a million years."

But I couldn't distract her. "Tommy!" Tom's eyes did not meet mine, but they met hers. "It's me, Tommy! Mrs. Bernstein." He nodded. The corner of his mouth moved; my mother took it as a smile. "See?" she said. "It is him." Before Ben or I could grab her, she scurried around the grave and began to shove, pushing aside other mourners, making her way to see Thomas Driscoll, venture capitalist, cover boy for *Business Week*. "Tommy! Is your mother dead?" she was hollering, when Ben and I reached her.

Ben took hold of her arm. "How are you, Grandma?" He hugged her tight against him, obscuring her view of Tom Driscoll, which was good, because then hardly anyone—not Gevinski, not Cass, not Stephanie, not Jessica, not Hojo, not Tom—heard her.

Only Ben and I did. "Rose," she boomed, the

sound muffled by Ben's massive chest. "What were you? Seventeen years old? Eighteen? Oy, I thought I would die when I caught you and Tommy Driscoll stark naked!"

Eight

Tennis season was over; Carter Tillotson's fair skin had lost its summer scarlet and reverted to its normal waxen no-color. If he'd had a wick growing out of his head, he could have been a Plastic Surgeon candle.

Carter, I'd assumed, understood that social convention required him to say something in a house of mourning. Yet all he'd done was sit in belligerent silence for five minutes. Finally he blurted out:

"Rough. Richie. And then if you go to jail . . . " Since my eyes had been downcast while reading over Stephanie's list of criminal lawyers, I was able to catch the motion of her black lizard pump swatting his cordovan wing tips in a swift kick. I stopped reading and just watched feet. Carter toed in but said nothing more. Stephanie got his ankle with her next kick, so he said: "The police knocked on our door two minutes after we got home from the funeral. A sergeant and a detective. They just left."

"Carter, for heaven's sake," Stephanie said.

"That's okay," I told her. The Tillotsons had come over with a bottle of red wine and a plate of goat cheese and biscuits to let me know they were with me, although it was clear from the instant he walked through the door that Carter was with me only because he'd been dragged. "Hadn't the police been to see you before?" I asked.

"The, um, morning after," Carter said. I knew women were supposed to be crazy about him, but frankly, I never got it. He was bland beyond belief, as if he'd been born without a personality. His life-lessness was so profound that he never, ever became animated, not even when he talked about his grand passion, nostril shapes. Over the years, I'd seen him often enough in tennis shorts and bathing trunks to know there wasn't anything great to write home about in the body department to compensate for his being so monumentally blah. Cass said his blahness was the point: His first name was Doctor, and he was six feet tall. Women saw a blank screen and projected onto it whatever man they most desired.

"The police kept asking over and over if we'd

seen or heard anything, which of course we hadn't,"
Stephanie added.

I was alone with the Tillotsons. Suspicious had
taken the train back to Philadelphia. Ben and my
mother were in the library with some relatives who
had stopped by to offer sympathy. Alex was there
too, but when I'd excused myself to speak to
Stephanie about lawyers, I'd left him stretched out in
a club chair and ottoman, his chin on his chest,
dreaming Quaalude dreams.

The living room was a huge, stiff space the decorator had convinced us we needed. She'd said: You
need one serious room for formal occasions. What
the hell is she talking about—"formal"? I'd said to
Richie. Are your aunt Bea and uncle Murray going to
present their calling cards on a silver salver? In the
end, naturally, we'd gone along, and the decorator
had created a room George III could call home.
Stately English furniture. Couches and chairs upholstered in beige silk and damask. Gilt frames on
extremely minor Dutch still-life paintings. The only
life came from the swaying trees beyond the silk-
swagged windows.

"You didn't see anything at all that night?" I asked.
Stephanie shook her head. "Hear anything? Anything
at all, Stephanie? I'm not just talking about the middle
of the night. Anytime after nine-thirty."

"No."

"Did anything strike either of you as unusual, or
even a little different?" Neither of them responded.
They were taken aback by my interrogation. Carter's
excellent posture got better; Stephanie had a blinking fit: blink, blink, blink, blink, as if she couldn't
believe what she was seeing. But they were too

well-brought-up to object. And I wasn't well-brought-up enough to lay off. "Carter, what time did you get home that night?"

I sensed a reluctance to talk when he answered me with his teeth clenched. "About ten after eleven. I saw nothing. Heard nothing."

"You were home the whole night, Stephanie?"

"No. I was speaking at the garden club meeting on indoor foliage plants. Remember?"

"That's right."

"I guess I got home around ten, ten-thirty. But I didn't see anything. Sorry, Rosie."

"It's okay. Now, both of you. How did you come home?"

"By car," they said, not quite in unison.

"I mean, did you go along Lighthouse Point Lane and then up Hill Road?"

"It's the most direct route," Carter said, still through his teeth.

"When you passed that spot where everyone parks to play tennis at your house, did you notice any cars?"

Carter shook his head. Stephanie said: "That's where they found Richie's car."

"Right. But when I walked over to your house, the cops were making molds of the tire marks. *I* think there might have been another car there."

"What do the police think?" she asked.

"They say the marks were probably made earlier. Or made by anybody who'd spotted the reflector on Richie's car and wanted to check it out—even a police car."

"I didn't notice anything," Stephanie said. "I'm sorry. I just wish I'd been more alert."

"It's not something you'd be looking for. Come on, Stephanie, don't feel bad." She wriggled way back into her chair. She was still upset. "Let's move on," I told them. "What did the police want today?"

Carter glared at Stephanie. God, did he want out. Well, he had been Richie's closest male friend—which meant they sat side by side at Knicks games. Richie had said they'd had some good talks. Knowing the two of them, that probably meant they revealed their most intimate feelings about Financial Planning in the Post–Tax Shelter Era. In his own way, though, Carter did seem to have cared about Richie.

And he did seem to believe I had murdered him. He couldn't wait to leave. His hands rested on his legs, just above his knees, ready to push him up and out. He had small, stubby-fingered hands, hands you'd expect to see finger painting, not performing delicate surgery.

"The police wanted to know about you and Richie," Stephanie said. "If you'd had any big fights. They're looking for a history of physical violence—on your part or his—that can go to motive. Right, Carter?" He nodded. Barely. "Now, Rosie," she went on, "while they were interviewing Carter I told them I had to punch down some dough, which I did. But I also went to the phone, made some calls, and drew up that list. I told all the litigators I spoke with: 'Bottom line: Who's the best?' "

It was after seven and dark outside. "I'll call them tomorrow," I said. "See how the chemistry is with each one."

"Trust your gut reaction, Rosie! You have great instincts." Stephanie used her we-can-win, captain-of-the-field-hockey-team voice. She hesitated and then added: "Wait. I should be with you when you call. . . . No, do you know what would be better? If I went along with you—" But Stephanie never got to finish her sentence.

Carter grabbed her arm and hauled her off her chair with such force he ripped the sleeve of her basic-black dress. Her smart and beautiful face turned stupid as she stared down at her bare shoulder through the torn seam. "We're getting out of here!" he shouted at her, dragging her toward the door. Was she too shocked to object? Or was she grateful to be dragged out, pulled away from my ugly mess, from me?

"Stephanie," I called out.

"Forget it," Carter yelled at me, just before they disappeared. "Don't call us or come near us again!"

I should have been shattered. Except I wasn't. My despair was so intense, my terror so profound, that being treated as the devil incarnate by a schnook whose life was dedicated to reconfiguring the faces of Greater New York so everyone looked Episcopalian didn't bother me one whit. Okay, maybe half a whit, but I forgot him completely when Ben slouched into the room.

"We have to talk," I said.

"I was just coming in to say good night."

"It's not even eight o'clock."

"Mom, I'm exhausted." His eyes were everywhere but on me.

"Ben, listen. Please believe me about Grandma. Whatever medical name you want to give what she has, she's crackers. You know that."

He shrugged, trying for a nonchalance only his

brother could get away with. "What about Mr. Driscoll?"

"History. We grew up together. We lived in the same apartment house. We were great friends as kids, but by high school we hardly saw each other." He waited. I took a deep breath. I had to explain the naked business. "Senior year, we ran into each other on the way to the library. We got to talking." I examined the ceiling, looking for a maternally correct response. I couldn't find any. "Ben, you're twenty-four years old."

"So?"

"So you can take it. Mr. Driscoll and I fell for each other. We had sex."

"And Grandma caught you?" For that one instant, he was smiling. Enchanted. Delighted.

"She caught us once. After that we were much more careful. Anyway, we had a lovely relationship until he went off to college, and that was that. No big deal." Tom Driscoll broke my heart. "No hard feelings. We said hi, how are you, during school vacations, but we were leading different lives. And then I never saw him again until he was a hotshot. He made a fortune at some private bank. Then he quit and started investing in sick companies. He turned them around, then sold them for tons of money. And that's when I called and asked him out to lunch."

"You just called him out of the clear blue sky?"

"What did I have to lose? We were both married. It was all very proper. Not much fun, because he'd turned from a wonderful person into a stiff. But he did become a client. The four of us socialized on occasion, although he never referred to the past. He behaved as if I was a business associate's suburban wife, which I was. More than polite, less than friendly."

"Did Dad know about you and Mr. Driscoll?"

"He knew we'd been friends as kids. That's all he needed to know."

"And Dad and Mrs. Driscoll?"

"They became good friends. Phone friends, mostly. I think they talked almost every day, and no, I don't think Dad was sleeping with her. She was his mentor. She guided him into a new life in New York."

Ben's smile was gone. His athlete's shoulders sagged. "I thought we were such a happy family," he said.

"We were. It's just the last few months—"

"Mom! Do you think the day after your anniversary party he suddenly woke up and decided he wanted out?"

"How come I'm to blame?"

"I'm tired." He started to go.

"It wasn't my fault, damn it! Everyone's always saying, 'It takes two to tango' and all those smug clichés about women who get dumped, but why am I responsible for his adultery, for his abandoning me?" Ben kept walking. I ran through the too-big room after him. "Ben, you tell me. What evil did I do that my life has turned to shit and I'm going to jail?"

And very softly he said: "I don't know what you did, Mom." He turned his back on me and walked away.

All my life, when bad things had happened—a miscarriage two years after Alex was born, my father dying of cancer, even Richie leaving—they were not unfathomable bad things. Embryos do fail, parents die, husbands leave. I understood there was no immunity from sorrow. But within forty-eight hours I would be in a six-by-eight-foot cell. I don't know why, but I didn't conjure up barred windows or even a psychotic cellmate: only a filthy, seatless toilet. The picture made me so weak I wanted to go up to bed under quilts and never, ever get out. In truth, I wanted to die. I thought about how many Xanax were left in the bottle. But I was already so dead inside that I simply did not have the strength to haul myself upstairs to overdose.

I was in the middle of a nightmare. And what made it even more horrible was that with the exception of my best friend, no one seemed to find my nightmare unacceptable, disgraceful, absurd, or, when you came down to it, unjust. No one would help me. My own kid! My tenderhearted one. Flesh of my flesh telling me: "I don't know what you did, Mom."

Not an absolute accusation but, by God, a doubt. How could he? Were we all so capable of murder that we could willingly accept the notion that any one of us might snatch a knife and impale our recently dearly beloved? Or was it me? Was there some peculiarity in my personality that made my own child, the teachers I'd worked with for eighteen years, my next-door neighbors, believe I could take a life?

Or was the circumstantial evidence against me so persuasive that it had to be believed by any rational person?

I leaned forward to bury my face in my hands,

certainly a gesture appropriate for existential angst, but then I remembered I had left Alex snoozing in the library; I wanted to make sure he wasn't in a too-deep, chemically induced sleep. To be perfectly honest, I was like a nervous mother with a new infant. I just wanted to make sure he was breathing.

He was. His cheek was warm. A strand of black hair hung over his face. I pushed it back. He blinked open his eyes and said: "Hiya, Ma."

"Are you okay, Alex?"

"Fine," he said, which with his rocker inflection sounded like "fahn."

"Everybody's gone. Want to go upstairs and go to bed?"

"Doin' fine here." Before the sentence was complete he closed his eyes again.

"I love you, Alex."

"Love ya too, Ma," he mumbled.

What would happen to him if I weren't around? Then I asked the question more directly: How would Alex survive the murder of his father, the conviction and imprisonment of his mother? Because, as I climbed the big staircase to go to bed, my going up the river was, if not inevitable, at least damn likely. How could I believe I would be exonerated by a jury of my peers if I could count on one finger of one hand only one person who thoroughly believed in me: Cass.

God knows why, but I was drawn into Alex's hellhole of a room. Undershorts, shirts, socks, books, crushed soda cans, two empty bags of cheddar-cheese popcorn, newspapers with enraptured accounts of Richie's murder, a brown apple core, sheets of music-composition paper littered the floor. His guitar, plugged into his old amplifier, rested on the bed. I went through his guitar case and backpack. Nothing. I finally found a bottle of large white pills in the pocket of the jeans he'd worn home. The bottle was one of those brown ones that vitamins come in, but of course, there was no label. Before I could tell myself he was twenty-one and old enough to make his own mistakes and that my protecting him would, in fact, insulate him further from reality, I went into his bathroom, shook the pills into the toilet, and flushed.

I didn't doubt Alex would find something else to relieve whatever pain he was in, but when we said goodbye, I wanted him to feel something. Anguish. Anger. I didn't want him to write a dissonant song about Pa's got a knife in his gut and Ma's stampin' due dates in the prison library. I wanted Alex to show some emotion. I wanted to leave knowing that he wasn't dead from the ass both ways.

I never thought I would look back with fondness to the way he was in high school. Angry. Purposeful, even if only to defy authority—outwitting Richie's fancy magnetic window sensors, climbing down the Sav-Ur-Life ladder to go wild with his friend Danny and the rest of his band. I could use an angry young man on my side, a man as clever as his father had been, a born manipulator.

But then I looked at Alex's pigpen of a floor, at the clothes and nail clipper and hair gel thrown on his chair, at the chaos he had created out of order in just twenty-four hours. I had to stop living a fiction. He was my son, not my hero-detective.

I pushed his grungy T-shirt and a couple of pieces

of popcorn off a corner of his bed and sat down. What happened next? I don't remember. Maybe I prayed and got an answer. Maybe I just sat for a while and concocted yet another fiction. But when I got up, I somehow knew in my heart that in a week or a year or a decade, Alex would be okay.

I felt so much relief I sank back down on his bed. I glanced out the window. The moon was a sliver, but the stars twinkled at me.

My foot drifted back and forth on his rug, then under his bed. It was still there: a Sav-Ur-Life twenty-foot ladder.

And then I knew I had to save my life.

Nine

A plan. I needed a getaway plan.

I shook my head: Pathetic. A joke. Someone like me actually running.

Money. I couldn't get too far without cash; I'd need a place to stay, traveling money, food. The zipper compartments of all my handbags yielded about thirty dollars and change. I added that to the eighty in my wallet. My cash card too, although not my bankbook, because unless the police were total toadloads, there would be a computer warning flag on all my accounts by the time the banks opened in the morning. Ditto with credit cards.

But for my last birthday, Richie had given me a ring; the sapphire was the size of a small plum. In hard-boiled mysteries, ingenues are always offering to hock something to pay the private eye—who always says, Nah, kid, forget it. Life is like that for eighteen-year-old blondes. But if they could consider pawning the family jewels, why couldn't I?

Then I asked myself: What do you think you could accomplish by running away?

I answered: Maybe nothing. Maybe this is some sort of pitiful diversion, an escape fantasy for someone who cannot escape.

A change of underwear. My Filofax. A little makeup. Xanax: I clutched the bottle and pressed it against my chest—salve for the heartsick. But I could have peace of mind only at my own peril. Also, if I had any hope of saving my life, I had to be tough; I could not allow myself to give in to despair should things get ugly.

My grace under pressure lasted about three seconds, but in that time I poured the evening's second dose of pills down the toilet.

As I raced around my bedroom, looking for my travel toothbrush, I told myself: This is some Stoopnagle plan. Forget it. Get some sleep, although that would be a neat trick, what with my anxiety running amok and every sedative in the house dissolving in the septic tank. I demanded: No more evasions. Be specific; what do you think you can gain by running away?

I answered myself: Richie's murder was not a random act of violence. I truly believe that. To absolve myself, I have to find out who done it. But this is not a John Dickson Carr mystery, with a clever deduction revealed in the penultimate chapter. Since catching the killer is not a realistic goal, at least let me learn what was going on in my husband's life for the past few years. More than anything, I need an alternative to offer Gevinski. And the only way I can do that is to get to know what Richie was doing, seeing, thinking. Since he had moved to the city long before he actually moved to the city, I have to follow him there.

The wind howled like sound effects in a cheap horror movie—*wooo-wooo*—and rattled the windows. A cold night, a harbinger of winter. I wondered: How does a fugitive from justice dress? I had a fast vision of jeans and a black turtleneck. But in Richie's world, I decided, fugitives would dress like everyone else—expensively. So I went into my closet and picked out a pair of charcoal tweed slacks by some French designer. They were cut so tight in the crotch that if I sneezed, I'd probably get aroused. Still, they were, for me, shockingly fashionable. Then a ninety-seven-ply cashmere cowl-neck and cardigan in pale gray I'd bought when shopping with my sister-in-law, Carol of the Frosted Hair—who observed, as I pulled it over my head: "It doesn't scream 'Quality,' Rosie. It whispers it." A pair of low leather boots. I scooped everything into an immoral but beautiful ostrichskin shoulder bag, a soft, generous thing I bought one month after we'd become rich, which was about two years before I started getting animal rights papers about screaming minks from the kids in my expository writing classes.

I turned off the hall light. Treading as softly as I could, I slipped past the open door of Ben's room. Mets banners and shelves of athletic trophies vied for wall space with Islanders and Giants posters. In high school, he'd added a *Young Einstein* poster. No rock stars, no political slogans. His old lacrosse stick was still propped up in a corner.

I moved down the hall and stood before the doorway of Alex's room. All along I'd known I was scared, of course. But I realized that I was in a state of absolute terror only when I heard my own panting.

Alex's room was still empty. With any luck, he would wake up in the library about noon, unless someone shook him hard, demanding: Tell us where your mother is! I slipped inside, locked his door behind me, and sat on the hard mattress of his narrow, teenage bed.

I said to myself: This is too dangerous. What if Alex wakens and comes upstairs? Are you going to force him to choose between you and the law? I felt the chances of that actually coming to pass were close to zero, but to err on the side of caution, I counted one-banana, two-banana until I reached three hundred, which—believe me—is the second most boring occupation in the world, the first being engaging in a conversation about cheese allergies with Suspicious Foods.

All was quiet. No Alex. I pulled back the shade so I could peek out. No cops that I could see, although I knew there were at least two around the house and two more in a car at the end of the driveway. I hauled the ladder out from under the bed. Oh, God! The chains that held the rungs rattled like Marley's ghost. I waited. No shouts, no police whistles. So, centimeter by centimeter, I eased open the window.

I warned myself: Don't do this! You'll just make it worse. They'll say you took off because you did it. An innocent person wouldn't run. And they'll catch you. You know they'll catch you.

I replied: So they'll catch me. What can they do? Add a couple of years to my sentence? When I'm sixty-five or seventy-five, what's another year or two? I'll have green teeth, gray pubic hair, and no hope. Go for it.

I told myself: This is reckless behavior. You are a responsible citizen.

I answered: They're going to drag me off to jail. I'm getting out of here!

I shook my head: No, wait. The night was too young. All those jaunty, thirty-year-old, blue-eyed cops on surveillance were probably still bouncing on the balls of their feet outside, nauseatingly alert. They needed an hour or two to get sleepy. I lay down. Alex's pillow smelled from his hair gel, watermelony. I was so tired, and I knew that fatigue could do me in. Too weary to cope, I would give myself permission to take a nap—and wind up waking at dawn. So I forced my eyes wide open and stayed awake by reciting, twice, all the poems I'd ever memorized. A dozen Shakespearean sonnets to begin. Then I skipped through a little Donne, a little Adrienne Rich, then some of the Romantic odes. Then on to Yeats. Eliot: "The Love Song of J. Alfred Prufrock." I eventually wound up with "Invictus" and "Casey at the Bat."

But I avoided "Dover Beach." Late one night, a few months after we moved to Gulls' Haven, Richie and I made sure the boys were asleep. Then we sneaked out of the house and made love down on our beach. Great sex deserves to be commemorated: I recited "Dover Beach." Sure, it's hokey, but it works, and by the time I got to "Ah, love, let us be true / To one another!" I was crying. Richie held me in his sandy arms and stroked my hair.

At eleven o'clock, I hooked the metal anchors over the windowsill and let down the ladder as carefully as I could. Still, the sound of metal against brick was louder than I could ever have imagined. Each clang brought new heart palpitations, and it didn't help that a dog howled in the distance. Finally, though, there was silence.

I sat on the sill. Slowly, I drew my legs outside until they were dangling against the brick. I could feel its coldness against my calves through my wool slacks. I was gripping the sides of the window frame so tight I'm sure I left my prints embedded in the wood. Don't look down, I commanded myself. Naturally, I looked down. The lawn was a gaping black hole, the entrance to hell. I squeezed my eyes shut and held on for dear life. The chains jangled in the wind. I forced myself to study the ladder. I wondered: Even if I really wanted to escape, how could I get on this thing?

Somehow I pivoted and got one foot on a rung, then the other. Oh, God, this thing was not steady! The ladder swung side to side through some malevolent will of its own. It scraped my knuckles against the brick. Even in the dark I could tell they were bleeding. No one ever died from bleeding knuckles. Move. Down another rung. Tendrils of ivy reached out for my wrists. Another rung. I couldn't. My arms were trembling. If I fell . . . I pictured my shattered body, my broken limbs, my skull cracked and oozing like a three-minute egg.

No, I could not do it. So I started to climb back up into the house. But as I pulled myself up one rung, the hooks that held the ladder gave a jolt of protest, as if ready to come loose. I hung on, breathless. My fingers were growing numb. If I couldn't go up, where could I go? Once again, I started down. I didn't dare look, because I was afraid I'd see four cops with guns drawn.

But then I peeked. I couldn't believe it! Almost there. Six, seven more feet: that was all. The black lawn turned into soft grass.

At that last moment, I did not think of the sons I was leaving behind. I didn't think of my mother. I thought of my students. I offered them a fast, silent apology and hoped someone would find the twenty-two "The Gamut of Love in *Pride and Prejudice*" papers under a "Knowledge Is Power" Data Associates paperweight on my desk and bring them up to school so Adam Gottfried would know he got an A– and not aggravate his colitis. And then my right foot hit the ground.

What was either the Hound of the Baskervilles or a gigantic Nassau County Police Department German shepherd come streaking across the lawn in my direction. It was barking loud enough to wake the dead—except for Richie.

Anyway, this dog, which looked as if it would be happiest curled up at Himmler's feet, was heading straight toward me! Could I outrun it? Just at the point where it was so close I could hear its footsteps, or pawsteps, I slowed down. The dog came up beside me! "Good boy," I gurgled hysterically. I glanced down. "Girl." For a growl that came from so deep inside the dog's thick chest, it was very, very loud.

When I was training one of our dogs, either Irving, the beagle who'd died in August, or Blossom, a cognitively impaired puli, I read that if a dog threatens you, stand still. Don't run. If the dog makes a move, however, like going for your esophagus, try yelling—ideally, before it rips out your esophagus.

"Jaws?" a man's voice called. It seemed to come from the steps near the beach, but the wind was still *wooo*ing, so I couldn't tell the exact direction of the sound. "Jaws!" The wind drowned out his whistle, but not before Jaws heard it and barked a response.

"Good Jaws," I whispered. The dog cocked her head and stared at me. "What a wonderful dog you are. *Such* a good dog," I babbled, as softly as I could. "Niiice. Gooood." I prayed she wouldn't sniff out the blood on my knuckles and decide it was snack time.

Despite Jaws' size, her legs had that slightly outward slope of a dog just emerging from puppyhood. Only her youth—she must have been a raw recruit to the K-9 Corps—could explain her forgetting to bark or bite. "Come on!" I urged, with the lunatic enthusiasm I'd always employed when coaxing pets or children to do something they did not want to do. "Let's go for a walk!" I took the first two steps of a brisk stroll. Either Jaws would sink her teeth into my thigh or . . . She stayed by my side! Not with what I'd call rapture, but as the wind blew away another cry of "Jaws!" my flesh was still intact.

I plunged into the woods that lay between my house and the Tillotsons'. It was rough going. Worse. I tripped over rocks and vines, turned my ankle as I slipped into a hole. Jaws stayed by my side. It was so dark I walked smack into a waist-high barricade of a dead tree and its branches. I took small side steps, feeling my way with my sore fingers, until I finally made my way around it.

The dog had stopped following me! She growled with each step I took, but she wouldn't come any farther than the roots of the dead tree. "Come on, Jaws!" I entreated. "You can do it!" I have to admit I am a born teacher, a great motivator. The dog, I finally realized, was dying to come. I could barely see, but she seemed to have caught her rear leg or legs trying to jump over the dense roots. She raised her neck and let out a howl of outrage. I started to feel so bad for her I was about to go back, but then I told myself: Jerk, this isn't a Rin Tin Tin movie. Then I was off through the woods, dogless through the dark night, on my own.

As I made my way, I worried about rabid rats. I worried about trigger-happy cops. I worried about poison-ivy juice that would slowly permeate my slacks. A coarse, hairy nettle rubbed against my neck, leaving a raised welt. Another anchored itself to the rough tweed of the cuff of my slacks and jerked me back. I fought it, kicking four, five, six times, a demented Rockette. At last I got free.

Back where I'd left her, Jaws was now barking in fury. From somewhere, probably on the lawn between the beach and the woods, I heard voices. Were they simply looking for Jaws, or did they know by now I was gone? I had taken off without looking back. I had no idea if the Sav-Ur-Life ladder was hidden by the dark night—or glinting in starlight against brick and ivy. Too late to think about it. I lumbered through thickets, through slimy patches of rotting leaves. I had to keep going.

But I simply had no strength left. I couldn't go on. I leaned against a young, not-too-steady tree. I was so sweaty that my sweater clung to my back and midriff. I shivered. My fingers weren't throbbing anymore; they were numb. But even as I exhaled a sigh of defeat, my mind cleared. Two significant events had taken place, I realized. One, Jaws had shut up. She'd probably gotten free and was, at this moment, salivating all over her master's trousers. No more growls and barks, and, best of all, no more voices. And two, I had come so far! Just beyond the tree in front of me was the spot where Richie had parked his car. I was about twenty feet from the road.

My long-range planning had included getting to Manhattan and, equipped with a rock to hock, to stay there awhile and do some investigating. But I saw that while I'd thought I was so damn smart, I had only made a handbag plan.

I had no real escape plan. How was I going to get away? At just that moment, the beams of two headlights lit up the road that led from my house to Stephanie's. I dropped to the ground. Don't get crazy, I calmed myself. It could just be one of the neighbors coming home from dinner and the theater. But it had been—what?—fifteen minutes since Jaws and I first met, when she'd broken away from her handler and come running toward me. Time enough for the police to figure something was up. And, I had to concede, the headlights appeared to be moving at

a speed at which cops probably move when searching for an escaped felon. They could be all over the
Estates by now. All over Shorehaven. Where should I
go? What should I do? The headlights came closer.

I could not go forward; that much was obvious. So
I fought my way back through the woods. I was less
afraid this time. Well, except when I saw the glowing devil eyes of some animal—a raccoon, or maybe
a feral cat.

At last, I was back at Gulls' Haven. I edged closer.
I could see the ladder. Yes, there it was, hanging
from Alex's window, bright silver.

Keeping hidden behind the first line of trees, I cir-
cled the house and the lawns until I got to the front.
All was quiet, eerily so. No cops, no cop cars. No
Jaws either. Where were they? Waiting to gun me
down when I walked out of the woods onto the
gravel drive? No, I realized. They're not here. They're
where I wanted them, out looking for me!

How did I know? Well, to be honest, I was no
expert. Except for what I read in Ed McBain novels
and true-crime books, I was not what you'd call con-
versant with the subtleties of real-life police procedure. Still, I had read enough to know that even if
they realized I'd taken a powder, they wouldn't all
go looking for me and leave the house unguarded.
There had to be at least one cop close by. Standing
around back, within running distance of the ladder?
Circling the house? Inside?

No, probably not inside. The house was as dark as
I'd left it—unless they were all using those infrared
goggles like in *The Silence of the Lambs,* which, I
decided, was overly cinematic, extremely expensive,
and highly unlikely. But soon someone with a badge

would make his way to the front of the house again and I'd be stuck in the woods—that is, until they started searching the woods.

I studied Gulls' Haven as I never had in all the years I'd lived there. What could it do for me? A beautiful, graceful brick box with a gently sloping slate roof. No help there. A covered breezeway, built in the same weathered brick as the house itself, with three small arches mimicking the grander front entrance. No place to hide. But the breezeway led from the left side of the house, where the kitchen was, to a side door to the three-car garage. A garage! Could I do it? *Drive* away? A second later, I was racing across the open stretch of lawn.

I admit I did not have it planned, but when I got in and saw Ben's Jeep with its Pennsylvania license plates, I knew it was the only real chance I had. A four-wheel drive through the woods, along the beach. What a getaway! Except, naturally, I had no key. I sincerely regretted all the time I'd spent on trigonometry, which had nothing to do with life, when I could have been hanging out with greasy-haired Brooklyn bad boys, learning how to hot-wire a car. These were my choices: crawl, Vietcong style, through the cutting gardens of Shorehaven Estates, then around the swing sets and barbecues of Shorehaven Acres, and down Main Street, past Dunkin' Donuts, to the Long Island Rail Road station—or take my red Saab the police knew so well from having followed it.

Ready, set, go. I hit the garage door opener just as I started the Saab's ignition. The big door rolled up in arthritic slow motion. Loud, too. I backed out the car, closed the garage door, opened my window, and listened. Nothing. I put the car into gear and, to a cacophonous grinding of gravel, started down the drive.

I'd seen enough detective movies to know not to put on my headlights. What the movies don't show is that, lightless, the way you know you're heading toward something is when you hear the sickening crunch of your fender as it implodes to accommodate a ginkgo tree. The noise! Better than a siren for summoning the police.

Sure enough. A voice sounded from far away. I couldn't make it out, although it sounded like "Potato!" which I sensed was highly dubious. I shifted into reverse. The car was willing to disengage from the tree, so I was out of there, putting on the low beams until I could navigate to the end of the drive. "Potato!" The voice was fainter. Then I turned off my lights again and drove into the darkness.

On Anchorage Lane, no cops. And as I crept out of Shorehaven Estates on the most rambling route I could devise—down Sandy Nook Drive, up Zephyr Court, around the old Whitney estate, along the rutted service road behind the Wagners', the Changs', and the Schaeffers' properties and across the Gillespies' cut-for-croquet lawn and around their poolhouse into a small copse of trees, at last emerging in the parking lot of Christ Our Savior Lutheran Church—I kept seeing headlights on parallel streets. But no cops.

At ten minutes before midnight, I pulled into the drive-in window of the Marine Midland Bank and punched in $300 on the cash machine. A police car with a giant shield on its door sped by. It did not stop for a closer look. The screen of the cash machine flashed: "Your transaction is being processed ROSE MEYERS." Clearly, it didn't yet know that Rose Meyers was on the lam, about to be number one on Nassau County's Most Wanted list, because after a moment of mechanical indigestion, it spit out the fifteen twenty-dollar bills.

I would love to write about a car chase, except there was none. After the bank, I turned on my headlights and drove through back streets until I was out of Shorehaven. I headed east, though, away from Manhattan, through the business district of Glen Cove, along the water and into the two-block-long business district of downtown Port Adams. It was five after midnight. The next day! So I stopped at another drive-in bank and withdrew three hundred dollars more. And then I parked beside the town dock. With any luck, the police would think I'd jumped, and they'd spend the next day or two dredging the inlet.

I found an unlocked pickup truck in a boatyard about two minutes away. I climbed into the driver's seat and contemplated my future.

First of all, I had to quit thinking of myself as an English teacher. What was I, then? Since murder suspect is generally a pejorative, not a job description, I had to see myself in a new role: detective. The only problem, I thought, as I ducked down below the dashboard while something—police car? fire truck? ambulance?—screamed in the distance, was that as a detective, I was stuck with myself for a client.

I sat back up. The owner had ground out his butts on the truck's floor and attempted to hide the cigarette odor by hanging a particularly revolting deodorant in the shape of a pine tree on his rearview mirror. He was not merely a slob; he was a moronic chauvinist, with a 3-D decal of a naked woman on the upper right of his windshield. When I turned my head, or moved in any way, the decal's mammoth pink iridescent breasts appeared to sway back and forth.

Second, then, I needed a list of suspects. I tried to generate a Hercule Poirot–style roster, full of blatantly homicidal types as well as genuine long shots, but all I could come up with were two names: Mitchell Gruen, who truly had a reason to hate Richie, and Jessica Stevenson, who, as far as I knew, had no reason, but I put her on my list because I wanted her to be guilty.

As far as questioning Jessica went, I had a little problem; my last appearance at Gracie Square had not exactly won me a standing ovation. It could be dangerous to try an encore. Besides, her doting daddy would very likely hire bodyguards once he'd heard I was loose. I would probably meet Gevinski and his pal in the maroon suit the minute I put one foot on her block.

And what about Mitch? How could I get to see a man so reclusive he ordered his dinners by fax so he wouldn't have to talk?

Then whom could I speak to? Who would know what Richie had been up to? Hojo Driscoll, of course. Tom? No. To him, Richie was probably just another business acquaintance. Carter Tillotson? Perhaps. He and Richie did have their semiannual lunches. But I doubted that he'd be any more willing to talk to me in Manhattan than he had been in Shorehaven. Richie's sister, Carol, Our Lady of the Bikini Wax? She might know something, but not much, and I had to choose my subjects wisely. Each person I spoke with meant potential peril. Even if no one tried to stop me, my freedom would be more and more in danger. The questions I asked and the answers I received would tell the cops where I was going to pop up the next time.

Time to move. I hadn't driven to Port Adams because it was a quaint town with a cute fish restaurant. I was there because it was on another line of the Long Island Rail Road from Shorehaven. The Shorehaven line would be crawling with cops. But the Port Adams train began twenty miles east, in Suffolk County, and traveled along older tracks through central Nassau and Queens. It was my only chance.

However, as I gripped the Big Mac–splattered handle of the truck door, I realized that whatever advantage I might gain by taking a different train I would lose by walking down a suburban street at 1:30 at night, waiting in a railway station, then boarding the 1:43 in my fancy French slacks and being the only passenger on the entire trip to Penn Station.

I spent the next half hour brushing off my sweater, picking thorns and twigs out of my slacks. I gave up and slept a little, but woke with a terrible start to the sound of sirens. This time they were only in my dreams.

I bought the *Times* and *Newsday* at the station and boarded the 6:32 along with a thick pack of commuters. Like them, I kept my head buried in the paper. Except I couldn't read.

Ever since Richie left me, I'd been trying to figure out how much I'd loved him and how much he'd loved me—if he ever had. How could he betray me?

And even if he had an affair, why couldn't he have done it on the sly? Then, like so many men, he could have come home. We could have grown old together. How could I have known him so little after all those years that I was so stunned when he told me about Jessica? Had I ever really known him? Or had our marriage been hot sex, tolerable companionship, and two mutual interests: Ben and Alex.

I thought of Jessica in her froth of gray silk at the funeral. Stunning. Sad. She'd gotten everyone to think of her as Richie's widow simply by sitting there all alone.

Alone? Wait a second. Where was her father? How come, just two days earlier, he was staying with her, hanging around in Richie's bathrobe, for God's sake. He had clearly been at her place the whole night. And the way he had held her in his arms: He was her protector. So how come, at the most traumatic moment in his daughter's life, instead of being by her side at her husband-to-be's funeral, he took a powder? For such a caring guy, not very paternal.

Unless he wasn't Daddy Stevenson at all. And if he wasn't, who the hell was he?

Ten

MURDER SUSPECT SLIDES DOWN SOCIAL LADDER. The Sav-Ur-Life ladder contrasted nicely with the ivy-covered brick wall of Gulls' Haven; it looked pretty impressive on the front page of the *Daily News*. My photograph, inset beside it, was a little blurry. Also, my hair was hideously short, the style I'd tried the previous spring, when I made the mistake of wanting to look natural. The haircut probably hadn't made Richie decide to leave me, but it no doubt strengthened his resolve.

For anyone on the lookout for an alleged perpetrator, however, the photo—chin up, eyes squeezed shut, with such a phony laugh that my uvula was practically on display—was clearly, recognizably me. And by the mere fact of being on the front page of a tabloid, I looked psychopathic. Someone at the *Daily News,* working fast, had found the damned thing in the yearbook. I was faculty adviser for *Kaleidoscope,* the high school's alleged literary magazine. I'd been standing next to Sunshine Stankowicz, the editor in chief, an annoying high school intellectual who spent most of her time sitting on her *tuchis*-length hair in the cafeteria, ostentatiously reading Virginia Woolf's diaries. The photographer had barked "Smile!" I'd overcompensated in a big way.

The ventilation in Penn Station was so deficient that there was no escaping the battle between human and hot dog smells, but what got me wasn't the odors; it was the thousands of commuters who seemed to be snapping up the *News* with unseemly glee. "Dead Millionaire's Ex Flees While Cops Patrol Mansion," the subheadline shouted. My fellow citizens were enthralled.

In that instant, seeing my thirty-two-tooth guffaw on page one, I knew the plan I'd hatched on the train was blown. It had been such a smart plan too: take a hotel room, where I could nap, eat a huge breakfast, and then, refreshed, outline a proper investigation. But having read every Rex Stout novel, I was an N.Y.P.D. expert; the New York cops would be cooperating with the Nassau County P.D.: my picture could be on its way to all the hotels, airports, and, yes, maybe even train stations in the New York area that very minute. So, keeping pace with the fastest commuter, a tall man clenching the *Wall Street Journal*, who looked as if he were going to cry, I raced up still another flight of stairs, to the sidewalks of New York.

The griddle in the coffee shop where I had breakfast looked as if it hadn't been scoured since early in the Carter administration, so I made do with a bagel. After all the years of being rich, of going with Richie to Four Seasonses and Ritz-Carltons, where breakfast was, inevitably, a minimalist arrangement of whole-grain food garnished with jewel-like berries, it was good to have a waitress in a hair net slap a prefab wedge of high-fat cream cheese on my plate.

I went over my mental list of people I had to interview: Jessica was too dangerous right now. Ditto Carol of the vegetable-dyed lashes. I'd have to speak to Hojo, to Mitchell Gruen. Maybe one or two of the Data Associates executives—the ones whose dreams of corporate glory had been cut short by Jessica's ascendancy.

I brushed my teeth in the coffee shop bathroom and tried, unsuccessfully, not to gag at the black hair and brown mineral stain in the sink, to say nothing of the roach traps in three of the room's corners. As I reapplied my blush, it hit me that the person to speak to first was the only one who might not give me away to the cops: Mitchell Gruen.

So fifteen minutes and a taxi ride later, I was downtown, in a gritty area just past the perimeter of SoHo, which had managed to remain ungentrified. No avant-garde shops for all-beige clothes, no restaurants with new thoughts about legumes. Mainly plain old ugly brick buildings: warehouses, small factories. One exception, perhaps a onetime private school or library, had a bas-relief of the Muses—or at least nine women in one-shoulder gowns—over the double entrance doors.

Mitch's building, like his other investments, was a loser; three of the four floors had boarded windows. On the second floor, the blinds were drawn. Red blinds. I stepped up to the door and buzzed all four buzzers. No answer. I tried again. Silence. Mitch had to be up there. Unless his body was putrefying on a pile of microchips, he was simply ignoring the buzzer. I held it down. Finally, a tinny, ticked-off voice demanded over the intercom: "Wha' you want?"

"Package from"—I thought fast—"Digit-Tech." I prayed that sounded computerish enough.

"Wha'?"

"Package. Looks like something for a computer."

"Leave it."

"Can't. You have to sign for it." A nasal buzzer honked for a second or two, but that was all I needed. I was in, and I ran up the stairs to the second floor.

Mitch's head, with its halo of gray frizz, stuck out through the narrow opening of the chained door. "Rosie?" he asked, incredulous. A second later, he added: "Boy, are you in trouble!"

"Hi, Mitch," I said brightly. My luck held. He took off the chain and opened the door another fraction of an inch, presumably to see if I was hiding an Uzi behind my back. I put my shoulder against the door and pushed, hard. I was getting good at this: The force caused him to stumble backward.

"What do you want with me?" he asked, not all that impolitely, considering I'd just shoved my way into his house. Except for getting a lot balder and a little grayer, Mitch hadn't changed much since he'd left Data Associates.

It was remarkable how undistinguished his features were: a nose neither thick nor thin, upturned nor hooked; small (but not remarkably small) eyes that might have been gray but could have been brown; a forehead not too high, not too low; a mouth so forgettable that you knew he had a mouth only because you would have noticed if he hadn't.

"A carving knife!" Mitch exclaimed, as he bounded back to close and bolt the door. Now, at age fifty-eight, free from the adult demands of teaching and corporate life, he wore play clothes: gray sweatpants and a too-tight undershirt. An inch of hairy belly peeked out around his waist.

"It's been a long time. How are you, Mitch?"

"Not dead, like some people I could mention."

Mitch's loft, the entire second floor, was one immense room. Walls, carpet, couch, and chairs were a vivid red. He'd bought the building and fixed up one floor as a present to himself after he'd made his first million with Data Associates. The place was a preadolescent boy's concept of a bachelor pad; the only relief from the flagrant redness was provided by a smoked-glass cocktail table on frail-looking wrought-iron legs and, of course, Mitch's stock of pale computers. "Would you mind getting out of here, Rosie? Don't make me be rude. I just have a lot of stuff to do."

"Soon." I strolled through the loft and took a seat in front of one of his five computers, a monster of an

IBM. Mitch followed and stood right beside me. "Don't you want to know how I am?" I asked.

"You think I want to get mixed up in this murder stuff?" He turned and gazed longingly at a smaller computer that had three saw-toothed lines on its screen; he was clearly aching to get back to it. "I've got things to do, and whoever did it to Richie, let me be the first to say"—he blew a loud, wet kiss into the air—"Thank you very much!"

His bare feet did a fidgety mambo as he waited for me to go.

"I'm in trouble, Mitch."

"No kidding."

"Were the police here?" He shrugged. "What did they ask?"

"You know."

"Tell me."

"Where I was when he was killed."

"Where were you?"

He emitted a fast, humorless laugh. "Here."

"Alone?"

"Alone." He busied himself retying the drawstring of his sweatpants. His head was down, so I couldn't see his face.

"Do you know who killed Richie?"

"Of course not." He lifted his right hand in a swear-to-God gesture.

"Do you have any idea who might have had a grudge against him?"

"You!"

"You too," I replied.

He sat on a desk chair with little wheels and rolled toward me until our knees touched. But I knew this from the old days: while Mitch had mastered rudimentary social skills—he knew not to pick at any of his orifices in public—he had never been able to judge social distance. He always came much too close, making whomever he was with uncomfortably aware that this middle-aged child prodigy was at least mildly disturbed.

"I need your help, Mitch."

"*Please*. Get out, Rosie. I'm busy."

"Should I remind you about the times I helped you when Richie started trying to force you out?" I asked.

"Some help *you* turned out to be." He chuckled. Planting both feet on the floor, he crossed his arms over his chest and swiveled his body back and forth. With each swing, the chair made a flatulent sound, which delighted him. I reminded myself that this jovial flake had—with a great deal of malice afore-thought—wiped out Data Associates' entire computer library in an attempt to destroy Richie's company.

"Maybe I wasn't able to help you in the long run, but I tried damned hard," I reminded him.

"Yeah, sure. So how come he got rid of me?"

"He got rid of me too."

"And now someone's gotten rid of him. But not me. It's 'Rose Meyers! Wanted dead or alive.' You're all over the TV, you know. If I call the police, I bet they'd be here in two seconds."

"But then you'd have to talk on the phone. You never liked that much—and I hear you've gotten worse."

"Yeah?"

"Yeah."

"Who do you hear all these things from?"

"Richie had sources." The source was Jane Berger,

Richie's public relations person. Jane had always been too important and too busy to remember my name; she called everyone who wasn't rich, important, or powerful "Snooky." For some obscure reason, though, she found time to maintain a modem relationship with Mitch. "I know you've been ordering your dinner by fax, not going out for months at a time," I told him. "Do you really want a dialogue with the police? You'd have to go down to headquarters to be interviewed. You'd have to testify in court."

Mitch furrowed his brow. His eyes darted from computer to computer. He looked angry and a little nuts, like Nixon in his final days. "Outta here, Rosie."

"Mitch, I didn't kill Richie. I ran from the police because I needed a chance to prove it."

"How are you going to prove a negative?"

"I have some good leads to the killer," I lied.

"Ho-ho-ho. Tell me another."

"Listen to me. Once I prove I'm not the murderer, that it had to have been someone else"—I paused for effect—"do you know who they'll turn to?"

"Bull!"

"They'll turn to the other person who had a grudge against Richie. Once I'm out of the picture"—I tried to sound as if this was an immediate prospect—"you'll be the center of a lot of attention."

"You're not getting out of the picture so fast, Rosie, and you know it and I know it."

I got up but didn't back away from him. "All I need is a few minutes of you on your computer. Come on. For old times' sake."

"No."

"If you help me, it will take—tops—a half hour."

"No way."

"Fine. I'll stay here."

That did it. He plopped down in front of a laptop, opened its lid, and demanded: "What do you want to know?"

"All the Data Associates executives keep their calendars and interoffice memos on a computer."

"So?"

"So I'd like you to bring up Richie's appointment calendar for the last three or four weeks. Can you do it?"

"His calendar at Data Associates? They put in a whole new security system after I messed it up." His pallid skin lit up with pleasure at the recollection.

"You didn't answer my question. Can you do it?" Instead of answering, he sat down and pounded the keys, a two-fingered Rachmaninoff. After a minute, the screen filled with numbers, then blackened, then filled up again. "What's happening?" I asked.

"Shush. I'm working," Mitch said. "I can't have anybody rushing me."

"But I'm in a rush."

"So go." Instead, I wandered around the loft for a few minutes, then finally fell asleep in a red chair shaped like a cupped hand. I woke about an hour later, when the click of computer keys stopped. Mitch was standing beside a printer that was spewing out pages. "Calendar *and* phone log," he announced, tearing off the pages and pushing them into my hand. "It wasn't easy, but I did it. Now would you get out?"

"I have to study this."

"Study it somewhere else."

I ignored his invitation and moved twenty feet or

so, from the red-hand chair to the red sectional couch. Easing off my boots, I began to read. For a minute, Mitch glanced from me to the door, but then he gave up and sat down at the computer with the saw-toothed lines and soon was lost in the world on the screen.

On the day he was murdered, Richie had a 10:00 A.M. meeting with Chemical Bank, a noon fitting at T's, whatever "T" stood for—maybe tailor—a 12:45 lunch with someone named Joe Romano from InterAmerican Tool. His afternoon was free. I checked the calendar against the phone log. Richie hadn't made any outgoing calls after 11:49 A.M.

However, there was a long list of incoming calls that afternoon, calls he would never return. One, at 3:15, came from Hojo Driscoll. One from Carter Tillotson, at 5:23, had the notation "PCB" beside it: Please Call Back. There was an unfamiliar number beside it. I went to Mitch's phone—red—and dialed. "Good morning. Dr. Tillotson's office," a voice that had taken elocution lessons said. Well, Carter and Richie had at least been pals, if not genuine friends. Why shouldn't they call each other? Still, under the least-likely-character-is-the-murderer theory, I considered Carter for a minute or two, but then dropped him because he was too least-likely to make any sense.

No calls from Tom Driscoll that afternoon, I noticed. Two with "PCB" from Jane Berger. Several from within Data Associates, although none from Jessica. I assumed Richie and she had spent the afternoon together after lunch, probably having sex in a position he had never wanted to try with me.

There was not much to go on: I read an entire

month's worth of Richie's life. From what I could tell, the calendar and phone log seemed appropriate for a busy-but-not-overburdened company president. Lots of internal calls between him and Jessica. One call a day—usually after lunch—from his great friend Hojo. Those calls lasted between ten and twenty minutes. He had lunch with Hojo the last week of September. Not a single call from Tom, and no others from Carter. But over the last month, there were two, three, or four calls a day from Jane Berger, the PR lady, all with PCBs.

"Mitch," I called out, "bring up the phone log again on your computer."

"Shhh! Leave me alone."

I walked over and stood beside him. "Access it and I'll leave within the next ten minutes." He left his jagged lines and moved back to the other computer. Seconds later, the phone log appeared. "Tell me the last time Richie made an outgoing call to Jane Berger."

He typed for about four seconds. "September fourth."

"Wow!" I breathed. "Don't you see what that means? I remember the date because that was when school started, the day after Labor Day. Six *weeks* before he was killed. She was his PR person. Richie was a major publicity hound."

"Big deal," he mumbled.

"How often did Richie speak with Jane Berger when you were there?"

He swiveled around to face me. "Beats me."

"Was she at the office a lot?"

He reached down to his foot and twirled the hard nub at the end of a shoelace between his thumb and index finger. "A lot? A couple of times a week, I guess."

"She called him at home almost every night. They were obviously discussing the business they'd talked about earlier in the day."

"So?"

"So they spoke a *lot.* How come all of a sudden she's pursuing Richie? And why wasn't he taking her calls?"

"You said you'd go."

"I'll go." I paused. "When I get a commitment from you."

"That's not fair!"

"I know. I stopped being fair last night. I need your word you won't call the police."

"Rosie . . . "

"Your word."

"Okay."

But then I had an idea. "One more thing. A big favor. Call Jane Berger's secretary for me."

"Are you demented or something? *Me?*"

As Mitch was shaking his head and saying "No way!" and "I don't talk on phones!" I looked up Jane's address. I wrote on a piece of computer paper: "This is the super from Ms. Berger's building. There's a terrible problem with a burst pipe. I'm in the apartment under hers. Tell her to wait in front for the plumber. He's got a green truck. She should bring him up to her place." After another five minutes of head shaking and foot stamping, Mitch read my script to the secretary. His delivery was wooden, but he got his point across. As I'd coached him, he hung up fast, before Jane could get on the line.

Before I left I asked: "Do you think I killed Richie?"

"Yeah." He offered an embarrassed, almost boyish smile. "Nothing personal, Rosie."

I arrived at Central Park West approximately ninety seconds before Jane Berger leapt out of a cab and headed for the long canopy of her apartment building. She was a Weight Watchers success story, a tall, now strikingly slender woman in an outfit with an ankle-length orange skirt that only the color-blind or the fashionably flamboyant would consider. Like some grand Spanish dancer, she flung one end of a purple shawl over her shoulder. Pausing for a second, she searched for a green truck.

Since I was not a green truck, she did not notice me, even as I hurried up beside her. "Hi, Jane."

"Hi, Snooky." It was only when I didn't move on that she glanced at me. Her eyes widened until her purple-shadowed lids disappeared. And then her mouth widened. She actually got off the beginning of a scream, until I said: "I've got a gun." My hand was in the pocket of my cardigan. She stared at the bulge made by my Elizabeth Arden Bronze Lamé lipstick, then at my face. "I really don't want to hurt you, so don't test me, Jane." In tight formation, we marched past her doorman, a tiny, elderly, Irish-looking man who was probably sick and tired of comparisons to a leprechaun. He nodded automatically but in a sweet, leprechaunesque manner.

Jane Berger herself was now bordering on willowy, but everything in her apartment was still oversized. She sat in something that looked like the offspring of a chair and a rhinoceros. I stood before her on a carpet so thick it made my ankles quiver.

"You should know," she proclaimed, "that I have *very* high blood pressure."

"As soon as I get the information I need, I'll leave," I assured her.

"One-fifty-five over one-ten. It used to be worse."

"Tell me about Mitchell Gruen."

"What's there to tell?"

"You kept in touch with him?"

"We talked on our computers every couple of months." She started gnawing off her nail polish, starting at the cuticle and working down to the tip.

"Were you friends with him?"

She gave the busy business woman's version of an amused laugh, a rapid "Huh" sound. But she got serious fast when she glanced at my lipstick bulge. "If I drop dead from a stroke," she said, "you know whose fault it'll be."

"You won't have a stroke. Tell me why you kept in touch with Mitch."

"An accommodation—to Rick." I waited, so she went on. "He wanted someone to monitor Mitch's hostility level."

"Well, how hostile was he?"

"What do you mean—'how hostile'? How hostile would *you* be if your partner ruined your life? Very hostile."

"Did it change at all in intensity? I mean, did Mitch seem to get angrier over time. Or was it the opposite: did he act as if everything was peachy keen?"

"No, he just plain and simple hated Rick. But if you're thinking . . . " She smiled for about a millisecond. I wished she'd be a little more terrified. "I'm *trying* to be open and honest with you. You're obviously trying to pin this on someone else, but you're talking about an agoraphobe here. Do you think anyone will believe Mitchell Gruen would leave his place and travel to Long Island to kill your ex-husband?"

Could Mitch have done it? I wondered: Could his rage have overcome his fear? Or could his phobia be part of an exquisitely constructed alibi by a master programmer and planner?

"What happened between you and Richie?" I asked.

"Nothing." She looked at my pocket. Her eyes narrowed. "Let me see your gun."

"Cut it out!" I used my tough voice, the one I used to convey the possibility of a trip to the assistant principal's office. Jane blanched. "Technically, it's not a gun, by the way," I told her. "It's a revolver. Now tell me about you and Richie."

"He let me go."

"Fired you?"

"Yes."

"When?"

"Right after Labor Day. Why do you care about this?"

"Because I'm trying to reconstruct Richie's life." I must have had a hysterical note in my voice. Jane averted her head so she would not have to gaze into the eyes of a maniac. Except one of her dangling amethyst earrings caught on the weave of her mohair shawl, so she was forced to confront me while she extricated herself. "I didn't kill him," I told her. "I have to get a lead on who might have."

"Well, *I* had nothing to do with it." She glanced at her watch. Her shoe started tapping. For a person who believed she was being held at gunpoint, Jane Berger was pretty testy.

"I didn't say you did. Just tell me why he let you go."

"He *said* all I had to show for six months of billings was one 'Heard on the Street' and a cable TV show. But that was CNBC. And I can show you a stack of clippings, a dozen proposals he turned down. It really had to do with *her*."

"Jessica?"

"Of course with Jessica, Snooky. I'm the best business publicist in town. I *made* his reputation. Did he ever tell you different?"

"He thought you were terrific. You got him that nice article in *Fortune*." She nodded, acknowledging the accolade.

"But *she* wanted to be in"—Jane threw aside her purple shawl in anger, revealing a peasant blouse that would cost a peasant a lifetime's wages—"the *columns*. She *had* to have Liz Smith," she explained. "What would Liz Smith want with her? Oh, and she wanted a spread in *Town & Country!* I'm a business publicist, not a magician. Did she think I could wave my wand and turn her into a celebrity? What did she ever do to deserve big ink?" Jane stared at her watch. "I *had* an important lunch date," she observed tartly.

"Keep talking," I suggested.

She combed the fringe of her shawl with her fingers. "Jessica obviously spent all Labor Day weekend working Rick over, because he called me first thing Tuesday and terminated me *over the phone!*" She grabbed a fistful of fringe and pulled so hard it nearly came off.

"And you've been trying to get the account back ever since, and he wasn't interested. He didn't even return your calls."

"What are you trying to say, Snooky?" She dropped the fringe but got busy removing filaments of mohair from her palm and trying to flick them onto the carpet. "That I killed him? Publicists don't kill. You know who kills? Wives kill."

She was getting a little too comfortable, so I wiggled the lipstick in my pocket. "Tell me more about Jessica."

"What do you want me to tell you? That she's a tough, cold bitch? Fine. She's a tough, cold bitch."

"Good at what she does?"

"So far. She was brilliant the way she opened up new markets for Data. She felt their business wasn't growing because of the business economy here."

"Here?"

"In the United States," she explained, not very patiently. "She pushed Rick to go international."

"Did he want that?"

"Yes, he wanted that. Even with the start-up costs, it made sense for the company. But if it hadn't, he would have wanted it because *she* wanted it." The tapping of Jane's shoe was silenced by the lush carpet, but I could see it moving impatiently. "The man was besotted."

I found I couldn't swallow. "Was she besotted too?"

"No."

"What was she?"

"Bored," Jane replied, sounding pretty jaded herself.

"I don't think so," I challenged her.

"Please!"

"How do you know?"

"I'm a woman. I know when another woman is full of shit, and believe me, that bitch could do the Nancy Reagan number—gaze at him adoringly until her eyes crossed—but she'd . . . " Jane stopped and bit down on her lip thoughtfully. "You know what it was? He wasn't all that boring. It was that he wasn't important enough for her. Once he left you and the excitement died down, she wanted something bigger, better."

"But she wasn't going anyplace, was she?" I asked.

"She hadn't put out a press release."

"What does that mean?"

Jane considered my question while she scrutinized a minuscule pucker in her panty hose; she wasn't one to waste time. Finally she said: "Jessica wasn't trying to hide her boredom hard enough—and that was the end of the summer, before he let me go. I bet it's even more obvious now."

Was Jane telling me the truth—or what she thought I wanted to hear, to get rid of me? The truth, I decided. If she just wanted me to be happy, she'd have told me Richie had grown weary of Jessica.

I was trying to figure out how to get out of Jane's apartment without tying her up, gagging her, and ripping out her phones. Which made me remember how I'd gotten out of Jessica's: thrown out by Daddy Dearest. "By the way," I asked, "do you know anything about Jessica's parents?"

"How should I know? Listen, can I just call my office, see if I got any calls?"

"No." But what was I going to do with Jane Berger? Hit her over the head with a lamp—a Corinthian column wearing a coolie hat—and run, thereby adding assault and battery to my list of felonies? The thought of whacking her over the head until the word "Snooky" was expunged from her memory was almost too enticing. As I was savoring it, Jane bounded out of her chair. She ran to her phone, pressed one button, and screeched: *"Help!"*

"Don't!" I screeched back, and wiggled my lipstick, even though deep down I knew I had no hope.

"Help!" Boy, did she have a set of lungs!

So I ran. Not the elevator, I decided quickly. Jane had pushed one button, so either she had one of those fast-dial things to the police—No, wait. She hadn't identified herself, so the one button was probably to call the doorman. A light would flash on his console, he'd pick up his receiver, hear her cries, and be waiting for me as I got off the elevator.

I spotted a red Exit sign, made for the stairwell, and dashed up two flights of stairs. I stood huffing, watching my watch. Okay: The police would take at least five minutes to get there. The doorman? Would he wait for the cops to come? Had he seen me as I walked in with her? Could he identify me? Or would he dash upstairs to see if he could help the hapless Ms. Berger?

Three minutes. I tore down to the lobby floor. I inhaled a chestful of air. Then I rushed out the stairwell door, screaming, into the lobby. The doorman was right there, standing guard, hands on hips, facing the elevator. "Miss," he called to me, in a very big voice for such a little man. "Stop!"

"Please," I begged. "I heard a woman screaming for help! It was awful!"

"Oh." He clearly thought I looked frantic. I was. "It's all right, dearie. The police are on their way."

I clasped my hands to my heart. "Thank God!" He smiled. After I said goodbye, I sauntered out the building, down to the corner. The second I was out of his sight, I ran like hell.

Eleven

I ran west, away from Central Park, hoping to get lost in the crowd. But at two o'clock on a Thursday afternoon, the crowd was just a couple of women in their eighties hauling shopping carts and a plaid class of mainly Hispanic third or fourth graders, led by a nun. I slowed to a brisk stride to save what was left of my antiperspirant.

Someone blew a whistle. In a flash of suburban stupidity, I immediately associated the sound with football practice and glanced over my shoulder, half expecting to see the apoplectic face of Coach Kramer, ready to *klop* one of the kids with his clipboard. Instead, I saw Jane's doorman sprinting—or trying to sprint—up Eighty-eighth Street, chasing me, shouting "Stop in the name of the law!" With what little breath the poor old man had left, he was blowing his taxi whistle to summon the cops.

In the same instant I spotted him, it hit me that I'd left my handbag in Jane's apartment. I was so overcome with horror I couldn't see straight—and went crashing into a Clean Sweep for New York litter can, which appeared to contain the paper-towel-wrapped feces of every dog on the Upper West Side. Meanwhile, the doorman had taken up a new cry, which sounded a lot like "Murder!" The tiny, white-haired whistle-blower was now no more than a half block away from me.

And the gap was narrowing; I could even hear his brogue as he got closer. What he actually was yelling was "Murderer!" My smashup with the litter basket momentarily knocked the wind out of me, but I charged onward, trying to look nonchalant—or at least not blatantly homicidal.

The doorman's voice began to fade. Without taking time to turn back, I knew I must be gaining on him. I could still hear his accusation, although in an increasingly weak, froggy voice: "Mur . . ." I offered up a prayer that the old man's heart would not fail, because if he died, it would be my fault.

God almighty, what was I going to do without my handbag? Everything I had was in it. Well, I couldn't pound on Jane's door and demand it back. So I pressed on, across Columbus, gradually picking up speed. Back down Eighty-ninth Street, past crumbling brownstones, past restored brownstones with the last of the year's chrysanthemums in stone boxes on window ledges. Displaying a grace I never knew I possessed, I darted around plastic garbage bags and bikes chained to lampposts. For a few seconds, I was moving with such thrilling agility that I ran for the sheer joy of it.

Naturally, at that exuberant instant, as I was transmogrifying into Jackie Joyner-Kersee, reality intruded. A police car squealed over to the curb. "Lady!" a New York basso profundo called out. It belonged to a very big cop. "Whatsa matter?"

"What?"

"I said, whatsa matter?" I had to get the cops out of there. Any second, the doorman would again be heard.

"My purse!" I panted. "A guy . . . " I rested one hand on my chest to ease the pounding of my heart and, with the other, pointed he-went-thataway toward Central Park. "Everything I had was in there!"

The cop looked at his partner. The partner looked me over, his eyes sliding up and down. It wasn't my middle-aged sweater-girl figure—although that was nothing to sneeze at—that was attracting him. No, he munched on the tip of his thumb, clearly thinking: Something about this woman rings a bell.

Suddenly, without a word passing between them, the giant cop got out and pulled open the back door. "Get in," he boomed. The seat faced a wire partition: a mobile cell. "Come *on,* lady," he urged. You know how characters in mysteries are always getting paralyzed with fear? Well, I truly could not move. "Fine with me," he growled. I stared up at him. "But if it just happened, maybe we can find the guy."

My throat swelled, my eyes grew moist. "Thank you!" I nearly wept with relief as I climbed into the car.

He took my emotion for gratitude. "That's what we're here for." Then we took off like a shot.

If I hadn't been teetering on the brink of hysteria, the ride would have been unmitigated joy, a car chase with the good guys, a siren blasting. Except I was a basket case. I had to impersonate an outraged but grateful citizen while recovering from not only my narrow escape from Jane Berger but also my flight from Gulls' Haven. What the hell—since I was in the recuperation business, what about my trauma at finding Richie's body? And what about the blow of his leaving me?

That wasn't all. I had facts to face. The jig could be up at any second. I told myself: There had to have been an all points bulletin about the Menopausal Maniac broadcast by now. These two guys just hadn't associated it with me—yet. The next second, the police radio's adenoidal announcer might offer an explicit description of my slacks and sweaters based on information from Jane.

The big guy turned around. His head puffed out at the jaw and narrowed alarmingly as it disappeared under his hat, like a head of garlic. "What's he look like?"

"He's white," I said. "Dressed in black." That sounded a bit dramatic, but having said it, I was committed to a vision not unlike Olivier's Hamlet.

"Early to mid thirties," I added. "His hair was combed down over his forehead."

We passed one white man dressed all in black, but he bore more resemblance to the Macy's Thanksgiving Day parade's Bullwinkle balloon than to Olivier, so at least my No sounded convincing. "I don't see him anywhere," I told them, with what I hoped was finality.

"Keep an eye open," the big one suggested. "Don't give up."

His partner added: "We'll drive around the park a couple minutes."

The city was flat, gray, but Central Park was three-dimensional. And the colors! The grass was a rich golf-club green, the trees flames of red and gold against a cerulean sky. This might be the last time I would see such a panorama of beauty. Any minute, the radio would give me away: Wanted for murder. May be armed and dangerous. They could drive me straight to jail in my back-seat cell.

"You've been so nice," I babbled. "Really. Thanks *so* much. But I'm late for a doctor's appointment." I lowered my voice to its most somber pitch. "A specialist."

No problem, lady, the big guy said. They even let me off on Fifth Avenue, where I told them the doctor's office was. They wanted my name. I was tempted to say Moll Flanders, but decided the way my luck was running, I'd get a cop who was writing his doctoral dissertation on Defoe. So I gave them my mother's maiden name, and for my address, I gave them the old Brooklyn apartment building where I'd grown up. I swore I'd phone the precinct in an hour to file a formal report.

Brooklyn worked its magic; when I got out of the car, the king-sized cop climbed out as well. He pulled a handful of change from his pocket, searched through it, and handed me a subway token. "Here, Pearl," he said. "So's you can get back to Ocean Avenue."

But I had no place to go. The afternoon curved off into infinity. I walked up one block, down another, my eyes on the cracks in the sidewalk to hide my face, to look like just another distracted New Yorker. By four o'clock, I was so hungry I couldn't stand it. I yearned for hamburgers. Giant pastrami sandwiches. Chinese food. Hot French onion soup crusty with cheese. I passed sidewalk food carts and was riveted by stacks of salt-studded pretzels.

The cold made my misery worse. I shoved my hands into my pants pockets, but that was little comfort because my fingers kept probing, futilely, for a forgotten coin or an old stick of gum. By the time I'd trudged about two miles and reached a chair in the main reading room of the New York Public Library, I was taking the wobbly steps of someone attempting to walk after a long illness.

The sour, satisfying library smell revived me a little. I hadn't been whistling "Dixie" while Richie and Mitch founded Data Associates; I was a good, if not a great, researcher. And I had work to do. After five minutes of explaining how my wallet had been lifted, my library card and all my identification within, and after three quarters of an hour of waiting, a library assistant with an American flag and the words "God Bless" tattooed on the back of his hand finally brought out *Who's Who of American Women, Who's Who in Finance and Industry,* and *Standard & Poor's Directory of Executives.*

Okay, what didn't I know about Jessica Stevenson? According to the books, nothing that would mark her as a born killer. "Born: Dayton, O." and "Parents: Arthur and Penelope (Winterburger) Quigley." Quigley? Could that mean there had been a marriage to a Mr. Stevenson? An intriguing possibility, because right before Jessica came to Data Associates, Richie and I had taken her out to dinner; she'd made a big deal of how much she regretted never having married or had children. I'd nodded and tried not to feel patronized. Still, if she'd been trying to hide a marriage, why would it be so evident from her *Who's Who* listing? If there had indeed been a Mr. Stevenson who'd made her his Mrs., why had she lied about never being married?

When I left my purse behind, I may have lost everything—but at least I knew my telephone credit card number by heart. Sitting in the warm, dirty comfort of the phone booth, I resisted the nearly irresistible urge to call Ben and Alex just to hear their voices and assure them that I was fine. I didn't call Cass either, even though I longed to. Everyone knew what good friends we were; her phone might be tapped too.

Instead, I dialed every Quigley listed with Dayton information. Trying to sound simultaneously chirpy and trustworthy, I pretended to be Mary Quigley of Orlando, Florida, who was researching her family tree. No luck, just answering machines and Quigleys who were strangers to Art, Penny, and little Jessica.

So I became Mary Winterburger and tried the one

Winterburger in Dayton. Pay dirt! A first cousin of Penny's told me she and Art were both dead. Cancer for her. And an accident with a propane-fueled barbecue for him. Terrible, terrible. I agreed. As for Jessica, she'd gotten married soon after college. There'd been a divorce. Oh, and a child. Where was the child? Back East with Jess, she supposed.

I wandered around the darkening streets. A child! The possibilities warmed me for almost a half hour. What if Richie had found out? Liar! he'd have yelled. To think I left a fine woman like Rosie for *you*. Maybe he'd threatened to fire her. Maybe she'd killed him before he could kill her career.

As the day dimmed, the comfort of my fantasy could not fight off the cold. Icy blasts of wind whipped grit and newspapers against me. What the hell kind of weather was this for October? For a few moments at a time, I was able to thaw out my ears by standing in the lobbies of office buildings, studying the listings of tenants. But I couldn't risk attracting the attention of security guards, and I'd return to the safety of the bitter streets and walk again.

My thirst was awful. My hunger was worse. In the twilight, every building on Lexington Avenue seemed to be a restaurant, or a drugstore with a flamboyant display of Kit Kat bars. I passed a mom-and-pop grocery with mountains of shining apples set outside, but the owner, a short Korean man in a long white apron, must have sensed my desperation, because he crossed his arms over his chest and guarded his fruit until I moved on.

A little before seven, I was chilled and exhausted. I had no choice; I used the token the cop had given me for a bus ride just to get warm again and to get off my feet. The ride helped, but not much. At the last stop, in Greenwich Village, I wandered into Washington Square Park. It had grown dark, and the only people there were a drug dealer with shoulder-length dreadlocks and a few others, like me, home-less. A woman in a torn down-filled vest and a wool beret sat on a bench cross-legged, to keep her feet warm. Her arms embraced herself, and she soothed herself with an almost inaudible lullaby. She looked my age. I heard footsteps behind me. A man came up behind me. I felt his breath in my ear as he crooned: "Babe, I got what you need."

I got out fast, but my feet were swelling in my boots, and each step I took hurt. I wondered if the homeless ever grew hardened to their pain or if their misery never subsided.

I got jostled by an army in suits on its way home from work, by legions in jeans toting backpacks, going to night classes at NYU and the New School. I had no strength left to shove back. Toughen up, I warned myself. It's going to get worse. But I wasn't prepared for a tough life; I had been soft and subur-ban and rich far too long. Food smells and sewer smells assailed me, traffic startled me, people fright-ened me.

At twenty-five minutes after eight, as I was follow-ing the sweep of the second hand of my watch to kill time, I spotted a flash of red out of the corner of my eye. A Burger King bag, a big one, in the clutches of a young woman in an NYU sweatshirt. She stood trans-fixed before the window of a science fiction book-store, staring at a display of stacks of a novel, *Atlantis 2000,* arrayed before a backdrop of what looked like a middle-income housing project surrounded by fish.

She was about eighteen years old, with the straight hair, exquisite posture, and slender form of a ballerina. I wondered how she ever expected to do a *grand jeté* after a Bacon Double Cheeseburger.

I swear to you I didn't plan it, because if I'd given it the least consideration, I would have been appalled at such a notion. But I wasn't thinking: I just snatched the bag and ran.

Amazingly, or perhaps not so amazingly, the Village being a neighborhood where sociopathic visitors were not unknown, the young woman didn't follow me. She screamed—well, a loud yelp—but as I glanced back, she was not racing to a phone to call the cops. What might have been considered a capital offense on Long Island—theft of fast food—was apparently treated as a mere nuisance in Manhattan.

The bag radiated heat against my chest; the aroma of beef and onions warmed my soul. I put a few more blocks between me and the scene of my crime. Then I hunkered down on the bumper of a parked gypsy cab and gobbled my dinner.

Somewhere between the french fries and the so-called apple pie (as, with rising guilt, I was imagining the dainty ballerina's pig of a boyfriend smacking her around for losing his dinner), the NYU sweatshirt appeared in my mind's eye. And that image immediately brought to mind the only person I knew at NYU, my favorite no-good kid, Danny Reese.

Danny had played bass in Alex's high school band and gone on to NYU. I'd once overheard Alex telling Ben that Danny had built up a lucrative business selling fake IDs to his fellow students, kids eager to part with big bucks for the privilege of getting into bars to drink and to vomit before reaching their majority. This new venture was probably the moral equivalent of his previous job: hawking marijuana in the boys' locker room at Shorehaven High School.

Danny Reese was a bad egg with good luck: no arrests, no convictions. Well, he had more than good luck going for him. He had a clever mind, a considerable amount of charm, and a sensuous handsomeness; if Elvis Presley had been born intellectually gifted in Nassau County, he would have been a ringer for Danny Reese. But behind Danny's sharp and sneaky mind, behind his facile smile, I'd always sensed sweetness. Okay, maybe not sweetness, but niceness. Certainly no meanness. The kid was damaged but decent. With a sultry mouth to die for. Which was why, in spite of his aiding and abetting Alex to climb out of his window and carouse night after night, I'd always had a soft spot for him.

And so in junior year, when, despite all his elaborate excuses (including an exquisitely forged doctor's note), Danny was about to flunk Cass's Introduction to Theater class because he hadn't written a term paper, I made it a point to grab him and Alex one night after band practice. Under the guise of having them help me rearrange furniture in the sun porch, I offered them a monologue, a critique of *The Glass Menagerie*. Alex found my babbling not only boring but mortifying; when his slit-eyed glare proved ineffective in silencing me, he tuned out. But slicko Danny knew precisely what I was doing. He listened intently. Two days later, he got an A on the final, thereby achieving a grade-point average sufficient to pass the course—much to Cass's annoyance. I had hoped my intervention would give Danny a second chance. What it had done was help enable him to get into college and use it as a base to further his entrepreneurial interests.

Rather begrudgingly, I thought, Manhattan Information gave me Danny's home address. By the time I found where he lived, on a run-down, block-long street near the Hudson River, it was almost midnight. The building itself was a two-story frame cube. A not-very-discreet sign, "Dawn L. Iannucci, Electrologist/Hair Removal/Cosmetician," dangled over a long-since-abandoned store that appeared to take up the entire first floor. A scrawny cat bolted by. It was chasing something I sensed I did not want to see.

Since midnight was Alex's noon, and since he and Danny had been such tight late-night pals, I had no qualms that I would wake Danny—although I had plenty of qualms about the kid himself. Adorable? Sure. And crooked as hell. However, as any mystery reader knows, a dame accused of murder can't be too persnickety about the company she keeps. So I tried to ring his bell—except there was no bell. I knocked, then pounded, on the door. No answer. But a dim light glowed up on the second floor, so I did what we did in Brooklyn when we wanted to get a friend's attention; I yelled "Danny!" at the top of my lungs.

As someone in another building yelled back "Shut up!" a window on the second floor opened. Danny leaned out, shirtless, his thick dark hair hiding his eyes. He did not seem thrilled to have company. He raised the sash higher so he could lean out farther and get a closer look.

"Danny," I said, moving closer to a street light. "It's

me." No recognition, no response. Since I was now a media event, I couldn't exactly shout out my name. So I called out, "Alex's mother." The window slammed shut. Seconds later, Danny came racing through the store and jerked open the door. "I hate to drop in on you this late," I said. My voice sounded gravelly and estrogen-deficient. "But it was too complicated to discuss on the phone." He grabbed me by the sleeve, pulled me inside, and led me toward a staircase in the back. "Um," I began. "Uh, have you heard about . . . ?"

Danny nodded. He'd regained his cool fast and was combing back his hair with his fingers, in the leisurely, self-aware manner of a backup vocalist between songs. In high school he'd been a hunk, but a small hunk. He still wasn't much taller than I, but he'd filled out, and his body now formed the ideal, broad-shouldered male triangle.

"You were just on the eleven o'clock news," he said. "They got one of the prom videos when you were a chaperone. You were laughing about something with Dr. Higbee and Mr. Perez, and then when you saw the camera you waved."

"I don't want to get you in trouble." I swallowed. "But I have nowhere to go."

"Come on up."

I was grateful he didn't say "After you," because my muscles were so sore and my feet so swollen that I had to grip the banister with two hands and drag myself up the stairs like an old lady. Also, I figured: better that I should be looking up at Danny Reese's taut ass in a pair of frayed Levi's than he at mine in a pair of French slacks that, from the rear, no doubt emphasized how far I'd traveled since my days of tautness.

He closed the door to his apartment, turning three locks, sliding a dead bolt, and shoving into place a metal rod that was bolted to the floor. Danny had a lot to protect—although definitely not the couch he told me to take a seat on, all lumps and extruding springs draped in someone's old yellow-and-blue tie-dyed wall hanging. But what electronic treasures he had! A movie-sized television, two VCRs, a mountain of stereo components, monolithic speakers.

"Mrs. Meyers." He enunciated my name slowly, dragging out each syllable. I assumed this was the new, hip salutation.

"Danny."

"Guess I shouldn't ask you what's new," he observed.

He was too cool to wait for my response. Instead, he disappeared into another room and returned buttoning the cuffs of a silky black shirt. He rested his back against the doorframe, crossed his arms over his chest, and peered at me. The shirt remained unbuttoned, but that was clearly the thing to do, since even in high school Danny had been so hip he made the hippest MTV hipster seem an incorrigible old fart. "What can I do for you?" he inquired.

"Nothing." I braced my hands on my knees and tried to push myself up. It didn't work. "It was wrong for me to come here. I'm sorry. Just give me a minute." He sauntered across the room and sat beside me. I could barely talk. "I'm so tired I can't think straight. I saw a girl in an NYU sweatshirt, and then I thought about you—that you were the one person who might not turn me in to the police."

"Mrs. Meyers."

"What?"

"That's not good thinking."

"It's not?"

"Not for someone who's wanted by the police. You should be thinking: Mr. Meyers' girlfriend—or his company—might be offering a reward for information leading to your capture. You should be thinking: If there's a reward involved, Danny Reese would sell his grandmother's wheelchair out from under his grandmother." He put his feet up on his coffee table, an upside-down wastebasket. He was wearing cowboy boots. Cowboy boots for a very prosperous cowboy: coffee-brown alligator-skin.

"I don't believe that of you. The Danny Reese I knew may have been a little off center, but he wasn't twisted."

"You really believe that?"

"My guess is, you don't care whether or not I killed my husband, although you have my word that I didn't. I suppose I hoped you might help me because you and Alex were once friends. Or because you think I'm a nice person. Or just because you like being . . . " I didn't have the heart to say it.

"Come on. Being what?"

"Being an outlaw."

He rested his head on the back of the couch. A small smile softened his lips for a second, then disappeared. "I'll help you," he said.

"The last thing I want to do is condescend, but I have an obligation to tell you . . . " I hesitated. "You could get into trouble. Of course, you know that."

"Of course. An accessory after the fact."

"You've become a mystery-reader, Danny?"

"No, Mrs. Meyers, I'm not a mystery-reader. I'm

what you'd call"—he gave me the smile that had made high school girls dizzy with desire—"a consumer of legal services. My lawyer tells me I'm a felon. But even *he* admits I'm a smart felon. A careful felon too. A felon who's never gotten caught."

"But they're not accusing me of selling pot in the locker room." Although he was too hip to ever look dumbfounded, I saw him fight the desire to turn and gape at me. "I'm a good teacher. I know my kids, and I keep my ears open. I knew about the pot. I knew about the pills too. And if someone had told me you were selling a little cocaine, I wouldn't have dropped dead from shock."

"I gave that up."

"Good!"

"I'm into fake ID. Not passports or anything like that. Passports, currency—they're dangerous unless your suppliers have state-of-the-art equipment. But I know a guy—"

"I don't want a passport. I don't want counterfeit money. And do I look as if I'd have the *chutzpah* to try and pass myself off as a twenty-one-year-old with one of your phony college IDs or driver's licenses?"

He swung his feet off the wastebasket. "Don't think I'm being impolite or anything, but what do you want?"

"I need a place to sleep tonight."

"So far this isn't much of a challenge."

"How about this, Danny? I need you to get word to Alex that I'm all right and to find out from him what's been going on at the house. But the phone lines will be tapped."

"Don't worry."

"No! Please don't call the house—"

"Listen." He cut me off. "You think I'm going to call Alex and say: 'I hear a certain Mrs. M. is alive and well and had a great night's sleep in Greenwich Village'? No. I call Alex, tell him I'm sorry about his old man. We bullshit a little about the Seattle music scene. I reminisce a little about our old days in the band, with him lead singer and me on drums—"

"You played bass."

"You know that. I know that. Alex'll know that. But the cops won't. And if Alex doesn't have the IQ of a sardine, he'll know to get to some other phone and give me a call." He stood and carefully arranged the bottoms of his jeans over his boots before going into his room and returning with a pillow and a quilt that might have been white when he began NYU four years earlier. "If you want to stay up all night worrying I'll turn you in, be my guest. But if I were you, I'd get some sleep." He didn't even hesitate before adding: "You look like hell."

I was exhausted enough not to be revolted by the lipstick smears and the suspiciously stiff patches on the pillowcase. Danny Reese made Alex, a master of piggishness, look like a compulsive cleaner. I almost sliced my shin on a compact disk wedged between two of the sofa cushions: the wound would have gotten infected by the years of accumulated Twinkie crumbs, grit, grime, and what felt like a random dusting of parakeet gravel. And the floor: even in the faint light from the street, I could make out a greasy paper liner from a pizza box, used tissues, wads of discarded notebook paper, beer cans, a wine bottle—and dirt.

Dirt. I could see the dirt on the kitchen floor of Gulls' Haven as I fell asleep. Dirt from the doorway all along the floor to Richie's shoes. Shoes or shoe? I pictured the bottoms of his expensive sneakers, a contoured design that looked like a field tilled by an advanced agricultural society. Lots of dirt in the grooves of the left shoe. But hardly any dirt on the right. Was that because the dirt from the right sneaker had come off all over the floor? Or because only one foot had really gotten into the dirt when he parked his car.

I turned onto my back. I should wash out my underwear, I thought. But I was too weary and weak to get up off the couch. I couldn't stand the thought of my sore feet pressing down on Danny's filthy floor.

Dirt, I told myself. Think about dirt. Think about the tire tracks in the dirt. The way Richie's car was parked, he wouldn't have stepped out into dirt. He would have stepped ... I squeezed my eyes tight, adjusting the focus on my image. He would have stepped onto a narrow carpet of autumn leaves. Dry leaves. They had to be dry; it hadn't rained for two or three days before that. One step. His next would have been onto the road. How did his sneakers— sneaker?—get so muddy?

How come the cops hadn't asked themselves that question? Had they taken soil samples from Richie's soles and matched them to the dirt on the floor? They had to have. And to the dirt where the car was parked? Of course. And the dirt from all three places was a match.

But they'd been making molds of tire tracks—not footprints. There weren't any footprints near Richie's car.

So where had the dirt on my kitchen floor come from?

From the person who was with Richie, or who tailed Richie and tracked it in.

From the person who saw the trail of dirt from the door, who realized there was none on Richie's shoes and decided it was important to put some there.

That way, it would appear that Richie had been alone—and there was only one person who could be accused of killing him, the only other person in Gulls' Haven.

The accused had a good night's sleep.

Twelve

Danny Reese's bathroom was about as immaculate as his living room, but at eight-thirty in the morning I couldn't afford to be finicky. I actually took a shower—after swearing to myself that no matter how irresistible the temptation, I would look neither at the drain of his tub nor at the inside of his shower curtain. I was drying off with the only clean terry-cloth object I could find, a washcloth, when Danny called through the door: "Give me your clothes."

"What?"

"I'm going out to get some coffee and stuff. I'll drop your clothes off with my stuff at the Chinese laundry."

"My slacks and sweaters have to be dry-cleaned," I explained through the door.

"Okay, but that'll take the whole day." Just as I was worrying that Danny was conning me out of my clothes, he called out: "I bet you're worrying I'm going to con you out of your clothes. You know, so you can't run while I'm out picking up the reward for turning you in." Then he added: "Open up. I've got something for you." I opened the door a crack. A hand slid through with a pair of corduroys and a chenille sweater. They were beautifully laundered and smelled of fabric softener.

"I haven't been watching the news," I said. "There's really a reward?"

"It's been on the radio. Fifty big ones leading to the arrest and conviction of the killer."

"Fifty *thousand?*" I couldn't button the corduroys. However, considering that Danny's ass was approximately the size of my two fists, it was a victory, and a miracle, that I was able to get the zipper more than halfway up.

"Mr. Meyers' company put up the money."

I pulled Danny's sweater over my head. Even before I had nursed two kids, I had never been one to yearn for the freedom of going braless; age forty-seven did not seem an apt time to reconsider. Still, I didn't have much of a choice, so I bloused up the oversized sweater, hunched over like Quasimodo so my shoulders would obtrude farther than my breasts, gave my head a what-the-hell toss, and opened the door.

"I'm not going to turn you in," he informed me. "You can believe me or not." He took my dirty clothes without so much as glancing at my breasts, which, while not a major blow to my self-esteem, was nonetheless a direct hit.

"I believe you," I told him. So there I was, with my life in the hands of a twenty-one-year-old amoral ex–drug pusher dressed in tight black jeans and a black shirt buttoned all the way to the collar; and I hadn't the slightest idea if I had just made a wise decision or the most deadly mistake of my life. "Oh, since you're going to the laundry . . . ," I added, and grabbed the quilt off the couch.

"Mrs. Meyers." The tone was frigid.

"I know. I'm not your mother. But the quilt's dirty."

"It's my quilt, Mrs. Meyers."

"Of course it's your quilt. It's just that if I'm ever your houseguest again, I'd prefer it a little cleaner. And call me Rosie."

After he left—with the quilt—I phoned the school. As I'd hoped, the secretary in the main office, Carla, answered. Since she was without question the most self-involved human being in the middle Atlantic states, it didn't matter whether or not the washcloth I'd put over the telephone mouthpiece muffled my voice; she didn't care who I was or what I wanted, because my call did not concern her, her boyfriend Kyle, or Kyle's Dodge Stealth. I gave her Cass's and my prearranged signal, saying I was the nurse from Dr. Goldberg's office calling to confirm Cass's appointment for one-thirty on Saturday. The message itself, of course, was meaningless; it simply signaled Cass to be at our agreed-upon pay phone near the cafeteria at one-thirty—she was off seventh period—and await my call.

For approximately a half second, I considered calling Stephanie to see if she'd gotten the name of a Nassau County attorney, but although I was ninety-eight percent positive she wouldn't turn me in, I couldn't afford a two percent risk. More important, Stephanie's last recommendation, Forrest Newel, had been so astoundingly unimpressive that I had a couple of doubts about her judgment. On the other hand, I didn't exactly have a list of criminal lawyers in my back pocket (or, to be accurate, in Danny's back pocket), and I needed help.

Danny returned about fifteen minutes later with two containers of coffee. "You're still here," he observed coolly. His eyes were always half closed, in the studied, sexy, sleepy manner of teen-dream actors on moronic TV shows.

"Did you think I'd run away?"

"Well, some people have doubts about my character."

"Danny, come on. I've known you for years."

He grinned. Wow, was he cute! "All the more reason for you to run."

"Probably, but I needed you for something else."

"Oh. What?"

"Do you know anything about criminal lawyers on Long Island?"

"Like what?" He eased the lid off his container of coffee and ripped open two packets of sugar with his teeth.

"A name, Danny."

"Oh." He nibbled on his plastic stirrer for a minute, deep in thought. "Vincent Carosella," he finally announced. "Ever hear of him? He's pretty famous." The name did sound vaguely familiar, probably from News 12 accounts of gruesome Long Island murder trials; well, at least he didn't sound like another prig with a watch fob. "None of my friends ever used him, because he doesn't do drug cases. But for heavy-duty—" Danny hesitated for a fraction of a second, deciding between "stuff" and "shit." But since we were pals on a first-name basis, he chose "shit." "For heavy-duty shit"—he bunched his fingertips together and gave them a passionate kiss—"Vinnie is the cream." Then he was off to call Alex—and offer an old customer a great deal on a mint Rutgers ID card and a pristine New Jersey driver's license.

When I called, a few minutes after nine, Vinnie Carosella was already in his office. We went through the preliminaries. His background: he'd gone to Adelphi College and Saint John's Law School and had been head of the Homicide Bureau in the D.A.'s office in Nassau County. His fee: as an afterthought he mentioned that he charged three hundred dollars an hour. He did not ask me if I'd killed Richie.

"Rosie," he said, "I got to be honest with you. Running away doesn't help."

"Vinnie, you tell me: If I turn myself in, what are the chances the police will keep looking for Richie's killer?"

"Small to nil." What a voice he had! Deep, ardent, a voice that could leave a jury in tears. The voice jogged my memory. I recalled seeing him on TV on some courtroom steps, telling a reporter or two that his faith in the American legal system would be vindicated by the not-guilty verdict he was certain the jury would bring in. He'd appeared to be in his late fifties, a snappy dresser. "Keep one thing in mind, Rosie: the longer you stay a fugitive, the harder it's going to be for me to convince people you're innocent. Okay?"

"Okay."

"Now tell me everything."

So I did. He assured me that as soon as he received my retainer he'd hire an investigator to look into Jessica's background, especially to see if she was hiding a child—or a lover—from Richie. As far as the dirt and the tire tracks, he wouldn't be able to get copies of the lab reports until I was indicted. At least, he added, not kosherly. However, he'd talk to a buddy of his, a detective lieutenant in Mineola, and see if he could come up with a few pieces of paper.

"Who knows?" I said. "Maybe you'll find something that will exonerate me."

"These things can happen," Vinnie agreed politely. "You want to give me a number in case I have to reach out for you?"

"I'd rather not. Not that I don't trust you. It's just that I don't know where I'll be from one day to the next."

"So you call me every day, around this time. Or earlier. I'm in by seven-thirty. I stay till about nine, ten at night. Don't worry about bothering me. I have no life."

It was almost half an hour, and Danny still wasn't back. Maybe he was turning me over to the cops.

Maybe he was watching the rinse cycle in the laundromat. In either case, I had time on my hands. I slipped into his room to see what I could find out about my *parfit gentil* knight. The bed, not surprisingly, was unmade, but at least, unlike the living room, the area did not qualify for federal disaster relief funds. His textbooks were piled on the floor so neatly it was clear they had not been touched for months, maybe years. No indication that he read for pleasure, even boy books: sports trivia or rock biographies. Naturally, nothing remotely resembling fiction. His black-and-white bass rested on top of a massive Marshall amplifier; back issues of *Bass Player* magazine and a songbook from Red Hot Chili Peppers were piled haphazardly beside it. The magazines weren't too dated, but when I ran my finger over the bass, there was a layer of velvet New York dust. I found signs of female company: a tortoise-shell barrette under the radiator and, in the back of his closet, a tiny white thong bikini.

But the rest of his closet was pristine. Danny clearly loved his clothes. And he had lots of them. The colors ran the gamut from charcoal gray to ebony to jet, a pretty narrow gamut. The only exception was a couple of pairs of blue jeans.

But he kept no samples of his merchandise: not a single fake driver's license, not one spurious identity card. The only drugs I found were ostentatiously legal, in drugstore vials with his name—although if he'd actually needed those amounts of Valium and Halcion to relax and get a good night's, he probably would have been institutionalized. I appropriated a few Valium, but considering that there was a fifty-thousand-dollar price tag on my head, I felt remarkably tranquil. Why not? If Danny didn't betray me, I was in damn good hands. He was a most careful felon; if the cops got onto him, they could bust in with warrants, smash down the doors—and find nothing. However, I did find something in his fastidiously hung pants. Pocket money. If my instincts about him were right, the sixty-three dollars I came up with had been forgotten long ago. I felt shame, guilt, and even some anguish over my skulduggery, but not enough to keep me from taking the money.

I called Data Associates. I couldn't ask for Richie's office because his secretary would know my voice. Instead, I asked for Jessica's. I told her secretary, Helen—who either smoked too much or was a transvestite—that I worked in the newsroom of the *Hartford Courant* and was checking facts for an article. Was it indeed a fact that Ms. Stevenson had approved a reward for fifty thousand dollars? Ms. Stevenson had. And her title at Data Associates? President. President? Well, technically, acting president, the secretary said. Since yesterday afternoon.

I remembered Gevinski assuring me that Jessica would have no reason for killing her megabucks boyfriend. Well, what about this? Richie was dead, and she'd been made president of a multinational corporation—with salary and stock options. She was now a woman with her own megabucks. And with her new title, she'd become a power in her own right. So yes, Sergeant, she'd had motive.

And speaking of motive, what about Daddy Dearest? If he wasn't her daddy but a richer, more powerful, more aristocratic, and—although I doubted it—more exciting lover than Richie, wouldn't that give her additional incentive to try out my kitchen knives? Take a stab at this: Kill Richie and she gets a raise, a promotion, and a newer, more important, if not more potent, lover. Forget lover. How about husband? Mr. and Mrs. Daddy. And the beauty of it was, Jessica *knew* she could get away with murder. With Richie's death, she would become a member of the Young Presidents Club—while I'd get to join the Great Books group at the Bedford Hills Correctional Facility for Women.

Confidential secretaries are paid to keep confidences. No matter if Helen loathed Jessica; she would not blab to me. But a few minutes later, I got to thinking: what about an *ex*-confidential secretary? Richie fired Frances Gundersen about six months before he'd fired me. Could Frances be persuaded to blab?

Maybe. When Fran Gundersen was fifty-three years old, Richie had given her a severance check and put someone named Daphne in her swivel chair. Daphne actually looked like a Daphne: small-boned and saucer-eyed, and with an English accent. I should have deduced then that the betrayal of Fran might foreshadow big-time treachery. But I hadn't; Richie was my husband, and while a husband may fudge a little about how much he lost at the blackjack table on the family vacation in Puerto Rico, for the sake of sanity a wife must assume her life is based on truth. So maybe I hadn't been such a consummate dupe when I believed him that Fran had grown grievously absentminded—the way some women do when they go through their change—and what choice did he have except to get rid of her?

I remembered she had lived in a part of Brooklyn unfamiliar to me, a section called Sunset Park, which had a sizable Scandinavian community. I offered a cruel little prayer that a woman her age would have trouble finding another job and she'd be home.

She was! She answered the phone the way she had all the years she'd worked for him. "Hel-lo-o!" She hit a high note on that third syllable she'd always added. I hung up and left a quick, unsigned I'll-be-back message on top of Danny's phone. In lieu of the dramatic sunglasses I was sure he had but I couldn't find, I hid as much of myself as I could under the brim of a black vinyl baseball cap, a hideous, trendy, sweat-provoking thing. I left the house and spent about three minutes on a street corner, paralyzed: Subway? Too many people who watch the eleven o'clock news. Taxi? All I had in the world now was sixty-three bucks; my profligate days were over. Subway? Taxi? Taxi? Subway? I became unparalyzed damned fast when I spotted a couple of neighborhood cops sauntering down the block. "Taxi!" And I was off to Brooklyn.

I will not discuss how long it took the cabdriver to find Sunset Park, or the fact that the ride there cost twenty-seven dollars and forty cents. Fran's tiny attached house was one in a long ocher brick row, probably built in the late thirties, around the time *The Wizard of Oz* came out, and in fact, her whole street, with its diminutive maples and itty-bitty lawns, had the resplendent cuteness of Munchkinland— although God knows Fran was no Munchkin.

When she opened the door, I had to look up; she was almost a head taller than I. Once she'd had the glowing skin and robust body of a roller derby queen, but in the time since Richie had fired her, she'd become what charitable people might call husky.

When she realized who I was, she quacked with astonishment.

"Sorry to drop in on you like this, Fran."

She looked all business in a gray flannel skirt, a long-sleeved blouse with starchy cuffs, and the small, floppy bow she'd always worn under her collar. An invisible boss might be saying, "Take a letter, Miss Gundersen," except that when I glanced down, I saw her white legs were stockingless. She was wearing pink satin ballet slippers with tiny bows. I felt relieved—and sad—that my prayer had been answered.

"I'm not going to hurt you," I told her. "I'm not armed. I'm not dangerous."

"That's a laugh and a half!" Fran sniggered. Her teeth had a lipstick coating; she was still wearing too much of the same bubble-gum color. But now the bright pink seeped into the tiny lines that radiated from her lips, making her mouth appear blurry. "You stabbed your husband to death, and you say you're not dangerous?"

"I didn't do it."

Instead of screaming "Police!" or slamming the door in my face, Fran stepped back and pressed herself against the wall so I could enter the narrow hallway. Since she couldn't pass me to lead the way, I invited myself to go right into her living room and take a seat. Fran followed and sat across from me, primly. Her hands stayed in her lap, but she crossed and recrossed her legs so often that her skirt worked its way up her sturdy thighs.

The little house was a beautiful surprise, filled with classic, light-wooded Scandinavian furniture and paintings of dawn on the fjords and hazy fields of flowers. Beautiful paintings, actually. "I'm glad I found you home," I said.

"I've had nothing but free time for the last year." Then she gave me one of those confrontational I'm-not-afraid-to-look-you-straight-in-the-eye looks. "So let's be honest here. He traded you in for a different model, and you killed him. Period."

"Could you consider making that a question mark, Fran?"

"No. But you know what? I thank you for it." She got up, grabbed my hand, and shook it. "I wish I'd had the guts to do it myself." She got busy straightening one of her paintings. "One day everything was hunky-dory for me. And the next . . . It's not just that I was an old dishrag. It's that I was *fired*." She turned back. Her fair complexion was mottled with angry blotches. "Kaput! Out on the street." Fran had been such a pretty, hearty woman; in the old days, Richie said he could picture her, her hair plaited around her head, yodeling. Big blondes like Fran are supposed to be jolly and generous, so for the first few minutes, her bright facade had obscured the magnitude of her bitterness. Now her hands, at her sides, squeezed tight and became fists. "A knife in his gut," she snapped. "Between you and I, the bastard got off easy."

"I thought . . . He told me he gave you a nice settlement."

"He gave me money. Conscience money. But what am I supposed to do with the rest of my life? You're a college graduate; you may not think being a secretary is such a big deal, but it was my *job*. I was good at it. All my friends were secretaries. And all of a sudden, all I have is a 'settlement' and nothing to do. I go out on interviews and no one wants me because the economy stinks—and I'm too old. No one wants an old woman around."

"You're not old."

"Oh, cut it out! I'm old. You're old. If he didn't want me anymore, why didn't he transfer me to one of the other execs? Or pick up the phone and get me a job with one of the corporations we deal with? How can you just say to a person who's been with you for years: 'You're a nothing'?"

"I don't know," I replied. "But it couldn't have been that painful an experience for him. He went out and did it again, to me." Fran crossed her arms, crossed her legs, then hunched over and rocked herself, as if easing a pain deep in her gut. I went on: "Think about it for a minute. This was a pattern for him. What if he did it to her too? Jessica. I mean, maybe you believe I killed him, but just assume for a minute that I was set up. Okay? By her. He could have thrown her over. Maybe she decided to avenge herself."

Fran sat up and let loose with another one of her raucous laughs, tossing back her head and opening her mouth in a capital O. She said: "He never did anything to her except whatever she wanted done!"

"How do you know for certain?"

"How do you think I know? Data Associates was my life. I still keep in touch with all the girls. Oh, excuse me: women. Laurie and Claire and Helen and the two Marys."

The secretaries to all the top executives at Data Associates! A gold mine of information.

"Please. I need your help to find out who did it. Look, if you really thought I was a murderer, you would never have let me in your house."

"You did what you had to do with him. I know you're not a homicidal maniac or anything. You're not going to kill me."

"You knew me all those years. Think for a minute: if I was going to murder Richie, would I have done it so stupidly?"

She hesitated. "I don't think you planned it. I think you probably went crazy for a minute."

"But you think there's the slightest chance I didn't do it. I can tell." I couldn't, actually, but I kept talking. "Give me the benefit of your doubt. Answer my questions. *Please,* Fran."

She took her time aligning the edges of her cuffs. She seemed absorbed and very complacent. I didn't like the fact that she found my desperation so pleasing. What had I ever done to her? Sure, I'd been the boss's wife, but I'd been a decent, mannerly boss's wife. Friendly, actually, even though Fran herself would never walk off with honors in warmth. Or had I, in smug ignorance, said something condescending, from which she was still hurting?

"I need help," I pleaded. No answer. She looked up from her cuffs and waited for me to squirm. I needed her, so I offered a small squirm, a slight shift in my seat. I gazed beseechingly.

"Go ahead," she said at last, and amused herself by cracking her knuckles. "Ask." Crack, crack.

"Tell me about Jessica."

"That's not a question. I thought you were an English teacher." Crack.

"I'll rephrase it. Jessica's been named acting president. Do you think that's just a horrible benefit of Richie's death? Or do you think she was always angling for something bigger, wanting to take his place?"

"The answer," she proclaimed, with the insufferable brashness of a quiz show host, "is Always Angling!" I suppose Fran's gusto wouldn't qualify her as manic, but for some reason she was suddenly flying too high. "A born angler!" She laughed too long and too hard. "Have I got an angle for you!"

She tossed back her head and laughed at the ceiling. She scared me a little. I wanted to run, but instead I sat—and dredged up one of my classroom techniques; I lowered my voice to just above a whisper, so she had to concentrate to hear me. For some reason, it almost always transformed wise guys and tough girls into sober citizens. "How did you or your friends know about Jessica's ambition?" I murmured.

"What?" I repeated the question. "We take minutes at meetings," she responded with high seriousness. "We type their letters. We place their phone calls. We *know* them."

"Tell me about her business relationship with him."

"Your husband was terrific with people, a good businessman too. But to tell you the truth, probably not a great businessman. Too cautious. From day one, she was pushing him further than he wanted to go."

"Like what?"

"Like she got him to give Mr. Gruen the ax. Like

she got him to go international. You may not know it, but your late sweetie was scared witless of that. She got a whole army of experts to convince him that if he didn't open up in Europe and the Far East, someone else would."

"But that was a couple of years ago. What about now? Did you hear if she had any more big ideas he didn't want to go along with?"

"How about taking the company public? Is that big enough for you?"

Granted, no one would ever call me a wizard of Wall Street, but it didn't take a financial genius to know that going public would have meant a ton of money for Richie. I also knew it was an idea that had always unnerved him, in part because he realized that while he was a virtuoso of charm, he didn't have the guts it took to be a brutal, bottom-line executive. Also, going public would mean that Data Associates might no longer be his alone. With thousands or millions of shares floating around, it could be taken over by some outside predator—or even by an insider tougher than he. Interestingly, the only executive who met that particular standard was Jessica Stevenson.

"He was definitely going to take it public?" It was hard to believe; over the years, he'd rejected that idea again and again whenever his accountants or lawyers brought it up.

"According to Helen and Little Mary, they were just waiting for your divorce to become final. So's you couldn't horn in on the action."

"Gee," I said.

"Yeah. Gee." We sat in silence for a minute. Her anger seemed to fade. "You want some coffee or something?"

We wound up in her kitchen, a small but picture-perfect space with what looked like custom-made blond wood cabinets. The countertops and splashboards were covered with large white tiles, some with birds painted on them. While we were waiting for the coffee, she asked me if I was hungry. A little, I told her.

I wound up eating two bologna sandwiches and a thick slice of still-frozen Sara Lee cheesecake, which Fran offered with reasonable cordiality. For some reason, when my body should have been fortifying itself for flight or fight, it had absolutely no interest in complex carbohydrates; it craved any and all foods guaranteed to engender heart disease and gas. Between bites of sandwich, I remarked: "I get the impression you think Richie was more in love with Jessica than she was with him."

"No kidding."

"According to my sources, she's been seen with an older man. Old enough to be her father, except her father's dead. My sources are pretty sure he's her lover."

"Nicholas Hickson," she said with the bored expression of someone having to state the obvious.

"Are you sure?"

"Do you trust Helen Woolley to know what's going on?" Helen was Jessica's secretary. "Helen's a pretty smart cookie."

"I trust her. It's just that the name Hickson sounds so familiar. Who is he?"

"Only the head of Metropolitan Securities." Which even I knew was the second- or third-largest brokerage firm in the world.

"How do you know about his connection to

Jessica?" I asked, recalling the white-haired power-house in Richie's bathrobe.

"They've been having lots of very long lunches, Helen says. Very, *very* long. Until five o'clock. I'm sure they were discussing Metropolitan's underwriting Data Associates' stock issue, ho-ho-ho. And there were trips to London, to Washington."

"Was she open about traveling with this Hickson?"

Fran gave a loud *tsk* of disgust. "Of course not! But Helen got to be phone friends with his secretary. Do I have to spell it out for you? Same itineraries. Different hotels, but if you think he was actually staying at the Four Seasons in Washington while she had a room with a king-sized bed at the Madison, you're very . . . " She may have been trying to find a synonym for "stupid."

"Very naive. No. I'm not naive. Do you think Richie knew about the two of them?"

"I don't know. That Jessica's got brains enough for two men. But he wasn't anybody's fool either."

He wasn't. And he *had* to have known something was up with Jessica, because in the last few weeks of his life, he'd clearly ordered his divorce lawyer to change tactics. The haggling over who got the antique andirons ceased. Harmony, if not actual goodwill, suddenly prevailed, along with an eagerness to get this thing over with as soon as possible because it's been so damned ugly—and hard on the boys too.

However, I knew my husband. He loved his andirons; call me small-minded, but that's why I'd wanted them. I realized that Richie's willingness to let go of them did not mean he had become accommodating. No, he was simply desperate to get the divorce so he could be free to marry Jessica. I'd told

Honi, my lawyer, that I could guess what the hurry was: Jessica was pregnant. She'd said: These old farts with the new wives keep thinking having a baby will make them live forever. Ha! Those new kids take ten years off their lives.

But from what Fran had just told me, the rush wasn't because Jessica was pregnant. Richie had been deathly afraid that if he didn't move fast, he'd lose her to Nicholas Hickson.

Fran licked her index finger and began picking up stray graham cracker crumbs from inside the cake pan. Quite casually, she asked: "If she was going to leave your husband for this guy, why would she bother killing him? It doesn't make sense."

"It does if Richie was trying to stop her, or to force her to marry him when she didn't want to."

She gave a disdainful snort. "*Force* her to marry him. He put a gun to her head?"

"Maybe he had something on her. You know . . . he was blackmailing her."

"You think he'd be so dumb or so crazy in love that he'd *force* her into marriage?"

"Maybe." All I got for this was another snort. "Look, she was everything he ever wanted. Brilliant. Successful. Elegant. Sophisticated." Fran nodded. She knew Richie. "He was obsessed with her—maybe right from the beginning." I paused. "Were you there when she came to the firm?"

"Yeah."

"Do you think he was having an affair with her from the start?" She looked uncomfortable but then shook her head no. A strong no. "You sure?" She nodded. I took the plunge. "Do you think he ever had any affairs before Jessica?"

Fran's guffaw was a little cruel; a simple yes would have sufficed. She must have realized this, because she actually muttered: "Sorry."

"Do you have any idea with whom?"

Fran looked off into the distance, somewhere between her instant-hot-water faucet and a tile with a cardinal on it. Her lips puckered into a bright-pink blossom as she concentrated. Finally, in a quiet-for-Fran voice, she said: "I always wondered about one thing. Mandy. You knew Mandy, didn't you?"

"Mandy? No. Why?"

"Right before I left, he was getting a lot of calls from a Mandy."

Mandy? "There was a Mandy who was in my son Ben's year in high school. The only other Mandy I've ever even heard of is a lawyer. She runs with one of my neighbors. But I've never met her; they run when she gets home from the city." Could Richie have met this woman at some Open School Night? At Be A Sport, getting their rackets restrung? Had she approached him one Saturday morning on Main Street with a Citizens for a More Beautiful Shorehaven raffle book?

"Which neighbor did she run with?"

I'd forgotten for a minute that Fran, who'd been Richie's secretary for almost fifteen years, probably knew our entire lives. "Stephanie Tillotson."

"Oh. Dr. Tillotson's wife." I nodded. "You know," Fran drawled, "that's how he met Jessica Stevenson."

"That's how *who* met Jessica?" I demanded.

"Your husband; Dr. Tillotson brought her up to the office one day. They all went out to lunch."

I sat up straight. My stomach felt painfully full, but something beside the thousand grams of saturated fat I'd just consumed was causing my discomfort. I conjured up Jessica. Nice straight nose? One of Carter's? "Was it a business thing, Dr. Tillotson bringing her to the office?"

"They didn't ask me to join them."

"Did he and my husband call each other often?"

"No. Once in a blue moon. I mean, not like Mrs. Driscoll. *She* was on the phone with him every single afternoon—and that's only the times she called him. Sometimes I'd walk in during the morning and he'd be yakking with her." She shook her head. "What was it with those two?"

"Sex?" I suggested.

"No way!" She paused. "Well, I don't think so."

"I don't think so either. Believe it or not, Richie was quite a guy." She knew I meant sexually. Her fair skin flushed. It hit me in that second that she'd probably had a crush on him all those years. That would account not for the fact of her bitterness but at least for its intensity. "What were he and Joan Driscoll talking about the times you walked in?"

"Gossip. I mean, they were like two old biddies in a tearoom, except they went on about social stuff— people, parties you read about in the papers." She chewed off some of her lipstick. "She treated me like dirt. She'd call and say 'Mr. Meyers!' Not even a 'please,' much less a 'hello.' What a scrawny bitch!"

I couldn't believe Tom would be willing to caress protruding ribs, fondle breast implants, thrust himself against a knobby pelvis. In high school he had been one hell of a thruster.

"That bitch had nothing but time on her hands. I mean, she was always sending him little presents. Or leaving messages about where they were selling 'perfect' patent-leather tuxedo shoes! Or 'darling' Art Deco fountain pens. How can pens be darling?"

"Do you think it was just superficial chitchat? Or were they close?"

"I think he told her everything. You want my guess? She got her jollies from hearing about what he was doing, and he got his jollies from telling her."

"No. Richie wasn't like that."

"He changed, didn't he? Let me tell you something: You have no idea what he turned into. I do. I was there. Trust me. I bet she knew about this Mandy. And definitely about Jessica. You really want to know about the women in Mr. Richard Meyers' life? Don't ask me. Ask Mrs. Thomas Driscoll."

Thirteen

The medicine cabinet mirror was streaky, so Danny spit on a piece of toilet paper and wiped it clean. A courtly gesture. I could have lived without his following it up by lounging against the frame of the bathroom door, hanging out while I put on makeup. "Alex is fine," he again reassured me. "Don't worry about him. Worry about yourself." I peered into the mirror. Amazing: life on the lam might be cruel, but I hadn't looked this terrific in years.

I extracted a palette of eye shadow from its plastic prison after the usual struggle. In a flourish of gallantry, Danny had gone to his best supplier and gotten me a new identity: an American Express card and a Minnesota driver's license in the name of Christine Peterson, which declared my age to be forty-one. He said not to worry, they were clean, untraceable. He also shoplifted an astounding quantity of drugstore cosmetics. I considered my reflection: Did I really want to contour my eyelids with a green rainbow of emerald, kelly, and lime? I put down the shadow. Blatantly tasteless. But who the hell had to be tasteful anymore? Away from school, off Long Island, I could be any woman I wanted to be. Maybe I should consider indigo lashes, plucked sienna brows, vermilion cheeks, ruby lips. They could mark a sea change.

"Did Alex say anything about Ben?"

"Ben's fine. He's staying at your house with Alex for a few days. His girlfriend went back to wherever."

"Philadelphia. Did Alex sound calm?"

"You mean considering his father was killed and his mother's wanted for the murder?"

"Yes."

"He sounded pretty calm."

"Drugged calm?"

"Maybe he had a little help. Stop worrying about your kids, Rosie. They're men. They're not gonna fall apart. Alex isn't gonna fry his brains on drugs. Okay, I admit: they're both worried about you. They'd be pretty twisted if they weren't. But at least they knew you weren't doing the dead man's float in Long Island Sound; the cops told Ben that you got to the city."

In the end, I selected Maybelline's most genteel

brown. "The cops' knowing I'm in the city may not be the end of the world," I mused. "My address book was in my handbag. It has all sorts of out-of-town names—my cousins in L.A., Ben's college roommate's mother in Salt Lake City, every client of Richie's I ever sent a gift to. It would be natural for the police to think I skipped town."

"Not if you keep popping in on everybody who was ever on Mr. Meyers' Rolodex."

"Oh. Right."

As always, I tissued off most of the eye shadow I'd just applied. Danny watched me, seemingly engrossed. I selected a respectable eyeliner. No one had ever observed me this intently. Sure, in twenty-five years, Richie, on his way to shower or get dressed, must have seen me put on makeup thousands of times. But he'd never found what I was doing interesting. He certainly never stopped and watched.

"Rosie?"

"Hmm?"

"Want a gun?"

The eyeliner pencil dropped from my fingers and made a dark-brown stripe in the sink. "Are you nuts?"

"I'm just asking."

"I'm an English teacher, for God's sake." Danny smiled. The kid had beautiful teeth. And to tell you the truth, the rest of him was beautiful too. I picked up the pencil and put my face close to the mirror—to be able to draw a thin line right along my lashes, and also to banish him from my peripheral vision. I didn't want to get all flustered and have him think I'd gone silly over him, a prospect too humiliating even to contemplate.

Danny made me uneasy. I couldn't figure out what his attention was all about. Kindness? Cruelty: behaving seductively to get a few laughs when the old broad—his *teacher*—made goo-goo eyes at him? Was it simple avarice, keeping a close watch on his fifty-thousand-buck reward? Hey, how about genuine sexual interest? How about empathy for a fellow outlaw?

"Me with a gun! Danny, if English teachers were armed, you'd be a dead man."

After the bologna-cheesecake festival at Fran's, I remained a spectator while Danny ate his lunch—prefabricated, microwaved macaroni and cheese, washed down with beer. Now it was my turn to watch him. Everything he did was stylish, from flipping open the tab on the can with his thumb to settling back on a chair and stretching out his legs. He didn't cross his legs at the ankles, the macho position suburban studs take. Instead, without herniating a disk, he managed to sit relaxed while at the same time thrusting up his hips, thus creating an enticing sheath of fabric—or maybe it was just a shadow—around his genitals. In short, Danny Reese was a knockout. If Richie had had his looks, his style, he would have broken my heart years before.

He began his second beer. "All that time, you really never had a clue he was cheating on you?"

"No."

Apparently, Danny did not buy my denial. "Big bullshit."

"Look, everybody has clues: A husband works late, but when you call him at the office he's not there. Or all of a sudden a husband who has the sensitivity of a cockroach becomes a big feminist:

Women can be smart! That really burns you, because you and your hundred and forty-five IQ have been married to him for twenty years. So yes, you pick up those clues—and if you've got any guts you force yourself to play detective. And you know what?"

"What?"

"The husbands who want to get caught get caught; they stick matchbooks from obscure motels in Fort Lee, New Jersey, into their pockets and ask their wives to take their pants to the cleaners. The ones like Richie? They get away with murder, if you'll pardon the expression. They don't charge dinners at romantic restaurants. They don't get phone calls they have to lie about. They make sure to have sex with you—passionate sex, loving sex—just often enough that your mind turns to mush. You think: What a husband! You're so ashamed you ever doubted him."

"You ever step out on him?"

"Never."

"Come on, Rosie."

I couldn't believe I was sitting in Danny Reese's apartment in Danny Reese's clothes having this kind of discussion with Danny Reese. "I'm not saying I wasn't tempted a couple of times." He wiggled his eyebrows in a Groucho Marx leer. "Okay," I conceded. "Once I actually shaved my legs so close I got down to the last layer of skin cells."

He clasped his hands behind his head. "And?"

"Nothing happened. The man was perfectly proper."

"Were you disappointed?"

"Yes, but relieved—I guess. He was an old beau from my high school days. His name was Tom."

I suppose I was hoping Danny would want to do

a little probing about Tom Driscoll. What he said was: "Forget old guys. You ever get a buzz on one of the kids in your class?"

"Not really." Danny did not appear convinced. "I'm not saying I didn't admire an occasional brain or body." That could happen to anybody. One semester, Cass, of all people, suddenly developed a consuming interest in the fortunes of the swim team. She made me go to practice with her. "You want me to say that all your teachers had mad crushes on you?"

"Yeah." He looked up at me. "Especially you."

I averted my eyes. "It doesn't happen that way. Besides, it's pointless."

"Why?"

"Because that sort of liaison is unethical." Any argument based on moral scruples was not one likely to be comprehensible to Danny, but I felt obliged to make it. "I'm not saying there isn't an occasional obsession, but women . . . We want something we know boys can't give us."

"Like what?"

"Strength." Danny opened his cuff, rolled up his sleeve, and flexed his bicep. Wow! But I said: "No. You know the kind of strength I'm talking about. And we want intensity too, not adolescent fixation. And love, I guess."

"You honestly loved your husband?"

"Of course I loved him." Loving Richie had been the central truth in my life. "Yes. I mean . . . It's complicated now. When someone betrays you like that, you're wounded . . . no, forget wounded. You're so badly hurt you're almost dead. So you know you *had* to have loved him, because how else could he have had the power to inflict such terrible damage?"

Danny reached for his beer and concentrated on squashing the beads of moisture with his thumb. He said: "I heard a 'but' in what you just said. You loved him, maybe still love him . . . *but*."

"No. I didn't say 'but.' " I stood: time to get back to work. Danny left the macaroni container and beer cans on the floor. "Okay," I conceded, as he followed me out the door. "Here's your 'but.' When the man you married turns out to be so different from the man you thought he was, you reexamine your whole life. The last few weeks before he was killed, I think I was starting to ask myself: Did I truly love Richie Meyers? Or did I just love a character with that name whom I created?"

We got to the NYU library on West Fourth without incident. Well, I did flinch as we passed a UPS deliveryman on Christopher Street. Danny threatened to shoot me up with heroin if I didn't stop cringing every time I saw a uniform; the postal worker stopping to shake a pebble out of his shoe and the six-foot kid in a jacket from an army-navy store were not out to get me. I was calling attention to myself. He made me turn around; the UPS man was eyeing me curiously.

In the library, we found an isolated carrel not far from the main reading room. Sharing a chair, we sat head-to-head, going through a stack of reference books. Danny seemed pretty impressed by the entries I showed him for Daddy Dearest, aka Nicholas Hickson. Who wouldn't be? Chief executive officer, Metropolitan Securities; graduate of Bowdoin; seven honorary LL.D.s, including one from Brown; trustee of Sloan-Kettering Hospital and the Museum of Modern Art; recipient of the Order of Merit, Italy; member of the Council on Foreign Relations; and the entry that would have killed Richie if the knife hadn't, Hickson's club memberships—Union, University, Century, Links, Knickerbocker.

"Not just your run-of-the-mill big shot," Danny said. He drew *Who's Who in America* onto his lap and, keeping his eyes on me as if nothing at all were going on beneath the table, ripped out Daddy Dearest's entry.

"Stop that!"

"Stop what?"

"You're mutilating a book!"

"Relax. I'm just borrowing a page. Now listen: Your husband might be considered a heavy hitter in some circles, but compared to this Hickson, he was minor league. Am I right? This guy is major power."

"But a married major power," I noted. "See? 'Married Abigail Wright, June 8, 1957.' Of course, 'married' is a green light for our Jessica."

"You think she wanted this Hickson guy? He's even older than your old man," he said, his thigh pressing against mine.

"If you were she," I responded, easing my leg away, "and you wanted to align yourself with money and power and position, would you be dying to marry Richie Meyers from Rego Park, Queens, when your alternative was Nicholas Charles Bromley Hickson from Darien and Manhattan?"

"What we've got to find out is what was going on with Hickson," Danny said. "He's some powerhouse.

Was Jessica a fast hump for him—or the real thing?"

"I vote for the real thing. You should have seen how protective he was of her."

"Your vote doesn't count, Rosie. You're wacko when it comes to her."

"I am not wacko." I closed the book on Hickson and went on to point out Carter Tillotson's entries in *Directory of Physicians* and the *American Medical Directory*. "He's my next-door neighbor."

"The gorgeous one's husband? I saw her when I was over for band practice; she was in the kitchen, cooking with you. Great face. Really nice body. But not hot."

"That's what Richie said. But her husband is the one who introduced Jessica to Richie. The missing piece is: How in God's name did Carter know Jessica?"

"Did he give her a face-lift or something?"

"Possibly. But all of Carter's noses turn up two degrees at the tip. And the woman's version of his chin is the bottom of a perfect oval. As far as I can tell, there's no feature on Jessica that has the Carter Tillotson label."

We went over the Carter-Jessica possibilities until Danny, who was not a big fan of speculation, announced: "Let's haul it, Rosie." He pulled me out of our chair, out of the reference room, over to a pay phone. Naturally, he didn't bother to check his pockets for a quarter; he punched in a credit card number I doubted was his and phoned Carter's office. No, the doctor was unavailable. In surgery? Yes, he was told.

"I'm calling from the University Club," Danny said, in an accent that sounded directly descended from

Governor Winthrop. "Miss Jessica Stevenson has applied for membership. She has given Dr. Tillotson's name as a reference. No, of course you cahn't speak for him, but he does have knowledge of her, does he not? Excellent. I shall ring back later this week. Thank you so much. . . . Oh, by the by," he said, suddenly wary, "was she a plastic surgery patient? Oh, good!" Then he added: "Thanks awfully."

" 'Thanks awfully'? That's overkill."

"Listen, Rosie, the babe thinks she was talking to the real thing, and 'thanks awfully' probably made her double-come—which she deserves because she told me Jessica *wasn't* a patient. *And* she told me that she was positive Dr. Tillotson would recommend Jessica, because—are you ready?—they were good friends."

I squeezed Danny's hand in thanks. He responded with a you're welcome in the form of a feathery kiss on my lips, just enough to reveal how warm his mouth could be. Maybe that was the casual kind of kiss college kids conferred on each other all the time. For just a second, though, it filled me with desire. I hadn't felt the touch of a man's mouth since June.

To cover up any detectable desire vibes, I got busy dialing Nicholas Hickson's office. Inspired by Danny, performing for him too, I suppose, I got Hickson's executive secretary and announced I was Ms. Mary Wollstonecraft, calling from the White House. Danny rewarded me with a huge grin. The secretary asked: "How may I help you?" I explained I was compiling a guest list. Although it was an awkward question, times being what they were, I was obliged to ask: was there still a Mrs. Hickson? "No," the secretary breathed. "Well, there is, but they're legally separated." I told her I wasn't sure if Mr. Hickson was being invited with a guest or not, but if she wouldn't mind, so we could begin Secret Service clearance . . . "Jessica Stevenson," the secretary said eagerly. "She's president of a company called Data Associates. Would you like her address?"

Although the library was fairly quiet, it was too public for me to hang out in too long. Also, it was getting close to one-thirty, the time I was due to call Cass. So we hurried over to Danny's office, which turned out to be a high orange leatherette stool at the bar in a small Chinese restaurant on Bleecker. The place was empty. Curtains were pulled closed across the window. While Danny checked at least a dozen messages written on the back of squares of pink paper that touted the previous week's specials, he sipped another beer and snacked on pitted olives from a metal container on the bar. I sat on a stool near the cash register and called Cass at school.

"You are alive!" she said.

"And well too. Except when I look ahead and see myself on line with a gray metal tray in the prison cafeteria; then I'm not so well."

"It might not be so bad. You could institute a reading program that will be hugely successful. Your life could become a movie of the week."

"I guess I wasn't looking on the bright side."

"Rosie, I wish you could resolve this nastiness so we could get on with our friendship."

"Me too. By the way, who's subbing for me?"

"An extremely young person who seems to know *David Copperfield* by way of a Saturday-morning cartoon adaptation." While Cass paused, I concentrated on spearing orange slices with a miniature paper parasol to keep from crying; I missed her so much. "Have you any notion when you will be coming back?"

"No."

"Oh."

"But I've learned a few things."

"I am all ears."

"Jessica came to Data Associates as an *enfant terrible* investment banker, remember? She made some terrific suggestions, and Richie decided to lure her away from her firm with a big salary and benefits. Except at that point, when they started working together, he wasn't one of the benefits."

"How do you know that?"

"From someone who worked there, who knew him fairly well. Anyway, Jessica stayed and put the company on a much faster track. First she gained Richie's trust. Then his love."

Cass sighed. "I wish God had created an interesting alternative to men. They never astonish, do they?"

"Speaking of men," I said, "listen to this: Jessica had a new boyfriend." I offered a synopsis of Nicholas Hickson's life. "Don't you think she would have gone for him over Richie?"

"Unquestionably."

I chewed on the toothpick handle of the parasol. "Let's dope this out. Jessica wants to find a way out of their engagement, but Richie senses something's up."

"How do we know that?"

"All of a sudden, after months of belligerence, he

backed down. Essentially, he agreed to give me everything I'd been asking for. More than that: everything my lawyer had been asking for."

"You were not bringing extraordinary pressure to bear?"

"No. You know that. I kept holding Honi back. I was still hoping Richie would change his mind, and I didn't want to seem too greedy. I actually wanted him to admire me. Can you believe how stupid I was?"

"Yes," she replied. "Well, in that case, it would seem the pressure on Richie did come from Jessica, not you."

"Right." The restaurant owner, a man with dramatic Rudolph Valentino hair, came over to the bar with a dish of dried noodles, set it before Danny, and gave him a snappy military salute. Danny saluted back, and the owner retreated into what I assumed was the kitchen. "The clock was ticking for Richie," I went on. "Jessica was going to choose between him and Nicholas Hickson—except how could there have been any doubt which one she'd choose? What I don't get is how come Jessica just didn't dump Richie."

"Richie Meyers himself was not the reason for her indecision," Cass said thoughtfully. "Her job was."

"Her job? So big deal, she gets fired. She goes to Metropolitan Securities and—"

"My dear, this Mr. Hickson is not, if you will pardon me, a nouveau-riche he-goat like your late, about-to-have-been-former husband. Mr. Hickson is, above all, classy and clearheaded. He might be mad for Jessica, but he is not so insanely in love as to be willing to offend his colleagues and stockholders by offering his lady friend—his prospective wife—a half-million-dollar position. Jessica surely knows this. But further, she understands that her position at Data Associates is unique."

"How is it unique?" I asked. Danny slid the dish of noodles down the bar to me. They looked too crunchy for a phone conversation.

"She works with a chief executive who is intelligent but not, shall we say, savvy in the ways of the international marketplace. She can bend Richie to her will. And Richie needed her. Not merely for emotional support. They had transformed the company together, and he would have been hard-pressed to run it without her."

Danny pulled out a brown envelope from a low shelf behind the bar and dumped the contents, Rhode Island driver's licenses, out before him. He held each one up to the neon light of a Miller Lite sign. Most of them were dropped, dismissively, back into the envelope. A few made it under the coin tray in the cash register drawer.

"Look at their business relationship from Jessica's perspective," Cass continued. "How many men are willing to cede that much power to a woman? Where else could she exercise her full range of talents? The woman was at a crossroads in her life." It was such a pleasure listening to Cass again, and such a help. Danny, who winked when I glanced at him, was canny. Cassandra Higbee was intelligent. "Listen to me, Rosie. Jessica was being forced to choose between a life she'd always wanted, the life Mr. Hickson could offer her—scads of money, social position—and her life's work."

"What about the sex with Richie?" I asked.

"I believe his talents meant a great deal more to you than to her. Perhaps she is one of those rare women who settle for nothing less than brilliant sex and, amazingly, always seem to find it; frankly, I regard them with awe and envy. More likely, what excites her is the ancient double whammy, wealth and power. But you are not asking yourself the crucial question."

"What is it?"

"*Why was Richie at your house?* Are you any closer to answering it now than you were when you climbed down that ladder?—the thought of which makes me quiver with horror."

"I know now his being there had nothing to do with me. The last thing in the world he wanted was me back in his life. No, he had to have been there because he was in a rush to marry her. So okay: what would he need that was in the house?"

"Certainly not a wedding suit," said Cass, who'd seen the walk-in closets stuffed with clothes he'd abandoned. "Cash?"

"I doubt it. Data Associates was never a cash business."

"What is left, then? Papers?"

"No. I looked to see if I could find what he came for. I couldn't find anything. He never kept much at home, and he took whatever there was when he left."

"How do you know?"

"I watched him pack up. I followed him from room to room, weeping, begging him not to go. God, was I pathetic."

"Rose, listen to me. You were never pathetic. The man was a rotter."

"Thank you."

"You are welcome. Now, try to recall: With you trailing after him, keening, is it possible he became rattled and overlooked something?"

"Like what?"

"Something that might be to your advantage in the divorce proceedings? Something that might be embarrassing or dangerous to him in business?"

"I think my crying probably did get to him. He grabbed all his stuff and got out in record time." I thought: Could I have missed something in my search? Could he have hidden something somewhere in the house? Whatever it was had to be important to lure him back. Admittedly, Richie was sexually daring. He'd been an entrepreneurial risk-taker. But he'd begun his career as an algebra teacher, not as first mate on a pirate ship; he was not adventurer enough to break into his old house on a lark.

I glanced at my watch. Cass had already missed five minutes of her eighth period AP English class. "Listen, I know your class is dying to discuss *Go Down, Moses,* but give me another two minutes."

"As long as you need."

"Guess who introduced Jessica to Richie?"

"Will I be amazed?"

"Yes. Carter."

"What?" she demanded, clearly amazed. "Carter Tillotson? How did he know her?"

"Not by doing a breast augmentation, that's for sure. Besides, I know she was never a patient."

"How can you be certain?"

"Trust me. I'm a good gumshoe. So the question is, could Carter have been carrying on—"

"How could he have met her?"

"He socializes with the entire Upper East Side of Manhattan, or the ninety percent of it with surgically altered body parts. You know how Stephanie is always getting annoyed that he fills up on canapés at cocktail parties and doesn't want to eat her stuffed quail at eleven at night. The question is, could Carter have had an affair with Jessica?"

"What would have prevented him from doing so?"

"Our friend Stephanie. His wife. He's a married man."

"Pish-posh. Have you ever believed that he's bobbing noses three or four nights a week?"

"He might have evening office hours."

"I am sure he does," Cass agreed. "But does Stephanie seem the genuinely happy wife of a busy doctor?"

"Cass, she's a woman who can spend half a day in the woods between our houses picking tiny pine cones so she can spray them gold to put in her potpourri at Christmas. How the hell would I know if someone like that is genuinely happy?"

"Well, I know. Stephanie has not been herself the last—let me think—the last year or so. She has been excessively cheery. In a white Anglo-Saxon Protestant, that is always a sign of a fairly severe depression. Think about it."

I thought. In the past year, Stephanie *had* been more nauseatingly chipper than ever, full of new enthusiasms—fashioning her pots-de-fleur, decorating cakes, taking up cross-country skiing. For a few months, she'd seemed almost manic, waking before five to pick flowers or knead dough before walking with us. Then, after a day filled with her usual frenetic activity, going on a five-mile run with her friend Mandy three or four nights a week before Carter came home around eleven to the exquisite dinner she had waiting. She'd slowed down a little in the last few months; no one, not even Stephanie, could keep up that pace. But had all the activity been a means of exhausting herself so she was numb to her own pain?

"What about her and Carter?" Cass asked. "You saw them together. Did they seem under a strain?"

"It's so hard to tell. They've always seemed like characters in a Coward play—superficial, although without the wit. They look great, they say the right things, but there doesn't seem to be much emotional content. And don't keep telling me it's because they're WASPs."

"It *is* because they are WASPs."

"Please. Shakespeare was a WASP. No, Stephanie and Carter seem to have something missing because there *is* something missing—in both of them. The question is: Is something wrong?"

"I think I will ask Stephanie to tea," Cass said. "Perhaps we can exchange girlish confidences about our husbands."

"Good." Passing up the dried noodles, I reached down the bar and took another slice of orange and, as an afterthought, two maraschino cherries. "One more thing," I told Cass. "Carter called Richie the day he was killed. It could just be coincidence, but maybe there was some business going on between the two of them. Or the three of them, if you add Jessica to the equation. I want to find out." The cherry was about a year and a half past its peak, but I was too far away from the cocktail napkins to spit it out. "By the way," I added, "have you seen my kids?"

"Of course. They came to dinner the night before last. Both displayed healthy appetites and made pleasant conversation. They neither dribbled nor spat. They remembered to say thank you as they left. You have been a good mother."

"Cass."

"What, Rosie?"

"You're too damn blithe. I know something's wrong."

"Perhaps there is," she said softly. My stomach contracted into a knot. "It seems that your nemesis, Sergeant Gevinski, has developed a new theory."

"What is it?"

"That your part in this business—your fingerprints on the knife, your fleeing—was your way of drawing attention away from the real murderer."

"And who is that supposed to be?"

"Alexander," Cass said, almost in a whisper.

"What?" I must have screamed, because Danny turned to stare at me.

"This Gevinski knows there was bad blood between Alex and Richie. Alex has a history of truancy, drinking, drugs, emotional problems."

"That makes him sound so goddamn pathological! He's not. He's just a normal, screwed-up rich kid."

"Apparently, the sergeant has interviewed several people who will vouch for Alex being terribly angry about Richie's leaving you. And then . . . "

"Don't protect me, Cass."

"It seems that once Richie cut off Alex's allowance, Alex was close to broke. The life of a future rock-and-roll legend is not an easy one. Sergeant Gevinski suggests Alex was fearful that Jessica would get her hands on Richie's money and that the temporary,

punitive financial cutoff would become permanent—
especially if she and Richie had a child."

"But Alex was up in New Hampshire when it
happened."

"Alex claims to have been in New Hampshire. The
sergeant believes he was in New York. Alex does
concede he was alone, wandering, composing a new
song in his head, the night of the murder. And he
admits he did not take the shuttle from Boston to
New York as he originally said he did; he claims he
hitchhiked but had you reimburse him for plane fare.
All he remembers about the ride was that the driver
was a man with a beard, in some sort of a sports car.
In other words, there is no tangible proof Alex was
in New Hampshire when Richie was killed."

That a son would murder his father for money? In
life as in fiction, such murders have been committed.
I knew that.

But, damn it, not by my son Alex!

Fourteen

"Get the hell out of my way!" I shouted at Danny, who was blocking the door. "I mean it!"

"Chill," Danny said, in a tone so placid it made me want to scream.

The restaurant owner hustled out from the kitchen. "Chill!" he repeated, except he had a loud voice and an old-country accent.

"Stay out of this!" I bellowed. "Both of you!"

Danny took a microsecond to pass the owner

some subtle signal known only to co-conspirators in the fake-ID underworld. The owner scooted behind Danny, locked the door, pocketed the key, and returned to the kitchen, although not before passing me and grunting a brief "Hah!" of triumph.

"You're not going back to Long Island," Danny told me.

"I am. Get him to open the door. *Now*."

Okay, so maybe I sounded a bit schoolmarmish. Still, I didn't think it was necessary for him to say: "Fuck off, Rosie."

"You fuck off, you little stinkpot. Do you think I'm going to let my kid take the rap for a crime he didn't commit?"

"Calm down for a minute . . . " He grasped my wrist. I yanked it away. "Okay, for half a minute. Don't you get what Gevinski's up to? This is a trap. I thought you were smart."

"I am smart."

"No, because if you were, you'd know you're doing just what this turd wants you to do: turn yourself in. Think about it." With his hand between my shoulder blades, he propelled me away from the front door, toward a large round table in the rear. Behind it was a black six-paneled screen covered with trees, mountains, birds, deer, elderly scholars, and Chinese characters, a garish, peaceful universe. "Sit," he commanded me. "Listen: Gevinski's got zero to nail Alex with."

"Alex lied about coming down from Boston by plane."

"Holy shit!" Danny said. "That'll definitely put him on death row." I managed a semismile. "Let me give you the script of what happened. Besides the hundred-to-one odds Gevinski's got your phone tapped, he's probably been having Alex and Ben followed in hopes that they'll lead him to you. It doesn't happen. *But,* when the guys go to Dr. Higbee's house for dinner, a light bulb goes on in his pea brain that you and her —"

" 'You and she.' "

"—are big-ass buddies." Yesterday's soy sauce formed a Rorschach blot on the tablecloth, a fleur-de-lis or an amputee starfish. "So he pays her a visit, pretending to want some information. He lets it drop that he thinks the real killer is Alex. He knows the best way to grind your gears is to threaten your kid; you'll be back in Shorehaven on the next train, begging him to arrest you." I didn't know I was biting my nails until Danny reached across the table and drew my hand from my mouth. "Look at it another way: Alex did a few drugs in his day, maybe shoplifted a little in junior high. Amateur stuff. But still, he's a guy who's got a certain sensitivity when it comes to cops. Don't you think he'd have sensed it if this Gevinski was crawling up his ass? Don't you think he would have mentioned it to me when we talked?"

"If Gevinski was crafty enough, Alex would never know."

"Crafty? Is he crafty trying to pin it on you? Is that an exercise in police genius? Or is it a lazy cop's easy way out?"

Just before twilight, when the first dinner customers banged on the door to be let in, the owner sent us off with a Chinese banquet in a shopping bag. Out on the street, Danny took my hand. I didn't pull it away. We passed modest brownstones, a bookstore, a shop that sold used records. Passersby glanced at me in the way passersby do, but no one blinked, much less froze with an "Aha!" of recognition. We stopped off at the dry cleaner and the laundromat. "Seek English Teacher in Husband's Slaying" seemed to be yesterday's news.

We strolled into a stiff breeze, toward the river. Neighborhood people—Italian families, NYU kids, poets, artists, academics, gay men, lesbians—hardly took notice of a forty-seven-year-old woman holding hands with a twenty-two-year-old boy. An elderly woman in jeans and a denim work shirt sat on a stoop with her cocker spaniel. The dog nodded; the woman concentrated on scraping pigeon droppings off the top step and didn't even notice us in the dwindling light. The Village was growing on me, its casualness and urbanity, its diversity and tolerance, its filth and elegance, its quaintness and cool. Shorehaven, in contrast, seemed merely exceedingly nice, a pale materialization of an Eisenhower-era dream.

Back in the apartment, I put steamed dumplings and General Tso's chicken in the refrigerator. For the next couple of hours, Danny and I worked on a list of all important people in Richie's life, arranging them in order of how crucial it was for me to interview them. Then we debated how to get to them without attracting the attention of undesirables—i.e., the police.

It was so cozy. Danny microwaved dinner. I washed some dubious-looking plates he swore he'd washed, put the clean quilt on the floor in front of the couch, and set up on it. When I returned to the kitchen to look in the cabinets and see if I could find anything resembling wineglasses, Danny came up behind me. He lifted my hair and kissed the back of my neck. This was no routine kiss; this took a very long time. My spine melted. Finally I was able to say "Don't."

"Why not?" he breathed onto my neck.

"I don't know. Because I don't understand what you want."

"I want you."

It is very difficult to say "Don't" to a young, handsome, and virile green-eyed male who, with exquisite slowness, is snaking his tongue from the back of your neck up and around and, finally, into your ear when your entire being—except for two or three rational neurons—is shouting: Fabulous! Wonderful! Gimme more! Even more difficult when his arms encircle you and his body presses against your back.

I tried to cool myself down. I told myself the attraction had less to do with my lusty, Semitic earthiness than with the fact that the kid had a couple of details to resolve in the Oedipal department. His hands slid down between my thighs. I told myself: This is plainly a Fuck the Establishment gesture.

Neither technique worked. I turned to face him and reached around him, cupping his perfect, tight ass. I kissed him. It was lovely. So I made myself meditate on how promiscuous he must be. I thought about all the young women—and perhaps young men as well—who dropped by to discuss obtaining proof of age and wound up on the not-so-clean sheets of Danny's unmade bed. On the other hand, I remembered that when I'd searched his room, there had been a box of condoms in his sock drawer. I kissed him once more. Then I allowed myself the pleasure of rubbing and squeezing the majestic bulge beneath his stylish black pants.

We left a trail of shirts and slacks on the way to his bed. Monogamy may have its limits, but with an ingenious and ardent partner like Richie, who showed me the delight of making love not only in the security of the marriage bed, but on a blanket spread for a picnic on the shores of Saranac Lake, in a seedy motel off the Expressway that offered X-rated movies *and* a complimentary continental breakfast, in the Queens-Midtown tunnel during a particularly onerous rush hour, I was not merely uninhibited. I was accomplished. After all those years, I had learned more than enough to knock the kid's socks off. And if I'd had socks, Danny would have blown them away with his raw energy.

"Rosie!"

"Danny."

"Fantastic!" he said later. "The best!"

"I'll show you something better."

And I did.

After the final fortune cookie, it was time to call number one on the list, Hojo, to find out if she was home—and if Tom was too. "He travels a lot," I explained. "Going to board meetings. Checking out new companies. So I have a fair chance of finding her alone."

"There's a shot she'll know your voice. And think about this, Rosie. She was great buddies with Mr.

Meyers. The cops could have warned her that you're doing a lot of sneaky shit around town. Let me do it." As Danny picked up the phone, he asked: "She's the social-climbing puker?" I nodded. "Mrs. Driscoll, please," he said. "Oh. Is this her husband?" Danny asked. Tom was on the phone; I felt my cheeks flush. "This is Chip at Park Avenue Wines," he said. "We're closing, but that case of champagne Mrs. Driscoll asked me about just came in. Would it be all right if I sent it over tomorrow?" He covered the mouthpiece with his hand. "She's away, at a spa."

I thought so fast I didn't even have time to hyper-ventilate. "Get the doorman's name," I whispered into his free ear. "You'll deliver."

"I could give the doorman a call before I send my delivery boy over, Mr. Driscoll. That way the champagne will be waiting for Mrs. Driscoll when she comes home. Thanks. Do you have a number where I can reach the doorman? And his name?"

After he hung up, I said, "I can't believe he gave you all that information."

"Why not? Number one, I'm *incredibly* credible. That's what my philosophy professor said after I tried to talk my way out of having to hand in a textual exegesis on Socrates. It's the secret of my success—except when it comes to the Philosophy Department. And number two, Driscoll sounded really fogged out. I couldn't tell if he was fucking or if I woke him up."

You woke him up, I decided silently. To rein-force my decision, I tried to imagine Tom asleep, a lock of dark hair, etched with silver, whorling on the pillow.

All of a sudden I was so weary I could have cried,

except I didn't even have the strength to squeeze out tears. I took Danny's hand and explained I would rather not have any surprise visits during the night. I could tell I'd knocked him out; he didn't put up much of an argument.

I slept better than I had since the night of Richie's murder, in large part because I was starting to accept the unlikelihood of Danny's turning me in to the cops. He liked me, of course, but it wasn't his sentiment that comforted me. It was the knowledge that my game of cops and robbers was far more exciting than his own and he would be loath to give it up.

I had a nightmare and woke around six, but I was unable to recollect what had caused my heart to pound in terror.

I sensed that I was getting near the end of my rope. I needed help. At seven-thirty, I called my lawyer, Vinnie Carosella. He agreed to meet me in Washington Square Park late in the afternoon. At ten, ten-thirty, and eleven I called the Driscoll apartment, just to make sure Tom wasn't there. Then I phoned the doorman. Please let this work, I prayed. "John," I said, "this is Mrs. Driscoll." I tried for the Hojo mix of ennui, cigarettes, and disdain. "I'm at the spa in Arizona."

"Yes, Mrs. Driscoll." I'd done it! I flashed a Churchillian V for victory to Danny; he assumed I was making a late-sixties peace signal and offered one in return.

"My friend Mrs. Peterson is flying out today to meet me," I told the doorman. "I asked her to pick up a few of my things. You'll let her in?"

"Yes, Mrs. Driscoll."

There was a risk, I acknowledged to myself, as I emerged from the subway at Fifth Avenue and Sixtieth and walked uptown, past people who actually looked like people in *Vogue*. The risk was that Tom had been neither sleeping nor philandering but had been alert to Danny's doorman scam, and the instant I arrived at his building and introduced myself to John, he'd give some prearranged signal and fifty cops would surround me.

But John handed me the key without so much as a glance at my face. When I told him I might be a while, since I had no idea where Mrs. Driscoll kept her things, he shrugged. Is the maid in today, John? I asked offhandedly. Maybe she can help me. The doorman shook his head and accompanied me to the elevator.

The elevator man, a merrier soul, brought me upstairs with a wink and a smile. Once he'd descended, I pulled out Danny's gloves from under my waistband and put them on.

The apartment was cooler than the hallway, and the chilly air made me aware of the sweat coursing down the sides of my face. I wiped off my forehead. Even through the thick wool of the glove, I felt a pulse in my temple thumping much too fast.

It took a minute of Inhale ("I am . . . "), Exhale (". . . relaxed") before I could collect myself enough to look around. The Driscolls' apartment took up an entire floor of the building. I'd been there twice with Richie and recollected that it had the chichi European atmosphere of a place designed not so much to be lived in as to be photographed. I couldn't believe that the Tom Driscoll I'd known, no matter how rich and stuffy he'd become, would agree to reside in such high style. The floors were covered with sisal, the stiff brown stuff they use for making rope, something no human being in bare feet would ever want to walk over. The windows were shaded by wooden venetian blinds, filling the huge living room with a wintry yellow light. Hojo had jammed the place with an awe-inspiring amount of expensive furniture.

Since the last time I'd been there—for a dinner that on the invitation had been described as "festive," a code word for almost-but-not-quite-black-tie, something I hadn't known until I arrived, over-dressed, in glaring, festive red taffeta—she seemed to have been bidding successfully at too many antiques auctions. In addition to her silver cigarette boxes and miniature marble busts of bald composers, she'd cornered the market in still more collections of useless objects. Antique pens. Crystal inkwells. Balls—marble, crystal, metal, wood—on wood stands. Small, exquisite china pots holding plants that looked as exquisitely cultivated as the specimens Stephanie and her garden club friends would grow; nestled among the gleaming leaves were small glass vials that held a single orchid each.

I checked out the bedroom first. Actually, the closet. Pure curiosity, but I was mesmerized by the display of self-indulgence: a warehouse of clothes, furs, handbags, shoes, belts, scarves, crammed together in a closet that was actually a separate room—a room the size of a studio apartment. Three gray skirts, two still with price tags, were on the floor. An ivory silk blouse, ripped from its dry cleaner's plastic bag but still on its hanger, had been tossed on top of them.

It didn't surprise me that the walls in the bedroom were upholstered in silk. The bed itself was a giant iron thing strewn with lacy pillows and draped with enough mosquito netting to protect the entire southern hemisphere from malaria. The skirted table on the side of the bed had a small silver tray filled with body cream, hand cream, throat cream, and eye cream. Not a book in sight. Not a sign of a masculine presence anywhere.

That was because the masculine presence had his own room down the hall. I stayed only long enough to ascertain that Tom slept in a mahogany four-poster bed, that he was reading a thick book about airline deregulation in the eighties, and, after a quick look-see in his tall chest of drawers, that sometime between senior year of high school and the present, he had switched from briefs to boxer shorts.

There were no kids' rooms, because Hojo and Tom had none. Hojo had confided to Richie that Tom was sterile, but by the time they'd both been through all the medical tests and discovered it, they no longer had any desire for children.

Hojo carried on the business of her life in an overdecorated office, from a desk Louis XIV himself might have thought too fussy. The drawers were chock-full of invitations to dinner parties and benefits. There were a few yellow Post-it notes: "Dartmouth 4/25," "Cancer 10/11." I felt a shiver of recognition: Tom's handwriting. I couldn't believe how familiar it looked. I hadn't seen it since we'd traded notebooks when we studied Latin together. But I didn't find a calendar; I guessed it was with Hojo at the spa.

However, the history of Hojo's social life was amazingly intact, as if, momentarily, she anticipated an invitation to donate her papers to the Smithsonian. Behind a small couch, a gilded table was piled with large boxes—ivory, mother-of-pearl, wood, lapis, malachite—one for each year since 1983, filled with clipped-together Filofax calendar pages, invitations, bread-and-butter notes, and laminated clippings from the occasional society column in which her name appeared.

I looked at my watch, then looked again. I couldn't believe only five minutes had passed. I lifted the bottom desk drawer onto my lap. Bingo! A note from Jessica, dated May 14. A month before Richie had told me he was leaving me. "Darling Joan, How can I thank you? Dinner was marvelous and so were you. I can't tell you how much your supportiveness means to both of us during this trying time. Fondly, Jessica." Richie had never been one to live dangerously. He would never flaunt an affair; if Hojo was having clandestine dinners with the happy couple, then Richie really must have trusted her.

I held it while I examined the pictures on the desk. In frames more suited to Caravaggios than snapshots, there were predictable pictures of over-dressed women on benefit committees, their too-coiffed heads so huge compared with their starved bodies that they appeared extraterrestrial. But there was also Hojo with Tom at some ski resort, smiling into the camera. I looked closer to see if the smiles were phony, but the picture was slightly out of focus. There was Hojo with three other stick-armed women in sleeveless dresses with palm trees in the background in what may have been Palm Beach or, for all I knew, Marrakech. Another picture of Hojo with an older woman, either her mother or some friend who had also been done by Carter and, thus, had the same face. There were framed snapshots from the summer: Hojo with Richie at a party at an oceanfront house; Hojo with Richie and Jessica on a dock—there were sailboats in the background, and Jessica was wearing shorts.

Seven minutes. I put Jessica's note back in the drawer. My mouth was so dry I couldn't swallow. What if Hojo called Tom and he said: By the way, your case of champagne is coming today. Or what if he routinely came home midday for a fresh pair of boxer shorts?

I flipped through the clipped calendar pages. A fair number of "Call So-and-so" at 516 numbers, the area code for Long Island, but most of them must have been friends in the Hamptons. There was one Shorehaven number written down the Wednesday after Labor Day. I didn't even have to look at the name: Tillotson. But considering the quantity of surgical alterations Hojo had sustained (including her most recent, the spectacular knockers I'd spotted at Richie's funeral), the entry didn't surprise me.

According to the calendar, Hojo had lunch with Richie at least once every two or three weeks. But there were also dinners: "Rick Cote Basque 8:00" in January. And "Rick, etc. Bouley" in February. I didn't get a French dinner in January. And I definitely wasn't et cetera in February.

But wait a second: The day Richie told me he was leaving, he had poured out his heart about his love affair. So I knew et cetera couldn't be Jessica Stevenson. Because Richie and Jessica had fallen in love—deeply, profoundly in love, as he'd told me in an unsuccessful effort to quell my hysterical pleas for him to stay—just two months before he decided to move out. It happened at a Data Associates corporate retreat in a resort near Santa Fe. "I *asked* you to come with me," he'd said, demonstrating how he'd given me every chance, "but you said you couldn't take time off from school. Remember?"

Twelve minutes. I stuffed the calendar pages into my pocket. For good measure, I snitched the previous four years of Hojo's life as well and dumped them into a lizard tote bag I took from her closet. Done! I closed the front door, removed Danny Reese's smelly gloves, and took the elevator back down to the lobby, where I handed the doorman a twenty-dollar bill. "Thanks a lot, John." He was very surprised.

He was even more surprised when, a minute later, I called him from a pay phone near Madison Avenue. "This is the woman who just gave you twenty dollars," I said.

"Wha'?"

"Listen closely. Mrs. Driscoll did not call you to give me permission to go into her apartment. I called you and imitated her."

"Huh?"

"'John, this is Mrs. Driscoll.'"

"Oh, Christ!"

"I was only looking around up there. I didn't take anything, so there's no need to tell anyone that you let in Mrs. Driscoll's friend. That would get you in big trouble, and I wouldn't want that. Goodbye."

What the hell had I gained from this foray except a social climber's chronicle of a meaningless life? How I envied Hojo her whiter-than-white, pillow-strewn bed. I wanted to go back upstairs, lie down, luxuriate in sweet-smelling sheets, sleep. No, in truth, what I really envied Hojo was her husband. I didn't want to believe that sometime in the last thirty years the real Tom Driscoll had died and left his soulless body in boxer shorts in that solitary bedroom.

On my way back downtown, the rhythmic clacking of the subway, the gentle jolting I'd known since childhood, comforted me.

Jessica had Nicholas Hickson to comfort her and, before him, Richie and maybe Carter. I closed my eyes. Richie: What a lover he had been! He had grace, imagination, and a first-class dirty mind. And Jessica had grabbed him. But not only Jessica: I remembered Fran Gundersen's smirk. And I'd never had a clue. All right, I'd never had a clue I'd followed up on. But who the hell was the et cetera in Hojo's calendar? Was it possible she could have been Mandy, Stephanie's friend? A whole damn borough of chic, anonymous Manhattan women available, and Richie picks someone from Shorehaven! Had there been others? Did it really matter? And even if it did, how could I ever find out?

"*Fran* told you Richie was having an affair with someone else—before Jessica?" Mitchell Gruen was snickering. Although it was early in the afternoon, his grizzled hair was still tousled from sleep. He was wearing a faded, shrunken sweatsuit, which, for good reason, looked as if it had been slept in.

"You don't think Fran would know?" I asked.

Mitch padded across the floor, past his computers, to his galley of a kitchen. He put a red bowl on the red Formica counter and poured in Lucky Charms. He sniffed a container of milk, thought better of it, and returned, feeding himself cereal with his fingers. "Don't you get it, Rosie? It was Fran."

"What was Fran?"

"The affair before Jessica."

"Oh, come on!"

He seemed annoyed at my pique. "Richie was doing it with Fran for *years*." Suddenly I couldn't respond, because my heart knew that what he said was the truth. "Fran was beauti-ful," he said.

"No she wasn't," I managed to say. If, by some miracle, Richie had come back to life at that moment, I would have taken a knife and stabbed him to death.

"Yes, she was beauti-ful—at the beginning. A big, beauti-ful broad. Richie set her up—you know—like a sugar daddy."

"He told you that?"

"Are you crazy? No. She did. But she was living in a dream world, Fran was. She should've known the score. For their fifth anniversary, you know what he did? He paid off the mortgage on a house she had in Brooklyn. Of course, she expected something more, in the line of an engagement ring. She came into my office, blubbering, begging me to talk to him."

"Did you?"

"You *are* crazy! I don't mess with that kind of

thing. I was having my own problems with Richie anyhow."

I waited to throw up, or to weep. Nothing happened. So I tried to calculate the chronology of Richie's adultery. First Fran, for years. "When did it end with her?" I demanded. "When Jessica came to work there?"

"No. Fran and Richie were still going at it when Richie threw me out."

But assuming Richie had thrown over Fran around the time he'd fired her (which, I felt, had to be a fairly safe assumption), there had been time for a breather. Or for another affair, sandwiched in between Fran and Jessica.

But it was just at that time, the first part of the year, when I'd started thinking our life together was getting better. Richie was acting more comfortable with his success. It seemed like the old days. For a few months, he stopped calling to tell me he was taking a hotel room for the night because he was too exhausted to drive home. Instead of dragging himself in around one, he'd be home by nine or ten. We'd sit on the couch in his den, his head in my lap, and we'd watch TV or talk. Look at us. An old married couple, he'd said once. Between Fran and Jessica.

But could there have been a third affair at that time? Well, it would explain why Richie tossed Fran. She could not be isolated from hurtful knowledge the way I could, tucked away with my own career, my own life in Shorehaven. Fran would have had to go because she was too close; Richie could not carry on another liaison under his personal secretary's personal gaze. Also, to give him credit, for an adulterous, libidinous shit, Richie was fairly monogamous. Before Jessica, we had enjoyed a glorious sex life. Even after, it never disappointed entirely. The night of our silver anniversary party, for example, we'd begun on the bed, moved to a chair, and wound up on the floor. If he'd been giving Fran even a tenth of what he gave me, he couldn't have taken on a third woman without risking death by coronary. He would have gotten rid of Fran before going—if he did—to the mystery woman.

Who the hell was Mandy?

I thought about what he'd given Fran. A house. Expensive furniture. And, I bet, the gorgeous landscapes on her walls. My gut told me they were the real thing, and I had a pretty good gut. Fran hadn't been a mink and rubies kind of dame.

Maybe the name Mandy was just a coincidence.

Or maybe the Mandy whom Fran had wondered about *was* Mandy the running lawyer, but she was doing some legitimate work for Data Associates.

"Time for you to go now!" Mitch sang out. "I have to work."

"Access Jessica's calendar for me. Then I'll leave."

"You did this to me the last time, Rosie!"

"And you let me back in, Mitch. You know why? Deep down you really want to help me."

"I do not," he huffed.

But he padded over to one of his small computers and, after less than a minute, asked: "What do you want to know?"

"The day Richie was killed: Where was Jessica?"

He tapped a few keys, then cursored down a column. "Morning, she made lots of calls from the office. You want to know who to?"

"Later."

"She had an eleven-thirty meeting in her office with Liz, the assistant general counsel."

"And then?"

"Twelve-thirty. It says 'Nails.' And after that, a two o'clock meeting at Metropolitan Securities."

"With Nicholas Hickson?"

Mitch spun around, his mouth twisted in annoyance. "If you knew that, Rosie, why did you bother me?"

Fifteen

Vinnie Carosella had soulful brown eyes. "You don't have the money for my retainer," he said, as I sat beside him on the park bench in Washington Square Park.

"Hello, Vinnie," I responded.

"Nice to meet you, Rosie."

"How do you know I don't have the money?"

"I heard from one of my police pals. You forgot your pocketbook—at the lady who used to do PR for your husband. I guess you were in a hurry when you left."

"I guess I was."

"Hey, it happens. And one of my other pals, in the D.A.'s office: he tells me they've frozen your assets." Vinnie Carosella wore magnificently polished black tassel loafers. He was as I'd remembered him from TV. Spectacles made his intelligent face appear intellectual. He was closer to sixty than fifty, but without a wrinkle, or even a laugh line: a dermatologist's dream face. The only feature at odds with his baby smoothness were large, weathered ears that looked as if they'd been bequeathed to him by Lyndon Johnson. "We have a little problem," he said. "I can apply to lift the freeze to pay for legal fees, but I have to produce you. You want to be produced?"

"Not yet."

"I was afraid you'd say that," Vinnie said. Skaters whizzed by on Rollerblades, swirling to music they alone could hear. "You know, I shouldn't even be here, what with you taking a powder. They could get me for harboring a fugitive. But even an old poop like me gets curious every now and then. I had to meet you. Our secret."

"Our secret," I agreed. "But if you knew I didn't have the money, how come you came?"

"Beats me. I like your story, I guess. It intrigues me. I'm a sucker for a good story."

"Do you believe it?"

"Not yet." He must have seen my face collapse, because he added: "It has a certain charm. Elsewise I wouldn't be risking a run-in with the powers that be, would I?"

"All this trust for no money."

"Oh, there's money floating around. Sooner or later, someone will pay me. You, one of your kids. Can you get word to them?" I nodded. "Let them know I'm representing you and that I'd feel better if I had a ten-thousand-dollar retainer." He patted my hand. "Don't take offense, Rosie. Criminal lawyers get paid up front."

"No offense taken." Down the path, at least ten dogs and their owners trotted back and forth behind a chain-link fence in a dog run. Just before Richie was killed, I'd been thinking about getting another dog.

I was pining for normality. For a dog. For a change of underwear, so I wouldn't have to contemplate washing my things at night and putting on a damp bra in the morning. For my students. For time to read. But most of all for a dog, who would bark with dumb delight every day when I came home from school.

I turned away from a particularly wonderful basset hound to discover Vinnie staring at me. "Amazing," he said. "I saw your picture in the paper, on TV, but until you sat down right beside me, I didn't notice you. You're doing something right."

I pushed up the sleeves of one of Danny's black sweaters. "I'm invisible. No one notices middle-aged women."

"Stop it. You're a good looker. Prettier than your pictures." It was a fine compliment, because it was offered as fact and not flirtation. He reached into the inside pocket of his camel-hair topcoat and removed what looked like a three- or four-page business letter. He handed it to me. "Autopsy report. From a pal at the medical examiner's."

I started to skim. "The cause of death was found to be: Exsanguination due to stab wound to abdominal aorta." I made myself read on, but the present-tense narrative on the following page did me in: "The deceased is admitted to the autopsy room in a morgue wrap. A nasogastric tube is in place, four EKG electrodes are present on the chest, bilateral chest drain tubes are present. . . ."

I handed it back to Vinnie. "I can't. Will you tell me about it?"

"Very cut-and-dried. Oh, jeez, no pun intended. Basically, the pathologist said what pathologists always say: If he wasn't dead, he'd be in great shape. Just the one wound, but it did the trick."

"Any clue whether it was made by a man or woman?"

"Can't tell. Very sharp knife, struck downward with a fair amount of force. Clean wound. Sorry. Wish I could offer you more to go on."

I told him all about Jessica and Nicholas Hickson. Vinnie said his best guess was that Hickson's firm was underwriting the offering of Data Associates stock. Conceivably, Jessica and Nicholas might have been plotting to violate a few SEC regulations: have their friends buy up blocks of the stock, or stack the board of directors so they could force Richie out. He thought it unlikely, but if true, Jessica would have less, not more, of a motive for murder. She could simply give him the heave-ho and he'd be out of her life.

"Have you been able to get any of the lab reports?" I asked.

"Not yet. They're not all in, and they're hard to pry out of official hands. I'm working on it. Sooner or later I'll probably get lucky. But don't hold your breath."

"I can't stop picturing how it was when I found Richie—"

"You shouldn't," he cut me off. "Too upsetting."

"Vinnie, I have to. I keep thinking maybe I saw something the police didn't."

"Maybe." He crossed his legs, his arms, and sat back on the bench with his head tilted upward as if he were on the Coney Island boardwalk on a bright July day. "I'm listening."

"There was dirt in the treads of Richie's sneakers, especially the left one. And there was an irregular path of dirt from the kitchen door to his sneaker. Right? With me so far?"

"I'm with you, Rosie."

"The next morning, I walked over to my next-door neighbor's."

"Why did you leave the house?"

"I had to get out. And I needed comfort. My neighbor isn't the type to smother anyone with affection, but she's so sensible and solid. A really decent person. Anyway, on my way over I passed Richie's car. Now picture this: it was fairly well hidden behind a line of trees, although if someone had been driving by at night, they could have seen the reflector light on the side bumper toward the rear of the car. The way it's parked, though, you really can't see the car itself. But the driver's door is only a few steps from the road."

Vinnie put both feet firmly on the ground. "Keep going."

"First of all, it hadn't rained for a while, so even if Richie had taken another step or two into the woods—to relieve himself or whatever—there was no reason for huge amounts of dirt to stick to his sneakers. The only place it stays muddy is all the way into the woods, where the trees are so thick there's hardly any sunlight. But even if it had been muddy, why weren't there bits of dirt on the road between the car and the house? I swear I didn't notice any, and I was extremely keyed up, very alert. How come the dirt makes its first appearance inside my kitchen door?"

He said slowly: "I don't know."

"Also, the dirt was pushed into the treads of the sneakers. But the rest of the shoes were clean."

"What are you saying?"

"I'm saying that there's a good chance Richie didn't go into the woods, that instead he did just what you'd expect: opened his car door, walked a few steps over dirt covered with dry leaves. Then he went along the road until he came to the drive that leads up to our house. Vinnie, it makes sense that he walked on the road. First of all, Shorehaven Estates is so damned old-money elegant: Street lights are considered vulgar. The only light at night comes from the moon—or a flashlight. By the way, did they give you a final list of his personal effects? I don't remember seeing a flashlight on it."

"No flashlight. Clothes, keys, watch, wallet with the usual credit cards and cash. Pretty much what the cops told you."

"Okay, so listen. Richie walked up the drive—it's gravel, not dirt—then continued past the front entrance, around to the kitchen. I doubt if he'd come in the front door, because that was closer to our— my bedroom. He came in through the kitchen; turned off the alarm and came in."

"He had a key?"

"I never changed the lock," I admitted.

"Hoping he'd come back?"

"Yes." I was so relieved he understood. "My matrimonial lawyer insisted I change the alarm, which I didn't. She didn't say anything about locks. I guess she assumed I had the sense to change them. Her mistake. I was in such terrible shape all summer. And even after, it took all the energy I had to get out of bed and get dressed for school. I couldn't deal with alarms."

"What about the lights outside the house? Could he have seen enough that way to get through the woods?"

"No. I always turn off the floodlights before I go to sleep. And Vinnie, think about this: I was alone with his body for five, ten minutes—I don't know how long—until the police came. Wouldn't I have noticed if his clothes looked as if he'd cut through the woods? But there was no need to; he knew he could march right up the drive and I never would have seen him. He also knew what even a sophisticated crook wouldn't know: that our alarm system didn't have a motion detector—you know, to sense if someone is coming up the drive. We installed one, but the kids and the dog and the raccoons kept setting it off."

"All right. If Richie didn't get dirt on his shoes coming through the woods," Vinnie asked, "how did it find its way onto them?"

"Before I answer that, ask yourself this: If I was the one who killed him, why would there be dirt on our floor?" He massaged his chin. "Let me tell you what I think. Someone was with Richie—or more likely, someone followed him to the house. That someone either went through the woods—the way I did on the night I took a powder—or stood way back from the house, beyond the lawn, a few feet into the trees, in a muddy patch, and watched him in the house."

"But you said there were no floodlights. And you had to turn on a light when you got to the kitchen."

"I did. But Richie *must* have turned the lights on. Because he didn't have a flashlight. Right? And he had to see whatever it was he was looking for. Also, the killer needed the light to see the knife—and Richie. There weren't a lot of stab wounds, were there? No, just one that was right in the middle, right on the money."

"Go on," Vinnie said.

"Let's get back to the dirt. Let's say the killer tracked it in. *After* the murder, he, she, whoever— let's make it he, for argument's sake—noticed the dirt on the floor. What a shock! But he's too cool to panic and too smart to do anything grossly amateurish, like try to sweep it up; maybe he'd know the police would find traces and would be doubly suspicious if it looked as if someone had cleaned up. So he went back outside, got some dirt—probably from right near the car—and pressed it onto the bottom of Richie's sneakers. And most likely, he kicked around the dirt on the floor, so the footprints he made wouldn't show. That way, it looks as though Richie was the only one to track in the dirt. And if he came in by himself, who could have killed him? Only someone inside the house. Me."

"Who would do such a thing to you?"

"Are you kidding? Do you think anyone who

would commit murder would have scruples about implicating me? No: he'd be thrilled there was a live-in patsy to get him off the hook."

"Do you have any sense as to whether the killer was male or female?"

"I wish I knew. Richie didn't do as well with men as he did with women. No really close male friends. He was a good enough father, but not one who relished the company of his sons. I'd say it was a woman—*except* Richie might have done something in business, or to a woman, that got some man very, very angry."

"Any candidates yet? Besides the girlfriend." I shook my head. Over at the dog run, the basset hound and its owner, a genial, broad-shouldered kid, an Asian version of Ben, jogged out the gate and up the path; the low-slung dog was so filled with delight with the kid's company that it kept trying to leap into the air. "You know, Rosie," Vinnie said quietly, "anyone in your position—a woman alone in a great big house—could have panicked if she thought she heard a burglar."

"What are you saying?"

"You know what I'm saying."

"That I should try to cop a plea? 'Your Honor, I heard a man in the kitchen and I didn't call the police or press the panic button on the alarm. No, I went downstairs and didn't recognize the man I'd been intimate with for more than twenty-five years. I mistook him for a prowler, so as I was looking straight at him, I stabbed him right smack in his abdominal aorta.'"

"What I'm saying is, the time is almost past where I can make any sort of deal for you. Listen, here's the situation as I see it: The cops are angry at themselves that you got away. But let me assure you, they're angrier at you. So far you've gotten some good breaks. And you're pretty darn clever. But you seem to think you've become invisible. You're not. You're resourceful and—so far—blessed with dumb luck. If they pick you up before I can come to some agreement with the D.A., it won't be good for you."

I patted his hand. "But no matter what happens, you'll do the best for me, won't you, Vinnie?"

"Yes, Rosie," he said, full of seriousness. "I will."

I watched Vinnie get into a cab and drive away. Then I sat and looked at the dogs for a while, although none of them had the tail-wagging, life's-a-party exuberance of the basset hound. The late-afternoon light softened and began to fade. People my age were hurrying home. High school and college kids slowed their pace; couples leaned into one another, relishing each other's warmth as the day's crispness turned to cold.

A half hour later, I went back to Danny's. He was lying on the couch, blasting a CD I couldn't like even if I'd yearned to be open-minded and young at heart. I blew a kiss to him. He stretched out his hand toward me, lazy, sensual. I wanted to leave before he stopped regarding me as a lover and remembered how in third grade I'd been den mother to his Cub Scout troop.

I went into the bathroom and exchanged his black sweater for my gray sweater and cardigan. When I came out, the music was off. He stood, waiting. "Where you going, Rosie?"

"I've got people to see."

He was still for a second. Then he put his arms around me and rested his head against mine. "Let me go with you," he entreated.

"I can't do that."

"Don't take this the wrong way, but if you go it alone, you'll fuck up. If that old secretary of your husband's called the cops . . ."

"I don't think she did."

"*That's* why you're going to fuck up, Rosie. If she did, they'll have their men stationed at every possible place you might show up. They'll grab you in a second."

I stroked his hair. It was silky, like a young child's. "I'm not going to the obvious places."

"Where are you going?"

"I have a plan."

"Let me help you."

"You *have* helped me."

"So why cut me out now? Come on, Rosie. It's been so much fun. Hasn't it?"

Before we kissed goodbye, Danny offered me money. I turned it down. I did accept a key to his apartment, although I knew in my heart I would never go back. As I eased out of his embrace, he said: "If I thought you'd killed him, I'd feel a hell of a lot better. I'd think: She's got balls. She can take care of herself. This way, I'm scared for you."

"Don't worry, not even for a minute. I'm very good at taking care of myself." I was far more scared for me than he could ever be. But I gave him a great big smile. Then I kissed him one last time, for good luck.

* * *

Carter Tillotson did his serious surgery at New York Hospital, ten blocks south of his office, but eye bags, thigh fat, and those other small, vexatious signs of being human were excised in his very own operating room. It was a perfect setup: a forty-minute drive from his estate in Shorehaven to the garage on East End Avenue where he parked his Mercedes, then a quick cup of coffee, a brisk hand-wash, and he had time to suction a couple of chins from a department store president or to give a thin-lipped model a juicy kisser before going to check on his hospital patients at 8:30 A.M. The only shadow cast across Carter's perfect life was Emerald Point. While one of the architectural gems of Long Island's North Shore, it was an enormous sponge that existed solely to sop up money. It never, ever became saturated. So Carter operated like mad all day and saw patients until ten or ten-thirty five nights a week. At least that's what he told Stephanie. I wanted to know if it was the truth.

So three hours before his scheduled departure, I stationed myself outside the garage nearest Carter's office and waited until the attendant left his glass booth for what I prayed would go into the *Guinness Book of Records* as the world's longest pee. With a hammering heart and a very dry mouth, I careened down a steep ramp and squatted behind a fat Cadillac Brougham. No people. Unfortunately, there were enough Mercedeses to open a small dealership. But after twenty minutes, on the next level down, I spotted a familiar dark blue Mercedes with M.D. license plates. Had I found my man?

Thank God the car was unlocked. I lay on the floor below the back seat of the car with the driest mouth in America. My throat was parched too, and I couldn't stop thinking of a diet Coke with ice and a slice of lemon. The thirst was, frankly, hell. But besides that awful discomfort, I had actual pain. Sure, I'd had backaches before, but never terrible soreness surrounding every single vertebra. I cursed all of the twenty or thirty movies I'd watched in which a lithe, well-quenched, pain-free gun-toter pops up behind the driver and puts a gun to his head. By the time the attendant came to drag-race the Mercedes up to street level, I had to bite my lip not to cry out with every lurch of the car; but at least he didn't spot me.

Please, I prayed, as the car screeched to a stop in a terribly well lighted spot, *please* don't let Carter see me. And please, let this be his Mercedes. Let me not wind up driving to Ardsley with an otolaryngologist. The attendant climbed out. "Here ya go, Doctor," I heard him say. Then nothing. I pressed myself even flatter on the floor. Soft dust streamed into my nose; bits of grit scratched my cheek. Was the attendant signaling Carter? Someone's in the car! Quick, call the cops! Just as I was conjuring up the cold metal of a police revolver butting against the nape of my neck, a man slid into the driver's seat and slammed the door. I looked up. Blond, clipped, Republican hair. Carter!

I took out my weapon. After having rejected the orange and chartreuse and purple plastic water guns in three different five-and-tens, I'd finally found a shiny, stubby metal cap pistol in a decrepit toy store in the Village. But my back was so stiff and painful, and I was so terrified by my own audacity, that I couldn't pick myself up off the floor until Carter was on the FDR Drive, speeding toward the Triborough Bridge. I put the barrel against the side of his head.

"Keep driving, Carter."

The Mercedes swerved! Both of us screamed as we felt the car surging out of control, first toward oncoming traffic, then—aaah!—toward the East River. But a surgeon has to have a certain cool, and within seconds, as hysterical car horns blared at us, we were moving straight ahead. Keeping the gun to Carter's head, I climbed into the front passenger seat.

"Get off at the next exit," I ordered as I pulled off the receiver of his car phone, opened the window, and flung it out.

"Are you crazy?" he shouted.

"This exit. Over and out," I told him, pressing the gun a little harder against his head, although not so hard that he could sense it was tin, not solid steel.

"Here?"

"Here."

"We're in Harlem," Carter breathed.

"I know exactly where we are." So we exited at 116th Street and parked two blocks from the drive. I ordered him to turn out the lights and switch off the engine.

"I hope you realize—" he began.

I finished his sentence. "—I won't get away with this. Maybe not in the long run. But if *you* want to get out of here in the short run—alive and intact—I think you should answer my questions fully and truthfully. If you don't"—I drew back the gun from his head—"I don't know if I'll be able to kill you,

Carter. But trust me, I'll shoot you in the hand." He didn't flinch. He sat, rigid, staring out the windshield at a motorcycle parked ahead of us. It was chained to a fire hydrant.

"Ready?"

"Yes."

"You introduced Jessica to Richie?" He nodded. "Tell me about it."

"There's nothing to tell. She was a friend. A casual friend. An investment banker. We'd met at a cocktail party one of my best patients threw. I mentioned to Jessica that I had a neighbor who'd had a huge overnight success. She'd heard of Data Associates and asked that I arrange a meeting. I did. And that's all there was to it."

"That wasn't all!" I yelled. He breathed in with a yelp, trying to control his terror that Woman Scorned was about to shoot off his scalpel fingers. "Calm down, Carter," I said, much more gently. "Just tell me the truth. Okay?"

"Yes. Okay."

"Were you and Jessica lovers?" His head whipped around, his shoulders grew even more tense, but he didn't answer. "Carter?"

"Yes."

"Were you still lovers when you introduced her to Richie?"

"Yes."

"What was the point of the introduction?"

"What I told you. To steer some business her way."

"Did Richie know you and she were lovers?"

He turned away from me and looked straight ahead. "I have no idea."

"Truth," I barked.

"I assume so. I mean, I would hardly introduce her as 'This is my lover, Jessica Stevenson.' But I'm sure he knew. He was an adult."

"Did you know that he was cheating on me?"

"I suppose so."

"What does that mean?"

"I don't know. I just assumed he was. The way he talked about women. Too aware of how they reacted to him. He was always looking. Very responsive to uh, physical nuances."

"Tits and ass?"

"He was more sophisticated than that." Considering Jessica's submicroscopic tits, I suppose that made sense.

"Had Jessica ever been married?"

"Two times."

"*Two?*"

"Her last year of college, to one of her professors. And then to a lawyer. Neither of them lasted very long. She was just reacting to family pressure."

"Any children?" Carter swallowed hard. "Answer my question."

"She never talked about it. I only found out because we came into her apartment one night and she played back her messages on the answering machine. There was a message from her ex-husband: She was four months late with her child support payments."

"Was this the lawyer?"

"The professor. A history professor. The boy lives with him and his second wife. Jessica says she was so young when it happened. She knows now she should never have left the child. To this day she mourns his loss." I had to hand it to him; he said it with a straight face and absolute conviction. Well, why not? The catch in his voice gave him away. He was still in love with her.

"Do you keep in touch with her?"

"Just as friends."

"How often do you speak?"

"Once, twice a month."

"Who calls whom?"

"I call her," he said, embarrassed. "But it's not the way you think. We're friends. My schedule ... It's easier if I call her."

"Did Stephanie know about you and Jessica?"

"No!" he practically shouted. "And don't you dare ... " His eyes moved to the gun. "Stephanie's been having a tough time lately. Please don't ... Our couple quit." His voice rose. "She's so frazzled. And then the murder. Leave her alone!"

In profile, the lower half of his face had all the definition of a cotton ball. He could have used one of his own chin jobs.

"If you knew Richie had a roving eye, how come you introduced Jessica to him?"

"It was business. Besides, it never occurred to me. She was way out of his league. He'd be too in awe of her. At that point, he was going for secretaries."

"I thought you didn't know for certain that he was having an affair." He just shrugged. "Did you know about Mandy too?" He shook his head. "She may be the same Mandy who's a friend of Stephanie's. A lawyer. She lives in Shorehaven. They sometimes run together at night." He shook his head harder. "Do you know what she looks like?"

"I've met a lot of Stephanie's women friends. I'm not sure which one she is."

"Did Richie steal Jessica away from you?"

"No." He clenched the steering wheel. "She and I just drifted apart."

"You mean she dropped you like a hot potato for someone else."

"Yes."

"Before she took up with Richie?"

He wanted to punch me, but he said, "Yes."

"For whom?"

"An older man."

"Nicholas Hickson?"

His hands dropped into his lap. "Yes."

"Why didn't that work out?"

"He couldn't bring himself to leave his wife."

"So she moved on to Richie. Tell me about their relationship."

"There's nothing to tell. They fell in love, but there were problems."

"Like what?"

"Jessica felt Richie was nickel-and-diming her. She didn't like it. She was disappointed in the ring he gave her."

"The ring was the size of the Rock of Gibraltar!"

"It wasn't a first-quality stone."

"I see."

Carter didn't seem to think I had the proper attitude. "It wasn't the ring itself. It was that he wasn't going into the marriage with a full heart."

"So she started up with Hickson again?"

"No. Hickson came back to her. He said he was willing to divorce his wife."

"And what did Jessica say?"

"She was torn. She'd made a commitment."

"But?"

"Your husband kept holding back," he said hotly. "The ring. And he gave her a gift. Art." I could see the shimmering landscapes on Fran's walls, the scribble picture on Jessica's. "It turned out the painting wasn't free and clear."

"What was the problem?"

"I don't know." I waved the gun so that if he had any peripheral vision, he'd see it. He saw it. "He'd paid for it with a check," he blurted.

"So?"

"Jessica had loved it at first. But then she decided it was too minimalist. Richie had made over ownership to her. But when she went to sell it, she needed proof of purchase. It turned out it had been paid for with a check on a joint account."

"Mine and Richie's?" I whispered. Carter nodded. "He was buying art for us," I said. "For the house, but also as an investment. He told me some of it was pretty avant-garde, not right for Gulls' Haven. I said, 'Let me at least look at it.' But he said the modern paintings were in storage at the auction house, in a dehumidified vault. He said he'd be glad to arrange for me to see them. But then I forgot. I was so busy being rich. We . . . no, *I* was buying so much, nothing had value."

"Hmm," said Carter, about as interested in my musings on social mobility as Richie had been during the last few months of our marriage. Only the silvery pistol an inch from his scalp kept his attention.

"Carter."

"Yes?"

"Why did you call Richie the day he died?"

"What?"

"You heard me."

"Oh. I forgot for a second. His chin. It was his chin. He called me a couple of days before, wanted me to clean up the jawline. He was in such a big hurry. I didn't have any cancellations, but I decided to squeeze him in that night anyway; I'd told him I wouldn't schedule anything without examining him first. But he never returned my call."

"Why did Richie come to my house?"

His jaw slid back and forth as if he were breaking in a fresh stick of gum.

"I know you know. There's no way you didn't call Jessica after the murder. You wouldn't miss a chance to speak to her. And you were her link to Richie; she'd discussed him before with you, and there'd be no reason why she'd want to clam up. On the contrary." No answer. "Carter . . . " I clicked back the toy gun's safety catch. To me it sounded ridiculous, but Carter seemed impressed.

"He needed the bill of sale. It was in his name, but the check had been on your joint account."

"What was he going to do with it?"

"What do you think?" he snapped. "Pull a fast one. He said you never even saw the bill of sale. You didn't know who the artist was."

"Who was he?"

"Cy Twombly."

"How much did it cost?"

"Three million," he said coolly.

"*What?*"

"You just knew he'd bought some art for investment."

"Three million? That's way out of Richie's class."

"But Jessica fell in love with it. She knew he wouldn't say no to her. And if he got the bill of sale out of your hands, he had some lesser works he was

going to pass off to your lawyer as your 'art investment.'" He looked at me. His stare turned into a
glare. "She *begged* him not to go. Breaking and
entering."

"He didn't break. He just entered."

"She begged him. She pleaded with him. It was
terribly dangerous. What would you do if you caught
him?"

"Probably throw my arms around him and kiss
him. No, I'll tell you the real reason Jessica didn't
want Richie to go: because she didn't want him to
please her. She wanted an excuse to ditch him so
she could marry Hickson. She was just stalling
because she needed time to think of a way to keep
her job. That would have taken some doing, even
for her." My grip on the gun got so tight that if it had
been genuine, Carter would have been dead. "The
bitch! I hope she dies!"

Carter reacted as if I'd truly gone off the wall. I
can't swear I didn't. "Please let me go," he whimpered. "Listen, she was sorry about the whole thing.
Do you know what? She swore to me up and down
she was hoping he'd go back to you."

I felt such a chill. "Had he brought that up?
Coming back?"

"Of course not," Carter retorted. "Why would he?
Jessica was his life."

Sixteen

Carter turned even whiter than usual when I told him to drive me to 125th Street, the main drag of Harlem. When I got out of the car, he peeled off as if he were being pursued by a battalion of armed-to-the-teeth Black Panthers.

In fact, Harlem was pretty quiet. Five or six guys around Alex's age sauntered out of a bar; they did not look as though they'd been drinking Perrier. They eyed me strangely. I would have felt nervous, but before I could transcend my already off-the-chart anxiety level, they hurried away into the night. It was only after the first taxi driver I flagged down sped away that I realized why the guys took off; the pistol was still in my hand. I stuffed it into my bra. It didn't make for a sleek look, but at least the next cab stopped.

I covered my trail on Forty-second Street; I figured that when Carter went to the police, they might check with the cab companies. Anyone happen to see a white woman in Harlem around ten-thirty? What was her destination? Good: Let them comb Times Square, looking for me.

I hustled along an endless three blocks, avoiding clots of men who looked less than clean-cut, past prostitutes in massive wigs and patent-leather miniskirts. The hookers surveyed me with the disdain of the fashionable for the frumpy, and they hassled me with "Chick-ee," "Lady. *La*dy," and "Lose your man? Huh? Huh?" I couldn't make myself go down the shadowy stairs to the subway because I had a sense I'd find some of their colleagues, the less gracious ones. I rushed along a few more blocks and stood in front of a theater, a more natural habitat for a suburban type like me. With the remaining ten dollars of the money I'd taken from Danny's pants, I hailed still another cab and headed uptown.

A night in Central Park was not an alluring prospect. I was already shivering from the cold, from grief for the homeless, for whom this was a mild night, and for myself. Still, I had to be on guard early in the morning. I hid in shadows, leaning against the stone wall that separated the park from Fifth Avenue. The cobblestones gave off a spiteful chill that went straight through the thin soles of my boots. A sharp wind agitated the tree branches and the dry leaves. I kept swiveling around, peering into the park's gloom, half expecting to see some hissing Halloween horror scaling the wall to get at me. I knew I had more to fear from the police than from a bogeyman, but I couldn't make myself go into the park.

Across the street, taxis and an occasional limousine pulled in front of Tom Driscoll's building. The night doorman in his snappy uniform double-timed it to the curb to greet men in tuxedos, women in jewel-color gowns clutching their sable jackets and chinchilla capes tight against their stylish décolletés. Husbands gripped wives' elbows and steered them into the radiance of the lobby. I stuffed my hands into my pockets. The key to Danny's apartment was warm.

One by one, lights began to go out in the buildings along Fifth and across the park on Central Park West. It must have been after eleven, although it was too dark to see my watch. I was freezing, and so tired. How could I not have foreseen that I'd be out on the streets so long? How could I not have comprehended that autumn inevitably carries with it an icy foretaste of winter—I, who for twenty years called after the boys: "Take a jacket!" I conjured up thick sleeves, a hood with a drawstring so it would fit snug and warm. I couldn't stop my teeth from chattering.

So I tried an imaging technique I'd learned from a yoga video I'd rented a couple of weeks after Richie left, when I decided relaxation exercises might be preferable to suicide. I envisioned myself on golden Caribbean sand, the sun sending its heat through me.

Yes! For just a second, I had a day at the beach; the buildings across Fifth Avenue belonged to a world far out in cold space. I was so heartened I barely noticed the chauffeur-driven Lincoln easing to a stop across the street. But then the doorman raced over and, practically genuflecting, welcomed Tom Driscoll home.

This wasn't going according to my plan. Sure, I was keeping watch, but halfheartedly. I'd been so sure Tom would already be upstairs, asleep, having dropped off after reading a paragraph of his book on airline deregulation. I'd anticipated waking with the sun, alert for his exit.

I had no time to think. I strode toward the curb and, trying to combine Brooklyn volume with Manhattan refinement, called out: "Tom." He kept walking toward the door. I dropped the refinement. "Tom!" He turned. I waved. The doorman watched. Tom offered a reflexive wave in return: I was probably a neighbor walking a dog. Except I had no dog. "Tom!" Then he knew. He appeared to do nothing, although I knew he was calculating what his options were, computing the odds as to which choice would best serve him. I was so cold the bones in my feet ached.

Then, in a flash, he handed his attaché case to the doorman; he smacked the fender of the Lincoln, and the chauffeur drove off. Scrambling around oncoming traffic, he was at my side within seconds. "How are you?" he inquired.

"For a person being hunted for murder who has to go to the bathroom, not bad."

He didn't invite me up to use his marble facilities. "What do you want?" He really had become one of the privileged class. No need for a coat: A warm car and a deferential driver were always waiting.

"Tom, I realize this isn't fair, popping into your life like this, but I had no choice. I need your help."

"I'm sorry," he said brusquely, as if denying a panhandler's request. "There's nothing I can do for you."

"I just have a few questions for you. That's all. And then I'd like you to get some information from your wife."

"Absolutely not."

With his doorman still eyeing us, hauling the pistol out of my cleavage wouldn't have been a smart tactic. But since I was on the subject of phony weapons, how about a little blackmail? "You know, about a year ago, before things got bad between us, Richie told me he'd been doing some research on a company you were acquiring." Tom waited. "He came up with some information on you that the SEC might find . . . interesting." The corners of his mouth turned down. "I hate to do this, but I'm desperate."

"Desperate and stupid."

"What do you mean?"

"You have nothing on me."

"Don't push me, Tom."

"Okay, what information do you have?"

"'Stupid' would be to tell you."

"There's nothing to tell. I'm a straight shooter."

"Not all the time." I hoped I sounded as if I had sinister knowledge.

"You know what we used to say back in Brooklyn? Oh, of course. You of all people would know."

"What?"

"Rosie, you're so full of shit your eyes are brown."
He turned and moved toward the street.

I grabbed the back of his suit jacket. "What can I
do to get you to help me?" I pleaded. "Do you want
me to cry?"

"No."

"Good, because I'm not going to."

"Let go of my jacket."

I did. "Nice fabric."

"Thank you."

"I'm sorry, Tom."

He seemed to be considering how to respond. I
steeled myself for a scathing remark. What he finally
said was: "I'll buy you a cup of coffee." When the
flood of gratitude ebbed a little, I realized he wasn't
making the offer out of fondness or courtesy or pity.
He was stalling so he could think of an effective way
to turn me over to the cops.

"If you can find a place open, you can even buy
me dinner," I said.

He didn't look thrilled, but he didn't say no. We
walked up Fifth. My feet weren't quite numb, but
they were so cold that every step hurt. He said: "You
shouldn't have tried to blackmail me. That was
beneath you."

"I know. I apologize."

"Fine." We each retreated into the awkward
silence of people who had once seen each other's
genitalia. The afternoon I'd taken him to lunch, our
time together had been marked by exaggerated courtesy and intense perusal of menus. Over the years,
we'd managed to make polite chitchat, but we'd
always been protected by the presence of our
spouses and business associates. I'd never even got-

ten close to him; the last time I'd actually stood beside him, we were barely eighteen. He'd grown a couple more inches and now was so tall I had to tilt back my head to see his face. "Why are you walking funny?" he finally asked.

"My feet are freezing. Don't worry about my feet. Will you help me?" Maybe Tom had traded his heart for a block of ice, but I didn't think he had it in him to become an easy liar; he wouldn't say "Oh, sure. Glad to," if he was planning to tap out a Morse code signal to a passerby: Call 911.

"Why should I help you?"

"Old acquaintance?" His stiff posture got even stiffer. "Because I didn't kill Richie." His eyebrows went up a fraction of an inch; evidently, this was a possibility he had not considered. "Because I don't deserve to go to prison for the rest of my life for a crime someone else committed. I have to find out who did it."

"Rosie, please don't do this."

"I don't have any choice, Tom."

"What do you think I can tell you? He was a friend of my wife's. I only had a business relationship with him, and I almost never spoke to him directly. My people dealt with his people."

"I know Joan"—I was extremely careful not to call her Hojo—"spent time with Richie and Jessica Stevenson while he and I were still a happily married couple."

"So?" he snapped.

"I also know Joan and Richie were dear friends, as they called it. But between Jessica and an earlier affair with his secretary, I think I've discovered a gap in his life. I want to be able to account for it, because I can't afford gaps. What I want to know is: before Jessica, did Joan know about Richie and some other woman?" He didn't answer. "Tom, I'm not engaged in some masochistic act; I don't get a sick thrill hearing stories about my husband's adultery. I'm trying to fill in the blank spaces because I need a full, coherent theory to bring to the police. I'm trying to save my life."

"You don't think the police can be coherent?" We waited for the light to change. I was breathing hard and sweating.

"They already have a theory they think is just dandy: I'm guilty. Why would they bother investigating any further?"

Tom took a deep breath and let it out slowly. "Joan and I had dinner with him and some other woman—before Jessica. I couldn't wait to get out of there. I couldn't believe he could be so low-class, so foolish in a business sense, as to bring along a woman he was . . ."

"Screwing," I suggested.

"Involved with." Well, Tom had gone to parochial school. "And I couldn't believe Joan knew about the plans and agreed to go. She may be a lot of things, but I'd always believed being tacky was never one of them."

"Who was the woman?"

"I don't remember." I was sure he was telling the truth. I knew him.

"Are there any details at all that you can recall?"

He concentrated by rubbing his forehead. "Pretty. Nicely dressed, although nothing fancy." Tom could not remember what she did, where she came from, or, for that matter, anything substantive about her. He'd been too steamed to concentrate on the conversation.

"Do you remember when this was?" I asked.

"This past winter. Probably February. Maybe March."

"Did you get the impression it was primarily a sexual relationship? Or something more?"

He gazed up toward the starless sky. "I don't know about him. Her? I suppose she was taken with him." He gave his forehead another rub. "No, more like crazy about him. And excited by the illicitness of the evening. I assumed she was married."

"'Crazy about him'? Does that mean smitten or in love with him?"

"I don't know."

"If you had to pick one?"

"Love."

"Did he love her too? Don't worry about my feelings."

"I couldn't tell. He was smoother, hard to read. He worked on not giving himself away. I'd say, if he wasn't in love, he was seriously attracted."

Tom seemed to have a certain restaurant in mind, but then I tripped over my own now numb feet. Without actually touching me, he shepherded me into an upscale pasta joint on Madison Avenue.

All of a sudden, a day came back to me, the day after he'd gotten accepted to Dartmouth. We'd cut school to celebrate. After a morning and afternoon of sex in the electric-meter room and the bicycle room in the basement of our apartment building, we'd been starving. He took me out to dinner. "Meatballs and spaghetti," he'd announced grandly. But I knew how tight money was for him, so I'd told him I wasn't in a meatball mood.

This time, the waiter, an older man with a clean red jacket and a neat white mustache, pulled out a chair for me. Without my having to say anything, Tom shook his head and indicated the chair opposite, where I'd be facing away from the other diners. The waiter raced around the table to comply. Tom ordered a bottle of Barolo and told the waiter to bring menus right away.

"I have to go to the ladies' room," I said.

"Okay," Tom replied.

"No, it's not okay. Do you still believe in God?"

"What?"

"Answer me."

"I suppose so."

"Fine. Then swear to God that you won't call the police or anyone else when I'm gone. Oh, and that if you do change your mind and don't want to help me, you'll leave enough money so I can pay for dinner."

He actually started to laugh, but I didn't join him, so he made a quick cross over his heart.

"You do realize you're harboring a fugitive, don't you?"

"When a man's just made a deal with you, Rosie, you don't remind him what a lousy bargain he's made."

When I returned, I sensed an easier atmosphere at the table. True, Tom wasn't the outgoing, sympathetic Irish charmer he'd been in Brooklyn. He'd gotten where he'd always wanted to be on top of the world, but his pinched, pale mouth, dull eyes, and too-austere dark-blue suit showed he hadn't gotten there for free.

When you hear the plunk of ice cubes hitting the

bottom of a glass forty feet away at the bar, you know you're dealing with a major lull in the conversation. I wanted to say something but was afraid Tom would start speaking at the same instant and we'd both sputter into red-faced mortification. Just as I was getting desperate for any simple declarative sentence to break the ice, he spoke. "I always valued our friendship."

"Me too. We had fun." He nodded but didn't look at me. Perhaps "fun" was a poor choice; I had no doubt that he would have paid big bucks to edit our history and erase the sex. "What about now? Are you happy, Tom?"

"That's a question women ask each other."

"Men don't care about being happy?"

"It's not the big deal it is to women." He signaled the waiter, and we ordered. Then he added: "I'm happy enough."

"Good. Can we talk about the relationship between your wife and my husband?"

"What do you want to know?"

"What was it all about?"

He exhaled, the sigh of a man to whom conversation meant a discussion of Bundesbank interest rates. "He was dying to be—how the hell can I put it?—a sophisticate. She taught him the ropes."

"Why did she bother with him?"

He shifted his glance to the waiter, who hurried off into the kitchen. "I don't know. What do you call it? The *My Fair Lady* syndrome."

"She was Pygmalion to his Galatea."

"That's right."

"Except in the myth," I noted, "they marry each other."

"Well, I suppose she found him appealing."

"Sexually appealing?"

"Probably."

"Do you think they were having . . . ?"

"No."

"Why not?"

"The man has to ask the girl to dance."

"Woman," I muttered automatically.

In a million years, I could not imagine Richie asking Hojo to dance. She was less a woman than a face-lift covered by makeup topped by a hairdo so perfect it could have been molded plastic. Despite her new balloon breasts, there was nothing remotely sexual about her. She had reduced herself to a head hovering over a Chanel ensemble.

"Rick, Richie, whatever he was called," Tom went on. "If that Jessica is the standard, he seemed to go for younger women."

"You're telling me! Well, except for his secretary, although she was pretty attractive at one time, a Gestapo calendar girl type." I thought about Hojo, with arms so thin you could see the interplay between the radius and the ulna beneath her sun-dried skin.

"My guess is he never thought of Joan in a carnal way. She had to settle for friendship." Tom shifted in his chair. He examined the contents of the bread basket. Suddenly his eyes met mine. "They needed each other. I think he got his kicks by telling her everything. And I think she was titillated, not just by stories of his catting around, but by his skill in hiding his cheating, in leading two lives. She got some kind of charge out of seeing him with other women. His girlfriends. You." I pulled over the bread basket and got involved in a silent debate between a salt stick and a hard roll. "I'm sure it's tough for you, having to hear this," he added.

"I'm in a tough situation. I can take it." The waiter came and set down bowls of thick minestrone. The steam warmed my cheeks. The rich aroma brought tears to my eyes. I told Tom how my hunger had overpowered my sense of decency and my fear, and how I'd snatched the Burger King bag from the young woman in the Village. He stared down into his soup. When he lifted his head again, his eyes were misted too. He glared, exasperated that I had brought him to this. The waiter, hurrying back with a bowl of grated cheese, saw our tears. He stopped short, then about-faced. Tom didn't even notice. He was lost in thought.

At first I was grateful for the silence. I spooned my soup. It was the most delicious I'd ever had, savory, hot. I could taste every carrot, bean, tomato, each spice. It was more delectable than my mother's chicken soup, more soul-satisfying than any bisque or bouillon I'd had with Richie in three-star French restaurants.

But I was afraid I was losing Tom; I couldn't tell if he was reconsidering the wisdom of helping me. "You don't owe me anything," I told him.

My voice startled him. He dropped his spoon into the soup bowl. Dots of red spattered the front of a white dress shirt fine enough for God to wear. "What did you say?" he inquired.

"I said you don't owe me. We were good pals, and we had some good times. But neither of us pledged eternal love or loyalty. You know I'm up a creek without a paddle. You have no obligation to come along."

He withdrew to the back of his mind again. The waiter came and saw he hadn't touched his soup and turned away, but Tom gave him a take-it-away flick of his wrist.

He barely touched his linguine, but his silence, even though it was becoming oppressive, didn't stop me from glomming down every last strand. Frankly, I was just as glad he didn't notice that I had the appetite of an offensive tackle. His wife was so flesh-less, so urbane. Early in their friendship, Hojo had confessed to Richie that she'd been bulimic for four-teen years and that other than her psychiatrist, Richie was the only person she'd ever confided in. I won-dered if Tom knew, or if he was so gullible or detached that he thought her thinness, if he thought about it at all, was due to a vigorous metabolism or wondrous self-control.

He raised his hand and made a squiggly writing motion, and the waiter hustled over with the check. Tom glanced at it and slapped down a credit card. When the waiter left, he said: "You asked me if I was happy." I nodded. "I like what I do. I've given some companies a second life. I've created jobs." He sat back, exhaling his fatigue, as if he'd just finished hours of filibustering.

But I didn't want the conversation to die again. "Are your parents still alive?" I asked. Except for his father's white hair, Tom could have been a clone: the same lean, squared-off black-Irish face, the same brown eyes. His father was jollier than Tom had ever been, though. A beer-truck driver, an easygo-ing, outgoing, ain't-life-grand man, Mr. Driscoll would greet me with "Ring-around-a-Rosie, Rosie!" He'd tousle my hair. It goes without saying that he didn't know that when I was supposedly tutoring his son in Latin and Tom was allegedly helping me with physics, we were actually up on the roof, trying to create a Kings County *Kamasutra* on a sheet we'd snitched, shamelessly, from some neighbor's laundry line.

"He got laid off when he was fifty-eight, couldn't find another job. Knocked him for a loop. Two years later, dead."

"I'm sorry. What about your mother?" I barely knew her. She was a plump hen of a woman, who read four or five newspapers every day. When she wasn't reading or busy with housework, she was pinning on her hat and rushing off to Mass.

"She's fine. Living with my sister Cathy in Garden City." He hesitated. "At the funeral, your mother seemed a little . . . strange."

"Senile dementia. I'm so sorry about how she carried on."

"No problem," Tom murmured.

The waiter returned, and Tom filled in the charge form. "Thank you, sir," the waiter said, showing enough enthusiasm over the tip to indicate that he was happy but not thrilled.

"I like making lots of money too," Tom told me as he stood.

"Good," I replied.

As we approached the door, his brow furrowed. He spoke so fast I almost missed what he said. "I was happily married for six months." He peered off to the side, then behind him, disoriented, searching for the ventriloquist who had just uttered those words.

"Which six months?" I asked quietly.

"The first six." He ran his finger under his collar, pulling it away from his throat. "Then she went down to Palm Beach, to visit a friend from school. I came home from work one night late, around eleven. I saw her suitcases in the hall."

"And?"

"I felt sick."

Out on the street, the temperature had dropped even more. We shuddered, simultaneously, as the near-freezing air hit us. "What went wrong?" I asked.

"I realized we'd gotten married because each of us thought it was time to get married. I guess she liked me because her old man told her I was a comer. He was a lawyer in a firm I'd retained when I was still with the bank. He was no legal genius, didn't have much money, but he'd gone to all the right schools and looked great in a dinner jacket. I thought that meant he had class. A couple of years later he introduced me to Joan. I'd come so far by then that I honestly didn't know what to do with all the money I'd made."

"But she had a few ideas."

"Yes. And I welcomed them. I knew one thing: I didn't want to spend my life going to country club dances. I wanted more." Tom folded his arms and stuck his hands under his armpits. "And Joan was perfect. She was so not-Brooklyn. She was elegant and much too ambitious to want to get stuck up in New Canaan or one of those places. She had a funny, wicked mouth. And she was well-connected. That's what I thought a wife ought to be.

"The thing of it was, whenever I pictured us together, I was in a tuxedo, she was in a gown, and we were always with other people: never watching

TV, or trimming a tree, or taking kids to church, the kind of life my parents had together. Joan had gone to Spence, Joan had gone to Holyoke, Joan had spent her summers in Provence. She'd grown up in another world—and that's just where I wanted to be." He stepped over to the curb and looked up the street for a taxi.

"Did you think about divorce?"

"Yes, but it went against my grain, my upbringing, so I tried to look on the bright side. Things would get better when we developed some mutual interest besides my money. Like kids. It didn't work out, but we stayed together."

"Why?"

"Why not? By that time I realized it was mutually beneficial. Still is. My life is my own. I'm always on the go, but I have a wife when I need one."

Tom waved, and a taxi appeared. He held the door open for me. "We can go back to my place, I guess." I shook my head. "You don't have to worry about being seen," he assured me. "Joan's out of town."

"What about your being seen?" I asked. Tom's face was so vacant he appeared momentarily dull-witted. "I'm a woman. What about your doorman? Your neighbors?"

"Oh." He seemed so surprised at this notion that I knew he had not been fantasizing about a night of lewdness and lust. It was as if, as a man, Tom had become so clean-minded that he'd cut himself off completely from the eighteen-year-old boy who'd walked around Flatbush with an unflagging hard-on.

The cabdriver rolled down his window and

groused in an accent I'd never heard before: "You going? Come on! What? What?"

"Across the park," Tom said, "down Broadway." He pushed me into the cab as if I were a particularly unwieldy package.

"What's there?" I whispered, as the driver pulled into traffic, not bothering to look in case anyone might object.

"I don't know. We'll find something. What are you whispering about?" I pointed to the cabdriver. Tom knocked on the scratched and yellowed plexiglass partition between the front and back seats. "How long does it take to get to Broadway?" he demanded loudly.

"What?" the driver shouted. Filtered through the partition, the word was little more than a gurgle of sound.

"Never mind," Tom called out, and settled back, making sure there was enough room between the two of us for an extremely obese person. "Tell me everything," he said quietly. "If I'm going to help you, you're going to have to trust me. Don't spare the details."

I began with the morning after our silver anniversary party. I told him everything that had happened since Richie's murder—except for Danny's name and the fact that he was a friend of Alex's and had hung around the house all through high school; I just said he was a kid who'd been in my class. I finished by telling him what I'd learned after I put a gun to Carter Tillotson's head. I would have offered him a peek at the pistol, but he was no longer the kind of guy who'd be delighted by an invitation to look down my sweater.

Tom didn't close his eyes or purse his lips or give any other sign he was deep in thought. In fact, he appeared normal, as if he were still listening to me—except I hadn't spoken for five minutes. I passed the time looking at the silvery swirls in his dark hair until, at last, he glanced at me and cleared his throat.

"Did you figure out who done it?" I asked.

"Are you kidding? You're nowhere near the 'who' yet; you're still getting information on people, figuring out relationships. You're at the 'how.'"

"What about the 'why'?"

"The '*why*'?" he repeated, as if I wanted information that wouldn't be available until the middle of the twenty-first century.

"Okay, forget the why."

"Now, could anyone have seen Rick's car in that spot where it was parked?"

"Not the car itself, but someone driving up the hill or walking along with a flashlight could have seen the reflector light—the little red thing on the side of the car."

"So if someone did see it, why would he—"

"Or she."

"Not now, Rosie! Why would this person bother to pull around the far side of Rick's car? Why not just pull over to the side near the road and check it out?"

"Because he or she didn't want to be seen."

"You can do she," he grumbled. I didn't give him an argument only because I suddenly realized I was stretching his composure, if not his goodwill, to its limits. "I'll do he. All right?"

"All right," I conceded.

"Back to those other tire marks near Rick's car.

Your Sergeant Gevinski keeps saying they could have been made by the local cops," Tom said. "But that doesn't make sense."

"Why not?"

"Why wouldn't the cops just stop on the road, alongside him?"

"That's right!" I was thrilled with his answer. I was also aggravated at myself for not having come up with it days earlier.

"All right," he said, very businesslike. "Let's move on to the dirt. There was dirt on Rick's shoes and on the kitchen floor. Correct?"

"Correct," I told him.

"Any footprints?"

"No. Just random dirt."

"You'd think sneakers with deep treads would leave footprints."

I nodded. "I think whoever killed him messed up what footprints there were because they obviously wouldn't have been a match for Richie's."

"And there was no dirt in any other part of the house?"

"No, none."

"So either Rick never got to another part of the house or he did and you're right: the dirt was applied to his shoes later."

"But if he was coming back to the kitchen, how come there were no papers or anything on him?"

"Either the killer took what was on him—"

"Oh, boy! That's right!"

"—or he hadn't found what he was looking for. Now, what about outside the house?"

"What do you mean?"

"You don't live in a log cabin in the middle of a

clearing. You have steps, paths leading to the house. Was there any dirt there?"

"No. Wait, let me think." I tried to picture the steps that led to the kitchen door, but I couldn't. It was then I realized I hadn't seen the steps that night or the next day. "I don't think I ever went past Richie, toward the kitchen door. And when the police came, I took them in through the front door, so . . . I guess I never saw what was outside. But wouldn't they have told me about it?"

"Are you serious?" Tom demanded. "You're the suspect. But if you want my guess: I think if someone else's footprints had been there, they wouldn't have been in such a rush to make you the prime suspect. But if there were footprints in the kitchen, it follows that there must have been footprints leading up to the house. The killer probably messed up the dirt outside, so it's natural the cops would think it came from Rick's shoes."

"Or they might not have noticed it at all, and the wind blew it away."

"Maybe," Tom muttered as he retreated into thought again. When he came back, he asked me what else I was planning to do. I told him I needed to speak to Jessica, Hojo, Stephanie. Madeline Berkowitz too; she might have heard some gossip about Mandy, Carter, or Richie around town. By the time we got to Madeline, we were all the way downtown, past the World Trade Center, and Tom was paying the driver.

We walked a block or two down streets so deserted they weren't at all scary and wound up in the first place that was open, Big Bob's, an old beer joint—all dark, gouged wood and disintegrating

Budweiser coasters—that with the addition of four
TV sets was now a sports bar for alcoholic yuppies.
The last patrons clustered at the bar, watching something—soccer or English football—on a TV that presented the world in an extremely green state. We sat
at a booth so far back it was close to invisible. Tom
had a brandy. I ordered a Scotch and soda, mainly
because ordering it made me feel like Barbara
Stanwyck, strong but still steamy.

Tom didn't notice. "We can stay here until they
close. Then we'll move on."

"To where?" I asked.

"We'll play it by ear. Meanwhile, let's go through
your list: I can speak to Joan; you'll tell me what
information you need."

"Thank you."

He nodded. "There's no safe way you can speak
to Jessica. She knows you're on the run. I'm sure she
feels you're a threat. If she doesn't have police protection, she'll have hired private guards. Let me think
about how to handle her. Now, as for your two
friends on Long Island . . ." I'd known how bright
Tom was; what impressed me at that moment was
his ability to assimilate and evaluate so much information in so short a time. "I'd advise you to wait.
First, you ought to tie up as many loose ends as you
can here. Second, you live in what is essentially a
small town. You teach at the local high school;
everybody knows who you are. When you do go,
you'll have to slip back in, sneak up on people. Of
course," he added, "that seems to have become a
specialty of yours."

We left about fifteen minutes later, right after the
last yuppie, and headed south, toward the Staten

Island ferry. I had to scurry to keep up with him. He had such long legs.

A memory flashed, like the blaze of a flashbulb: Tom and I at eighteen. We were walking past the ape house in the Prospect Park Zoo; I had to trot to keep pace with him. The gorillas and chimps were hooting and hollering as if they were auditioning for a Tarzan movie when, suddenly and offhandedly, Tom remarked that he was taking a girl from Queen of All Saints to his prom. His friend Bobby's girl-friend's best friend, he explained. He kept walking.

How can you do this to me? I demanded. But not out loud. We don't just have sex, Tom. If we lived in a garret in Greenwich Village, people would take one look at us and call us lovers. It's not only physi-cal. We *are* lovers. We *talk*. I read Aquinas's proofs of the existence of God because you told me they were harmonious. Harmonious: I'd loved that word. You read *The Tempest* for me. I couldn't get over how insightful you were.

But all those years ago, the only thing I could get out was to ask Tom the girl's name. Peggy, he said, in his breezy way. Then he said: Hey, Rosie, want to split a Fudgsicle with me? I shook my head.

Tom asked: "Are you sure you want to stay in New York?"

Thirty years later, I was so angry I could hardly speak. "Do I have another choice?"

"Yes. You can go anyplace you don't need a passport."

"What are you talking about?"

"I'll take you somewhere on a private plane, so no one can spot you. I'll see that you get settled, give you whatever you need to make a go of it. You have my word I'll never tell anyone. You can slip into a whole new life."

I should have wept with gratitude or gawked with surprise. "Why didn't you ask me to your prom?" I demanded.

"Rosie!"

"Why didn't you?"

His finger jabbed at my shoulder. "Keep your eye on the ball, for Christ's sake."

We waited in silence by an empty taxi stand, although I had no idea where he or I would go.

After about ten minutes, I said: "Your offer . . . I don't know how to thank you. I'm sorry I was so ungrateful."

"It doesn't matter," he muttered.

"It exceeds any generosity that's ever been extended to me."

"Do you want to take me up on it?" he asked, his eyes searching for headlights.

"There can't be any new life for me. I'm a mother. How could I give up my sons?"

We lapsed back into silence for another minute. The wind coming off the water was sharp, damp, icy cold. I was picturing him putting his arm around me, drawing me close to keep warm, when he jammed his hands into his pockets. Then I said: "What you're doing now is risky enough. If I took you up on your offer, you could ruin your whole life."

"I'm forty-seven years old," he announced.

"Of course you are. So am I."

"I have no children to worry about. All I ever risk is money, and there's always more of that because I've always hedged my bets. It's funny: people see me as a gambler, but I'm really very cautious by nature."

"So how come you're gambling now?"

Tom spoke hesitantly, as if every word had to pay a toll before it came out. "I suppose I want to see if I'm capable of a grand gesture, if I can even begin to approach being the man I'd always hoped to be."

"Who is that?"

"A man with guts."

When a cab finally came, Tom told the driver to take us to the best motel around La Guardia Airport. I shook my head vigorously. "Relax," Tom said. "That's not on my agenda."

There were no adjoining rooms left at the Airport Highlander. The bridal suite offered a king-sized bed with a mirrored canopy. Tom paid cash for what the desk clerk called the Presidential Suite and registered us as Mr. and Mrs. Thomas Smith; the clerk cared neither about the obviously phony name nor that we had no luggage.

Whatever sexual tension might build up when a man and a woman—former lovers—enter a motel room was dispelled before it could happen. The second Tom closed the door, he strode over to the phone. He put on a pair of tortoiseshell reading glasses, then called his office to listen to his voice mail. "Make up a list of what you want me to ask Joan," he told me. Cradling the phone between his chin and his shoulder, he punched the tiny keys of an electronic diary. I finished before he did; he was a man with many messages.

The Presidential Suite had not been dusted for

some time, but the living room was nonetheless pleasing, full of simple but massive furniture that, despite its owing more to plastic than to mahogany, looked White Housey enough. A soft green couch, with its bird-claw-clutching-a-ball legs, was so comfortable that I had to keep both my feet on the floor so I wouldn't slouch into sleep.

Tom took off his jacket and hung it over the back of his chair. "Joan and I are not a couple who have long conversations. I'm going to have to give her a song and dance about why I want this information."

"I'd like to listen in on the extension," I told him.

"I'd rather you didn't." Boy, was that understatement.

"Something you might not even notice may grab me," I explained. Tom shook his head and pressed a few keys in his diary to access Hojo's phone number. I continued: "What's she going to say on the phone? 'Remember the night we had with the Great Dane?'" A hint of his old smile flickered for a second. "Look," I said, "I've spent some time with her. I know how caustic she can be. It doesn't matter. After tonight, you'll go your way, I'll go mine, and the chances that I'll run into either you or Joan again are close to zero—especially if I'm working the drill press in the license-plate shop. I just want to hear how she answers my questions."

He glanced at what I'd written down. "If that's what you want . . . " He placed the call. "Mrs. Driscoll, please. I'm not interested in what spa regulations are. This is her husband. Connect me." He covered the mouthpiece. "Get into one of the bedrooms and pick up the extension. *Now.*" I wasn't able to grab the receiver until Hojo was saying hello, but she sounded so groggy I knew I was safe. "Joan," Tom said. "Me. Hate to wake you, but I need some information."

"About what?" I heard the click of a lamp going on, the hiss of a butane lighter. I pulled off my boots and lay down on the bed.

"About Data Associates," Tom said. "You know, I stuck it out with them because you and Rick were such good friends—"

"You never told me you weren't happy with them," she snapped.

"Well, now you know." His tone was careless, even bored, but, most of all, glacial. In the years Richie and I had been married, even before Jessica, we'd had some big fights. Real lulus. He'd screamed at me and slammed out the door a dozen times. I'd told him to go to hell at least that often. Once, I threw an entire Grand Marnier soufflé at him and only regretted that he'd managed to dodge it. We'd gone for days when our only exchanges were essential marital information. But I'd never been treated with such coldness: Tom and Hojo were like employees of some enormous corporation who hated each other and yet, decade after decade, were forced to work side by side. Unlike Richie, however, who had no compunctions about telling me to fuck off and die, Tom was polite to his wife.

Hojo exhaled what must have been a long stream of smoke. "Go ahead," she said.

"Can this Stevenson woman run a company any better than he did?"

By this time, all that was keeping me awake was dim hope and sore feet. "Jessica's supposed to be stellar," Hojo responded. "Rick swore it was she who took a one-man band and transformed it into an international corporation."

"He was sleeping with her. Was he going to say she was a dope?"

"If you remember," she said wearily, "he wasn't sleeping with her until fairly recently. He fell head over heels in love with her practically overnight. It only took him a couple of months after that to finally kiss off the little *hausfrau*." I'd always had a degree of compassion for this brittle woman with her silicone breasts, her plastic cheekbones, and her sad compulsion to stick her finger down her throat. It vanished then.

"So Rick and Jessica had a good working relationship before the affair?"

"Yes."

"Was it understood that if anything happened to him, she'd take over?"

"I haven't the foggiest." Hojo discharged what I assumed was a chuckle. "So accommodating of Rick, to agree to get stabbed so Jessica could play president."

"I thought you liked her."

"She's divine."

"You're jealous," he said, a simple statement of fact.

"Don't be a ninny, Tom. Rick was my *friend*. It so happened she was cheating on him and breaking his heart." Joan turned coy. "Want to know with whom, duckie?"

"Why not?"

"Nicky Hickson."

"That pompous jerk?"

"He happens to be charming, and much richer

than you. Fourth-generation rich. Rick was desperate to finalize his divorce and marry her. He was sure if he could act fast, he'd win."

"Why did he go back to his old house?"

"You won't believe this. To get some bill of sale for a Twombly he'd bought and given Jessica. She wanted to sell it. She decided it 'bored' her. Can you *believe* that? But it was worth at least three mil."

"Did she know he was going to sneak into the house?"

"Of course she did. She was going to let him get the paperwork. Then she'd sell it. *Then* she'd give him the old heave-ho, but of course, when I told him that, he got all pissy at me. The man was absolutely bewitched. He was sure he could keep her if he did exactly what she wanted."

"Was he bewitched with the one before?"

"My dear, completely and totally. Although that didn't last." Hojo's flat voice took on an erotic dimension. "Before *her,* he'd been doing the secretary, Brunhilde or whatever her name was, for at least ten years—in the office, out of the office—and all the while keeping the home fires burning. But once the wife started whining"—she put on a nasal Brooklyn accent—"'Rich-ie, awl this mon-ney. Whaaaat will become of our values?' . . . well, he granted himself an emotional divorce. For a while, he thought it was true love with Brunhilde, but *merci Dieu* I was able to talk him out of that! I said, 'Can you imagine *her* on your arm at the next MOMA benefit?'"

"Who was the one he brought to dinner with us that night?"

Hojo emitted an awful noise, a blend of a snort

and a laugh. "You mean the night you cut my clothes allowance?"

"Yes."

"Really, Tom, you can be such a punitive shit. I couldn't *believe* how you carried on. Thomas, the Wrath of God."

He didn't like talking to her, and he definitely didn't like my being on the extension; for the first time, his voice had a nasty edge. "Who was she?"

"You spent an entire evening with her and you don't remember who she was?"

"No," he snapped.

"God! She was Rick's first real love affair. Well, not really love, but you have to admit she was acceptable. More than acceptable, actually, although mind-numbingly boring. Remember?"

"No."

"Rick was just looking to get out of that stifling marriage. But the affair was clearly a dress rehearsal for Jessica. He just loved them Protestant and well-bred . . . as did you, love. Remember?"

"What was her name again?"

"Why is she so important?" Hojo's voice grew even icier than Tom's. "Want to drop her a mash note, *mon ange?* Give her a little jingle?"

"No."

"You were such a bloody bastard. How can you *not* remember what went on? It's not as if you and I dine out together night after night, dear one."

"Tell me her name, Joan."

The Driscolls may have been locked into a marriage of mutual loathing, but it was still a marriage; she knew something was up. "Why do you want to know about her?" He didn't answer. "What is all this about? What does she have to do with Jessica?" Hojo demanded.

Drop it, I pleaded silently. She's onto you. He heard me. "It was an attempt at conversation."

"My sweet hubby! I'm honored. An *intime* conjugal chat. Next you'll be wanting to sleep with me again."

He slammed down the phone. So did she.

Tom must have known the last thing I wanted to do at that moment was face him, which was precisely why he called out: "Get back in here, Rosie."

What could I say to him? Sorry that you and the missus want to rip out each other's entrails. Or, Gosh, what a wily son of a gun my husband was! Able to satisfy three mistresses while making millions. And then to come home and satisfy me too, with a technique that would have taught Masters and Johnson a thing or two.

All those months after Richie left me, I raged, I grieved, but mainly I sat at the kitchen table eating my heart out—mainly with Häagen-Dazs Chocolate Chocolate Chip—and asking myself: Where did I go wrong? Should I have given up teaching as he begged me to do and moved to the city? Stuck my finger down my throat and become a size eight? Streaked my hair? Realized that a man like him would be stifled by someone like me and suggested an open marriage?

Hadn't I realized what the world was like? Each year, thousands of abandoned wives wandered blindly past shopping malls, stripped of their dignity and their credit cards. Millions of the menopausal, no longer warmed by the heat of their man's arms, found their only human touch in a sympathetic embrace by one of the other divorcées in their support group. They no longer had enough hope to dream of romantic love, but only had hopes of future grandchildren, who might want to hug them. How could I not have known this was possible for me?

"Rosie!" Tom called. I marched into the Presidential living room. He was standing near the door, jacket on, tie knotted, wallet out, counting his cash. His jaw was clenched; it could have been my imagination, but I thought I heard the grinding of teeth. "I'm going."

"Why?"

"I don't have much cash," he said. "A hundred and twenty. If you can stop by my office tomorrow morning, I'll leave an envelope with the receptionist. What name do you want on it?"

"I don't want your money." He couldn't look at me. Instead, he gazed at the doorknob as if it were the most desirable object in the world. "I need your help, Tom."

"I can't give you any more than I already have," he told the knob.

"Do you think I didn't know that you have a terrible marriage? Do you think it comes as a stunning surprise that you don't sleep with your wife? And do you think that with all my problems I give a damn about yours?" At least he turned around. He wasn't handsome, but his thin, hard-edged face revealed character and depth and sadness. "Well," I added, "that's not precisely true. I do give a damn. I have this nasty little fantasy that in the end, it will turn out that Joan became mad with jealousy over Jessica and killed Richie. I'll be absolved and can go on with my life."

"And me?"

"You could move to a monastery."

He started to laugh. "It's a thought."

"Or go on with your life. Do you have someone?" I asked. I think I managed to sound curious in the most casual sort of way. He shook his head. I couldn't believe that I asked: "What do you do for sex?"

"Work," he finally said.

My subconscious may have offered a few words of thanksgiving that he hadn't said "Boys." Or worse: "A twenty-four-year-old mistress with a doctorate in econometrics."

Tom glanced at his watch. "Jesus, it's late."

"I've never been this tired," I told him. "I have to get some sleep. I'm begging you . . . No, that isn't fair. I'm hoping you'll stay because I have to get to Jessica and I can't get there without your help." I paused. "Will I see you in the morning?"

"Yes," he replied at last, then turned, walked into the suite's other bedroom, and closed the door.

I went back into what had become my room and fell on the bed, barely managing to pull the cover over me before dropping into a deep sleep. It was only three hours later, when a toilet flushed in the room upstairs and the pipes screamed at the assault, that I awoke in a panic, so confused as to where I was that, for a moment, I was sure I'd had a stroke. Even after I turned on the light, my heart was still racing. I slid back under the warmth of the cover and bedspread, but it didn't work.

*   *   *

It's terrible to meet a wonderful boy when you're still a girl, because he becomes the standard no one else ever measures up to. Even after Richie and I were married, I had longed for Tom. It wasn't quite sexual desire; Richie more than satisfied me. What I yearned for was the mysterious merging of serenity and joy I felt when I lay in Tom's arms after making love. Both of us had been big talkers way back then, spouting opinions on art and life, arguing about politics, questioning each other at such length that we could have written each other's autobiography.

But after the talk and the sex, we were quiet. Those moments defined for me the word "sublime." My head would rest on his shoulder, where I could sniff the sweet and bitter scent of sweat and Canoe aftershave and luxuriate in our silence.

For all women, there is always the man that got away. But what a man Tom Driscoll had been! What a hurt, to lose someone so fine. And what a shock, to realize that you will never recover from the blow, not for the rest of your life.

I walked through the living room to his bedroom door, but I stopped, afraid he had locked it after I'd gone to bed. If I twisted the knob, he would know for sure that I wanted him. He'd pretend to be asleep.

But if I'd learned anything in the past week, it was that after all these years, I had turned out to be a gutsy dame. No, better than that: a brave woman. So if it had been last night when he'd told me he was taking goddamn Peggy to his goddamn prom, I would have demanded: "*What?* You're taking some Irish virgin from Queen of All Saints? You're afraid to say: 'This is my girl, Rosie Bernstein from Madison High'? Damn it, Tom! You're too good to be a coward." And then, not knowing whether he would follow me, I would have had the courage to turn and walk away.

Tom was sleeping so deeply he didn't hear me until I cracked my knee against the nightstand beside his bed.

"Rosie?"

"It's me," I said. The bad news was my knee hurt. The good news was that it was so dark he couldn't see the changes that all the years and two pregnancies had wrought. I felt for the blanket and lifted it so I could slip in beside him before he could think of a polite way to tell me to go back to my room. "Remember?"

"I remember," he said. He pulled me up against him so we were body to body, nose to nose, and then mouth to mouth. Our kiss was so familiar, the first soft pressure, the exploration that grew in intensity. Our last kiss might have been just hours before.

"I'm out of practice," he said softly.

"The last thing I'm looking for is practice."

He put one hand between my shoulder blades, the other on my rear, and pulled me closer. I rubbed my cheek against his, cherishing the roughness of his beard.

"I've thought of you so many times, Rosie."

"Me too, Tom."

Our timing wasn't what it had been in high
school. Our moves had far less grace. And he was
right: he was definitely out of practice. But our loving had never been so lovely. After, we rested until
the dawn lit up the Presidential Bed. It revealed us
in each other's arms, in perfect silence and absolute
bliss.

Seventeen

"Of course I didn't mind coming to your office!" Jessica assured Tom. She crossed her legs. "We've really only met socially. I'm glad to have the chance to talk." From where I was hiding, in the bathroom attached to Tom's office, all I could see was Tom's left sock and shoe, a sliver of his desk, and, in a strategically placed side chair, all of Jessica. She looked not merely none the worse for wear but downright stunning in a dark-blue suit the exact shade of Tom's. "The only reason I hesitated was because I'd called a nine o'clock staff meeting. But you sounded concerned over the phone, so naturally I canceled it immediately."

Her back was straight but not stiff. Her face wore the serious-but-congenial mien suitable for a major client. Only her hands, gripping the arms of her chair, betrayed any tension. Jessica, of course, was sharp enough to realize that being woken by a curt 7:00 A.M. phone call from Tom Driscoll demanding a 9:00 A.M. meeting in his offices was not good news. Tom's silence must have been unnerving; she drummed her fingers twice, then stopped herself. I noticed that the awesome but imperfect Meyers Diamond was no longer on her finger.

"I've had a long relationship with Data Associates," Tom said finally.

Jessica nodded. The light from a brass lamp near the edge of Tom's desk shone on her expensive panty hose; there was plenty to shine on, from the top of her spike-heeled pumps to the bottom of the brief skirt of her otherwise prim suit. Her crossed leg, which had been giving an occasional sexy swing, uncrossed and aligned itself with its companion. "I would hope it's been a profitable relationship for us both," she replied.

From the way Jessica used her body, you'd have thought she'd spent two years studying Lauren Bacall in *Key Largo* instead of earning a master's in finance. But if I had to put my money on what she had that hooked successful men like Carter, Richie, and Nicholas Hickson, I'd have to say that the erotic aspect—the legs, the sultry walk, the glossy, perpetually parted lips—was only the half of it. The other fifty percent was a cold mind so much like her conquests' minds that when they took her to bed, they could be making love to themselves.

"Profitable for you people," Tom told her. "Not for me." As she opened her mouth to express her dismay, Tom cut her off. "All my dealings were with Rick, but I feel I should give you a personal explanation as to why I'm dropping your services."

"I beg your pardon?" At least that's what I think she said; her voice was so faint I couldn't be sure.

"Your research on Star Microelectronics could have been done by a second-rate sophomore at any third-rate college in the country. And your so-called indepth profiles on the principals of Vancouver Associates made your Star report look like a work of genius."

Jessica did the impossible and sat even straighter than before. "I cannot accept that."

"That proves my point," Tom said.

"What point?"

"That you're no more fit to run a research company than your boyfriend was."

If I'd been in Jessica's high heels, I would have burst into tears. But credit where credit is due. She recrossed her legs and leaned forward. "I disagree. I am fit. But please understand: Rick kept research as his bailiwick. Frankly, his system of controls left a great deal to be desired."

"Your background is finance, isn't it? What makes you think you can oversee five hundred or so academic types?"

"By opening a vice-presidential slot solely for quality control. By randomly selecting a report each day and having it read thoroughly by two other senior people: one of our top researchers and myself. I guarantee you —"

Tom cut her off. "You can't guarantee anything."

"Give me two months," Jessica pleaded. Tom must have shaken his head. *"Please."*

"Not at these rates."

She didn't even hesitate. "Twenty-five percent discount on your billings for the next two months. After that trial period, a blanket ten percent off what you're paying now." She took a deep breath. "And I'll freeze your rate for the next two years."

Tom laughed. "You worked on those figures before you got here."

She offered a trace of a smile that said: We speak the same language, you and I. "You sounded a little bent out of shape, so I thought I'd better come prepared." Tom must have smiled or given some sign of indulgence, because Jessica settled back into her chair. Her leg began a leisurely pendulum swing.

She was good at finance, but great at seduction. Jessica trotted out all the old prefeminist tricks—the southern belle's we-have-a-secret smile, the call girl's stroking of her neck and calves, the teenager's toying with her hair—that no liberated woman would dare use in a business situation. Unseemly, unrighteous. Expedient, effective. If, at that moment, a mesmerized Tom had swept her up in his arms, called the police to haul me off to the hoosegow, served Hojo with divorce papers, and booked a suite at the Ritz in Paris for a getting-to-know-you weekend for him and Jessica, I would not have been surprised.

"It's an interesting offer," he responded. "I'll give it some thought."

"Thank you."

I felt so useless, hiding out in his utilitarian executive bathroom—gray tiles, with an Ansel Adams photograph of snow-capped mountains hanging over the toilet—while Jessica was free to be Jessica.

"I'm direct in my dealings," Tom was saying. "Maybe too direct at times. I apologize: I should have asked you how you're doing. This must be a bad time for you."

Jessica sucked on the fleshy pad of her thumb. "It's been your basic hell." She sucked a little more. "Not just Rick's death, but that he was *murdered*."

"And look who they say did it," Tom responded.

"How could they let her escape?" she asked, indignant. "They were going to arrest her right after the funeral, but out of decency to his sons, they decided to do it the next day. Can you believe the stupidity?"

"Just terrible," Tom sympathized. "Any news yet? Although if they'd found her, I suppose I'd have heard it on the radio this morning."

"They can't seem to catch her, which only shows their absolute ineptness. She's not a fool, but no one would call her clever. Although she did talk her way up to my apartment."

"You're kidding."

"No. She said she was Rick's sister, and the cretin doorman let her up."

"Did she threaten you?"

"Threaten me? She hit me!"

"Jesus H. Christ! She *hit* you?" I'd told Tom I'd smacked her. Big deal: He didn't have to carry on as if I'd beaten her senseless. "Do you have police protection?"

"They're useless. I have private security."

"Very smart." I wasn't able to work myself into a froth over their tone of tycoon-to-tycoon intimacy, because Tom kept moving along. "Has she been spotted anyplace else?" He sounded deeply concerned not only about the case but about Jessica's welfare. For all I knew, he was. I wished I could see him.

"Yes, she has. And with a gun."

"No!"

"Yes! She threatened the woman who used to do our PR. The woman didn't actually see any gun, so our brilliant men in blue didn't take her report seriously at first. But then she popped up—literally— in the back seat of one of her neighbors' car, a fellow who's an old friend of mine, who introduced me to Rick. But this time, she held a gun to his head!"

"I just don't get it. I knew her years ago. We grew up together."

"That's right. She was the one who steered Rick to you." Oh, yeah? I wanted to shout. "She" didn't steer "Rick." "She" was the one who, with intelligence, articulateness, and two coats of mascara, convinced Tom Driscoll to sign on as a client.

"She was such a nice girl," he mused. "Even now, I can't believe she could be capable of that kind of violence. I guess she went crazy."

"You're assuming that her story about Rick breaking into the house is true."

"What do you mean?"

"I think she lured him into the house on some pretext in order to kill him."

"You're telling me that the Rosie Bernstein I knew planned a cold-blooded murder?" Tom was amused.

Jessica wasn't: "Absolutely." Her voice took on a husky intimacy. Her hand dropped, and she began a sensuous exploration of her ankle. "Look, he left her for me. She was an older woman with no future."

"Husbands waltz out all the time and wives don't go homicidal," Tom interjected.

"What took her over the edge was knowing that Rick . . . " She took a deep, reluctant breath. "Rick didn't want her. First, there was his secretary. That one went on for years. She had to have known. God knows everyone at the company knew: He couldn't have tried very hard to keep it a secret. Then a woman from wherever he was on Long Island. You can't tell me she didn't catch on to *that* one. Do you know what I think? Beneath that nice, ordinary facade, there's a woman who slowly went mad. I think she'd been planning it for years. I was just the icing on the cake."

"I don't buy that," Tom told her. "You're a little more than icing." His voice had the resonance of a male who wants to mate. Jessica laughed softly, an appreciation of Tom's acknowledgment of her charms. I couldn't bear the thought that I'd gotten him interested in sex again and that Jessica would be the one to reap the benefits.

"All right," Jessica conceded modestly, "I may be more than icing. The difference was, Rick fell in love with me. The others were just . . . I used to tell him that once he got some money in his pockets, he just couldn't seem to keep his pants on." The two of them chuckled, simultaneously and delightedly.

"Do you have any idea why he went to the house or how she lured him there?" Tom asked casually.

"No. That's part of the reason I know she manipulated him. And she must have done a good job of it too, because he would *never* have entered that house again of his own free will." She smiled. "You know how he and your wife referred to it, don't you? Upwardly Mobile Manor."

"Charming."

Jessica picked up the sudden chill in the air. "I thought that was a little churlish myself. But Rick abominated the place."

Tom suddenly got sincere. "Tell me if I'm getting too personal." Jessica nodded, although from the way she was eyeballing him, there was no such category as too personal. "How does someone of your caliber wind up with a man like him? Weren't you concerned he'd keep fooling around?"

"Not really. For the first time, he'd met a woman who had the upper hand." Tom must have given her a heavy-duty leer, or at least a come-on smile, because Jessica suddenly stopped feeling up her ankle and began—with a fair degree of subtlety that made it all the more effective—to massage her middle and index fingers. She did it with such an enticing rhythm that I wouldn't have been amazed to see them ejaculate. "I did love him. But I've been doing a lot of thinking lately."

"About what?"

"Was it love? Or was I just obsessed with his . . . What's the word? Vitality? No, virility." I couldn't believe it! She actually ran her tongue over her lips! "He was quite the fellow, Rick was." So, to her mind, was Tom Driscoll, and her recollection of Richie's prowess was meant to telegraph the message that it took quite the gal to bring out the full potential of a middle-aged fellow. I had no doubt that Nicholas

Hickson had, momentarily at least, ceased to exist for her; Jessica had conquered him the moment he agreed to leave his wife. Now she was concentrating on Tom. True, as his own wife had pointed out, he may not have been fourth-generation rich, as Hickson was, but he was rich enough. Younger, too, than Daddy Dearest and infinitely more attractive. Also, he had a wife, so Jessica wouldn't have to miss her usual fun of busting up a marriage.

"You know my wife was drawn to Rick," Tom said, clearly irritated by such poor judgment.

"I know," Jessica consoled him. "Nothing ever went on between them."

"I'm aware of that," he said coolly. "He was a lady-killer, though. Not that you could tell from the look of him."

Jessica gazed at Tom. "Rick gave his ladies what most women never get. Not just lovemaking. He wasn't a Don Juan, not in the sense of being a satyr. But he was a hopeless flirt, and a great one. He turned his attention on a woman, and all of a sudden her life opened up. He gave them excitement. Attention. He made them come *alive.* But when he got bored with them, they stopped existing for him; they might as well have died. Even if it had only been a heavy-duty flirtation, losing him would have been bad enough. But can you imagine his walking out on an actual affair? If the wife hadn't done it, one of the other two might have. Trust me: he could drive a woman *crazy.*"

"It's an interesting theory."

"It's more than a theory. After he left the wife and moved in with me, I started getting beastly calls."

"From Rosie?"

"I don't think so. I have a feeling it was a disguised voice, but even then, it didn't sound anything like her. Besides, one of the calls came on a night she and Rick were meeting at her lawyer's office. When he came home, I asked if they'd been together the entire time, and he said yes. I remember he'd laughed: There was no way she'd have given up even a second of his company. Sad."

"Was it always the same woman who called you?" Jessica nodded. "Did she threaten you?"

"If I didn't stop seeing Rick, she'd, uh, cut off certain parts of *my* anatomy."

Easy: She could have done it with manicure scissors. But Tom sounded appalled. "Jesus!" he said.

"I told you he could drive a woman crazy," Jessica said.

"But not you," Tom observed.

He must have risen, because Jessica was suddenly out of her chair. "No," she said softly. "Not me." Tom strolled over to her. "It takes a lot to make me crazy," she added.

"I'm sure it does," he replied. He shook her hand. "By the way, I accept your terms. We'll speak again in two months." His voice fell to an even lower, more voluptuous register. "After the trial period."

"I'll look forward to that," she murmured as he escorted her out the door.

I emerged from hiding, expecting to see Tom come back in sweating, breathing hard, probably turgid. But he was one cool dude. "Do you know what my old Irish mother would say about a girl like that?"

"Woman. What would she say?"

"She'd say: '*That* is a wicked, wicked girl.'" He grinned. "Some piece of work, Jessica is."

"Tempted?"

"I'm human." He put his arm around me, kissed the top of my head, and added: "I'm not so sure about her." I hugged him for a minute, then plopped myself down on a seat of what might have been the world's longest sectional couch. It was an innocuous gray that repeated itself in the carpet and in the burgundy-and-gray-striped seats on two pull-up chairs. The entire office, including lacquered burgundy cabinets, had clearly not been designed by the person who had conceived the Driscolls' Euro-chic apartment. Rather, it showed the hand of a decorator for an office furniture store, whose lackluster imagination had been further constrained by being ordered: Modern, but not too modern, and stick to the budget. Tom sat beside me, and we propped our feet up on the low burgundy coffee table.

"Think she did it?" I asked.

"Hard to say. I'll tell you what does bother me. The police are sure it's you. So why does she need an elaborate construct that you not only did it but you planned out the whole thing? She made it sound inevitable that anyone who came under his spell could have done it because he drove them crazy— but that you were the craziest because you'd been with him the longest." He took my hand between his. "What did he have? Did he have to strap it to his leg?"

"No. He was a wonderful lover, though: imaginative, uninhibited. But we'd been married for twenty-five years. When he left, if I did go off the deep end, it wasn't because I'd lost my stud. Well, I have to admit that his studliness was nothing to sneeze at.

But the real hurts? My family broke up. I lost my life's companion. When the person who knows you most intimately says, 'No, thanks. I don't want any more,' it's the cruelest rejection."

"He was nuts, Rosie."

Oh, yeah? How about your tossing me over for the Virgin Peggy? I was tempted to say. But I stayed mum on that one. Nor did I point out that when he came home from Dartmouth for Thanksgiving his freshman year, he never called. I'd waited and waited, and when I finally phoned him late Saturday afternoon, he sounded surprised—not that I'd been brazen enough to call, but that I existed. He said he'd love to see me, but he'd already made plans.

But now he was my comrade, my co-conspirator, so I simply said "Thank you."

"What now?"

"I need a minute to think." I shut my eyes. Random images, stray phrases, half-formed notions, whooshed around. I remembered a steamy detail or two from my night with Tom. I brooded about whether anyone at home had remembered to take back "The Gamut of Love in *Pride and Prejudice*" papers I'd graded or to put more seed in the bird feeder. I recalled playing tennis, doubles against Stephanie and Carter, missing a game-winning shot because I was momentarily spellbound by Richie's incredible intensity, every muscle taut, every thought concentrated on winning, and how he'd smashed his racket against the net post in fury over my bumbling. I thought how dearly I would love a facial.

But once I opened my eyes, I was clear on precisely what I had to do. "I have to go back to Shorehaven, Tom. I have to find Mandy."

Parallel furrows appeared between his eyes. "I thought we'd agreed it was dangerous for you to go there. You're known."

"We agreed that I'd finish everything I had to do here in the city and then I'd go back."

"You'll be spotted in two seconds! Someone will call the police." He pulled a zinger out of thin air. "You'll be surrounded by a bunch of cops. One of them could be a nut case and pull out a gun and shoot to kill—and then claim you were going for a weapon or something." He was starting to believe his own story; his palms got damp, then wet.

"It won't happen," I reassured him.

"How the hell do you know it won't?" He let go of my hand.

"It's unlikely. Okay?" But I didn't exactly make a flying leap off the couch. I stayed put. I needed Tom's clear, tough mind. And I needed him too, sweaty palms and all. "You know everything I know," I told him. "Can we go over it one more time?"

Finally, reluctantly, he said: "All right." He took back my hand.

"Who had something to gain by Richie's death?"

"You're talking about a real motive now, not about this driven-mad-by-passion stuff?"

"Right."

"Well, you have the most to gain, namely by becoming a multimillionaire in your own right, gaining control of Data Associates—"

"But that's ridiculous. Why in God's name would I want a company?" I demanded, perhaps not the most diplomatic thing to say to someone who spent his life acquiring companies.

"You could run it. Sell it. Fire Jessica. Whatever

interested you. Also, as the police see it, there's the usual jealous-woman business as well. You were his wife, and he left you for someone else."

"Go ahead. Say it."

Tom obliged. "A younger woman. In their view, that's a heavy-duty motive."

And for the good reason that so often it *was* the husband or wife who shot, poisoned, burned, throttled, hammered, pummeled, stomped—or stabbed. "You're sure I didn't do it, Tom?"

"Are you sure *I* didn't?"

"Of course."

"Ditto. So if not you, who else has a great deal to gain?" He answered his own question. "Your sons." I didn't respond. He knew enough to move on. "There's Jessica. For all the reasons you've considered. And because if I'm any judge of business smarts, she probably slipped a couple of advantageous clauses into their prenuptial. Probably some division of shares so that she'd have an interest equal or almost equal to his in the company— although that wouldn't have happened until they'd been married for a specific period of time. But what might be in effect now is an agreement that if anything happened to him, she'd get to run Data Associates."

"Oh my God!"

"If she did kill him, then she planned it out very carefully to put the blame on you. Brilliant job." Tom was playing a silent game of This Little Piggy, and he grabbed my pinkie. "Nicholas Hickson. Jessica might have mentioned what Rick was planning to do— breaking in and taking the bill of sale."

"But why would he want to kill Richie?"

"Maybe he wasn't so confident about Jessica's leaving Rick. Maybe he felt she needed a little more incentive to become his missus."

"Do you think he'd have the strength? He was tall but kind of scrawny."

"All he needed was one good jab with a sharp knife. Or maybe he sent someone to do it for him. Hickson's got serious money and connections. He might be able to come up with a real assassin, not a goon who'd get skunked the next night and start to brag." Tom gazed at my hand, as if more information could be found in my palm. "That's it for logic. Interested in illogic?"

"Very."

" 'Revenge of the PR Woman!' The one he canned right after Labor Day." I shook my head: dubious. "How about the two other girlfriends the lady-killer drove to the point of madness. Or the girlfriends' husbands or boyfriends."

"Possible."

"The secretary? Or what about this Mandy? Where does she fit in?"

"That's why I have to go back."

Tom didn't like that, but he was objective enough to give Long Island yet another chance: "One more possibility. Remote, though."

"I'll take whatever you've got."

He decided that was a double entendre and winked before he went on. "Carter Tillotson is what I've got for now. His answer to you about why he called Rick that last day, about the presurgery exam . . . Was he making it up as he went along?"

"I'm not sure. He was hesitant, but I assumed that was because he was so surprised that I knew about the call. Plus he did have a 'gun' to his head, which doesn't make for smooth conversation." I chewed on my bottom lip for a while. "I'll tell you one thing that was weird. The night Carter came over with Stephanie, supposedly to pay a condolence call. He was his normal, nebbishy self—although people don't think he's a nebbish because he's tall and nice-looking and a doctor—but all of a sudden he went haywire."

"Right. You said he dragged his wife out, told you not to bother them again." I nodded. "That behavior makes sense if he really thought you were a psycho who might kill again. But if that was the case, why did he drop by in the first place?"

"I guess Stephanie talked him into it."

"Then why didn't he see it through like a gentleman?"

"That's what I don't get. He just got more and more ill at ease until he was practically twitching."

"Think back. At what point did he go over the edge?"

I couldn't be sure. "Maybe when Stephanie was talking to me about helping me find a lawyer."

"Now listen to me, Rosie. I've met this man. He's in the social rat race, or trying to be: cocktail parties, little dinners, a couple of charity events. He's trying to become society's darling, the face-lifter of choice, and he's making some progress. All my wife's friends go to him. He even has some of the women my wife aspires to be friends with going to him. And my wife, for God's sake: She's done everything but put him on retainer. Now I admit, he and I haven't said more than a couple of words to each other, but he never, ever struck me as excitable. And not the repressed type who could suddenly explode."

"I told you: He's a nebbish."

"But, at least since that afternoon, he has been a nebbish who is extremely agitated about you, for whatever reason. And your last encounter wouldn't make him say: 'Gosh, that Rosie is easy to be with!'" Tom took a couple of deep breaths; he was working on a sermonette, which had to be just right. "I know I can't tell you what to do, but it is my most profound hope that you'll stay away from him. Either he is a terribly dangerous man or he's convinced you are terribly dangerous. He's a man on the edge. There's no telling what he might do."

"I know." I did. I really did.

Tom walked over to his desk, picked up a phone, and gave his secretary a quick story about having come in early, before seven, with his sister-in-law Marge, from Seattle. Joe's wife. Clearly, the secretary was familiar with what must have been the never-ending saga of Joe Driscoll. Would you please bring in coffee? Tom asked her, and lowering his voice, he added: Cancel all my appointments for today. The implication was that whatever mess Joe had gotten into again, it was a major emergency and required immediate intervention. I felt bad that his brother Joe had turned out to be a problem. I remembered him as a sweet, dreamy-eyed boy who came in second in the New York City spelling bee.

Moments later, the secretary entered, a persnickety-looking woman who appeared as if no detail was too unimportant for her to love. She put down a tray with folded linen napkins, porcelain cups, and coffee service, asked if there was anything else, Mr. Driscoll. She offered me a terse Good morning, but assiduously avoided looking at what she probably assumed was my tear-ravaged face. Excellent: Tom had neutralized the one person in his office who might wonder about how odd it was that he'd come in early, before her—and with a mysterious visitor.

Tom got busy pouring himself a cup of coffee, and I escaped into my own thoughts. In a way, I'd done well. I'd gotten more information than I ever imagined I could get. But instead of narrowing the problem—Who killed Richie Meyers?—all those facts merely made the question more complex and unanswerable.

"Rosie." I was startled. I'd been looking inward and had forgotten there was anyone else in the room. "Did you ever get any threatening calls?"

"What?"

"Remember what Jessica said about getting those disgusting phone calls."

"Right, I remember. No. No one ever bothered me."

"He not only left you for Jessica, but he also left another woman for her. And when he did . . . Maybe that woman did go crazy."

"And if he did leave her for Jessica, then she *had* to have been the one before, the one who filled that gap in his life. She's Mandy!"

"Maybe Mandy," he said. "Don't get too excited. The worst thing you can do is say: 'Aha, the culprit!' and cut off all your other prospects. The name could be a coincidence. There was the Mandy Rick's secretary told you about. The Mandy in Shorehaven may be someone else."

"No, Tom. It *had* to have been someone in town. Listen: It all fits in. Richie was coming home early those nights. I was so thrilled. I thought he was really trying to stop being such a workaholic. He was the old Richie again. But he hadn't given up cheating; all he'd cut out were drinks and dinner."

Tom rubbed his forehead for a minute. "All right. Let's think about his coming home so early. It's not that he didn't want to spring for dinner. It's that the woman was married. She had to get back to her husband—in Shorehaven."

"So who was she?" I murmured.

"We have to go back there. We have to find out."

That's when I had to explain to the man I'd fallen in love with a second time that there wasn't going to be any "we."

Eighteen

om Driscoll had gotten cool in his first semester at Dartmouth. In the years since, he'd grown so self-contained that I'd completely forgotten he had a flash temper. But he reminded me by slamming his fist on the coffee table and barking "Don't be an idiot!" when I refused to let him aid and abet me any more than he already had: He could not come along to Shorehaven.

"If I get caught, they'll catch you too," I explained in my honors English class voice.

"Do you think I give a shit?" he yelled. He stood and kicked the couch. His face was red, but just behind the anger I spied the glow of an athlete who's just completed a great play. Tom's rediscovery of his rotten temper wasn't just satisfying to him; it was exhilarating. "As a matter of fact," he continued, "I don't give a flying fuck!"

"When you're doing five to ten you'll give a flying fuck!"

It took me a moment to summon whatever composure I had left and explain the logistics of my plan. I would take a New York City cab out to Great Neck, about ten miles due west of Shorehaven. Once darkness fell, I could stroll over to the railroad station and be another shopper or commuter hailing a suburban taxi to get home. "Shorehaven," I'd say wearily.

Tom perched on the edge of his desk and swung his leg, reminding himself how cool he was. "You want to talk with three of four people," he said, suddenly extremely serene. "You're no dope, Rosie. Use the brain the good God gave you. Think: How can you go it alone?" He was so reasonable. "We have to work something out so I can be there if you need help." I shook my head. "Why are you being so stupid?" he shouted.

"I'm being smart!"

Obviously the couch had proved unsatisfactory, because he gave his desk a swift kick. "You've got your head so high up your ass you can't see daylight! Doesn't it occur to you that the police will be waiting at your friends' houses?"

"Not necessarily."

"Did you forget about Carter? He's damn well

going to be watching out for you. And do you think his wife is going to be all nice and forgiving about the gun you put against his head?"

"It was a cap pistol!"

"How the hell would she know that? And what about your nut-job friend who writes that crazy poetry? Do you expect her to make a pitcher of martinis after you sneak up on her?"

I admit: The objections Tom was raising made me very shaky. More than shaky. I wanted out. I'd had it. All I wanted now was to find a rogue plastic surgeon, get an Elizabeth Taylor nose, and find a place to live that had palm trees.

I had been moving too fast to notice that I had burned the last of my energy reserves three days earlier. I was spent. Peace at any price. For one second, I did allow myself a daydream: Tom kissing off Hojo and his business and spending the rest of his life with me on a small island, in a house on a bluff above the beach, with white curtains that billowed in the tropical breeze and a great library.

But I couldn't kid myself for longer than a second. Tom Driscoll's Big Adventure had lasted almost twenty-four hours. He hadn't been a wild and sexy high school boy for thirty years. He was merely an important man having a brief lapse of judgment. His break with good sense would probably not last much beyond midnight.

Even if he made good on his offer to bankroll me, what life could I have if I took my new nose to some new, palmy town? How would I ever know whether Ben married Suspicious Foods and had whiny, lactose-intolerant children—or fell for a loving and lively woman? Who could tell me whether

Alex made a go of his music or whether he wound up on the street—or in a three-piece pinstripe, negotiating megadeals for rock stars?

"I've thought all about going back to Shorehaven, Tom. I agree: I'll need help when I get there. That's why I'm going to call my friend Cass."

This time he didn't bother to shout. "Rosie, it's important that you hear me."

"I'm listening."

"Your friend is a straight shooter. She's gone too far helping you. She'll have no choice now but to call the police. Maybe she's called already to tell them you're in touch with her. That phone at school you've been using could be tapped!"

"I know it's a risk, but I trust her. I really do."

"Should I remind you that you were the woman who trusted your husband?"

I don't know how long I remained paralyzed by indecision, but in the end I agreed not to tell Cass I was going back to Shorehaven but only to ask if she'd heard anything new. Tom, encouraged by my new prudence, said he was willing to call the high school and be Mr. Thomas, Cass's architect, who had to reschedule their ten-thirty appointment on Saturday. I prayed that Cass would drop by the office to check her box before ten-thirty.

Tom joined me again on the couch. We sat without speaking, holding hands, fingers laced, staring straight ahead, two teenagers transfixed by a movie in which something horrible was about to happen.

At ten-thirty, I called the pay phone near the cafeteria.

"Hello," Cass answered, almost as if asking a question.

"It's me," I said, committing an egregious grammatical sin.

"How can you say such a thing?" Come on, I told myself: This isn't a double-crosser cooperating with the police, agreeing to talk to me on a tapped phone and help them locate me and lure me back. "Are you still there?" Cass inquired.

"It is I and I am here."

Cass's voice didn't break, but it sounded very high, rising above tears. "Rosie, not an hour goes by that I don't grieve for the loss of you, that I don't fear for you."

I turned. I did not want to see Tom. I was so ashamed of doubting her. I recalled a line in a textbook I'd used in an expository writing class years before, quoting some French writer: "It is more shameful to distrust one's friends than to be deceived by them."

"I miss you too, Cass. You have no idea how much."

"Of course I do," she declared, sounding a bit more like her usual self. "Let me tell you what I learned from Stephanie: very little. However, it was obvious that she is in a dither. One would not imagine her WASP nervous system is sufficiently developed to register disquietude, but one would be mistaken. I dropped by right after school and barely had taken off my coat before she wheeled out her bar cart, Stephanie of the We-never-drink-before-five Tillotsons. I had a small sherry; she poured at least a double shot of vodka onto the rocks for herself. I've never seen her so pale! The woman was whiter than snow, whiter than one of her overrated blancmanges, whiter than—"

"Whiter than you. I know she's a white person, for God's sake. Just tell me what she said."

"That she is tense. Why, you may ask. She fired her couple and now can find neither a nanny nor what she refers to as a proper housekeeper, and we both know what 'proper' means."

"Not darker than her blancmange. What about Carter?"

"Oh, Rosie! What possessed you? Was the gun real?"

"Of course not. What did she say about it?"

"He's had the runs ever since."

"Good. He deserves them. Did she say anything about Carter and Richie?"

"They were primarily sports friends, playing tennis, going to basketball and hockey games. I tried to get her to be more forthcoming about Carter by letting on how stunned Theodore was by the murder: violent crime in a residential area with two-acre zoning! I intimated that he has been sleeping poorly."

"Really?"

"Of course not. Theodore is a blockhead; nothing touches him. He sleeps like a baby. However, guess who does *not* sleep?"

"Carter?"

"Stephanie admitted that he has not been himself since that night."

"There *is* no 'himself,'" I retorted. "Carter Tillotson was born without a personality. Stephanie's fiddle ferns are more interesting than he is."

"I am sure that is true, but she is convinced that he is troubled. She suggested to him that it was better to 'talk things out,' but he said all he wanted was to be left alone, which he has been. Since his joyride with you, he has been sleeping at his office."

"Considering he has the runs, that's probably a blessing."

"Without a doubt. He is also there because the police are examining his car, looking for clues as to your whereabouts, and he will not take Stephanie's BMW for obscure reasons that may have to do with male-machine bonding. Naturally, being in the house with no one to cook for has made Stephanie even more tense. She farmed out the tyke to her mother's housekeeper. She says she has barely left her greenhouse, because it is her only comfort." Cass took a deep breath and admitted: "Actually, I do feel sorry for her."

"Did you bring up Jessica?"

"Only to ask if she had seen her at the funeral. She said she hadn't but had heard that Jessica was wearing gray—which she thought was too self-conscious. She did not want to discuss Jessica. She was so adamant that it leads me to believe she knew about Carter's affair, although I cannot say for certain. Actually, she was too jumpy altogether for me to assess what she knows. If I had to guess, I would say she is deeply concerned about her husband. Every time I said his name . . . I couldn't actually *see* a change in her, but I sensed it. It simply may be that he's normally so stolid that any sign of emotion frightens her."

I transferred the phone to my other ear. "Maybe she's worried that since Jessica is free now, Carter may go courting again."

I glanced back at Tom. Before I called Cass, I had offered, *quid pro quo,* to let him listen in on my conversation. Unlike me, he declined to eavesdrop, a reaction completely alien to his old Brooklyn instincts;

Dartmouth had done damage. Now, of course, he was so curious he could barely keep his behind on the couch. He mouthed: "What? *What?*" I shook my head—not now—then stirred the air with my hand: This conversation's far too complicated to try and convey. Offering what I hoped was an apologetic look, I turned my back to him.

I was going to disregard his warning. Yes, I'd been wrong about Richie. Maybe I'd been wrong about other people too. But I had to take a chance on Cass. I did not want to live in a world in which best friends could not be trusted.

"Cass, Richie was having an affair with someone in town. I have to find her. I have to talk to her." There was stunned silence on her end. On mine, Tom, who had been pouring himself more coffee, slammed the pot back onto the table with such force that its bottom cracked; coffee streamed across the table and dripped onto the rug. I almost told Cass to hold on, when it suddenly came to me that Sojourner Truth and Elizabeth Cady Stanton had not lived in order that I should break off a conversation so crucial that my life might depend on it, race to the bathroom, and get a towel to clean up a man's mess. "Did you hear me, Cass?" I inquired.

"Yes. Are you quite sure?"

"Quite." Tom watched the coffee trickle onto the rug for a minute, then headed for the bathroom. "I have to find out about someone named Mandy. According to my sources, she's the woman Richie was carrying on with before Jessica. I'm pretty sure she lives in Shorehaven."

"Mandy?" Cass asked herself. "There is a Mindy

Lowenthal in the reference section over at the library."

"No. I'm pretty sure it's Mandy." Tom returned with a box of tissues and cleaned up the coffee mess, although not without leaving a few wet brown Kleenex shreds on the carpet. "I have a hunch she's the lawyer who used to run with Stephanie at night. Check with Stephanie, but *please* be circumspect. I don't want anyone to know you and I are in touch. People have to think I'm a lone ranger."

"Am I ever anything but circumspect? I shall speak with Stephanie and inquire among my sources about any Mandys—or Amandas."

"Most likely she'll be between the ages of twenty and forty, but knowing Richie, don't cross off anyone under seventy-five." I closed my eyes to concentrate on a lie for Cass. It took only a second to come up with a whopper; I was getting proficient. "You can tell Stephanie that Sergeant Gevinski was at your house, questioning you about where I might be, and he got a phone call. You overheard him talking about Richie and a woman named Mandy."

"An excellent lie!" Cass said, with admiration.

"Thanks. Will you do this sooner rather than later? It's very important."

"I feel a sore throat and a high fever coming on. I shall have to leave school immediately." In all the years Cass had taught, the only time she ever left school before three o'clock was to deliver a baby. "Can you phone me at home around six this evening? I should have something for you by then, if there is anything to be had."

"Maybe I can drop by," I said softly.

"Rosie, no! You *cannot* come back here."

"Don't you think I know how to be careful?"

"You cannot be careful enough! I saw Alex this morning."

"When?"

"As I was going up the hill to meet Madeline and Stephanie for the walk."

"What was he doing up at that hour?"

"I have no idea. However, now that I am no longer his teacher, I find him quite agreeable. In fact, I have come to like him. Rosie, he and I chat every day. He tells me your house is under continual surveillance. And I myself know that there are an inordinate number of police cars cruising about the Estates. You must not risk coming back."

Tom knew I had made my choice. He did not fly off into a rage. We stood beside the wet patch of carpet and held each other. My head rested on a perfect spot, where his chest and shoulder met. He asked if my decision to go it alone was final. I said it was. He said he would pray for me. I told him I'd need every prayer he could muster. He rubbed my back between my shoulder blades and said that when all this was over, I could rub his back. I told him not to expect anything more from me, not even back-rubbing; he was a married man.

He said that if I needed him, to call his private number and say I was his sister-in-law Marge. His answering service would reach him in minutes: Day or night, he would come for me. Then he opened one of his cabinets, twirled a lock on a small safe, and took out a stack of money. When he counted out ten hundred-dollar bills, I told him that was more than enough and I hoped when all this was over I would be in a position to pay him back.

He walked me past his secretary and a receptionist, down a long gray corridor to the elevator. When it arrived he tried one more time: "Come on, Rosie. Let me go with you." He was pretty choked up.

For all I know, I may have been crying. But I definitely did not lose control. I stepped into the elevator, pressed "L," and told him what I'd never had the guts to say in high school; I'd waited for him to say it first. "Hey, Tom."

"What?"

"I love you."

The door closed before either of us could say goodbye.

Almost as scary as renting a car with Danny's fake credit card and driver's license was giving myself a haircut. I wore it brushed back, long enough to pull into a ponytail for exercising or a snazzy topknot for black-tie nights. But I bought a pair of scissors, and in the bathroom of a shop just off Madison Avenue that specialized in exorbitant and hideous sports outfits—black and olive-drab sweat suits trimmed with enough grommets, nailheads and chains to please the most discriminating sadist—I hacked off so much that when I stopped to study myself in the mirror, I saw another woman, with a lopsided Dutch-boy hairdo.

After my eyelashes and legs, I'd always considered my forehead my best feature. So it wasn't Athena's brow. It seemed to have wisdom and even a trace of nobility. Now it was obscured with bangs.

I flushed away the last locks of hair, stuffed the toy gun I'd been toting around in my cleavage into a deep pocket in my new sweatpants. Then I put up the hood of a sickly-green sweatshirt that had thick industrial zippers at the neck and cuffs. It was the least belligerent article of clothing in the store. Once in Shorehaven Estates, I would fit right in, even pass as a devotee of serious style—except among the seriously stylish.

I studied myself. My green hue was a reflection of the sweatshirt and my queasiness, but if you disregarded the pea-soup complexion, I looked downright exotic. The love child of a Sicilian and a Cherokee. What an arresting face! If I hadn't become even more nauseated at the thought of what I was planning and started gagging, I might have been dazzled by the new me.

I drove the new me across the Fifty-ninth Street Bridge into Queens. The silver Sedan de Ville I'd rented was the sort of car usually owned by a tycoon whose arms and cigar were of equal length. I'd chosen it on the theory that if I had to stow it on some street in Shorehaven Estates where parking was illegal, the police would become instantly suspicious if they spotted a sensible Chevrolet, but they might overlook a ridiculously extravagant Sedan de Ville.

Once over the bridge, I got stuck in what appeared to be a long-haul truckers reunion and did not get out of Long Island City until three in the afternoon. On the Expressway, I met up with the beginning of rush hour. But one of the classical music stations was offering a salute to Bizet, so it wasn't the torment it usually was. In fact, I sang along with Carmen. By the time I got to Nassau County, Bizet had given me such a good time that when I turned off the radio I could actually hear my stomach making rumbling, hungry noises.

I sat in a corner booth at a Pizza Hut. Although I sensed it might be a mistake to finish almost an entire medium-sized Cheese Lover's pizza with pepperoni, I decided to risk it on the theory that New York State authorities probably had some regulation prohibiting convicted felons serving life sentences from ordering out. I had two Cokes too, not diet. Then I drove another ten miles to Vinnie Carosella's office, in one of those eighties brick, glass-brick, and glass buildings that overlooked other brick, glass-brick, and glass buildings.

The receptionist, a sturdy, frizzle-haired woman, the type who could be cast as the knowing big sister in a tampon commercial, seemed to accept my story that I was a friend of Rose Meyers. I gave her the name on my driver's license, Christine Peterson. She accepted the name and even accepted my sweat suit—with its equally atrocious matching down-filled vest. I was so excited: My bangs had worked! She led me to Vinnie's office. "Mr. C," she called out. He glanced up from a yellow legal pad. "Ms. Peterson. Rose Meyers sent her."

The bangs didn't deceive Vinnie. "*Peterson?*" he demanded after he closed the door. "If you're going to pass yourself off as something else, give Russo a shot. Maybe Garcia. Peterson's a stretch, Rosie."

Desk, tables, chairs, bookcases—every surface except the seat he'd been sitting on—was piled with letters, manila envelopes, legal briefs, memos, and Post-it–covered reports. Giant rubber bands secured each pile; thus chaos was thwarted. Vinnie cleared a chair for me, sweeping a bound sheaf of papers onto the floor. He held the chair chivalrously while I sat.

"What can I do for you?" he asked

"I came to give you a retainer. I don't have much, but—"

"Forget it," he interrupted. "It's a done deal. A cop who owes me a big one got word to your kids that you were all right—and that you'd retained me. They stopped by a couple of days ago. Nice boys. Yesterday the older one gave me ten, cash." Before I could ask, he added: "Sold his car. They're both fine. The medical school is being nice about his staying away so long. The younger one had to turn down a booking at a rock club, but the manager took that to mean he was suddenly hot, turning down work like that, and called back to hire him for a big pre-Christmas concert.

"So that's good, Rosie. But I couldn't pry the tire report out of the police lab—although that's not the end of the world, because I got a friend to give me the highlights orally." Vinnie walked to an armchair and, leafing through the stack of papers on the seat, extracted a sheet of yellow legal paper. "The tire tracks you thought you saw near your husband's car? Well, you weren't having hallucinations or anything. They were from Michelin MXV tires, probably made around the same time your husband's tracks were." He skimmed the page. "His car had Pirelli P-zeros."

An involuntary surge of hope passed through me. I was almost afraid to ask: "Is this good news, Vinnie?"

"It's not bad. I mean, it isn't like having his girl-friend, that Jessica, get a guilt fit and call the cops and offer a videotaped confession, but it's a helpful fact. Someone else was probably in the area when he was there."

"It corroborates part of my story."

"A very small part, to be honest with you. It's a start, though." On a corner of his desk, under an open lawbook, was a candy dish, a huge thing in the shape of a brandy snifter. It was filled to the rim with miniature Almond Joys, an assortment of Hershey bars, Snickers, Milky Ways, and Three Musketeers. He laid aside the book and scooped up a handful, offering them to me as though I were a trick-or-treater with an unfilled shopping bag. When I declined, he heaped them on his desk and, picking out a Hershey's Krackel, peeled off its wrap with the adroitness of a longtime lover. He popped the candy into his mouth.

"What kind of cars have those Michelin tires?" I asked.

"I figured you might ask that. The answer is, nice cars. Saabs, BMWs, Volvos, Mercedeses." I noticed a chocolate beauty mark on the side of his mouth.

"I have a Saab," I told him. "Two of my friends—Cass and Stephanie—have BMWs. Stephanie's husband has a Mercedes. Madeline has a Volvo. They're so common." For some reason, no doubt ignoble, people who lived in the Estates preferred Aryan cars; there were probably five thousand Michelin MXVs rolling out of driveways every day. "There's a woman named Mandy too. God only knows what she drives, but even if it's a tricycle, I'll bet it has Michelin MXV tires."

"What does all this have to do with the price of tomatoes?" Vinnie inquired.

It took a while, because he kept stopping me to ask questions and unwrap chocolate, but I brought him up-to-date on what I had been doing since our meeting in Washington Square Park, which seemed a lifetime ago. A lifetime? Richie's murder: that had been a lifetime ago ... except it had been only one week.

"Let's see," Vinnie said. "The Michelin lady—lady for the sake of argument—is driving along, following your husband or maybe just driving by. In any case, she sees where he parked his car. She drives up and parks on the far side of him, either to check out his car or to hide her car because she's seen him get out and go to your house."

"It's a few feet deeper into the woods," I reminded him. "Maybe it was muddy in there after all, the way it is when the trees are right on top of each other. Maybe she got dirt on her shoes. Remember the dirt that was on my kitchen floor?"

"No one picks up that much dirt on their shoes, especially if they got out of the woods and just walked to your house the way your husband did." Vinnie meditated by massaging the bridge of his nose. "I'm the D.A., okay? You know how I'd handle what you just told me? When I got the lab guy on the stand, I get his direct testimony that the ground near the other set of tires wasn't all that wet either. The dirt was your husband's dirt."

"But he didn't leave footprints anywhere near his car! There was no dirt there."

"There was some dirt on his sneakers, and from the D.A.'s point of view, that's enough. There isn't any evidence of a third party."

"Can he prove that beyond a reasonable doubt?"

"I might be able to do something on cross to confuse the issue. It sounds like the lab people were under orders to concentrate on your husband's car. They wouldn't win any prizes for being meticulous when it came to the other tires and the ground around them. That could help us—a little."

I edged forward in my chair. "What about this? If he—she—the killer—comes from Shorehaven, especially from the Estates, or has been to our house or the Tillotsons', he or she knows that spot where Richie parked. Now, where could the killer have gone? If you don't want to be seen on the road, you can walk through the woods for a very short distance; you'll come to the path that leads you up to the Tillotsons' tennis court. But don't forget, this was the middle of October, and it was night. It's very unlikely that anyone would climb up a narrow path, hide on a tennis court that's surrounded by trees, and wait there for Richie to come back to his car. Also, there are enough trees right around the car that you might not even see him when he came back."

"Just out of curiosity, can you see your house from the court? Could someone have seen your husband walking there—or even inside, in the kitchen?"

"Not unless you had binoculars. But listen to the second choice you'd have if you don't want to be seen. Forget the tennis court. You park so Richie's car is blocking yours, okay? Either you've followed him or you just happen upon his car and want to see what's doing, if Richie's in it. Well, he's not, but you can figure out where he's likely to be headed. However, you don't want to be seen. And if you weren't following him, you can't risk walking along the road and up along our drive, because you might bump into me, right? Or Richie: you don't know if he's alone."

"Right," Vinnie agreed.

"So what do you do if you want to see Richie but not have him or anyone else see you?"

"You cut through the woods," Vinnie said. "But you're the one who told me it was like going through a jungle."

"But it can be done, Vinnie! Look, I did it. Believe me, it was rough going. My boots were a muddy mess. There were vines hanging all over the place, like ropes—nooses. I got all sorts of twigs and briers caught in my clothes, in my hair. Of course no one would *want* to go through that place at night. But I knew where I was going, so I was able to do it. You know why?"

"Why?"

"Because it was war, Vinnie, and I was desperate."

Vinnie Carosella nodded. "And so was the killer."

I sat back and gazed at his chocolate mouth and into his chocolate-brown eyes. He gave me a chocolate smile. "Vinnie, don't tell me . . . "

"Yeah, Rosie, it's true. You convinced me. You didn't do it. Somebody with intent to kill dropped by your kitchen that night. You are innocent. And wronged."

"Thank you." I stood to leave.

"Or," he continued, "you are *the* most incredibly gifted liar I've met in my whole life. In either case . . . " Vinnie doffed an imaginary hat, swooped it through the air, and held it over his heart. "I am at your service, Miss Rosie. Right now, what I'm going to do is get over to the D.A.'s and sit down with him. Maybe get him to call in your friend Gevinski. Talk about tires. Talk about all the other leads, like cutting through the woods and getting shoes dirty. Talk about shoes that should have left footprints but didn't. I'm going to talk about all the evidence they didn't follow up on because they were so hell-bent on arresting you. And you know what you're going to do in the meantime?"

"What?"

"Stay put!"

Sure, Vinnie.

Nineteen

Theodore Tuttle Higbee III, in a robe with satin lapels, tamped down the tobacco in his pipe and puffed. A contented man, he sat back in his easy chair in his oak-paneled den and, red pencil in hand, returned to the galleys of his lamebrained magazine, *Standards*. On his feet were velvet slippers with gold escutcheons. At his feet was man's best friend, his collie, Ronnie.

I kept my fingers crossed that I could count on

Ronnie. The dog's nature was not dissimilar to that of the President for whom he had been named. Indeed, just before I ducked to pass under the window, the collie glanced up and wagged his tail in anticipation: Ah! Someone to scratch my head. A second later, forgetting why he was happy, he yawned and returned to his nap.

Edging back and forth in the narrow space between the hedges of spreading juniper and the Higbees' ranch house, I tried to determine which among several rooms with curtains drawn was Cass's study. This *has* to be the one, I told myself. There was a silhouetted shape: Cass at her desk? A large table lamp? I waited, getting up to "But thy eternal summer shall not fade" in Sonnet 18, when the shape shifted position. I tossed a pebble against the window. *Ping!* Nothing happened. If Cass was lost in a book, I'd need to hurl a boulder to get her attention. On the other hand, if she was lolling in the bath and the silhouette turned out to be her obsessive-compulsive housekeeper wiping finger marks off furniture, I could be in deeper shit than the pile of Ronnie's I'd stepped into a few feet back.

My heart pounded. I had parked the Cadillac in the most concealed spot I could think of—a quarter mile away, at the end of the twisting, tree-lined driveway of neighbors who spent most of the year in Florida. Not unclever, but it gave me too much to think about. What if I had to make a fast getaway?

I had other worries too. What if I'd overlooked some minor menace that, left uninvestigated, would grow and grow and finally do me in? Or what if there was a major menace—Cass herself? I exhorted myself: Don't worry about a trap. Trust Cassandra Higbee with your life. She will not call the cops. I tried another pebble, then one more. The silhouette moved! A hand, seemingly in slow motion, drew back the curtain. Before it had parted enough for me to see the face, I spotted her beloved reading sweater, a cardigan of the fluffiest wool, the color of rubies, with deep pockets for glasses and Life Savers.

Cass had no doubt that it was me out there, although I was still crouched at hedge level. She gestured with her thumb—go that way. A moment later, her garage door opened and I was inside, between her BMW and Theodore's Porsche, and Cass was hugging me. Then she pulled back and gawked at my hair. "You look like Zelda Fitzgerald!"

"Thank you."

"No, no. After she became deranged." Her eyes moved downward. She drew herself up to her full five feet three inches. "Of course, your coiffure is a thing of beauty compared to that costume you are wearing."

"This isn't a great time for a make-over."

"How unfortunate. Well, then, let me tell you what I have discovered on the Mandy/Amanda front."

Cass's mind was swift, but the rest of her had always moved at slug speed and moved only when absolutely necessary. She walked only under pressure from me, Theodore, and her doctor. She was never one to stand when she could sit, so she opened the door to her car. I moved around to the passenger side, and we climbed into the icy leather seats.

"Before I left school," she reported, "I spoke with Faith and Vivian in Guidance," she reported. "They were able to recall two students named Mandy." She patted her pockets until she found a Guidance Department Request for Information form; she glanced at her notes. "A Mandy Daley was graduated two years ago and went off to Oberlin. She was a cellist; they assume she is still sawing away in Ohio. The other is older, in her mid-twenties. Her name is Mandy Springer—"

"I remember the name from an old class list. I'm pretty sure she was in Ben's year."

"She was in my American Literature class. According to school records, she considered a career in dental hygiene but never applied to college. At least no school ever requested her transcript. Her whereabouts are unknown. There are no Springers listed in the telephone directory. If I remember correctly, she was plain, bashful, barely an average student. I cannot imagine Richie being involved with such a girl. Can you?"

"Where he's concerned, I can imagine anything. But . . . I don't think I should waste time on these Mandys. Am I making a big mistake?"

"I have no idea, Rosie."

Cass turned her head and checked out the door that led from the garage to her kitchen. I calmed myself by reasoning that she had not called in the cavalry; she was merely jittery over the possibility, however remote, that Theodore might decide to stroll into the garage to fondle his fuel injectors.

"What about other Mandys?" I inquired. She set down her notes on the dashboard.

"None—"

"*None?*"

"May I finish, please? Thank you. I made many calls. It is curious: Most people seemed convinced they know an Amanda. However, when pressed, they are unable to name one. I came up with"—she picked up her notes—"an Amanda Huber, sixty or so, who works the presser at Shore Dry Cleaners; an Amanda Chase, who is seventy-seven and a pillar of the senior citizens' creative writing class; an Amanda Conti, who is thirteen and the junior high school's long-jump champion. No lawyer Amandas. No other Mandys at all—until I finally reached Stephanie about an hour ago."

"Where had she been?"

"At a contest sponsored by her garden club, in which the participants displayed centerpieces that combined holly, flowers, and vegetables. She said the contest was 'super,' but then, 'super' is her only adjective."

"Except for 'icky.' "

"True." Cass, never one to expend an extra calorie unless compelled, was growing fidgety. She fiddled with the levers for the directional signals and the windshield wipers, cleaned imaginary dust specks off the air vents, polished the radio and tape deck with the cuff of her sweater.

"Who *is* Mandy?" I demanded.

She depressed a small button, resetting a mileage counter beneath the odometer to a row of zeros. "Mandy Anderson." She did not have to consult her notes. "A bankruptcy lawyer, Stephanie's age. They met while Stephanie was still at Johnston, Plumley and Whitbred."

"Does Mandy work there?"

"I did not ask. I assume she does. However, once Stephanie quit her job, they were unable to find time to see each other. To remedy that, they ran together at night."

"Have they done it lately?"

"No. Bankruptcy is big business; this Mandy has been working until eleven or even midnight. Stephanie says the woman is 'super-stressed-out.' She has not seen her in ages."

"Where does she live?" I asked

"Here in town."

"I know that. Where in town?"

"Sorry," Cass said. "I did not ask." She peered into her rearview mirror as if it were reflecting a glorious scene.

"Cass," I roused her.

"She said Mandy is a lovely person. Mandy is smart. Mandy is a master of law-firm politics."

"Pretty?"

"Not according to Stephanie," Cass said. "Come to think of it, that is somewhat odd."

"It *is* odd," I agreed. "Stephanie's always saying how pretty everyone is."

"It is one of the curses of great beauty: She feels obliged to endow every plain woman with loveliness. That way, people will think she is benevolent and unaware of her charms. Can you imagine feeling compelled to prove to others that you are not secretly mocking their appearance?"

"So Mandy Anderson is a major dog?" I asked.

"Or Stephanie may simply dislike her. That would allow her the freedom to be picky and small of spirit, the way we are. Why shouldn't she dislike the woman? How can anyone like a person who willingly runs five miles at nine o'clock at night?"

"But Stephanie runs at night, and we like *her*," I said. Cass made a lemon mouth. "We *do* like her."

"I suppose so."

Something was lurking on the edge of my memory. Something about Mandy. I unzipped two of the pockets of the down vest and shoved my hands in. "Mandy Anderson," I thought aloud.

"Heavens!" Cass declared. "I nearly forgot. There are seventeen Andersons listed in Shorehaven; they must breed like rodents. I called each one."

"Well?"

"Not a single Mandy. Of course, she might have an unlisted phone number. Or Anderson might be her maiden name. She could be Anderson amongst the bankrupts and Mrs. J. Harcourt Goldfleigel here in town. We will never know."

"Of course we will"—I slipped out of the car—"once I speak to Stephanie."

Cass jumped out too. "You *cannot* go back there!" she cried. "Surely the police who are at your house will be keeping an eye on hers as well."

The garage door was open; beyond the floodlights, all was darkness. "I've come this far. How can I not talk to Stephanie?"

"Oh, Rosie, aren't you afraid?"

"Of course I am. I've been afraid ever since I tripped over a big, lumpy thing on my kitchen floor and it turned out to be my husband. I've been living with my *kishkes* in a knot ever since then. But when you take risks, you live with knots."

Cass clasped her hands under her chin and considered what I'd said. "I understand. You took a risk coming here."

I could have given her a big fat denial, but instead I simply said: "A small one."

"You made a wise decision, though you cannot be certain of that now. Hear me, Rosie. This is a night that may be filled with peril. You are bound to need help."

"I'd like to leave you out of it, if at all possible." We moved toward the open door. "I don't know if I'll be able to get to a phone. How can I get in touch with you?"

"Do you know those stairs that go to my basement entrance? I will leave that door open and tell Theodore ... Ah! I will tell him that I am having a terrible period. He will be very solicitous, but the very idea of what he calls 'woman problems' makes him uneasy, the knucklehead. He will be thrilled to avoid me."

"You love him, you know. That's your dirty little secret, Cass. That's why you stay with him."

"Hogwash."

"But you always make him sound like the world's biggest fool."

"He is. He is the sort of man who would not think it queer if a woman sacrificed a flock of goats to the menstrual goddess at her time of the month. He will pay no attention if I behave oddly. I will visit the basement every quarter hour or so until he goes to bed. Then I will stay down there and wait for you, as long as it takes."

There is nothing as dark and dangerous as a rich neighborhood without street lights. Teenagers taking shortcuts across backyards climb over fences and fall into invisible black-marble-dusted swimming pools. Cracks that have widened into chasms on substandardly paved, smooth-asphalt-looks-nouveau-riche roads catch unsuspecting cars. Burglars are deterred as much by the fear of tripping over a toppled weeping cherry and tumbling into an open storm sewer—their shrieks unheard by Chardonnay-sippers in their houses hundreds of feet from the road—as by the frequent police patrols. I turned onto Hill Road, which led up to the Tillotsons' house, and crashed into a mailbox shaped like a mallard.

I looked over at Gulls' Haven. A lamp in one of the bedrooms spread a golden glow. If I were in a movie, a single violin would begin to play "There's No Place Like Home" on the sound track. But schmaltz could be lethal; if I imagined caressing my boys' rough cheeks, or sitting before a crackling fire, sharing a bowl of popcorn and listening while they hooted over terrible school assemblies they'd endured, I would be so warmed that I could not survive the night ahead.

When I reached the top of Stephanie's drive, the wind subsided and an owl fell silent long enough for the cold air to relay cop shouts from Gulls' Haven: "Hey!" "Jim? That you?" "Shut the hell up!" I veered off behind a copse of evergreens and examined the front and one side of Stephanie's house. There were no signs that her grounds were patrolled; I heard no footsteps, saw no flashlight beam flitting over the lawn. The outside of the great money-sucking Tudor, illuminated by floods, appeared flat, a piece of scenery for a very elaborate production. But then I sniffed cooking smells, something sweet, apple-y, and Stephanie's house swelled into dimensionality.

Inside, only the downstairs lights were on. I sidestepped through the spruce, into a grove of flimsy white birches that offered almost no cover. As more of the house came into view, I saw Stephanie's greenhouse. How could I miss it? It was so brilliantly lit it could have been a pavilion for Cinderella to dance in. Glass twinkled, diamondlike; gro-lights threw off sparks of refracted color. Stephanie was at her work sink in her denim gardening overalls, lifting a pot and trimming its hairy roots.

I edged closer, past terra-cotta tubs overflowing with her fall plantings: green and purple ornamental cabbages and trailing purple mum plants. First of all, I told myself, a woman who nurtures green things, bakes, cooks, does fine needlework, weaves, reads, listens to opera, invites the neighborhood two-year-olds in to spatter-paint, and works to improve groundwater is a good person. She will believe in me. She will help me.

On the other hand, I'd abducted her husband and held him at gunpoint. She might not be so delighted that I was turning to her in my hour of need.

I approached the garden door of the greenhouse on my hands and knees. The lawn was spiky and dry, but the path had been smoothed by hundreds of trips to the garden. I propped myself up and stretched out to grasp the handle of the wooden door. A single click of the latch was enough. Stephanie jumped as if an alarm had gone off. I pulled back and pressed myself flat on the ground, perpendicular to the path, my head several feet away from the door.

Stephanie's gardening clogs clopped toward me. I raised my head an inch or two as the door opened. She glanced around and down, but not far enough to see me. "Rosie?" she whispered into the night. The artificial sun of the greenhouse lights on her perfectly oval face revealed not one flaw; her skin made porcelain seem coarse. It was a sweet face as well as a beautiful one; if I read it right, she did not appear so much concerned about herself as worried about me. "Hello?" I could hear the tension in her voice. "Rosie, are you out there?"

On the other hand, if she believed I was a threat, she had a couple of gardening tools in her overalls pockets that could maim nicely. I had the toy cap pistol I had used on her husband.

I pushed myself up into a squatting position, ready to leap up to greet her. Ha, the advantage of surprise! However, when you've spent the last year being a forty-seven-year-old English teacher, sky-rocketing to full height from a squatting position is more an intellectual concept than an actual event. By the time I put my hands on my knees and pushed, Stephanie was right at my side—helping me to stand.

"Are you all right?" she asked. She was five feet ten, and an athlete. A sharp and sinister bulb planter sticking out of one of her breast pockets pointed right at my throat.

"Fine," I said, backing away.

"What's wrong?"

"Nothing. I just don't want to stand near the door-way, if it's okay with you. I'd be lit up so bright the cops could see me for miles." With one hand I brushed off the sweat suit. With the other I felt for the gun; it was still in my pocket.

"Let's go into the house, then. I'm making a *dartois aux pommes*. Flaky pastry with apples, applesauce—"

"For God's sake, Stephanie!"

She slapped her hand to her forehead. "Can you believe this? I don't know what I could have been thinking. You must be freezing. I'm sorry. Forget the *dartois*. How about an Armagnac? Come inside." I was doing fine in a sweat suit, vest, gloves, heavy socks, and a brand-new pair of running shoes. She wore only overalls and a cotton turtleneck. "How can I help you?"

"I'm okay. I don't have much time." I glanced toward the house. If the police were inside, they wouldn't hang crepe paper streamers and blow up balloons to welcome me; they'd be hiding. Still, Stephanie hadn't glanced in that direction, as she might if she knew help was just yards away. Nor had she shown any sign she was afraid of me: no heroine-tied-to-the-railroad-tracks scream when she spotted me. "Let's stay here and talk."

"Sure. Let me just get my jacket." She saw my objection before I made it. "Look, Rosie, I know you must be supernervous. My jacket's hanging in the greenhouse, on that poor dead magnolia. See it? It will just take me a minute to get it." While I hesitated, she crossed her arms and hugged herself. "Never mind," she said. "I'll make do."

"Stephanie, I'm so sorry about what I did to Carter."

She nodded but looked away. It's not easy to

come up with a socially acceptable response to a friend who has just apologized for pressing a gun against your husband's head. "I suppose you were under a lot of pressure," she said at last.

"I was."

Her generosity gave way to a certain testiness—not that I blamed her. "Where in the world did you get a gun?"

"From one of my old students who turned to a life of crime," I lied.

Stephanie had five inches on me, and she looked down, a picture of severity. "Do you know the statistics on the number of accidental deaths each year from unlicensed handguns?"

"I've had my death already. Except it wasn't from a gun. And it wasn't an accident."

Stephanie shivered so hard it was almost a spasm. "Did you do it, Rosie?" she asked. The wind almost blew her voice away.

"No!" Calm down, I warned myself. She's terrified. You don't want her to run or call out to the cops. You need her.

You *think* you need her. But what if Jessica was wrong? What if Jessica herself was the killer and her whole story to Tom was just that: fiction. What if I'd followed the wrong trail and the answer was back in the city?

"Do you have any ideas who did do it?" Stephanie still sounded frightened.

"Tell me about your friend Mandy."

"Why does everybody want to know about Mandy?" Stephanie demanded. She was still shivering, I noticed. She crossed her arms and squeezed them so tightly together that the pressure lifted up the bulb planter until it nearly dropped out of her pocket.

"Who's 'everybody'?" I asked.

"You and Cass. Why do you want to know about her?"

"Richie was having an affair with her right before he started with Jessica."

"*What?* With Mandy? I don't believe it."

"Mandy Anderson," I said.

"That's her name, but ... No way, Rosie. No way. First of all, she's superhomely. Not interesting homely. A really nice figure but crooked bottom teeth and icky skin with those giant pores. And the world's worst nose job. Carter says she looks like the next words out of her mouth will be 'oink-oink.'" She was about to chuckle at this example of rhinoplastic wit but stopped when she saw my expression. "Sorry. I mean, sorry for the remark, but also for all the hurt you've had. You know, on those stress indexes where they rate traumatic experiences from one to ten? You must have—"

"It's beyond counting," I cut in. "What is Mandy like?"

"Very nice. I like her a lot. Smart. She just made partner in her firm—and she's bringing in business on her own. It's great to see a woman being a rainmaker."

"Did she ever mention Richie?"

"No. Of course not. I doubt if she even knew him. I mean, she works almost all the time. The law is her whole life. She's not at all active in the community; they just moved here a year ago."

"Is she with the firm you were with?"

"No."

"Which firm?"

"A big Wall Street firm."

"Which one?"

"Kendrick, McDonald."

"Is she married?"

"Rosie, maybe I wasn't all that close with Richie. When you told me he'd fallen for someone else, that he was leaving you, I thought I'd faint. Richie Meyers? But I did know him well enough to know he'd *never*, not in a million years—"

"Stephanie, Richard Meyers was a man full of surprises. Please, just answer my questions." She nodded okay. "What's Mandy's marital situation?"

"She's married to a tax lawyer."

"What's his name?"

"Jim. I hardly know him. I mean, most of the time I spent with Mandy was at Women's Bar Association meetings and running." The wind ruffled Stephanie's hair; she ran her hand over it and, naturally, it retreated into absolute smoothness. Perfection. However, she was so flawless she seemed molded of peachy-white plastic, not made of flesh. "Jim is much better-looking than she is," she added.

"Any children?"

"Not yet. She's just thirty-two. She wanted to wait until she made partner and then get pregnant, but the way she's been working, she's not going to want to get tied down with a baby so fast."

"Where does she live?"

Stephanie sucked in a deep breath. "Let me think." I waited. Why was she taking so long? Come *on*. "She always meets me here, so I'm trying to remember. Oh, over in Shorehaven Acres, on Crabapple Road."

"Do you know the number?"

She shook her head. "It's a split-level. Coming from here, it's on the second block, I think the third or fourth house on the left, but don't quote me." Suddenly she gripped my arms. "Rosie, don't do anything rash."

"I won't do anything that's not necessary. Tell me how Carter knew Jessica Stevenson."

"What?" Stephanie demanded, thrown by the quick change of subject and the mention of her husband's name. Her head swiveled, as if searching for someone who had the answer. "I swear, Rosie, when Richie left you and you told me about Jessica, I swear"—she lifted her right hand—"I didn't even know that Carter knew her. You have to believe me." I didn't, but then again, I didn't actually disbelieve her. "She was working at the same investment bank as one of his patients. A man: Carter had done his eyes and jowls. Anyway, she was at a cocktail party this man gave. She was telling Carter about her work, about how she concentrated on helping small companies get capital and expand. It sounded right up Richie's alley, so Carter introduced them. That was it."

"Was Carter her friend?"

"No!" Stephanie's denial showed more spirit than I'd ever known her to display. "Absolutely not." So she *did* know about Carter and Jessica. "If he did see her at all after she started working at Data Associates, it was only when he was meeting Richie at his office before they went to a Knicks game or whatever."

I didn't want to humiliate her by making her acknowledge Carter's affair, so I took time before I spoke. "Was Carter upset when he heard about Richie and Jessica?"

"Well, I guess so. I mean, yes. You know, upset for you, upset that Richie had walked away from the marriage."

"What did he say about it, specifically?"

"Nothing. I mean, you know ole Carter Tillotson, our man of few words." She was lighthearted, almost giggly. "'Too damn bad,' or something like that." Suddenly she grabbed my vest and pulled me toward her. "Let's go inside, Rosie! Come on, before my *dartois* burns to a crisp." I grasped her wrist and jerked her hand away. "I'm sorry," she apologized. "I didn't mean anything by that. All I want to do is help you. It's so cold out here. It must be terrible for you. And . . ."

"And what?"

"I'm so scared you'll get caught, Rosie." Her bright eyes grew brighter. "I know what! You can have Gunnar and Inger's suite, downstairs, right behind Astor's Nintendo room. It's perfect! Out of the way. Carter won't be home till eleven, and if you come in now, he won't have a clue you're there! It's *really* pretty; I did the whole thing in a blue toile. You can get some rest. I can make you dinner, and we can figure something out."

She reached toward me again, this time not grabbing, merely imploring me, one hand outstretched, open. But I had too much left to do, and with the three-cheese pizza with pepperoni still sitting on top of my heart, I could not bear the notion of Stephanie hovering over me, an expectant smile on her humdinger of a mouth, waiting for me to laud her *dartois*. Also, I had qualms about going inside with her; I didn't think she was cool enough to keep a secret from Carter.

"Rosie," she said, and reached out with her other hand as well: Come, let me take care of you. A magnanimous gesture.

"Okay," I finally agreed. "Go get your jacket, and we'll take a walk around the house. No reflection on you, Stephanie, but I just have to be sure no cops are wandering around. For my own peace of mind."

"I understand. Please don't apologize," she said, and hurried into the greenhouse. Did she really forgive me for what I did to Carter? Could she really be that understanding? Or would she tuck me into a blue toile bed and call the cops?

Like a wild woman, I ran back into the woods.

I'd admitted to Cass that I was always afraid. True, for a few hours in the airport motel, with Tom wrapped around me, the fear had abated, but in its place came dread at the inevitability of resuming my quest: grief, too, that the little room in the back of my mind that I'd kept ready for Tom all those years would only be used for a one-night stand.

Nevertheless, between the time I galloped away from Stephanie and scrambled around the perimeter of the woods behind a dense row of trees, emerging to trot another half mile out of the Estates and over to Madeline's in Shorehaven Gardens, I lost my fear.

Why? How? Well, the only explanation I can come up with is a battle analogy. It's midnight. A soldier in a trench knows the shelling will not stop. She knows she may die before daybreak. Having accepted that premise and accepted that by some grace she has so far been spared, she throws back her head to gaze at the starry night, giddy and grateful. Hey, God! I'm alive! At that moment, she acknowledges that she has only the tiniest role in determining her fate. But what the hell, God has stuck with her so far. Nevertheless, it's a long time till dawn. She knows all the terrible things that might happen to her between now and then. What will she do? Surrender? Commit suicide? Not this soldier! She has only one option. For one second she manages a prayer of thanks in the form of a big grin. Then she grabs her weapon and fights on. Maybe she lives. Maybe she dies. But at least, all through the night, she's not afraid.

Madeline and Myron Michael Berkowitz, D.D.S., had built a house Anne Hathaway might have lived in if she'd divorced Shakespeare, gotten alimony, and moved to Long Island. It had crisscrossed beams, leaded windows, and synthetic thatch that conformed to the Nassau County fire code. When Myron left, he'd signed over the house to her. The following year, the real estate market dwindled to virtual meaninglessness. A couple of buyers had come to look, but no one other than the Berkowitzes, it seemed, had wanted to define the good life as living in an English country cottage with an in-ground hot tub in back. Madeline was stuck.

So was I: I tried to think of an imaginative way of sneaking up on her, but I was coming down with a cold and it was all I could do to keep from alerting her with a major "Achoo!" In the end, I simply walked up the path to the front door and rang the bell.

"Who's there?" Madeline called through her intercom, as I hoped she would. It wasn't very late, but her voice was soupy with sleep. There were intercoms all over the house; in the final years of their marriage, she and Myron had their only civil exchanges speaking to one another from different rooms.

"It is Cassandra," I announced. There was no response, so I added: "I have news"—I pronounced it "nyoose," in Cass's prep school way—"about Rosie."

When Madeline opened the door, even before she realized who I was, she saw immediately that I was a white person, not the black person she'd expected, and she started screaming. Up and down the scale—"Aaaaaaaaaaaaaa!"—while trying to shut the door. Then she cried "Rosie" and came close to passing out; her screeching stopped, her body went limp, and I bulldozed my way into her house. She recovered too fast. "Aaaaaaaaaaaa!" Her hair, mussed from the pillow, stood out in gray spikes, so it looked as if she'd put on a helmet. Her caftan, a tent of bottle-green velvet left over from her hostess days, was crushed from having been slept in. "Aaaaa—"

"For God's sake, Madeline. Get a grip!" I slammed the door behind me.

"The police are upstairs!"

"They are not."

That was probably not the smartest comment I could have made. Her face, glistening with night cream, fell into flaccidity. Her eyes welled up, acknowledging her imminent doom. All she could say was "Please . . . "

"Madeline, calm down. If I were a homicidal maniac, you'd be dead by now."

"Dead?" she whimpered. Shrinking back, she tripped over the saddle between the hallway and the guest bathroom. I caught her to keep her from falling. She tried a knockout punch at my nose, but as she was off balance, it hit the air. As soon as she was safely on two feet, I let her go and backed into the hallway.

"I have to talk with you, Madeline."

"I bought a can of Mace," she muttered, more to herself than to me. "I heard what you did to Carter."

"Where is it?"

"Where is what?"

"The Mace."

"Do you think I'd tell you?" It was probably upstairs, on her night table.

"You and I don't need Mace."

She laughed an ironic poet's laugh. "Of course not."

"I didn't kill Richie, Madeline."

"Right." She backstepped until she banged into the sink; it was shaped like a clam on a pedestal.

"Think, Madeline. If I were guilty, wouldn't I have kept running until I was safe? Why in the world would I have stayed around, trying to find out who did it?"

That stumped her, but only for an instant. "You were looking for a way to pin it on someone else."

"How could I do that, if all the evidence points to me?" Either she was being extremely cautious or the repartee had worn her out. She rested her hip against the sink. Her breathing came hard. She couldn't think of an answer. "Before Richie took up with Jessica, he was having an affair with someone else."

"Oh?" she asked, sarcastically. "Is that a surprise to you?"

"It was. I guess it wasn't a surprise to you."

"Grow up. That's what they do."

It did not seem a propitious moment for me to suggest that it was unjust to stereotype men. "The affair he had before Jessica: It was with a woman named Mandy." Madeline put her hand to her cheek. Feeling the grease of her moisturizer, she pulled off a couple of feet of toilet paper and wiped the stuff off her face. "Do you know a Mandy?" Madeline shook her head. "The one who used to run at night with Stephanie."

"I never met her."

"Do you know anything about her?"

"Stephanie says she's a great lawyer. And she has a twenty-three-inch waist. I bet Jessica's even more high-powered than this Mandy. But they're both the same type, aren't they?" Her apprehension was ebbing; her old, familiar anger surged. "Two peas in a pod. Self-possessed. Took every advantage of the women's movement but never paid their dues. Young. WASP. Arrogant."

Just then, something Hojo had said to Tom popped into my mind. She'd been talking about

Richie. Richie and who? Mandy? Something about Mandy? No, about Richie and Jessica: "He just loved them Protestant and well-bred. . . ."

"Oh," Madeline added, "One more thing. Stephanie says Mandy's *the* most oversexed woman she ever met."

Twenty

I left Madeline's house with a fistful of tissues and many doubts. Should I retrieve the Cadillac and whiz over to Shorehaven Acres to find Mandy? Go back and confront Stephanie? She'd known about Carter and Jessica and hadn't confided in me. Fair enough. Could she also have known about Mandy and Richie? Long runs on dark nights promote confidentiality; could her lawyer pal Mandy have been *that* close-mouthed about an affair with Stephanie's next-door neighbor?

I should have been in bed sipping hot lemonade and rereading *Bleak House.* My sinuses were clogged, my throat felt as if it had been filed with an emery board, my eyes watered, and frankly, I'd had it with heroics. I blew my nose, trying not to honk, thrust out my jaw a couple of times to clear those ear-to-throat tubes, and stole over to Madeline's toolshed.

The rubber doormat's no-skid bottom made a revolting thwacking noise, the sound of a hundred pacifiers being yanked out of babies' mouths. Just as I'd remembered, the key was right there. Inside the shed, I felt my way around the cobwebby murk, determined not to think of night crawlers and hairy-legged spiders. Finally I located the Berkowitz family bikes. Like a housewife evaluating cantaloupes, I squeezed tire after tire. I filched what turned out to be a mountain bike and took off into the blackness.

Naturally, riding back up to Stephanie's was no picnic, especially since I hadn't been on a bike since my sophomore year at James Madison High School, when I parked my beloved Schwinn for a minute to pick up a pumpernickel for my mother and a truck ran over it. Head down, pedaling like mad, I probably looked like Miss Gulch in *The Wizard of Oz.* Also, navigating in the dark over bumps and potholes with a drippy nose was not easy. At least I wasn't going downhill, where I could career out of control, fly through the night, land in somebody's artfully landscaped Judeo-Japanese willow/boulder/moss/wood bridge/babbling brooklet, and drown. My Schwinn hadn't had gears, but once I got the hang of shifting the mountain bike, I reached the summit in about ninety seconds.

Cops! The place was crawling with cops. Stephanie must have called them from the green-house, right after I bolted. I hauled the bike into the woods, stood it against a tree, and studied the entrance to Emerald Point, a hundred feet below. The police weren't announcing their presence. That is, there wasn't a single *whaa-whaa* of a siren. However, on either side of the tall entrance posts, there were enough patrol cars flashing hysterical patterns of red and white for the denouement of a Dirty Harry movie. Whether by craftiness or by disorganization, three more official vehicles raced past me at a velocity great enough to scatter leaves. Brakes squealing, the cars swung between the opened iron gates and up to the Tillotsons'.

Down in front, on the road, cops with walkie-talkies paced back and forth, pivoting once in a while to survey the darkness. Walkie-talkieless cops, deprived, eyed their comrades. Across the road, neighbors gathered, dressed in enough L. L. Bean and Eddie Bauer gear to launch a polar expedition. Soon someone's housekeeper would bring hot cider and doughnuts.

I stared down the hill: Two men were running up, toward the cops. Alex and Ben? Yes! Racing past the spot between our house and the Tillotsons', where Richie had parked his Lamborghini for the final time. Ben, the brawny college jock, fell behind. Alex, smaller, more lithe, his long hair flying behind him, passed his brother and, finally, came to a stop in the dazzling police light. They were so close! In two seconds I could touch them! Of course, in two seconds, with all those trigger-happy cops, I could be a human colander.

Mandy. I had to focus on Mandy. What *was* it that I'd heard about her? I set the bike flat on the ground, tossed some leaves and evergreen branches over the glinting handlebars, and walked through the woods— away from my boys, away from the Tillotsons'. Something about Mandy . . . Was it something Stephanie had said? Whatever it was, it didn't jibe with the truth. Why not? Because it contradicted something Tom had said about Mandy, and whatever Tom said was, ipso facto, the truth.

My progress was slower now, because I had to stay well into the woods. Although I needed to get back to Cass's, I couldn't afford to take the road and get trapped in the high beams of a police car. My chest and back felt as if malevolent hands were compressing them, squeezing out the last of my air. Breathless, I sat on a fallen tree. The dead bark grabbed at the thick cotton of my sweatpants. Take it easy, I chided myself. The answer will come if you relax. Just pose the question.

Okay, what had Tom said about Mandy?

The brain is a less than perfect instrument. What came to mind was not a couple of revealing sentences packaged in quotation marks but a remembrance of falling asleep in Tom's arms, his long leg draped over my hip. Comforting knowledge, albeit not precisely germane. One more time: What information had Tom Driscoll given me about Mandy Anderson? Had he heard Hojo talking about her? Overheard a mention of her in some conversation? Could he possibly have run into Mandy someplace?

Damn it! Was this to be my fate, the particular brain cell that contained the bit of information critical to my vindication dying of old age thirty years before the rest of me?

All of a sudden I said Wow! Double wow! I had it! And I flew through the trees back to Cass's, faster than anyone else in the world ever could.

"Stephanie told each of us how unattractive Mandy is, right?"

"Correct," Cass agreed. Simultaneously, we put our feet on the seats in front of us. When the Higbee kids were young, years before they'd gone away to school, Cass and Theodore had converted the rear of their basement into a theater, with a raised stage hidden behind a blue shower curtain and three rows of benches for the audience.

"Okay," I began. "If this Mandy has giant pores and a snout, then try to figure this: When Tom was speaking to his wife—"

"Tom who?"

"Tom Driscoll. High school Tom, remember? Big client of Richie Tom—"

"Fleet-footed, long-fingered Tom, with eyes like twin dark pools?" Cass demanded. The blessing and the curse of confiding in your best friend about your past is that she remembers what you tell her.

"Oh, cut it out."

"How do you know what Tom said to his wife?"

"Because I was listening in, and I'll tell you about it later, if there is a later. Anyway, this year, most likely in February or March—pre-Jessica—Tom's wife arranged dinner at a restaurant with Richie. She told Tom it was going to be a foursome, and since they probably allot three point two hours of social time per month to each other and he still owed her, he went along. But guess who he expected to be there but who didn't go ... because she wasn't asked? Guess who Richie took to that dinner in my stead?"

"That tacky, tacky man! He took a *date?*"

"Yes, and I'll tell you who it was: the woman who filled in that gap in Richie's life. Tom said she seemed crazy about Richie. Now, let's call her Mandy, because right around that time, when Crazy About Richie was shoveling caviar with him and the Driscolls by night, someone named Mandy was calling his office by day and asking to be put through to him—and asking with enough lack of discretion to clue in Richie's secretary that he'd found another source for nooky."

"Crude."

"But accurate. Also, Mandy Anderson makes sense in this context. Her appearance coincides with the time Richie started coming home early again. Remember, eight or nine months ago, when I convinced myself we were in our 'Grow old along with me! / The best is yet to be' phase?"

"I remember. You convinced me as well."

"The reason Richie was able to get home so early was because his lover, his Mandy, lived right here in town. *She* couldn't dally all night because she had a husband to get home to."

"What about that evening she dined *à quatre,* then?" Cass asked. "Doesn't that qualify as an all-night dalliance?"

"A Girls Night Out once in a while wouldn't make

a husband suspicious, especially not the husband of an emancipated woman."

Cass gazed at the tragedy mask her kids had painted on one side of the proscenium arch, its upside-down-U grimace lacking any ambiguity. "I'm not sure."

"So let me convince you. At first the only thing about the evening that came back to Tom was how uncomfortable it was—how vulgar Richie was to have brought his lover: the same tacky-man reaction you had. But he also was able to remember something else. The woman was pretty."

Cass caught her jaw before it could drop too far. "And Mandy is not!"

"Correct! Now, before Tom and Hojo reached their normal level of mutual loathing and hung up on each other, she made a couple of interesting remarks. One, that this was Richie's first real love affair, as opposed to a sexual relationship. Or, if it wasn't true love, it was a reasonable facsimile, a rehearsal for the real thing."

"Jessica being the real thing?"

"Yes," I conceded. Okay, it still hurt a little. But in time, maybe I'd come to see my years with Richie as an extended miscalculation. Well, at least I'd emerged from my marriage with two kids I loved, a great career, and a red convertible. Women have done worse. And if I was lucky enough to have a future, who knew the amends I could make?

"But if this lady at dinner wasn't the real thing," I went on, "she also wasn't just another tootsie. Hojo said she was *more* than acceptable. And one more thing: she was well-bred and Protestant."

"I cannot speak for her breeding or lack thereof,"

Cass remarked. "However, the name Mandy Anderson does not sound Latvian; why couldn't Mandy be the woman at that dinner?"

"Because Mandy Anderson has a face like Miss Piggy's. The dame Tom had dinner with was pretty. Ergo, either Tom has bad taste in women, or the dame at dinner was not Mandy, or . . . " I waited for Cass.

"Or Stephanie is lying! Mandy *is* pretty."

"That's right! Cass, you know that what Stephanie wants more than anything is a perfect universe. Beautiful houses, gorgeously-arranged food, exquisite gardens—and stunning couples who adore each other. Her heart must have been breaking over Carter and Jessica, but did she let down her hair and tell me?"

"No."

"Why not?" I asked.

"Because it was unpleasant. Yes, that makes sense! Denying unpleasantness is her life. It is her husband's lifework also: a crusade against reality, the creation of what he believes is beauty."

"Stephanie will do anything to avoid a mess. So how could she tell me my husband had been unfaithful with someone besides Jessica? But once she knew I'd found out, she did what she thought was a kindness: she made Mandy homely. Jessica is young and pretty, and Stephanie didn't want me to feel like an old bag who got tossed over *twice* for a smart, good-looking dame in her thirties. She protected me."

I got up and stretched my legs. It was hard to tell because of the baggy sweats, but I was convinced my thighs had gotten slimmer over the last week. I headed over to the wall phone, called Manhattan Information, and got the number for Kendrick, McDonald. "Those big Wall Street law firms are supposed to be sweatshops," I said to Cass. "Let's see how late a sweatshop stays open." But this sweatshop wasn't answering.

"Cassandra!" Theodore's voice exploded. I was frantic for a place to hide. No door to run through; the shower curtain in front of the stage was translucent; the stage itself had no backstage. "I've made you cocoa, Cassandra!" he called.

"I am on my way up."

"My God!" Theodore exclaimed. We whirled around and there he was, framed at the bottom of the basement stairs, his eyes darting back and forth between me and Cass, as if witnessing some shocking debate. Before I could think what to do, he tore across the long room. I scrambled to get away, but he grabbed both my arms and pulled them behind me, in a rudimentary but nonetheless effective wrestling hold. "Don't try to fight me!" He called out to Cass: "I'll hold her. Call the police!"

Theodore may have been slender, but did he ever have a grip! I tried to recall all the magazine articles I'd read about self-defense, but since he was behind me, protected by the bench I'd been sitting on, I couldn't kick him in the scrotum. "Let go!" I bellowed. He was really hurting me. "Theodore, let me explain."

"Cassandra!" Theodore shouted. "Don't just stand there! Get to the phone!"

"Let her go," Cass said calmly.

"What?" he asked, uncomprehending.

"Let her go." His thumbs dug into the pressure

points just above my elbows. "Rosie and I have plans for this evening."

"Have you taken leave of your senses?" he asked her, squeezing tighter. "Have you?"

"Ow!" That was me.

"I have not. Rosie is innocent. I am going to help her prove it."

Theodore stepped over the bench, presumably so he could steer me toward the stairs. I lifted my foot to stomp on his instep; I could escape while he was writhing in pain. But I missed. "You are *not* going to help her," he instructed Cass. "She is *not* innocent. Look what she did to her husband. Look what she did to Carter Tillotson. She is a madwoman. A killer." My forearms were growing numb. "Is she armed?"

I swiveled my head around. "Yes. I'm carrying a small neutron bomb."

Just as it hit Theodore that his wife had let me into the house of her own accord, not under duress, Cass announced: "If you attempt to call the police or impede us in any way, I shall leave you and renounce custody of the children as well. Think of Thanksgiving. No, think of Christmas. You with a bare Norwegian pine and three sullen adolescents, and I . . . " She reflected. " . . . the toast of Oxford."

"Oxford?" He smirked. "Who'd want to go to Oxford?" But he knew precisely who. He let me go.

With great tenderness, I massaged my elbows. "Let's all sit down," I suggested. "Please. I have something to say."

Cass complied. "Do you trust my good sense, Theodore?" He gave her a begrudging nod. "I vouch for Rosie. Listen to her." He smoothed the creases from his lounging robe and sat beside her.

"I've learned more about Richie in the week he's been dead than in all the years we were husband and wife," I began. "I've accepted the truth: He had wanted out of the suburbs, out of being a regular guy. He'd wanted out of our marriage for a long time.

"I forced him to stay. You know, last summer he wanted to buy a villa in Tuscany. I laughed at him. I mocked him: *Us* in an Italian villa? I laughed because I wanted to persuade him that he was still Richie from Queens. But he'd grown in a way I never could. He'd become a man who *could* live in a villa. Let me tell you: he wasn't just angry at me for keeping him down on the farm. He was enraged. He loathed Richie the Little League coach. He was sick of being the math teacher who by some fluke had made big bucks. He was desperate to be Rick. And the only thing standing between him and the life he wanted to lead was a suburban high school teacher with a bit of a Brooklyn accent.

"I was fooled by his tears that last day. Not that they were phony: I'm sure kissing me off wasn't easy for him. But he didn't just want to leave me and get on with his life. He wanted to pay me back for being a lower-middle-class outer-borough Jew and for never letting him forget he was one too. He had to hurt me and humiliate me.

"Look how he ended a twenty-five-year marriage. Not with regret. Not even with coldness. With a kick in the teeth. He encouraged the party, the charade of a silver anniversary with friends, relatives, neighbors, business associates. And remember when he toasted me? 'Rosie, it's been twenty-five years. What can I say?' I figured he'd wanted to say a whole lot more, but he got all choked up, poor guy. And then, twelve hours later: Goodbye, Rosie. Good riddance. I admit, he did meet his paternal obligation that morning; he spent an hour telling the boys. Then he just cleaned out his desk—although obviously he forgot a few items. But then he was ready to leave.

"You know what I still can't get over? His malice. He left it to me to tell all the people who were calling to say 'Thanks! Great party!' that it obviously hadn't been so great. He left it to me to pack up and return all the gifts he and I had opened the night before. Why did he let me do that? We sat up till two in the morning—just the two of us—ripping paper, tossing ribbons, laughing, having a great time."

"Six juicers," Cass recalled. She could also recall, because I'd told her, that Richie and I had made love—ardent, newlywed love—from two until after three.

"Seven juicers. I'm not saying humiliating me was his prime concern. But it was pretty high up there." I smiled at the Higbees. They smiled back.

They thought I was trying to be brave. What I actually was doing was thinking about how, one night after he left, when we were meeting at my lawyer's, shouting about whether I'd helped get Data Associates off the ground, Richie suddenly made a tactical decision to calm down. He reached out his hand across the conference table, and I, with equal guile, and some longing, took it. With a tenderness he hadn't shown me in a decade, he said, "You'll find someone wonderful, Rosie"—in the comforting knowledge that I would not.

I was thinking about the fun I'd had with Danny. I was thinking about my night with Tom and how, after the fun, he traced my features with his finger, kissed my cheek, and said: "You're my sweetheart, Rosie." He held me the whole night. Richie, you dead son of a bitch, I was thinking, in those few hours he gave me what you never could, not even in a quarter of a century.

"Time to go," I said to Cass.

"What are we doing?"

"We have to find out what Stephanie knows about Mandy and Richie."

"And after she tells us, we must ask her to introduce us to the lady."

Theodore's smile evaporated. He disengaged his arm from his wife's and stroked his Clark Gable mustache with his thumb and index finger. "Whatever you do, Rosie, Cass is not going with you."

Cass took a step closer to me. "Do not pay him any attention. You know he is not to be taken seriously."

"You had better take me seriously," Theodore warned her.

"Please! The only fiction you read are William F. Buckley novels. How can I take you seriously?"

"Consider yourself warned, Cassandra." With that, Theodore Higbee turned and stomped up the aisle beside the benches, through the basement, and up the stairs. An instant later, I watched Cass's gray slacks and dark-red sweater hurrying after him.

Occasionally, clichés are necessary because they perfectly describe a feeling. So: My heart sank. The sinking had nothing to do with friendship, ditto for understanding and warmth; by this time, I had learned I could get through the night without them.

However, without Cass, I could never get past the cops to Stephanie's.

Before my heart could break as well, she called down the stairs to me. "Theodore gave me his word he will not call the police. He can be trusted. Now I am going to get my coat." Her words grew so hushed I could barely hear them. "And a gun."

"In your absence, the English Department of Shorehaven High School is having a rough patch," Cass said. "If both of us are arrested, it will be up shit's creek without a paddle." Then she closed the trunk of her BMW on me.

We'd agreed there was no alternative. I couldn't lie flat in the back of the car, as I had when I surprised Carter, not with scores of cops on the alert, brandishing flashlights. And after 11:00 P.M. on suburban Long Island, there was not a surfeit of horn-rims with false noses attached, so any notion of slipping into Stephanie's house disguised as an itinerant accountant was, at best, questionable.

In movies, characters are always hopping into car trunks to hide, or getting shoved into them for that last ride to the cement mixer. But neither a shot of the trunk cover descending, eclipsing the screen, nor a high-decibel sound track with mad pounding and muffled pleas for mercy can approximate the horror of being locked in.

I was living my worst death fear: not the end of consciousness but, utterly helpless, having to endure the persistence of awareness: living death. Even the darkest sky has a pinpoint of light from a random star, but I was entombed in blackness.

The trunk was what a good neighborhood in hell must smell like, a concoction of moldering paperbacks, a broken-ribbed umbrella that had never quite dried, and a shred of radicchio leaf, ripped off on the way home from the greengrocer's a year earlier, that had putrefied from solid to liquid and was on the verge of becoming gas. But at least the foulness that seared the back of my throat proved there was still air to breathe.

I lay on my side, my arms wrapped protectively around my head, getting smashed against the sides of the trunk with each bump. I agonized over Cass's fondness for grilled cheese sandwiches; she kept an electric skillet in her office and made grilled Swiss and tomato almost every day, except when a group of us went out for lunch. We'd have vegetables on pita; she'd order corned beef. Your arteries will shut down, I'd warned her a thousand times. Think about your heart. A bad shock might do her in. One glimpse of cops with assault rifles, and she'd understand that, after all, she should have listened to Theodore and stayed home. But by then it would be too late for her poor heart; it could withstand the thrills the Brontës offered, but this night was, simply, too exciting for someone with a doctorate from Columbia. She would not survive.

They would find me a week later. Cass's eldest, Kate, home to mourn, would open the trunk to sling in a bag of Dog Chow for Ronnie and shriek *Arrrrrgh!*

I was hurled forward. A piece of metal, maybe part of the car jack, slashed through the sweatpants and scored my knee. I would have wept at the horror of it all, but then I heard the crackle of gravel and realized: We were on the sloping drive up to the Tillotsons' house! Suddenly I was rolling toward the front of the trunk. We had reached level ground. At last, with a lightness of foot she had never before demonstrated in all the years I'd been driving with her, Cass braked and brought the car to a gentle halt.

We had rehearsed everything she was going to say: Officer, my name is Cassandra Higbee. I live on Bridal Path Way and am a friend of Mrs. Tillotson's. Cass would show the cop her driver's license and add: I was also a friend of Mrs. Meyers, and she was just at my house. Hey, Lieutenant! the cop would yell, and several policemen would gather around the driver's door. Cass, as chair of the English Department, would address her comments to the most senior officer. I knew the police were here, she'd say, so I decided it would be faster to drive by rather than call. Mrs. Meyers left my house about two minutes ago. While she was there, she kept asking if I knew about her late husband and a woman named Mandy; I told her I did not. Here Cass might want to rest a hand on her chest and take a deep breath to compose herself. Mrs. Meyers was agitated, she'd go on. I inquired if I could help her in any way. She said no, that she had to get back to the city. I offered to drive her to the station, but she said she had a rented car. A Cadillac, I think.

Here, Cass was to pause for four seconds. Then she would add: Oh, yes! I almost forgot. Mrs. Meyers did mention that she'd parked the car at the Rothenbergs'. That big ranch over on East Road. They're in Florida.

Cass and I had decided that the car, with my fingerprints all over it, would keep Gevinski and his men satisfied and, more important, get some of them away from the Tillotsons' house. It was worth having to give up my means of escape. A vague "Rosie Meyers is in the neighborhood" would be just another routine lead for the cops; it wouldn't get them off and running.

If the revelation of the Cadillac caused the commotion we hoped for, Cass would get out of her car and ask one of the cops, who was rushing off, if she could please see Mrs. Tillotson. What a fright this has been for all of us! she'd say to him. Perhaps Stephanie Tillotson and I can comfort each other. With any luck, the cop would be grateful for Cass's visit, or at least wouldn't say no for fear of seeming racist in front of someone who appeared self-confident, substantive, and well-to-do.

Cass would exit the car. Once she determined that the coast was clear, she'd press the lock of the trunk, causing it to open a fraction of an inch. She'd head for Stephanie's front door. If it seemed safe—that is, if only Stephanie, and not a cop, came into view— Cass would say Stephanie's full name: Stephanie Tillotson!

I would come flying out of the trunk. Cass would react with shock and chagrin—What? Rosie? In my trunk?—as I herded them into the house. However, if Stephanie was under a police guard, Cass would use the first name only: Stephanie, what a nightmare! In that case, I was to remain in the trunk. Cass would drive us away as soon as she could.

What was taking so long? I got up to "Deep into that darkness peering, long I stood there, wondering, fearing . . . " in "The Raven." The poem, so bleak, was a foolish choice, although, for the first time, I truly entered into the spirit of Poe's unholy dread.

Click! Cass unlocked my prison. An exhilarating blast of air hit me in the face. The narrowest stripe of midnight blue appeared, and although I could see nothing, I heard the baritones and basses of cops—but not too close by. Their low sounds were soon followed by the notes of Stephanie's door chime.

I reached into my left pocket and hefted the nearly weightless cap pistol. I had no need to touch the gun in my right pocket; I could feel its heaviness.

Cass had swiped it for me. Here, she had said, when she returned to the basement. I don't need it, I told her. I still have my phony one. I patted my pocket. She shook her head: Maybe it fooled Carter, because you held it against his head and he couldn't really see it. But if any police should surprise us, they would know immediately that it was a toy. Both of us paused. Holding the police at gunpoint didn't sound particularly prudent. Let's not, Cass said. She hung the gun on a hook with a billiards rack. It did look like an extremely authentic gun.

No, I countered. Let's—unless Theodore will miss it. He's probably forgotten he has it, Cass admitted. He keeps it in a strongbox in his desk, along with stamps with no mucilage. He only bought it because it is de rigueur for reactionary, NRA-loving buffoons. He hides the bullets on the top shelf of the linen closet, beside his snorkeling mask. Burglars and the KKK always phone before dropping by, of course, so he would have time to load up. Then she added: I did not bother bringing the bullets, Rosie; I assumed you would not want to handle a loaded weapon.

A heavy door opened. "So good to see you!" I heard Cass say. A woman's voice murmured a reply. "Surely the police are still guarding you?" Cass inquired. A long, digressive murmur. And then: "What a dreadful time this has been for you. Poor Stephanie Tillotson!"

And I popped out of the trunk.

Twenty-one

"Please," I begged Stephanie, "don't call for help. I swear I won't hurt you."

"Rosie is innocent," Cass said. "I will vouch for her."

"How can you?" Stephanie demanded. Her face was ashen. Even in the subdued light, pearly-blue veins shone on her temples. A muscle beside her right eye twitched. For a second I thought she was winking at me. She wasn't. "I never thought she killed him until tonight. But then she sneaked up on me! I was so scared, Cass, especially after what she did to Carter."

"I apologized for that," I whispered, a consequence of prudence and a sore throat. If I hadn't been in the middle of my defining moment, I would have excused myself and gargled. "And I'm sorry I ran. I don't know why I did it."

"She did it because she is a nervous wreck," Cass explained to us both. "Look at her!"

If you discounted congenital differences in beauty, at that moment I actually was looking a lot better than Stephanie. It wasn't just her pallid face. Her hands were filthy from working in the greenhouse. She'd bitten her nails too, and there were bits of potting soil on her mouth and chin.

Stephanie finally managed to look at me. "I called the police," she said.

"I can see that. There are at least a hundred of them."

"What did you expect me to do? When you ran off into the woods . . ."

"How could you think that I was guilty? You're a lawyer, Stephanie. You're supposed to be rational. If I'd murdered Richie, what possible motive would I have had to hide in Carter's car to get information?"

"I don't know!" Her voice echoed off the stone walls of her entranceway.

"Shhh!" Cass and I hissed together.

The entranceway was a cavernous hall broken only by a chandelier suspended from a twenty-five-foot-high ceiling and a grand stained-glass window above the front door. It was such an imposing and

solemn place that if someone had stuck up a cruci-
fix, Thomas à Becket could have said Mass.

"Sorry I was so loud," she whispered.

"Mrs. Tillotson?" A cop, probably calling from her
music room.

"Tell him it's one of your neighbors, checking to
see if you're all right," I said. Stephanie swallowed
hard. "Please, Stephanie, be convincing!"

She looked at Cass for reassurance. Cass gave it:
"Go ahead."

Stephanie repeated what I'd said, although not
convincingly. Her voice cracked too much. She
wiped her hands along her gardening overalls, leaving a dark-brown stain on top of paler brown gardening smears.

"Tell him you're going upstairs to take a bath, to
try and unwind," I entreated. "That way we can talk.
Hurry."

We were about to sneak upstairs, when it hit me
that the music room the cop might be in was right
across from the great staircase. I glanced around
the huge, empty hall. "Mrs. Tillotson?" the cop
called.

"Come on!" I said, and ushered them into the
guest closet. Seconds before the cop's "Mrs.
Tillotson? Where are you?" I closed the door. "Mrs.
Tillotson!" the voice, although muffled, seemed
closer this time. "You there?" Louder. The voice!
Gevinski! Finally softer, heading for the stairs.

I left the door open just a crack, so the light
remained on. Notwithstanding, it was probably a
hellhole for Cass and Stephanie. For me, after my
time in the trunk, it felt like Radio City Music Hall.
Cass maneuvered into a corner. Stephanie inched

toward the rear of the closet, until she backed into her red fox coat and could go no farther. I grabbed onto the knob to make sure the door didn't fly open.

"We need information, Stephanie."

"I don't *have* information."

"Tell us about Mandy," I said.

"Again?" The long fox hairs were annoying Stephanie; she kept shrugging and shaking her head to rid herself of their tickle. "I told you, both of you."

"You told us Mandy was homely. She isn't."

"How do you know what she looks like?"

"Trust me," I said, probably a little coldly. "I know. And I know she was having an affair with Richie."

"Rosie, I *told* you Richie would never have anything to do with someone like Mandy." She didn't look angry, but she was spitting out her words so fast I knew she had to be. "Can't you drop it?"

"No, I can't. Listen to me, Stephanie. I don't care if what you have to say is pleasant or ugly. I just want the truth. Tell me about the affair."

"I don't *know* about it. Even if she did . . . "

"You do not have to worry about hurting Rosie," Cass chimed in. "She has taken a beating and survived. She will survive Mandy." At some point Cass had taken her sweater off. I hadn't noticed her doing it, but now it was tied around her shoulders in that secret knot only people who have gone to prep school know.

"Where does Mandy live?" I asked. The closet smelled of apricots. The walls were covered in a gold foil. Apricot-colored satin covered the scented hangers. Tiny, lacy pillows of apricot-scented pot-pourri, in circle and heart shapes, hung from tiny brass hooks.

"In the Acres. I told you. On Crabapple."

"Can you take us there?" Cass inquired.

"What?" Stephanie seemed stupefied.

"Not now," I said quickly. Cass had pushed too hard. It was going to be rough enough for Stephanie to admit she lied. I wanted time to allow the old friendship to warm us, so that when we did go to Mandy's, we could go as the Three Musketeers. "She works in the city?"

"Yes. She just made partner. She does bankruptcy work."

"Right. I think you told me that."

"How does she commute?" Cass broke in, just as Stephanie was getting comfortable again. I wanted to bop her. "Car or train?"

"Car," Stephanie said. "We used to ride in together, until I left the firm."

"Would there have been any reason for her to be driving here in the Estates the night of Richie's murder?" Cass asked. It was a good question, but I didn't like losing control.

"Not that I know of," Stephanie said. "I haven't seen her in ages, though. All she does is work, work, work."

Cass inquired: "What does her husband do while she works?"

"He works too."

"Where does he work?"

"Kendrick, McDonald. Major firm. Over five hundred lawyers."

"Does he ride home with her at night?"

"No." My heart thudded for no reason. Not enough air, I thought. The glow of the foil made Stephanie look like a golden statue. "Their hours are different, and he's down on Wall Street." She turned from me and pushed the fox coat over to the far side of the closet, but it met with resistance from her mink and a sheepskin jacket and popped back.

"In other words—" Cass said.

"Just a second," I said. "Don't push so hard, Cass."

"I am not pushing, and please do not get huffy with me."

"Can we get out of here?" Stephanie suggested. "Listen. That sergeant is looking for me upstairs." We could hear his heavy footsteps. "I know! We can sneak through the kitchen into the pool wing. Hide in the sauna."

"Just a second," I said. "You said you used to ride in with Mandy until you left the firm."

"Yes," Stephanie said, looking longingly at the door. "I think I feel claustrophobic."

"You worked where that Forrest Newel is, on Park Avenue."

"*Yes*." Claustrophobic and pissed off. The sweet smell of apricots was becoming overripe.

"So now," I pressed on, "Mandy is Forrest Newel's partner." Stephanie nodded an exasperated yes. "That's interesting."

"Rosie, you're wasting time. I don't hear him up there anymore. Any minute he'll be—"

"Don't worry."

"*I'm* not the one who should be worried."

"Stephanie, how could she be Forrest Newel's partner? You told me Mandy worked at Kendrick, McDonald."

"I did not."

"You did too."

Stephanie looked at Cass and then at me. "Her

husband, Jim, is at Kendrick, McDonald," she said firmly.

"He's *not,* Stephanie," I said. I saw her stiffen, and I sensed Cass, in her corner, going rigid too. "I need the truth. It's time you were straight with me." Suddenly Stephanie pushed against the closet door. She was strong, but by now, having been a menace to society for a full week, I was prepared.

"Don't do this to me, Rosie. Don't keep me here. You have no right."

I held tight to the knob, pulled back as hard as I could, and looked past her, to Cass. "Hold her!"

"Rosie!" Cass objected.

"Hold her, damn it!"

Cass grabbed the straps of Stephanie's overalls as she apologized to her: "Terribly sorry about this."

"Don't be sorry, Cass," I said as Stephanie struggled. "Right now, you and I could drive over to Shorehaven Acres and knock on every door on Crabapple Road. We could call up Johnston, Plumley and Whitbred *and* Kendrick, McDonald, and you know what? We wouldn't find any Mandy Anderson."

"She's crazy!" Stephanie cried out to Cass.

"Quiet," Cass snapped back.

"There *isn't* any Mandy," I said.

"Don't listen to her, Cass!" Stephanie pleaded.

"What are you talking about?" Cass asked me.

"Everything we know about Mandy comes from Stephanie. Right, Stephanie?" Cass kept holding on to her straps as I held the door closed. "I want the truth, Stephanie, and I want it now," I told her.

For a second, Stephanie's foot moved, and I thought she was going to kick me, but then she stopped fighting the restraint. She raised her head, so she was talking to three apricot-colored hatboxes up on the shelf. "Mandy's not real," she admitted to the boxes. "I needed a way to get out at night. When we lived in the city, I always used to run at night in the park, but Carter hated me doing it. So I made up Mandy."

"Why did you tell us the Mandy story too?" Cass asked. "Did you think Rosie or I would care if you ran alone at night?"

"I was mortified! How could I admit to you that I couldn't stand up to my husband?" She swatted away some more fur.

"So there was never any Mandy," I said.

"I shouldn't have lied," Stephanie said, now looking down at her socks. She must have left her clogs in the greenhouse. "It was a little lie that just grew and grew." She took a heart-shaped potpourri pillow off a hook and inhaled its fragrance. "I'm so deeply sorry, Rosie."

I spoke with extreme care. "Let me understand. The woman here in town whom Richie had an affair with . . . "

"She wasn't Mandy," she conceded, relieved. "There *is* no Mandy."

"Isn't it funny, then?" I remarked.

"Isn't *what* funny?" Cass asked. "Rosie, you are not being clear."

"Isn't it funny," I said, "that if there is no Mandy, someone named Mandy kept calling Richie's office?"

"I see," Cass said.

"There's not just *one* Mandy in the world," Stephanie said softly.

"From what I gather," Cass told her, "Richie's secretary—who had been his longtime mistress—sensed that this woman, Mandy, had a proprietary interest in Richie. She had a strong feeling that Mandy was calling to set up or confirm a tryst."

Stephanie didn't say a word. I spoke to Cass: "Stephanie earned her living as a litigation lawyer. She got paid for being confrontational. Do you really think she would have to lie to Carter if she wanted to go running at night?"

"No," Cass said. "She would just do it!"

"Damn right. See 'Mandy' for what she is, Cass: a story Stephanie made up to get out without arousing suspicion. She'd say ta-ta to her Scandinavian couple, lace up her sneakers, and out she'd go. She'd come back an hour later with a smile on her face."

"No!" Stephanie said.

"So what if she was a little disheveled?" I said to Cass. "And if it took longer than an hour, if she got home breathless, after Carter did? No problem. He'd be microwaving the four-course dinner she'd prepared. Sure, she'd be a little winded—but that glow! She probably said: 'Carter, this is a super workout!' Don't you get it? Mandy is Stephanie. And Stephanie killed Richie."

Stephanie screamed, and though her shrieks should have been absorbed by fox, mink, and sheepskin, seconds later the doorknob was jerked out of my hand—by Sergeant Gevinski. His gun was pointed at my nose. "Move!" he ordered.

But Theodore's gun was in my hand, and it was aimed at Stephanie's heart. "After you," I told him.

*   *   *

It was my party, so we sat quietly for five minutes. Then it began. "Where is Dr. Tillotson?" I asked Gevinski.

"Over where the little girl is staying."

"My mother's," Stephanie explained. Her tone was so friendly an outsider would have believed we'd come together to make pecan pie. "He went there to give her a kiss good night—even though she's sleeping." She seemed the old Stephanie: easy-to-be-with, bright-but-not-challenging, energetic, gorgeous Stephanie. I had to warn myself: This is a brilliant stratagem. Don't be a two-time sucker. This utterly agreeable woman with whom you've stretched strudel dough betrayed your friendship and murdered your husband.

A tender smile brightened Gevinski's moon face as Stephanie spoke. A second later, he was eyeballing me. But he widened his eyes into a stare from a glare so as to be in compliance with police guidelines on dealing with armed psychopaths. "Ms. Meyers," he said, very calmly. He turned his attention to his gun, which was now resting on the table beneath my left hand. "A couple hours ago, over at the D.A.'s, I got called in to speak to your lawyer. I've dealt with him before; he's very smart. He made a couple of good points. Maybe I *did* get the wrong take on things. Maybe you do have a credible explanation for a lot of this."

"I do," I agreed.

"Good," he said. We could be four old friends, sitting around a card table in Stephanie's gameroom playing Scrabble. Well, except for the guns. And in spite of her let's-bake-almond-crescents cordiality, Stephanie was sweating so heavily that a droplet of perspiration dribbled from her face onto the table-top. "I'd like to hear your explanation," Gevinski said to me.

"I'd like to tell it to you."

"All I ask," he said, with saintly serenity, "is that you put your gun down on the table. You can still have control of both weapons, but we'd all be a lot more relaxed—"

"No."

"Look, any minute one of my men is going to come looking for me."

"Tell him you're busy."

"You think he'd buy that?"

"Then tell him I'm holding a gun on all three of you. He'll have to cool his heels till the hostage negotiator comes. Meanwhile, you and I can keep talking."

I rested my gun-toting arm on the dark-red felt of the card table. This was Shorehaven Estates, so it wasn't just a regular card table; it was an eigh-teenth-century gaming table, the felt ripped in enough places to be truly impressive. Except for a leather couch and an electrified chandelier from some duke's billiards parlor, however, the rest of the gameroom was devoid of furnishings. The bil-liards table Stephanie wanted cost at least four breast augmentations and a month's worth of chemical peelings, and Chippendale dining room chairs and a rug for the living room were higher priorities.

"Let me tell you about Stephanie's brioche," I said. "It's wonderful. We used to bake together all the time. I'm good, but she's gifted." Gevinski wasn't paying attention. He was too busy watching guns, so I took his off the table and held it in my lap. "Listen to me, please. Brioche is a French egg bread. People usually make small, cupcake-size brioches, with a cute little twist of dough on top. They're nice for breakfast."

"Rosie?" Cass looked concerned.

"I found Richie's body about three-thirty in the morning. You"—I addressed Cass—"came by about a quarter to seven, after Sergeant Gevinski had interviewed me. You'd met Madeline and Stephanie for the walk, but once you heard what had happened, you came right over. About an hour after that, you had to leave for school, but I was still a basket case."

"Of course."

"So a little later, around eight-thirty or nine, I walked up the hill. I guess I was hoping to get some comfort from Stephanie."

I turned toward Gevinski. "But before I got here, I saw two men from your forensics unit or whatever you call it."

"Lab," he mumbled.

"They were making molds of tire prints all around Richie's car. They seemed most concerned with the tracks from the Lamborghini, but there were others as well. Check with them; you'll find out there were two different sets of tire marks." He nodded, not at all surprised I was bringing up the subject of tires. I knew then that he really had talked turkey with the D.A. and Vinnie Carosella. "One set was from the Lamborghini's tires, Pirelli P-zeros. The other tracks were made by Michelin

MXVs. They're on a lot of luxury cars: Jaguars, Mercedeses, BMWs."

Stephanie cleared her throat. "That's all anyone has in the Estates; luxury cars are a fact of life. Cass and I have Beemers, you have—"

"This isn't a chat, Stephanie. This is a monologue." I looked at Gevinski. "I have an idea. When Dr. Tillotson comes home, call one of your lab people over to check his Mercedes—and her BMW. Tires are almost as singular as fingerprints, right? You'll see: One of their cars will have Michelin MXVs that match the tracks next to Richie's car. Want to guess which one?" Cass was with me; she could barely stop nodding.

"Ms. Meyers," Gevinski said carefully. "This may be interesting. But so what? Nobody drove a car into your house that night, did they? Your husband had a knife in him. Tires or no tires, only the two of you were in the house when it happened."

"Sergeant, you and I know that both the Tillotsons have denied knowing anything about Richie being in the neighborhood that night. So if one of their cars pulled up beside his, it would indicate that one of them was lying. That's a little better than interesting."

Gevinski didn't respond. Stephanie puffed up her cheeks with air and then slowly exhaled through pursed lips. I waited for her to defend herself, but she just continued breathing and sweating.

Gevinski crossed his arms and rested them on his belly. "Is this all gonna connect up with egg bread?"

"I'll get there. But first let me tell you about what happened when I got here that morning. The house-man, Gunnar—he's Norwegian—answered the door. He doesn't speak much English, but he showed me in to see Stephanie. Later, his wife, Inger, brought in a tray of brioches."

"Good," Gevinski said.

"Not yet. What happened to Gunnar and Inger, Stephanie?"

"They quit." A scowl obliterated her bake-off affability. "I told you they quit."

"When?"

"I don't remember."

"It was only a week ago. Was it the day of Richie's murder? The day after?"

Gevinski was looking at Stephanie, but not skeptically enough for my comfort. "I can't say for certain," she told him. "They got another offer, a good deal more than we were willing to pay them. They packed and left right away." She leaned, ever so slightly, toward Gevinski. "I didn't send them away. She's trying to make it sound as if their leaving was an overt act in a criminal conspiracy, but it was a simple, everyday occurrence. Servants come and go all the time these days. Gunnar presented me with a *fait accompli*. They were resigning. I accepted his resignation." She sounded so rational—and so courteous—that Gevinski looked back at me as though I were a conspiracy theorist who, momentarily, would attempt to link Stephanie Tillotson with Lee Harvey Oswald.

"What was Inger and Gunnar's last name?" I asked her.

"I don't know," Stephanie snapped at me. "Olsen? Jensen? Something like that. Ask Carter."

"He made out the checks?" Gevinski asked.

"Actually, we paid them in cash. That's the way they wanted it. But I'm sure Carter will know."

"In case he doesn't," I broke in, "we can call the employment agency that sent them. Cloverleaf? Cloverdale?" Well, Stephanie did not bare her teeth at me; in fact, she nodded so cooperatively that, once again, Gevinski's mind seemed to turn to mush. "I used them too. Are you going to call them and check to see if they quit?" I asked Gevinski. "I don't think they did. I think she fired them. Maybe they saw something."

"I'll call them," he assured me. "I promise." But then, I had two guns and he had none. "Egg bread?" he prompted.

"Brioche. When I got to Stephanie's, she said she'd made brioche especially for me." This remark did not appear to cause a stir around the table. "I thought: how nice of her. But I didn't get the *meaning*. Of course, I had just found Richie's body five hours earlier, so I wasn't in peak form. Now I am. Listen: I make brioche the fast way—start to finish in three hours. But Stephanie would never take that kind of shortcut."

"I know you have a gun," Stephanie said harshly. "But I don't give a damn. This is so superdumb I cannot believe it."

"The classic recipe takes a minimum seven hours from start to finish. The dough has to go through three risings."

"What is this *crap?*" Stephanie shouted. Cass glowered at her.

"If Stephanie was baking brioche at eight-thirty in the morning, she'd have to have started working on it at one-thirty—maybe even before midnight." My arm ached from holding up the gun. I propped it on the table, then realized, a second before Gevinski did, that with one good swipe he could disarm me. I sat back and aimed for Stephanie's heart again. "How come you were baking so late at night?" I asked her. "Trouble sleeping?"

She shook her head, as much in pity as in anger. "The dough was frozen," she explained to Gevinski. "I took it out and popped it in the oven for a half hour." He nodded.

"It wasn't frozen!" I told him. "She'd freeze cheese straws, maybe *bouchées*—puff pastry shells—but *never* brioche dough. It only keeps for about a week. Even so, she's too much of a classicist to even consider freezing."

I'd convinced Cass. But Gevinski's eyes did a one-hundred-eighty-degree roll.

Stephanie put her hands together as if to pray; her cuticles were caked with dirt. "What the hell are you saying?" she growled. Well, she was finally truly, deeply, and overtly angry. "That I had an affair with your husband, killed him, and went home and made brioche?"

"Yes."

"*You're* the one who's been accused, you know. You're the one who's a fugitive. You're the one with the gun."

"I know."

"Do you think for a minute the sergeant—or the D.A., or *anyone*—is going to seriously consider brioche as evidence in a homicide investigation? I can't believe I'm being subjected to this." She turned to Gevinski. "This is sadistic."

"I'm being sadistic?" I laughed. "Sadistic is having an affair with your friend's husband. Sadistic is stabbing him to death and letting your friend take the rap."

She wasn't talking to me anymore. "This is obscene," she declared to Gevinski and Cass.

"You didn't have an affair with Richie?" I demanded.

"Of course not! I didn't have an affair with anyone."

"So when you found out he was leaving me to marry Jessica Stevenson, you weren't shocked."

"Of course I was shocked," she told Gevinski. "A good friend walking out on his wife is shocking."

"You didn't feel betrayed when you heard Richie was in love with Jessica?" I asked.

"No!"

I turned to Gevinski. He stuck his hand down the back of his collar and scratched his neck. "What if Richie had been having an affair with Stephanie and told her it was getting too dangerous, that he thought Carter or I was getting suspicious? What if he told her his twenty-fifth wedding anniversary was coming up and he felt obligated to see it through, and the two of them should lie low for a while? It wouldn't be at all like Richie to just tell the simple truth: that he'd fallen for someone else. My guess is, Stephanie lay as low as she could—and never heard from him again. She saw him at our anniversary party, but of course she couldn't make a scene, even when she saw him dancing with the woman her husband had an affair with, Jessica Stevenson. Do you really believe she didn't feel betrayed?"

Stephanie glared at me and smiled at Gevinski. "This is laughable. Laughable," she repeated to Cass.

"You don't think she was well-acquainted with who Jessica Stevenson was? Check with Dr. Tillotson," I suggested. "He'll confirm his affair. He's stayed in touch with Jessica, by the way. If he denies it, ask Jessica herself. She's not what you'd call honest, but she'd have to tell you the truth; too many people know about that affair for her to say it didn't happen." Gevinski loosened his tie, burnt orange, and opened the collar of his shirt. "The day after the party," I said to Stephanie, "when I called you and said, 'Stephanie, please come over. Richie's left me. He's going to *marry* a woman in his firm named Jessica Stevenson,' you didn't feel betrayed?"

"Damn it, do something!" Stephanie told Gevinski.

"Mrs. Tillotson, she's got two guns. Take it easy."

My head throbbed. My feet were hot; I was dying to take off my new sneakers. But what if I had to escape again? And even if I found the strength to get away, where could I run this time?

The sharp knock on the door made us all jump. All three of us looked to Gevinski. "Sergeant?" It was a very deep voice.

I turned the gun toward Gevinski, about to give him his lines, but he was looking at the door. "Turner? That you?"

"Yeah."

He closed his eyes and clasped his hands behind his head. "I'm busy. Gimme a few minutes."

"Okay."

"The husband home yet?"

"No."

"Knock when he gets in." He waited for the sound of feet shuffling off. "Ms. Meyers, Mrs. Tillotson here's an attorney. She could tell you that what you're telling us is a bunch of . . . details that don't mean very much in a court of law." Stephanie managed a flicker of a smile. "Even if you could tie it into a coherent story, which I frankly doubt, it would make such a weak case—I mean, *the* flimsiest circumstantial evidence—that the D.A. would be laughing from now to the Fourth of July." He mimicked a hysterical district attorney, even slapping the table before his final har-har-har. "Am I right, Mrs. Tillotson?"

"You're right." Stephanie was too smart to try to vamp him, although she did give him a hundred-watt smile. Not too much: just enough to come off as sincere and very grateful.

Nevertheless, at that moment I felt an almost imperceptible change in the atmosphere in the room. I think all of us felt it. It wasn't that Gevinski had started to believe me; maybe I should have cooled it with the brioche business. And it wasn't that he thought Stephanie was lying. It was simply that he'd moved beyond curiosity. Even if I hadn't been holding a gun on him, he would now be willing to listen to me.

"You say you got a coherent story?" Gevinski asked.

"Yes."

"Get on with it."

"I've done a lot of investigating. What I'm going to present to you is a synthesis."

"Combining different parts into a single entity," Cass suddenly chimed in.

"She's chair of the English Department," I explained to Gevinski.

"I spoke to Dr. Higbee a couple of times," he said. "I know how she talks. Go ahead with your synthesis."

"Stephanie was having an affair with my husband.

I don't know when it started, but by February it was going strong. She would sneak out of the house at night, claiming she was going to run with a lawyer friend, Mandy. She's admitted to Cass and me that she invented Mandy.

"Richie would park in the spot where you found his car. Maybe they had their trysts in the car, which, knowing my husband, is possible, but knowing how tall Stephanie is makes it unlikely. They probably went to a nearby motel."

"One of those places on Northern Boulevard, no doubt." Cass sniffed. "No sane person would lie on their linen."

"I'm sure, if you ask, you'll find someone from whichever motel it was who can identify Richie's picture and his jazzy car," I told Gevinski. "With any luck, this someone was curious—and might even be able to identify Stephanie in a lineup."

"You watch too much TV," Stephanie snapped.

"Second-rate movies," I corrected her. "In any case, in April, Richie's firm held an executive retreat in Santa Fe. I had piles of papers to grade, so I couldn't go. That weekend, he fell for Jessica. He fell for her hard; everyone seems to agree he was head over heels, that she was the love of his life. You ought to get the date of the retreat, because then you'd know when his affair with Stephanie was finished."

"So what are you saying?" Gevinski inquired. "Mrs. Tillotson lured him to your house and—"

"No. I'm sure she had no idea he would be here. I'll tell you why he had to get into my house. He'd bought a terribly expensive painting—three million dollars' worth—and given it to Jessica as a gift. There was only one problem. Maybe two."

"Must we?" Stephanie cried out.

Gevinski lowered his voice to a whisper, as if confiding only in her. "Better if she gets it off her chest." Then he turned his attention back to me.

"Jessica wanted to sell the painting. She was tired of it. She was tired of Richie too, but that's another story. The problem was, she couldn't sell it until he could come up with the bill of sale to prove ownership. He'd been in such a rush to leave me that he left behind some important papers."

Outside in the hall, a clock began to toll. It sounded muffled, ineffectual, but it cut off conversation. It was either eleven or, more likely, twelve. For no particular reason, we all glanced at the door.

"Richie and I weren't on speaking terms. It would have been difficult for him to call and invite himself over. Also, he was worried I'd find out about the painting; it would have added three million more to our joint holdings and brought the legality of the gift into question."

"So?" Gevinski asked.

"So I don't know what time he came in, because I went to bed that night around nine-thirty or ten. I guess it was sometime around ten-thirty."

"If he was going to break into your house," Stephanie said contemptuously, "why would he come so early?"

"Because he knew I went to bed early on school nights. He knew my habits. If all the lights were out, I was asleep, or at least upstairs. He also knew our dog had died, so there wouldn't be any barking. The house is so big; as long as the alarm didn't go off, I'd never hear anyone in the kitchen. And if for some reason I *did* come down, well, I'm sure Richie was confident he could get around me—probably tell me he ached for the house, which I'd interpret as a signal that he ached for me. If he had to, he'd have made love to me."

Gevinski looked as if he wished I hadn't said that. He sighed and said: "If this is your story, I gotta tell you—his getting there that early really doesn't make sense. Why didn't he wait till later?"

"Because he was desperate to get back to the city. He knew Jessica had someone else—"

"She had *another* one?" Gevinski muttered.

"—and Richie was afraid to leave her for even one night. He was under terrible pressure, doing everything he could to get our separation papers signed, to get free. Jessica had a very hot marital prospect, and he was panicked she'd find a way to wiggle out of their engagement. Anyway, let's assume he came in around ten-thirty. Does that contradict the time of death in the autopsy report?"

"No," he answered, not too reluctantly.

"That was the time when Stephanie came home too."

"What are you talking about?" she demanded. "I was home."

"You were at your garden club, talking about indoor foliage plants."

She backed down and nodded to Gevinski. "I was. I'd forgotten the meeting was that night. Sorry."

"S'okay." He smiled at her.

Before he could decide to pinch her cheek, I pressed on. "She was driving up the hill when, out of the corner of her eye, she saw the side reflector light on Richie's car. I'm sure she was filled with joy for that moment. She pulled her car into the spot on the far side of his. Remember, you're going to check her tires." I waited for Stephanie to break in, but she just sat expressionless; she might have been a mannequin. "She probably waited for him to jump out of his car and greet her. Nothing happened. She got out, looked inside his car. No one was there. She probably called his name. 'Richie.' "

Stephanie shifted in her chair. "This is some story," she said to Gevinski, a disgusted look on her face.

"Yeah, some story," he agreed.

Cass rapped the edge of the table. All of us sat straight. "A story is fiction," she declared. "This is nonfiction."

"Stephanie had to find Richie," I continued, "but she was dressed for her meeting. She drove back home and changed—and probably told Inger, who did speak English, that Mandy wasn't working late for a change, that they were going for a run.

"I'm sure she combed the neighborhood, but she couldn't find Richie. Where could he be? At his own house, obviously—my house. Maybe she walked over along the road or cut across the beach. But if she took either of those routes, she could be seen. Carter might spot her on his way home, or if he turned on the back lights and looked out the window. My guess is, she cut through the woods. If anyone knows those woods, Stephanie does. She's always going there for wild berries and pine cones for her flower arrangements. In any case, she got to my house and saw a light on."

"In the kitchen?" Gevinski asked.

"I'm not sure where Richie was at that point. He'd never have left the bill for that painting in the kitchen; that was my turf. But coming or going, he would definitely have used the kitchen door; it's the entrance that's farthest from my bedroom. And there's no reason why he'd be afraid to put on a light. I wouldn't see it and neither would anyone else; the house is isolated.

"Maybe she knocked on a window and he let her in. Maybe she let herself in. Or she waited till he opened the door to leave. But they must have talked. There might have been a terrible fight. Or maybe he was just dismissive: 'Are you kidding? Me leave Jessica? For *you?*'

"Stephanie gave up her job without too many regrets. My guess is, they told her she wasn't going to make partner. Her life at home became so busy—and so empty. But Richie was a thrilling man. For those few months, she must have seen what it was like to *live*." Stephanie eyed my gun. I tightened my grip. "When he dropped her, what did she have? A bunch of potted palms, a mixer with a dough hook, a child who didn't particularly interest her—and a husband whose only passion is for someone else. When Richie dropped her, it destroyed her happiness. And that last night, he took away the only thing she had left: hope. So Stephanie grabbed the knife and stabbed him to death."

Stephanie offered what I guess was meant to be a snort, but I thought it came out a whimper, a silent confession. I peered at Gevinski. Clearly, he hadn't heard the same sound I'd heard. His arms stayed crossed, as he waited for me to get on with it.

"Is that all you have to say?" Stephanie demanded, obviously encouraged by Gevinski's reaction. I have to admit, she still appeared composed. The whimper could have come from troublesome plumbing. "That's your whole story?"

"No," I told her. "That's the prologue."

Twenty-two

"After a woman stabs the man she loves with a carving knife, you'd think she'd be on edge," I said. "I'm sure Stephanie was. But she didn't lose her cool completely. My guess is, she acted fast. She didn't have to waste time wondering whether Richie was dead. One look and she would have known what I didn't want to know: it was over."

We all looked at Stephanie's blank face. Maybe

she was recalling the horror of looking into Richie's eyes, dark and dead, open so wide you could see the curvature of the eyeball, but no expression passed over her faultless features. For all anyone knew, she could have been contemplating how many varieties of lettuce to plant in the spring. Cass was probing in one of the pockets of the card table, most likely in an unconscious search for an overlooked cashew. But Gevinski remained one hundred percent alert.

"Unless Stephanie tells us," I went on, "we'll never know if she ever considered confessing. All we do know is that she stood in my kitchen and, like any amateur criminal who'd acted before thinking, realized she'd left fingerprints and footprints. Did you find lots of fingerprints around?" I asked Gevinski.

"You think I'm going to tell you that?"

"You'd have to tell my lawyer about it before my trial, wouldn't you?"

"But I don't have to tell you now."

"Don't you want to clear the air a little?" I asked.

"No."

"Move your chair two inches toward me," I directed him. "That's it. No more." I asked him to sit on his hands, so he couldn't grab the gun, and to lean his head toward me.

"Sergeant Gevinski, wouldn't it make sense to give me a break?"

"Why?"

"Even if you're not convinced, you know enough now to at least have serious doubts about Stephanie. Telling me about the fingerprints wouldn't be giving out any vital secrets. Your superiors over at headquarters, the press—they're going to be looking at how the case was handled. If I'm guilty, you've lost nothing. If I'm innocent, your being open with me now could help show you weren't vindictive. You can slide your chair back to where it was."

Stephanie spoke so fast her sentence sounded like one long word. "I know as long as she has the guns we're in danger. But I'm begging you: don't give in to her threats. Appeasement never works. She'll just ask for more."

"I'll take care of it, Mrs. Tillotson." He wiggled his fingers; maybe his hands were numb after sitting on them. "I'm not giving you anything your lawyer couldn't get on his own," he said, for me, for Stephanie, and for the record. "The outside doorknob was clean of all prints."

"Not even my husband's?"

"Not even his. Of course, he could have come in another way."

"Did you check the buttons on the burglar alarm?"

"Partial print on one of them," he muttered, maybe hoping I wouldn't hear.

"Whose?"

"Mr. Meyers' right index finger." The chairs were small for a man his size, and he squirmed around trying to center himself. "The print could have been from the time he was still living there."

"You know that couldn't be true," I protested. "He hadn't been in the house since June. I've been using the alarm every night. My kids use it when they're home. How could his print still be there?"

"Let's move ahead," Gevinski suggested. "The countertops were clean. The other knives and that wood thing they fit into were clean. There were lots of prints—mostly yours—on the stove, oven, microwave, fridge. That's about it."

"Except for the knife in Richie."

"The only prints on it belonged to you," he said to me.

"I told you I tried to pull it out of him."

"But you couldn't, right?"

"Right. If my prints hadn't been on the knife, would you have thought I was guilty?"

"Probably. I'm not swearing I would've had enough evidence to convince the D.A. he should bring the case before the grand jury, but I would've tried."

"Do you want to know what really happened after the murder?"

"You got the guns, you call the shots." He seemed pleased by his unexpected play on words and awarded himself a small smile.

"Stephanie wiped every surface she might have touched, including the knife handle," I explained. "In doing it, she probably used a towel or a rag to hold the top of the blade steady as she rubbed. She was either bending over or squatting or kneeling right beside him, and her weight forced the knife in deeper." I turned toward Stephanie.

Stephanie unbuckled her watchband and rubbed her wrist. "I don't think you planned to put the blame on me," I said to her. "Not then. You just wanted to save yourself. I helped you by trying to pull out the knife."

"She didn't just make this story up tonight," Stephanie announced to Gevinski. "She spent the whole week working on it!"

I tried to make her acknowledge me. "If I hadn't been their only suspect, if the police had taken time to investigate Richie's life, do you have any doubt at all that your name would have come up?"

"This whole 'affair' thing is totally in her mind!" Stephanie told Gevinski. "We were *friends*. The four of us were friends."

"Once she got rid of the fingerprints," I went on, "she knew she had to get out. That's when she must have noticed the dirt she'd tracked in. It was still caked in the treads of her sneakers. Richie's were clean. She kicked the dirt or pushed it around with a tissue or a paper towel to get rid of the prints of her sneakers. Then she ran out—probably to the area near his car—and got some more dirt. It was a terrible risk, but if she didn't take it, the police would realize an outsider had killed him."

Cass drew herself up to full stature. Obviously this was a matter that required a Ph.D.; my mere M.A. would not do. "In itself," she declaimed, "the trail of dirt was not threatening. It might have been brought in by a thief, or by a malefactor who had followed Richie from Manhattan. There is no reason to think that the police would have believed that the dirt necessarily came from a neighbor. Why should they? There would be no logic to such an assumption. Nonetheless, by that time, the killer realized the importance of dirt. Its presence had to be explained; if the authorities could be made to believe that Richie had tracked it in, they would not look beyond Gulls' Haven. The killer then made a choice: Put the blame on Rosie. Complete safety was possible only if the murder could be attributed to someone in the house."

"You don't think *I* did it, Cass?" Stephanie asked, incredulous.

"I do, Stephanie. If I am wrong, I will apologize, although obviously I would no longer expect an invitation to your open house on New Year's Day." She turned to me. "Forgive me for interrupting you, Rosie. You were talking about dirt."

"Thank you. Stephanie took the dirt and pressed it into the soles of Richie's sneakers. She may have sprinkled a bit more onto the floor, to add to the dirt she'd tracked in. One more thing: the dirt doesn't go any farther into the kitchen. It stops right at the bottom of Richie's shoes. Does that mean he never found what he'd come for? That Stephanie caught him leaving empty-handed and disappointed?"

Gevinski massaged his chin in a downward motion, stroking an invisible goatee. "Maybe he'd just gotten there himself," he mumbled.

"Maybe. In any case, Stephanie's work at my house was finished. All she had left to do was run home, wash up, and wait for her husband. Carter claims he got home before eleven. So if Stephanie first saw Richie's car at ten-thirty, she had time to kill him, wipe away her fingerprints, spread some dirt around—and still be home in time to make a fast vinaigrette."

Gevinski's face appeared beardless except for an oval of reddish-brown prickles around his mouth. I couldn't stop staring at it. It looked as if he'd tried on one of those gooey lipsticks the girls in junior high wear—Fudgy Cherry—and smeared it badly.

Gevinski was still on the fence. I had to have him

come down on my side. What could I offer that would have more weight than my brioche theory? What about the dinner that Stephanie, Madeline, and Cass had served to me and the boys and Suspicious? Alex had come in late, as usual, his hair pulled back; Cass and Madeline had been startled at his resemblance to Richie. But Stephanie? She'd been profoundly shocked—and mesmerized by my son.

What about how she'd not only given me the name of Forrest Newel, the lousiest litigator in America, but urged me to stay on with him. "He's supposed to be the best," she'd assured me. What about forcing Carter to pay a condolence call with her, giving me another list (probably the other nine of the Top Ten legal maladroits) and offering to go along with me to see them. Without calling attention to herself by being too inquisitive, what a perfect way to keep up with the details of the police case against me—and with my lawyer's defense.

Or would I be wiser to stick to the hard evidence and offer Gevinski a cogent, unemotional statement of facts. Yes, I decided, that was the way to do it.

Except before I could begin, Stephanie began to cry. Plaintive sobs, a waterfall of tears. Gevinski dug into his back pocket and offered her an off-white handkerchief. She shook it open and wept into it.

"I'm not a woman who uses tears to—" The rest of her sentence was, naturally, lost in another spasm of weeping.

"I know," Gevinski said.

Stephanie managed to bring her crying under control with a final shudder that made her broad, athletic shoulders tremble. "I want to defend myself, but how can I talk at gunpoint?"

"I understand," Gevinski said, his tone so Christlike in its compassion that he could have been Max von Sydow in *The Greatest Story Ever Told*. "You'll have your chance. I promise you, Mrs. Tillotson."

"I never had an affair with anyone," she told him. "And with Richie Meyers . . ." The way she said it, you'd have thought she was talking about anal sex with a sewer rat. "I wish I knew why she picked me as a scapegoat. I suppose after she ran, she must have realized it was only a matter of time until she was caught. She *had* to produce another suspect. So she constructed a case against Stephanie Tillotson. I have to admit, bits and pieces of it sound persuasive. But the whole story? Insanity. Going out to get dirt to put on the man's sneakers? Sergeant, *please:* isn't it crazy?"

"Where are your sneakers and running clothes from that night, Stephanie?" I asked.

Of course, she disregarded me. "And that story about my staying up all night to make brioche? It's the product of a diseased mind."

"Did my diseased mind make tire tracks next to Richie's car? Did it make the tracks that—I'll bet you anything—just happen to match the ones on your car?"

"She keeps harping on the tires," Stephanie said to Gevinski, hugging her arms to protect herself against the horror of what was happening. "For all I know, maybe she got hold of my car and drove it beside his that night. You know, I've been assuming this story was something she thought of just this week. Maybe she'd been planning this murder for ages!"

My perfect comeback never got heard, because just then a hamlike fist pounded on the door and said, "Sarge. Husband's here." I was about to tell Gevinski to have Carter come in, when the door sprang open. Sure enough, Carter—as well as his escort, a plainclothes cop, who almost dropped his can of orange soda when he saw me. "Holy shit!" the cop bellowed when he saw the gun in my hand.

"Wait outside, Turner," Gevinski said.

"Sarge. . . ?"

Gevinski motioned for him to shut the door.

"Why did you let him leave?" Carter burst out.

"For God's sake!" Stephanie said at exactly the same moment.

The Tillotsons waited for an explanation: How *could* you? They were appalled.

But I knew this was no victory. Who knew what was going on in Gevinski's mind? After all, Turner was free. The clock was ticking. I pictured a SWAT team in ribbed black turtlenecks breaking through the windows. Or could something simpler stop the proceedings—like Turner walking through the door again and shooting me between the eyes?

I asked Cass to move to the couch and motioned to Carter to take Cass's seat at the table. "Gunnar and Inger," I said. "Did you speak to them before they left your employ?" He pressed his lips together and shook his head: No, I will not speak! "Carter, have you gone batty?" I asked. "Answer me. I have a gun."

He pried apart his lips just enough to say: "I will

not be put through this again. Go ahead. Shoot me if you want to." There's nothing more irritating than a nebbish trying to be noble. If I'd have said 'Boo!' at that point, he probably would have soiled his pants.

I was about to stop his bluster. I glanced down at the gun to find the little piece you pull back with your thumb before you shoot, or if indeed this gun had a piece like that, but just then Gevinski intervened: "Tell her what she wants to know, Doc."

"What?" Carter was the Compleat Irate Citizen.

"You'll have to answer the question sooner or later, just for the record," Gevinski said reasonably. "Since she's brought it up, do it now. We don't have a train to catch."

Carter tried to buy time by running his fingers through his hair, but it was too short. "I did not see Gunnar and Inger before they left."

"What was their last name?"

He looked puzzled to be asked such a question. "I wouldn't know that sort of thing." He looked toward Stephanie, but all her attention was on Gevinski.

"Ms. Meyers, we can get this over with fast if you'd let me call in one of my men and have them check these people's name out," Gevinski suggested.

We finally agreed that Cass would use the Tillotsons' second line and call Turner on the first to tell him to track down the owners of the Cloverleaf or Cloverdale Agency in Manhattan and have them get Inger and Gunnar's last name and phone number. Tell Turner to do it ASAP, Gevinski directed Cass. ASAP? she inquired coldly. Forget it, Gevinski replied.

"When you came home the night of the murder," I asked Carter, "did you see Richie's car?"

"What?" he asked, as if the question was too complicated. "Oh, his car near the court. No."

He'd stalled before answering, and his answer was a lie. I knew it. I felt it. The problem was, I couldn't figure out how to get the truth out of him. What could I do? Assign him detention? Could I call him a liar? Give the gun another try by sticking it in his ear?

"Can I put my two cents in?" Gevinski asked. I nodded. "Maybe it would be better if I asked the questions, Ms. Meyers. And maybe it would be easier on the Tillotsons if I questioned them separately. I guarantee, you'd still be in control. But one could wait somewhere, like over in a corner of the far side of the room, while I asked the other—"

I was too exhausted to figure out precisely what he was up to, but I figured it had to be something. "We'll all sit right here," I said. "But you can ask some questions if you'd like."

Gevinski's shrug let me know I was doing something incredibly stupid, but he turned his full-moon countenance to Carter. "Ready, Doc?"

"I have to be in surgery at eight tomorrow morning."

"I'll do my best to be quick. Now, we've done a lot of talking here, so you'll have to go along with me even though it may not make too much sense."

"All right," Carter said.

"You introduced Jessica Stevenson to Richard Meyers?"

"Yes."

"How well did you know Ms. Stevenson?"

"Not very well. We'd met over drinks at one of my

patients'. She told me about her work. I suggested she and Richie get together and chat."

"That was it?" Gevinski inquired.

"In a nutshell."

"You didn't have a love affair with Jessica Stevenson?"

I suddenly saw the merit in questioning the Tillotsons separately. "You're not serious?" Carter asked him.

"Yeah," Gevinski answered. "I'm serious."

"No. I didn't have an affair with her."

"Why don't you give Jessica Stevenson a call and ask her?" I urged.

"It's late and you've got a gun, Ms. Meyers," Gevinski said. "It wouldn't be a bad idea to give your nerves a break and keep quiet. I still have some more questions; let me ask them." He clasped his hands on the table and leaned forward. I assumed this was his sincere posture. "I'm sorry I have to do this, Doc, Mrs. Tillotson. It's ugly, but that's what makes up a lot of this job: seeing god-awful stuff and asking people embarrassing questions. So . . . Doc, to your knowledge, did your wife ever have a love affair with Richard Meyers?"

Carter's mouth opened, but Stephanie spoke. "Carter, you know you don't have to answer *any* of his questions. You know that, don't you?" It wasn't as direct as a smack across the face, but it seemed to have the same force.

"I know this is a lousy question to have to answer," Gevinski said to Carter. "I appreciate the pickle you're in. But this isn't just a man-and-wife thing. This is a homicide investigation, so if you've got nothing to hide in that department, you really should speak up."

Carter's words were as clipped as his hair. "I'm sure Stephanie would never be unfaithful."

"Good!" Gevinski said, appearing delighted. "Good!" But instead of asking another question, he got involved pulling at his cuffs so that his shirt-sleeves would stick out a uniform half-inch beyond the sleeves of his jacket. He didn't seem to notice the way Carter's and Stephanie's eyes kept locking, pulling apart, and locking again.

Just then, I saw something out of the corner of my eye. A flash at the window. What was it? Nothing, I comforted myself, in the unconvincing fashion in which you deny what you don't want to see, like a mouse tearing across the kitchen floor and diving under the dishwasher: a shadow, you tell yourself. But it happened again. Not a shadow. A streak of light.

Cops were massing outside. Checking the layout? Planning the final assault? Gevinski saw the light, too, and, for a moment, fell into a tactical reverie: Should he go for my guns? Throw his body over Stephanie's in a one-on-one witness-protection program?

A disk of brightness—a flashlight held down-ward—shone on the grass. Then it vanished. Gevinski said, "Good," again, not for any reason but because he must have sensed the absence of sound and didn't want us to wonder what was going on. "What was I saying?" he mumbled.

"Stephanie," Cass piped up from the couch. For a second, Gevinski was confused at sound coming from an unexpected direction. "Why not tell the truth?" Cass asked Stephanie. "If you had an affair with Richie, it would not necessarily mean that you murdered him. Adultery ends in petulance and useless garter belts far more often than in homicide."

"I *didn't* have an affair," Stephanie barked at her. "And it's none of your business."

"You never went to a motel with him?" Cass persisted. Forget it, I wanted to tell her, but every particle of energy I had was being drawn out to the blackness where, seconds before, there had been a light.

"No."

"You never went out to dinner with him?"

"No. Now stop it, Cass!"

"No dinner," Cass ruminated out loud. But I knew Cass; she was not a ruminating-out-loud kind of dame. "No—"

Dinner! Oh, yes!

"What about the night you had dinner with Richie and the Driscolls?" I asked.

I thought Stephanie would be too smart to play dumb, but she said: "What are you talking about?" Then I thought: What if it *was* someone else? All Tom had said was "pretty." And Hojo had only mentioned "Protestant" and "well-bred." That narrowed the choice to about half a million women in Greater New York.

"What is this about?" Gevinski muttered.

"Another one of her lies," Stephanie spit out.

Right now, a platoon of cops could be putting down their flashlights and picking up their rifles while I was wondering if Ms. Pretty and Protestant was a horsewoman from Lloyd's Neck, or a five-foot-two Congregationalist minister from Park Avenue, or a chemist from Rye—or Stephanie Tillotson. Well, I had to put up or shut up. "In February," I began,

"Stephanie went out to dinner with Richie and one of his big clients, a man named Tom Driscoll. Driscoll's wife was a great friend of Richie's." I turned to Carter. "Joan Driscoll. One of your patients, right?" Carter swallowed, although that took a good deal of doing. I spoke directly to Stephanie now. "It's possible that Joan had met you before, at some cocktail party. But Richie confided in Joan about all his affairs, so whether she'd met you or not, she knew all about you even before the dinner, Stephanie. And once you showed up, there was no doubt she knew precisely who you were. Carter's wife. Richie's lover."

"A lie," she said softly.

"You obviously had some sort of relationship with her." When I'd gone through Hojo's calendar pages, I'd seen the Tillotsons' home number. I should have realized then how odd that was. Hojo's relationship with Carter was professional. If she needed him, she'd call his office. No, she had the Long Island number so she could get in touch with her dear friend's dear friend—Stephanie. "You gave Joan some of those pots-de-fleur you make up. Those pretty plants with a tube to stick a flower in. Did she tell you she uses orchids in hers?"

Gevinski's eyes were half closed and his mouth was slack, the detached, dozy expression the unsubtle employ when they want to appear indifferent to what fascinates them. "You have anything to say about all this, Mrs. Tillotson?" he asked.

"Nothing, except I deny it."

"What do you deny? The dinner? The plant things?"

"Everything. Rose Meyers murdered her husband. That's all I'm going to say to you."

Gevinski's posture grew expansive. He pushed back his chair, stretched out his legs; if he'd had a beer in his hand, he'd have been one of the congenial good old boys in the background of a pickup-truck commercial. "I know you're a lawyer, Mrs. Tillotson. The last thing I'd try to do is pull a fast one on you. But you should clear things up now, so we don't have all these details coming up at her trial. If you cooperate with me, no dirty laundry has to come out in public later."

I was glancing over at Cass to check if she felt as I felt: Gevinski was now on our side. "Steph!" Carter suddenly howled, as Stephanie pushed the card table over on me and ran for the window.

Gevinski's gun fell on the floor. As I tried to get it, and get the table off my lap, Gevinski landed a karate chop on my collarbone. "What are you doing?" I cried. "Get *her!*" He responded with one fierce punch to my solar plexus. I fell to the floor, truly unable to breathe. I doubled over to try and stop the pain.

"Steph!" Carter wailed over and over again. "Steph, don't!" I wasn't too clear what happened next, but Stephanie was at the window, kicking out the panes of glass. But the wood crosspieces barely splintered. She wasn't out yet.

My breath wouldn't come. I broke into a cold sweat and, in a panic, tried to plead for help, but I wasn't able to speak. Cass bent over beside me.

Gevinski was screaming, "Get in here! Get the fuck in here!"

By the time I was able to take my first breath, four uniformed cops were holding Stephanie. A second later, my view was blocked because twelve blue-clad legs and six drawn guns were surrounding me. One of them helped me up and over to a chair. Gevinski righted the table and sat beside me. He'd given his handkerchief to Stephanie to weep into, so he had to borrow Turner's so as not to smear any fingerprints I'd made on the gun. He opened it, said, "Shit! It wasn't even loaded," and handed it to Turner.

"You punched me!" I was able to gasp.

"I didn't crack your goddamn head open, did I? You should be goddamn grateful." But at least Gevinski waved some of the cops away from me, so I was down to two guns pointing at me.

The ones guarding Stephanie seemed embarrassed at having to restrain such a splendid woman; they didn't want her to think ill of them for manhandling her and kept muttering "Sorry" and "Scuse me" every time she tried to jerk out of their grip.

"Want to sit down and talk, Mrs. Tillotson?" Gevinski inquired. He allowed himself to be ignored for a moment and then turned to Carter. "Doc," he said, in the gravest of tones, "this is serious stuff here. Sit down." Carter was about five feet from Stephanie and her cops, gazing at them as if they were a museum exhibition. "Sit down!" Gevinski bellowed. Carter sat on my other side, so he was opposite Gevinski—and wouldn't have to look me in the eye. Tie perfectly knotted, hair impeccably cut, and no sweat: Yet behind Carter's expressionless gray eyes, he looked as though he'd seen a sight more harrowing than any he'd ever beheld in the emergency room. "Doc, did you see Richard Meyers' car the night he was murdered?"

"Yes."

"Shut up, Carter!" Stephanie called out. "Don't talk. Say you want to speak to a lawyer." I bet this time she wouldn't recommend Forrest Newel.

"I saw the red sidelight on his car on my way home."

"Shut the hell up!" Stephanie shouted.

"Do me a favor," Gevinski told the group holding Stephanie. "Mrs. Tillotson's upset. Take her in another room. Keep her company." He sounded congenial to the point of jollity, until he added: "Get a couple of female officers in there with you, in case she has to go to the ladies' room. If there's any problem and you think she'd be better off in a safer place, let me know."

As they led Stephanie out, Carter covered his face with his hands. He didn't cry; I guess what was happening was too painful for him to watch. Stephanie glanced in disdain as she passed him. At the door, she turned back and spoke to Gevinski. "There's nothing he can tell you."

"You never know," Gevinski replied.

"I do, and so do you. A husband can't testify against his wife." And she strode out the door, a queen with her palace guard.

"She might have apologized to you, Rosie," Cass remarked. "If not out of remorse, at least out of common courtesy."

"You want to stay here, Dr. Higbee?" Gevinski asked.

"I would like to."

"Then even though I like the way you talk, you got to keep quiet. Deal?"

"Agreed."

"Good." He took a spiral-bound pad and pen from

his inside jacket pocket and turned back to Carter. "Doc, I'll make some notes, but we ought to back it up." Casually, he waved over a cop in a backward baseball cap and a zip-up jacket. The cop double-timed it out of the room. When he returned, he handed Gevinski a tape recorder about the size of a deck of cards. "Don't let this hang you up, Doc. It's strictly routine. We use these all the time." He switched on the recorder. "You were saying you saw Richard Meyers' car on your way home, Dr. Tillotson. The night he was killed. Take it from there."

"I got upset because I thought it was starting up again."

"The affair between your wife and Meyers?"

"Yes."

"How long did you know about it?"

"After it was over. But it still got me very upset."

"How did you know?"

"Jessica told me."

"Jessica Stevenson?"

"Yes."

"Did you have words about it or discuss it with Mrs. Tillotson?"

Carter shook his head. "I knew she was paying me back because she found out about me and Jessica." Gevinski didn't even have to ask how; Carter volunteered. "Detectives," he said. "I'd always had long hours, but I suppose women can sniff out that sort of thing. She hired detectives. But Stephanie's affair with Richie ended because *he* fell for Jessica."

"Do you know if Mrs. Tillotson took it hard, his dropping her?"

"I guess so. She . . . withdrew I guess is the word. Then she started doing the opposite. Doing too much. Not sleeping. Too happy."

"What happened when you got home that night?" Gevinski said. "Was your wife there?"

"Yes, but she usually was, even during the time they were carrying on. She was opening a bottle of wine. Very happy to see me. Too happy. I went up to shower and get into pajamas and a robe—that's what I do when I get home—and I ran into Inger Jensen."

Gevinski nudged one of the cops guarding me. "Tell Turner the couple's last name was Jensen, and tell him to get a move on with the employment agency." He rested both arms on the table and leaned forward toward Carter. "Did they leave a forwarding address, Doc?"

"Inger called me at the office about severance pay. I told her I'd mail her a check. You can ask my nurse for the address."

Carter took a small leather book from the inside pocket of his jacket and gave Gevinski the nurse's home number. Gevinski sent another cop out with it. "So what happened when you saw this Inger?" Gevinski asked.

"She mumbled something that Missus went running. I think she knew what the running meant. It was her way of letting me know Stephanie was at it again."

"And they quit the next day?"

"No. Steph fired them. She's always firing the help, so I didn't think anything of it. She's a perfectionist. When she was a lawyer she worked day and night. When she decided to stay home and be a mother, she did the same thing."

I had a sharp pain near my collarbone and a dull ache between my ribs. But at least I was breathing almost normally. I decided to give talking a try. "When did you hear about the murder?" I asked.

"Quiet," Gevinski grumbled. "When did you hear about the murder, Doc?"

"I was watching the *Today* show, and the local news came on. I ran downstairs. But Stephanie had gone for her walk with her friends." He examined his snipped-down surgeon's nails. "I suppose that's when I understood."

"That she'd killed him?"

"Yes. She got home soon after that, and she was full of the story. High as a kite. About all the police and what could she do for Rosie." He said my name as if I were someone he'd heard his wife mention. He did not look at me. "I waited. After my breakfast, she went up to change. I began to look all over for the knife. They said on the TV he'd been stabbed. I didn't realize it was still in him. I thought she may have brought it here. It's a big house. She must have thought I left for the office, because I heard her go to the greenhouse. But I stayed and kept looking."

"What did you find?"

"Just running pants and a jacket. In the laundry room. They were in a pile of folded laundry. But I don't know if they're the ones she wore."

"Do you know where they are now?"

"I guess she put them away. We don't have a new housekeeper yet, so she's been doing all that work herself."

"Did you find her sneakers?"

"Steph's quite an athlete. She has four or five pairs

of sneakers in her closet. I don't know which ones she runs in."

"You asked that I not speak," Cass said to Gevinski, "but I will, briefly. Stephanie's running shoes are Sauconys."

Gevinski threw Cass a terse "thanks" as he ran to the door. "I need Turner," he boomed. Turner, a large coffee stain on his right sleeve, returned, looking harassed, which he must have been.

"The agency owner's over at her office now, Sarge. The nurse is going to Dr. Tillotson's office to get the Jensens' address, but she lives in the Bronx. I'll let you know, the first one who calls."

"You knew all this time," I said to Carter, but he was looking up at a corner, where two walls met the ceiling. "It wasn't even that you love her so much that you had to protect her. You love Jessica. But you would have let me spend the rest of my life in jail."

"Quiet," Gevinski said.

"I guess you thought the publicity would hurt your practice," I went on. Carter studied the ceiling as if he were alone, waiting for something interesting to happen. "You must have been terrified of Stephanie. That's why you left Astor at your mother's. That's why you slept in your office. But once they arrested me, you figured she'd calm down. Right, Carter? You could go back to the way it was again."

"Quiet!" Gevinski looked away from me, over at Turner. "I need a warrant. Get the A.D.A. on the phone." Turner used the gameroom phone and handed the receiver to Gevinski, who ended a two-minute harangue to the assistant district attorney with: "I want to see the judge's signature on the dotted line in a half hour from when I hang up." He slammed down the phone and sauntered back to my chair. "What do you say we go for a stroll, Ms. Meyers?"

We walked down the stone steps past clusters of curious cops, onto the beach. "Does it hurt where I hit you?" Gevinski inquired.

"I'll let you know how much after I speak to my lawyer," I told him. The wind was an endless breath exhaling from the north, blowing the tops of the breakers into a froth. "Can I go and see my kids now?"

"No. When we get back, you can call to say you're okay, but then I need your statement. But don't go getting your hopes too high. You're not off the hook yet. You ran."

"You were going to railroad the wrong person, and you're telling me I'm not off the hook? I just saved your career."

"You held me and the others against our will. That's kidnapping."

We walked over mussel shells; each step made a loud crunching noise. "How would you and the department like me to tell my story to one of those atrocious tabloid TV shows? You can watch me. I'll have a great hairdo and makeup. I'll sniffle into a hankie and be brave while they show a clip of the police commissioner and the D.A. mouthing off about Rosie Meyers, menace to society, about how once she's captured she's finished, because you have such an airtight case against her. How about that?"

Gevinski kicked a crabshell into the water. "You're too high-class for those shows."

"No I'm not."

"Yes you are. And if you stay away from them, I could recommend to the D.A. that no charges be filed against you."

"If it's okay with my lawyer, it's okay with me."

From the beach, Emerald Point was a castle lit up for a ball. The lights still blazed in the greenhouse.

"All that money . . . ," Gevinski muttered. He waited for me to acknowledge that it did not buy happiness.

Instead, I punched his arm, as hard as I could. It felt terrific! "What the hell are you doing?" he barked.

"Getting your full attention. Tell me: What do murderers do with their weapons and their bloody clothes?"

"You hurt me!"

"Good. Now answer me about murderers."

"I don't know. If they're dumb, right away they take the stuff to some big bridge, you know, like the ones going into the city, and throw everything into the water. If they're smart, they find some smart hiding place until the investigation blows over, because they're paranoid about being caught. They remember *Quincy*; they're big on forensics. And you know what? The dumb ones turn out to be the smart ones, because even if I saw someone toss a package off the Brooklyn Bridge, what are the chances I could ever find it? But the smart ones . . . To tell you the truth, that's my big hope with Mrs. Tillotson. That she's so smart she's stupid." He gazed up at the three-story mansion; the floodlights were brilliant. They obscured all the stars. "It's gonna be a miracle if I find anything. You'll pardon my French, but it's such a fucking big house."

"Fuckin' A," I agreed. "But want to bet ten bucks on where the sneakers are?"

They had gathered all eight of Stephanie's sweatshirts, three jackets, and a pile of spandex pants to take to the lab, but to Gevinski's naked eye, there wasn't a spot of blood on any of them.

After the search warrant arrived, it took nearly an hour, but they finally found Stephanie's sneakers buried in the dirt of a huge New Zealand tree fern—in the greenhouse, where I told them to look. A young cop came running in to Gevinski, who was taking my statement; Vinnie Carosella was at my side. Gevinski raced out. Since he'd forgotten to invite us to join him in the greenhouse, Vinnie and I decided to follow him.

"I don't know if we'll be able to pick up anything," the lab technician was telling Gevinski. She held the Sauconys up to the light by the laces and shook off some of the potting soil that adhered to them. She did not look optimistic. "See all this dirt sticking to them? Know why? They're damp. They might have got watered with the tree, Sergeant, but chances are . . ."

"She washed them before she put them in here," Gevinski said, shaking his head. "Shit-ass-rat-fuck!"

I echoed him silently.

"I don't know how strong a case you've got here," Vinnie commented to Gevinski, perhaps a bit unkindly. "A good lawyer could probably beat it." Vinnie's back was to the tree fern. He was inspecting Stephanie's tuberous begonias, and he looked impressed. "No fingerprints, no nothing." Gevinski pretended he wasn't listening. "So she had an affair and lied to the police about it. So the Norwegians said she went running that night. So maybe she drove her car up right beside his. I could have a good time with a case like this." He patted my hand. "But this is a better time, Rosie. This is the best. You're free!"

"Damn it to hell and back!" Gevinski was barking. "Let me see the damn things." The technician handed over the sneakers by the ends of the laces. Gevinski held them right above his face, but a moment later, his mouth twisted in disgust.

"Tough luck," Vinnie said.

"Yeah."

"You want her running clothes?" the technician inquired.

"Later."

"Why not now?" I piped up. "You don't exactly have rooms filled with other evidence."

Vinnie spoke to me out of the corner of his mouth. "Don't let's push it."

Gevinski gave me a disgusted look, but he did take the stack of running clothes from the technician. Then he had to stand there until a cop found a plastic sheet to cover the dirty floor. As if setting up for a fine picnic, Gevinski ordered the sheet spread out. Then he set down Stephanie's sweatshirts, spandex pants, jackets. Standing back, he studied the arrangement. "You two can go back inside if you want to," he muttered to us.

"That's okay," I said.

"We'll hang around," Vinnie agreed.

We watched Gevinski watch the clothes. "If she was running at night, she'd have worn one of the jackets," I advised him. "Probably not the one with the reflective strip. She didn't want to be seen."

I pointed to two other jackets. Gevinski took a magnifying glass from the technician and studied them, inside and out. "Zilch. Didn't she ever slobber anything on herself?" He unzipped the pockets. "More zilch."

"At least we found out who did it and I'm free," I said, trying to cheer him up.

"Yeah," Gevinski muttered, without much enthusiasm. But a second later he perked up. He pulled a pen from his pocket and, with incredible care and patience, extracted a fragment of paper. "Tissue," he grumbled.

"Least it's not used," said the technician.

"Can't win 'em all, Carl," Vinnie told him.

Gevinski examined the second jacket, a green so dark it was almost black. "Tweezers!" he suddenly barked. The technician slapped a pair into his hand. From the right pocket, he extracted a folded paper.

"What do you got?" the technician asked.

"Shut up! Leave me alone! Get outta here." She didn't budge. Slowly, Gevinski opened the paper with the tweezer and the top of his pen. "Check it out, Rosie," he exulted. "Check it out!"

Thin white paper does not launder well. It had come apart in seven pieces, faded from the washer, shredding and dusty from the dryer. Across the top was printed a bleached-out logo: Knightsbridge Gallery. A computer-generated receipt. The date of sale had dissolved away, and what seemed to be a lot number was almost as white and unreadable as the paper itself.

"Look at this!" Gevinski said. A description of an oil, colored pencil, and pencil work by an artist whose name had been expunged in the rinse cycle.

"She must have taken it out of Richie's hand!" I rejoiced.

"And stuffed it into her pocket!" Gevinski threw back his head and roared, a lion with its prey helpless at its feet.

Vinnie, standing behind me, began to hoot. The purchaser's name was perfectly legible. Richard Meyers, Gulls' Haven, Shorehaven, New York. The price was clear too. Two million eight hundred thousand dollars. Plus tax.

Vinnie walked me home. "Nice place you got," he commented, as we came up to the end of the drive. In the dawn light, the bricks were the color of red wine. The air was salty and delicious. Gulls squawked and swooped over the roof. "If you want to stay here and be one with nature," I advised him, "watch your head. Their aim is perfect in the morning." Without thinking, I felt in my pockets for my key. "Oh. I'll have to ring the bell. I told the boys to get some sleep. This has been terrible for them. Losing their father—and then the whole world saying I did it. I hate to wake them."

"Rosie, I don't think they'll object."

They weren't sleeping. The bell was still chiming

when they yanked open the door. Ben got to me first. He picked me up off the ground and hugged me. By the time he put me down, he was crying. "Sweetheart," I said, and reached up to pat his head.

"Mom."

"You should put something on your feet. The floors must be freezing."

Alex slid in between us, but Ben still held on to my hand. Alex kissed my cheek. "Hey, Ma," he said. His hair had just been washed; it smelled of one of Richie's fancy shampoos and fell over his shoulders in damp black curls. He gave me a shy, sweet smile that I hadn't seen since his Cub Scout days. "Ma, you okay?"

"Give me a hug and I'll be okay."

He did, and I was. Well, almost.

Vinnie said we'd speak later. The three of us closed the door behind us. "I thought you'd be hungry and want something 'hearty,'" Ben said.

"Remember when she'd call us in to dinner," Alex asked him, "and she'd say, 'Here's a hearty winter dish'?" He stuck his finger down his throat, "Lamb stew!"

"Cassoulet!" Ben one-upped him. "With those slimy beans."

"You guys don't know what's good," I told them.

"I made you baked ziti," Ben said.

"I grated the Parmesan cheese," Alex countered. "If you want, we can make you something else. Oh, Ma. Do you mind going into . . . " His voice trailed off.

"Is the kitchen okay, Mom?" Ben asked.

I took their hands. "Let's go."

It was a good thing I said yes, because when we got there, Tom Driscoll was standing by the table, waiting for me.

Twenty-three

The Twilight Gardenia bath oil formed a slick that glistened pink and yellow in the morning light. I lay back in the sweet, steamy water, watching the gulls plunge into Long Island Sound.

How come none of us ever saw what was within her, not even a hint of it? Did we think: Wow, if the outside is that beautiful, can you imagine what's inside? After more than a decade of public sleaze and greed and smallness of spirit, were we still so dumb as to think that blue blood was evidence of virtue? Were we still so cowed by right-wing flimflam that we believed the woman who pinches back basil and drives car pools has a purer soul and a gentler heart than the woman who is out in the world?

The sonorous notes of an electric guitar came up through the bathwater. I lifted my head and heard Alex singing, his lovely voice falling, then soaring. He was rehearsing for a demo tape. Tom had a friend on the board of Columbia Records.

Putting aside the murder, how could she walk with me five mornings a week, bake with me Friday afternoons, and screw my husband at night? If she could discount my friendship that easily, what did she value?

I thought about the married man downstairs. When I'd left them in the sun porch, Tom was consulting Ben about his bad knee, and Ben, after probing and taking a medical history, seconded Tom's doctor's opinion: osteoarthritis.

So big deal: a little degeneration. I wanted the man. And why shouldn't I have him? Hojo was, assuredly, not my friend. Still, did I owe her anything? No.

But had God been in a breezier mood when he chiseled Thou Shalt Not Commit Adultery than when he forbade murder?

I wrapped my head in a towel and stepped out of the tub; there were too many mirrors. It was not necessary to behold my unspeakable haircut right before I went to sleep.

Was she sick? Had anyone ever thought to themselves—for even an instant—that, hey, there's something not right with this dame? To the contrary;

they thought she was as right as they come. Perhaps she was sick. If she was, though, where did evil fit in? Or was evil irrelevant? Did Hitler's father abuse him? Was Pol Pot's mother self-involved? Maybe that explained them. Maybe nobody was to blame for anything.

But I didn't believe that.

"Rosie Posie," Danny Reese said, "you are a headline again! Who *is* this bitch?" Despite his exhilaration, his voice was still thick with sleep. But then, it wasn't even nine in the morning.

"I had to call to thank you."

"It was fun, wasn't it?"

I considered the question. Fun? "Let me get back to you on that."

I was rubbing White Rapture body lotion onto my feet, but after seven days of want, it was not so easy to settle back into luxury on three-hundred-count cotton sheets and drift off.

"Think about it some more," he said, full of confidence. "And while you're at it, think about you and me."

"*That* was fun," I conceded. "But beyond that, you were a great and loyal friend. I'll never forget what you did, Danny."

"No big deal."

"I want to pay you for the license and credit card."

"Are you kidding?"

"They were a big help."

"Holy shit! You actually used them?" My silence gave him his answer. "You are one lucky woman, Rosie."

"For God's sake, you told me they were clean."

"It depends how you define 'clean.' They weren't hot."

"Oh, Danny!"

"Well, not red-hot."

Now that I wasn't there, I was able to smile at the thought of his apartment, even his unspeakable bathroom. My smile grew wider as I thought of Danny: those green eyes and that spectacular ass. "I have a proposition for you."

His voice was pure velvet. "I'm listening."

"No, it's much better than what you're thinking. It's an offer with strings attached."

"I hate strings."

"If you go back to NYU and graduate—"

"Give me a break, Rosie."

"I'll buy you anything you want for graduation."

"Anything? A new sound system?"

"Easy. Or any car you can think of. Any trip you want to take. Or I'll buy you your own apartment."

Danny was speechless, but only for a second. "I have to actually graduate?"

"Bachelor's degree—and after I see the diploma, I'm going to the NYU registrar's office to check if it's for real."

"You're still such a teacher!" Danny told me.

"I know," I said, full of joy.

Fortunately, my nervous system being what it was, no one shouted "Surprise!" Fortunately, too, I'd slept for ten hours and put on silk slacks, a blue silk shirt, and enough makeup to make it look as if I really didn't need makeup—because my sons threw me a welcome home party.

Cass was wearing a glamorous aubergine pants suit and diamond earrings. She said she loved me—and that I could have the rest of the week off. Theodore gave me a hug and told me he was going to devote his next monthly column, "Right Turn," to Rose Meyers and her libertarian spirit. I reminded him I had no libertarian spirit, that in fact, as he knew very well, I was a liberal Democrat. He laughed it off.

Suspicious had driven up for the evening, but at least she refrained from kissing me, which I took as a hopeful sign. Madeline, in what looked like a Lord Byron costume, did kiss me, which was fine, especially since she'd brought a box of bittersweet chocolates and no poems.

Vinnie Carosella wore a blue blazer and a polka-dot bow tie. He told me, as he eyed Madeline's chocolates, that he'd heard that a neighbor of mine had been denied bail. Then he handed me a bottle of champagne and said he wouldn't bill me for it. I took him aside, mentioned I'd stolen Theodore's gun, and asked if he could get it back from the police as part of our peace treaty. And while he was at it, could he get my purse—and the sapphire ring that was in it—back from Jane Berger. Piece o' cake, he replied.

Tom Driscoll had spent most of the day doing business on the phone and going to the D.A.'s to report about the dinner he'd had with Richie and Stephanie. He took a nap on a couch in the library too. I introduced him as an old friend from Brooklyn who was a client of Data Associates. Not even Suspicious bought that story; like most of the others, she peeked at his left hand and seemed confused and annoyed to discover a wedding ring.

Alex and Ben augmented the ziti with a spread from a local housewife turned illustrious caterer. They had blithely given her carte blanche; I paled when I saw a blanket of shaved truffles on the sliced beef. Alex said: "Relax, Ma. It's a celebration." Ben added: "We can make sandwiches with the leftovers."

It took me until after dessert—pumpkin mousse, Halloween being less than a week away—to tell my story. I expunged the sex, excised the nastiness between Hojo and Tom, and deleted any mention of Theodore Higbee's gun and Danny Reese's traffic in stolen credit cards. Then, because the waiter from the caterer wanted to clean up and go home, I suggested we repair to the library for coffee.

Vinnie Carosella was a star. He poured brandies, sipped coffee, and fielded questions with such aplomb you'd have sworn there was an invisible television crew from *60 Minutes* recording it all. "She had to have forgotten the bill of sale was in her pocket," he was explaining. "There would be no reason for her to wash and dry it."

"Why did she take it in the first place?" Ben asked.

"She's a lawyer," Vinnie replied. "She must have sensed its value almost immediately. Maybe your father told her why he'd come. Or she figured it out for herself: if he'd broken into the house, it wasn't just to steal any old piece of paper. This was major."

"The price of the painting was major too," Tom observed. "She probably realized it was an asset he wanted to hide. If she had the brains everyone gives her credit for, she'd figure out that Rick wanted to sell it. Stephanie might have thought that if the painting was with Jessica, the two of them might make a nice deal."

"Stephanie was *always* poor-mouthing," Madeline said.

"Good thinking!" Vinnie said, smiling at her. "And she knew fifty percent of three million is a very rich number. But my hunch is, she realized almost right away that it was too risky." Tom nodded his agreement.

"How could she forget it was in her pocket?" Theodore asked.

"She had a great deal on her mind," Cass replied. "Once she dismissed the idea of making a fast profit, she had no need for it."

"She would have remembered it eventually," I suggested. "When things calmed down a little."

"When you were off to jail!" Madeline huffed. "This case will set the women's movement back a hundred years!" The statement was so patently idiotic neither Cass nor I bothered to dispute her. I reached out and took one of her chocolates and immediately felt more kindly toward her.

"The D.A. would have a pretty fair case even if it had never been found," Vinnie told us, eagerly waiting for me to pass the candy to him. "Wonderful chocolate!" he raved to Madeline. "Where do you get it?"

She gave him a Mona Lisa smile. "I'll send you a box." Vinnie beamed at her.

"Did you speak to the D.A. today?" Alex inquired.

"What?" Vinnie asked, still beaming. "Oh, yes, the

D.A. We talked at least once an hour. He's getting his pins lined up. The Jensens—the couple who worked for the Tillotsons—will both testify that Stephanie came home at or about ten-thirty and that moments later she went out to run. Mrs. Jensen can describe the jacket Stephanie wore, which is the same jacket we found the bill of sale in. And Tom here picked out Stephanie in a lineup. He can tell how he had dinner with her and Richie and his wife."

"The tire marks," I prompted.

"Right," Vinnie said. "They have to run all the formal lab tests before they can get the findings admitted as evidence, but it's clear the prints were made by her BMW."

"Good," Alex said. He sat on a tufted ottoman, watching me and Tom. The others may have suspected. Alex knew.

"And we have a bonus," Vinnie went on. "The Lamborghini was locked. The door handle and the area around it had been wiped clean. But Stephanie's fingerprints were on the windshield, which is consistent with her bracing herself to bend over and look into the car."

"But that doesn't prove she killed him," observed Madeline.

"Exactly," agreed Vinnie, clearly impressed with her deductive prowess. "But it does put her at the scene. It's another nice piece of circumstantial evidence." Vinnie poured himself another brandy and swirled it in the glass. He sat back and sipped. Everyone watched and waited; he was a great showman. "And then there are the phone calls."

"What phone calls?" I demanded. I would have

jumped out of my seat, but I was sitting beside Tom. "The threatening calls to Jessica?"

"No. Gevinski will check those, but he assumes she was intelligent enough to have made those from a pay phone. I'm talking about her calls to Richie Meyers' private line in his office."

"My goodness!" Theodore said, with great delight.

"They don't have the complete record yet, but their contact at the phone company said some of the calls lasted close to an hour. And they're checking to see if Richie placed calls to her from the private line as well."

Vinnie caught my eye, then shot a quick glance over at the boys. "Alex, Ben," I said, "please make sure the guy from the caterer takes the garbage outside. And make sure that he puts the lids on the cans very tight. The raccoons have been at it again."

When they left the room, Vinnie said, "He was their father. No need to rub it in. Mrs. Driscoll's testimony will be of great help. She was out of town but flew back and came to headquarters late this afternoon. She and Richie were good friends. He'd told her all about his affair with Stephanie—although those confidences may be excluded under the hearsay rule. However, what will be allowed is Mrs. Driscoll's testimony that at that dinner, she clearly remembers Richie showing Stephanie a great deal of affection, including kissing her on the neck. The defense will have trouble passing that off as a friendly kiss.

"Also, Richie bought her a diamond bracelet. Since neither of them could risk hiding it in their houses, he kept it in his office safe and brought it with him every time he saw her."

"How do you know about it?" Cass asked.

"Because they were showing it off, laughing about their little game, at that dinner. Mrs. Driscoll remembers it clearly."

Everyone turned to Tom. "I remember them talking about a bracelet she was wearing," he said, "but that's all. I tuned out the minute I walked into the restaurant and saw him with that woman."

When the boys came back, Vinnie told them he couldn't tell yet whether Stephanie's lawyers would want to go to trial or make a deal.

"A deal means she'll still have to go to jail?" Ben asked.

"Without a doubt," Vinnie replied.

Theodore looked at me and shook his head. "You liberals! Imagine how happy you'd be, Rosie, if there still was capital punishment in New York."

Cass patted his cheek and turned to me. "You never believe me when I tell you the man is a jackass. Now you see him for what he is—although he did refrain from his imitation of a condemned man in the electric chair."

Theodore reached for her hand and gave her a loving smile. "Let's go home, Cassandra."

After the guests left and the boys went up to bed, I told Tom it was time for him to go.

"What are you talking about?"

"Remember way back when?"

"Which when?"

"In high school. We had a couple of fights, but no matter how angry I was at you, all you had to do was take me in your arms and we'd be at it again."

"Was that so bad?" he asked, unbuttoning my blouse.

"I'm not the girl I was," I told him, taking back control of my buttons. "I'm not easy anymore."

"You're a hard, tough broad?" He laughed.

"No. Just not easy."

"You told me you love me, Rosie," he said, annoyed. "Look, if we don't sleep together tonight, I can live with it. But why are you sending me home?"

"You're married. I don't want a married man."

"You know I have no feelings for her. And vice versa. We've stayed together because there was no reason not to. But now . . . Don't you think I'm going to end it?"

"I hope you do. But let me tell you something. You've been with this woman about the same amount of time I was with Richie. It may not come as a surprise to her, but it's still going to be painful. Painful for both of you."

"We spend approximately two weeks a year as a couple, and even then we travel with other people. We can both be in New York for weeks on end and barely see each other."

"She's got to have feelings."

"She does, but love isn't one of them, at least not love for me. But she feels there's a certain social cachet to having a husband, and I suppose she's right. I look presentable and behave decently, which probably pleases her. Of course, if I were a billionaire, I could spit when I talk and scratch my balls in public and she wouldn't mind. But I'm not, although I do pay the bills. She has strong feelings about that. But Joan is a sophisticated woman; she realizes I'll be paying them for the rest of her life, no matter what."

Tom eased off his jacket, prepared to stay. I walked to the phone. He watched, steely-eyed, as I called the local cab company and asked them to send a taxi to take a guest back to the city.

"I love you," I told him.

"I love you too." He took me in his arms. Our bodies were molded in such a way that they still fit perfectly together. Tom lifted my face and kissed the bangs of my awful haircut.

"I'm sorry if you're angry at me for sending you away," I said. "But the only way I want you is free and clear."

"I'll be back tomorrow afternoon or tomorrow night. Free and clear. Well, except for the paperwork."

Then he kissed me until the taxi came. I'd forgotten how nice and dizzy it made me, standing on my toes, putting my head all the way back so our lips could touch.

"My sweetheart," he said softly. The cabdriver flashed his lights—Come on. Hurry up. I'm waiting, bub—but we stood in the doorway, holding each other. "We're going to be a great couple," he assured me.

"We'll give it a try," I said.

"Isn't it wonderful, Rosie? We have another chance."

"After all these years."

"Yes," Tom said. "But this time it's different."

"How is it different? Are you going to tell me we're older and wiser?"

"No. I'm going to tell you that this time around, we know that there's nothing in the world better than what we've got."

We held hands as we walked to the taxi. I turned away as soon as he got in, because I couldn't bear to see him leave.

"Rosie!" I looked back. He'd rolled down his window. What if he changed his mind? Well, I would survive.

"Yes?"

"Sorry about the prom."

"You were a louse."

"I know. Am I forgiven?"

I couldn't stop smiling. "Of course you're forgiven." The taxi pulled away, but I heard Tom call out: "See you tomorrow!"

And indeed he did.